NEXT of KIN

NEXT of KIN

JOSEPH SCHREIBER

G. P. Putnam's Sons
New York

G. P. Putnam's Sons
Publishers Since 1838
200 Madison Avenue
New York, NY 10016

Library of Congress Cataloging-in-Publication Data

Schreiber, Joseph.
Next of kin / by Joseph Schreiber.
p.   cm.
ISBN 0-399-13928-1
1. Teenage boys—United States—Fiction.   2. Kidnapping—United
States—Fiction.   3. Family—United States—Fiction.   I. Title.
PS3569.C529325N49   1994   93-31258 CIP
813'.54—dc20

Printed in the United States of America
1   2   3   4   5   6   7   8   9   10

for Beth

NEXT of KIN

1

They had come to expect Uncle Titus' phone calls at odd hours. Like a distant radio station, he seemed the most communicative on the outer fringes of daylight, late at night or early in the morning.

His very last phone call came on the brisk Tuesday morning of October 12, while the Danzigs were still eating breakfast. From where he sat spooning up a bowl of Frosted Mini-Wheats, fourteen-year-old Nicholas Danzig could see his mother, Shelley, reach for the receiver and tuck it underneath her chin. She was alert and agile for this hour of the morning, Nicholas thought, and always pretty in a way that emerged freshly each time she encountered a new voice or face, even over the phone.

"Hello?" she said. Nicholas took a spoonful of cereal and watched his mother's face brighten with recognition. She smiled and tucked a wayward strand of hair behind her ear. "Well, good morning to *you*." She listened, nodding, then glanced at his dad, who was sitting at the kitchen table reading the morning *Detroit Free Press*. "Honey, it's Uncle Titus. You want to say hello?"

"Titus?" Ian Danzig raised his eyebrows. "Sure." As he started to stand up he bumped his knee hard against the table. Coffee from his chipped *Good Time Dad* mug tipped and sloshed. Nicholas, his own eyes still a little swimmy with sleep, watched with waking interest as the dark stain spread across his mother's linen tablecloth like the shadow of an object falling fast.

"Oh, Ian, *look*—" Shelley grimaced at the spill. "Never mind, I'll clean it up." She reached, stretching the phone cord over Nicholas' head. "Here, take it quick so I can grab the tablecloth before the stain sets in."

Ian Danzig took the receiver. "Morning, Titus!" he exclaimed, practically shouting. He was a tall, rather soft-spoken English teacher, but he spoke into the phone with the same bluff, hearty-sounding voice that Nicholas had always heard him use around his great-uncle. "We're— well, we're all fine, sure. Say, can you hold on a second and I'll go pick up the extension? Yes, just a minute."

He glanced over at Shelley, who was busy bundling up the stained tablecloth, and then handed the phone down to Nicholas, seeming to notice him for the first time. "Here, champ, you want to hang this up when I get it upstairs?"

Nicholas nodded and took the phone, feeling the familiar sensation of being an extra in a busy scene. The whole big production—Uncle Titus calls, Mom chirps, Dad spills the coffee and runs for the extension—wasn't anything unusual. In fact, it was so familiar it seemed a natural sequence of events. His parents had never kept many secrets from him, but a phone call from Titus had always been kept somewhat clandestine. It was just the way things were.

Most mysteries never lasted long in the Danzig family. Two of the classics, sex and Santa Claus, had bounded in and out of family mythology in a single night when Nicholas had stumbled downstairs on his fourth Christmas to find his parents, naked and bodily entangled, among a pile of half-wrapped presents. After that occasion they seemed to have loosened their rein over his thoughts and his inevitable enlightenment. They still took him to church, but he harbored secret doubts about the existence of God. All his life he had been quiet and thoughtful and solitary, and he felt quite certain that he could imagine almost anything except perhaps death.

Or the idea of spending any length of time with his great-uncle.

The old man's full name was Titus Heller, but because he was such a close friend of the family, all the Danzigs referred to him as Uncle Titus. He was a large, broad-shouldered man of rudely carved features, huge ears and a slightly bulbous nose mapped out with broken capillaries. His matted gray hair was as thick as a dog's fur. Nicholas thought he always reeked faintly of motor oil and the cold autumn wind, even in brightest springtime. For the last several years as his arthritis and emphysema had taken their toll he seemed to have aged whole decades between visits. His face had been enmeshed with wrinkles when he frowned, looking at Nicholas' mother's portfolio of card designs or talking with Ian Danzig about what Titus invariably called "the kid business."

"So, Ian, how's the kid business going?" Uncle Titus would grunt, and since this was before the arthritis and emphysema, he would even scoop Nicholas up in one muscular arm as he passed. He always pretended a familiarity with Nicholas that even as a boy Nicholas never felt. His uncle's bulk scared him, and the ancient, blue tattoos of naked women across his hairy forearms, and the dirty coveralls and flannel shirts he favored. In the winter he wore a heavy, wretched-looking cattleman's coat with the collar turned up over his thick neck.

"Well, *this* kid's fine," Ian would say, rustling his son's hair and sounding a little nervous, "but the students . . . well, you know, Titus. It's a job. A person has to have his work."

"Sure, I know all about it." Uncle Titus would grin, showing teeth as yellow as corn kernels. "Was in the kid business myself, you know. At one point. I've been known to continue with it. Upon occasion."

Uncle Titus had visited them frequently back then. He had all kinds of routines he used to show his strange affection for Nicholas, sweeping him off his feet, throwing him high up in the air, manipulating his body under one arm and then the other like a soldier with a rifle. Once, Nicholas' father told him that Uncle Titus had been in the Army. Titus' body seemed to still be rehearsing the motions, slowly and reflectively, as if the routines would not die until he himself was gone. Even after his arthritis forced him to limit his visits, he still stayed longer than either Ian or Shelley Danzig might have wanted, eating dinner and belching, whispering lewd jokes, lighting and grinding out the Marlboros that it took Shelley years to tell him to smoke outside.

Now Nicholas stood next to the bare kitchen table, waiting while his father bounded up the stairs two at a time to the study on the second floor. What was taking him so long?

In the meantime, he knew without question, the old man was going to talk to *him*.

"Howdy there, nephew," Titus' voice rasped from out of the receiver. In the background Nicholas could hear the sound of seagulls squeaking and waves bursting. Titus owned several houses, but he spent most of his time up in the village of Burns Mills, Michigan, on the shore of Lake Superior, a full day's drive from the Danzigs' home down in Portage. "How you doing?"

"Fine," Nicholas said. "How are you?"

Instead of an answer, the old man erupted into coughing, which produced little static bursts across the phone line. Because of the emphysema, he was hooked up to a variety of rusty oxygen canisters that he toted along in the back of his wheelchair. He hadn't seemed to hear Nicholas' inquiry through his coughing fit. "I'm out on my porch with the portable phone lookin' at the lake," he said with a sawdusty wheeze. "Fresh cool air's good for the lungs, you see."

Nicholas swallowed. "Uh—"

"You're goin' to school today, aren't you, Nicky?" Titus asked him. Static crackled and hissed. The connection seemed to be deteriorating by the second. "Walking? It's fine weather for walking, you know. Makes me wish I was a kid again."

He chewed at the side of his lip, wishing he had never put the receiver up to his ear in the first place. "Uh—"

There was a sharp click from the extension upstairs. "Nicholas?" his father's voice intruded, sounding reassuringly clear and nearby compared to Titus' galaxies-away crackling. "You can hang up now, son, I've got the phone."

Nicholas hung up the receiver, closing the circuit between the two grown-up voices. But hanging up didn't bring the rush of relief that he'd hoped for. Whenever his parents' routines seemed too familiar to him, he was always left feeling unnerved and maybe a little cornered besides.

He sat down, took another spoonful of Frosted Mini-Wheats and chewed them down. Actually he didn't need to chew them much at all. They had gotten quite soggy in the unmistakable way that Frosted Mini-Wheats did if you didn't take them completely seriously from start to finish. *That's what you get for thinking when you should have been eating*, he told himself. *Better get busy before they turn to mush.*

But he didn't lift the spoon to his mouth again. He just looked down into his cereal and thought about all the rituals his parents went through every day. He could name a hundred of them, just for starters. Just a few minutes ago his dad had been complaining about all the problems he'd been having with the new Mercury Tracer, and his mom had been thinking out loud about the three of them driving up north for the autumn Color Tour through Canada, as they did every year, when the phone had rung.

A phone call from Uncle Titus? It was just a variation in the routine. His father always stood up too quickly, banged his knee, bumped his coffee. Whenever Titus called, the well-rehearsed scene would begin to run. Nicholas wondered if his parents really thought they were fooling him.

He stood up and carried the bowl over to the sink. His mother already had the coffee-spattered tablecloth submerged in cold, sudsy water. She had pushed her sweater sleeves up to her elbows and there was a little dab of bubble-froth on her chin as she struggled with the fabric. Her cheeks were red with determination.

He observed for a long moment. "Looks like you're trying to murder it or something."

"Nicholas, honestly, I really don't have time for your smart remarks." She wrung the suds from the tablecloth without looking up. "Did you pack your lunch?"

He nodded. Making his lunch was the first thing he did in the morning, usually before he was even fully awake. That way he often forgot what he'd made and surprised himself by noon. But even that little spark of spontaneity was becoming tragically predictable, just another part of the routine. He glanced at the clock over the stove, saw that it was almost seven-thirty and got his brown bag out of the refrigerator, then pulled on his windbreaker and picked up his backpack. "I'm leaving now."

"You don't want to wait to get a ride with your father?"

"Nah." He hoisted his backpack up over one shoulder. "Gonna meet Louis down at the corner." Louis Skye was the closest thing he had to a best friend in the world, and the two of them had fallen into the habit of walking together on the rare days when Ian Danzig didn't drive them. "See you later."

"All right," she said, looking up at him with a harried-looking smile. The soap was still daubed on her chin like a little white goatee. "Have a good day, kiddo."

"Okay." He opened the door and escaped out into the cool morning air.

The morning was cold and mirror-bright, made all the brighter by the dry October leaves. As Nicholas watched they tumbled and scudded across the street in front of him on an invisible river of wind, eddying into an occasional autumn dust devil. Last night their neighbors, the Howards, had set an entire pile of them ablaze in their backyard, and Nicholas could still smell the rich, pungent aroma lingering very faintly but unmistakably in the air. It was a good smell. He inhaled deeply, imagining that he was cleansing his lungs of the dusty captivity of homelife, and cut diagonally across the front yard, trailing a jet stream of his own breath behind him.

He leapt across the sidewalk and started walking up the street.

He never walked on the sidewalk. Instead he hung along the edge of the curb, with the iron-grated sewer drains gurgling as he walked over them. The gutter was littered with a patchwork of damp leaves and fragments of a smashed jack-o'-lantern that somebody had foolishly put out on their porch a full two weeks before Halloween. He shook his head. People and their rituals. Someday—

His thoughts broke off with a nearly audible snap, and all at once he was aware of a vehicle whipping around the corner behind him, shocking him back into the real world. He heard brakes squeal, laying twin strips of black rubber across the road. He looked over his shoulder to see the black van as it swung up alongside of him, close enough to touch, and skidded to an ear-piercing halt, engulfing him in its shadow.

"Hey!" he shouted. "What the—"

The driver's door flew open. The woman herself he saw only for an instant—a flash of blond hair, glasses, a navy-blue sweater and jeans—before her right hand shot out in a flicker of red fingernails and snatched his wrist, yanking him forward toward the back end of the van. He dropped his lunch and felt his backpack slide off his shoulder as the other hand clapped over his mouth, stifling a scream that wasn't quite there. All his senses sharpened. He heard the paper lunch bag hit the pavement and felt the tips of his sneakers scuff the curb as the woman whisked him forward, down the walk and, with a final swoop, up into the open side door of the van. He sat up in time to see the door come sliding shut behind him.

The woman climbed up into the driver's seat ahead of him, threw the van into reverse and pulled back into the middle of the street. He heard a shriek of brakes, tires laying more long black strips across the blacktop. The woman shifted again, and his head snapped back as the van roared up the street.

His heart began to beat again. He swallowed, his throat so dry that it felt parched. "What's going on?"

She turned around for the first time and with the same urgency that she'd used in sweeping him off the curb, swung her right fist back and cracked him across the chin, laying him down into darkness.

2

Portion of the testimony of Louis V. Skye, October 23.
Nick wasn't at the corner waiting for me. I didn't see him coming up the street either. Usually he's ready for me to show up in the mornings. Even when I'm a little late he'll wait for me, if it's not too cold. It's weird that a kid like Nick who isn't crazy about school can't wait to get there in the mornings, but I guess he doesn't like sitting around the breakfast table with his folks either, having those weird sort of conversations that you have when their brains are going twelve different ways at once, saying, "Well, are you up for the morning?" and asking if you got all your homework done, I mean, as if you'd have time to do it now before school. Dumb stuff like that.

Anyway, Nick wasn't at the corner. Like I said, that was unusual. He hadn't said anything about going on vacation or anything, but I wasn't too worried about it at the time—Nick's a weird kid. He's told me some stories sometimes you wouldn't believe, out of his own head.

I didn't think too much about it until his folks asked me about it later. I don't know. He never had a lot to say to me. I hadn't known him that long. Now I can't believe I thought like that. Now I feel so dumb. So dumb.

The fact is, I didn't hear any more about it until I read in the paper on Saturday that my friend Nicholas Danzig was dead.

3

Nicholas opened his eyes slowly. He was sprawled on his stomach across the metal floor of the van, his cheek mashed against cold bare steel. He was shivering and he heard himself thinking crazily, *I hope we aren't going far. I didn't even bring my toothbrush.*

He took a shallow breath, and brilliant pain flared in his chin and jaw so sharply that he gasped aloud. Slowly he began to remember that he'd been hit. He prodded at the tip of his chin with his fingers and flinched, his eyes already brimming with tears of pain. Only once before in his life had anyone hit him in the face, during a playground brawl two years ago, and that mild pain seemed to have affected an entirely different nerve branch than the cabbage-sized throbbing in his jaw and temples now. It was so powerful he could almost hear it each time it rose up, driving tears from his eyes. A deep bruise had begun to form across the lower half of his face.

He pushed himself up into a sitting position and looked around.

The windows of the van had been blacked out with thick, sloppy strokes of a paintbrush. Also, during the moments that he'd been unconscious, the woman had inserted a sheet of plywood between the front seat and the rear. A thin slit, only two or three inches wide, permitted a narrow stream of daylight through to the back. But the plywood gave him a little courage. At least she couldn't clobber him again while it was between them.

"Hey," he said loudly. His jaw delivered an ugly dose of pain down his spine, all the way to the heels of his feet, and he swallowed as much of it as he could. "What's going on here? Where're we going?"

No reply. Just the busy humming of the van's tires on the roadway.

"What's going on?" he repeated, and brought his face close to the slit in the plywood. "Hey!"

Before he could see anything more, the slit went dark, as though she'd slapped a strip of tape across it. Blackness dropped over his shoulders and face. He felt panic start to well up somewhere inside of him, his throat constricting and his stomach aching as if in the grip of a cold hand. Stop, he told himself, and he heard his mother's voice in the back of his mind, its cool, reassuring tones: *You're more intelligent than most kids your age, Nicky, and that can work against you if you allow it to. But if you can go placidly amidst the noise and haste—that is to say, if you can keep a cool head when everybody else is going crazy—then the battle has already turned in your favor. Believe it, kiddo.*

But could she forgive him a little panic? After all, this was—

The chill of the steel floor ran through his entire body.

This was kidnapping.

He gasped for another breath, hugging himself, clenching his sweatshirt in his fists. Abruptly he was fighting back tears again. He was inside the black van with the blacked-out windows, cruising down some nameless freeway, and nobody in the world knew about it. Not the police. Not even his parents.

He envisioned it with the clarity of an episode of *America's Most*

Wanted: that afternoon his parents would figure he had gone to Louis' house, but by dinner they would be worried and by nightfall they'd be outright scared. Somebody would finally decide to call the police. They'd find the brown paper lunch bag spilled open across the sidewalk halfway up the street, his backpack lying lopsided in the gutter, a skid mark running slightly askew to the curb. But he was not there. He was *gone*.

His lungs filled themselves to scream.

If you can keep your head . . .

He bit his lip, hard, almost until blood came, until he knew he was not about to startle himself with a scream. He forced himself to take a deep breath, then another, then another, then the next and the next.

Finally he said, in a voice no more than a croak, "I think this is a mistake. My name is Nicholas—"

"—Nicholas Danzig," a voice on the other side of the plywood finished. It was the woman, and his first impression was that she sounded very casual, even kind. "Yes, I know what your name is."

"Where are we going? Can I ask you that? I mean, what are you going to do to me? Are you going to kill me?"

"No." The voice sounded mildly bemused. "No, I'm not going to hurt you anymore."

He held himself, carefully poised, listening.

Finally she released a long, cautious breath. "I do hope you'll be able to forgive me for my rudeness," she said. "It might not have been the best way, but it was the quickest."

"Look," he said, clinging as tenaciously as he could to whatever facts were at hand, "I don't know who you are or what you want, but in civics class we learned that kidnapping's a federal offense. It's a capital offense. They *execute* you for it. And my mom and dad—"

"Nicholas, please."

He drew back from the plywood. Instead of exasperation or anger, what he heard was the firm but somehow gentle tone of authority and purpose. The voice and the words themselves seemed to swell with their own sense of righteousness. He was reminded absurdly of an angel's voice, or his own mother's voice when he had been very young, and for an instant he sat, overcome with a rush of confused feelings.

"Don't tell me about those people you call your parents," she said. "I'm going to ask that you don't mention them again. They aren't your mother and father. They're strangers. They've been deceiving you all along."

"They *are* my mom and dad," he said with his face against the plywood again. "If you just take me back to them right now, they probably won't press charges against you for kidnapping me."

This time she actually laughed, a soft and chimelike sound. "What makes you so certain you're being kidnapped?"

"I don't know what else you'd call it," he said, "when somebody grabs you off the street, throws you in a van and drives away all before noon on a school morning."

"What if the stranger is your sister?"

"I don't *have* any sisters. My mom and dad—"

"I told you, those people are not your mom and dad," the voice said. "They adopted you. They raised you, you grew up in their house and ate their food and lived by their rules, but those people have no children of their own."

"That's a stupid lie!" he said, and drove the flat palm of his hand against the wood, feeling the impact reverberate through the entire sheet. "You can't take me away from them, they're my mom and dad! They'll catch you! Whoever you are, you can't take me away! *You can't!*"

He slammed his palms against the plywood. He pounded on it with his fists until he was sobbing too hard to pound anymore, until all he could do was rest his shoulder against the plywood and cry. His nose and fingertips were cold, his hands stung, his face was throbbing.

"I HATE YOU!" he shrieked.

His words rang in the silence for a few seconds.

"But I love you, Nicholas," the voice murmured back at last, with its strange, sweet patience. "You're family."

4

For a long time after his initial outburst, Nicholas sat perfectly still, listening to the tires thrumming along the road and thinking about what the voice had said. He didn't want to think about it—he would have preferred to devise some means for his escape—but the darkness inside the van seemed to welcome all his doubts, all his uncertainties, amplifying them over any plans he tried to make.

The voice said he was adopted, which was impossible. His mother had told him all the usual childhood stories about himself, about when she found out she was pregnant with him. They were stories he knew well.

"We lived in an apartment in Detroit then," his mother had said, "and things were rather dismal, as I recall, what with your father teaching in the city and me doing secretarial work for General Motors. But you were our first sign of good hope, Nicholas. Here was God giving us the thumbs-up and letting us know that the hard times were coming to an end."

Nicholas had always thought that was kind of reaching. Making a baby, as he understood it, was quite nearly the easiest thing in the world. But he had never had the heart to ruin the narrative flow.

His mother told him about driving home from the clinic that day, singing along with "Good Day, Sunshine" on the radio, so happy that she thought she might explode with love for him, this unborn child inside her. It was 1978, and he was the sign of a brighter future for the Danzigs. His mother said that by the time he was born in October, his father had found a more lucrative teaching job outside the city, and Uncle Titus had talked to some people he knew at Hallmark, getting his mom started designing cards. It wasn't exactly what she had gone to school for, she said, but it made a lot more sense than waiting tables, which she had done for a while back in Detroit. The family moved to a newer, larger house out in the country with a huge oak tree in the backyard and an old tree house he remembered from all the—

"—pictures?" the voice from the front of the van asked.

Nicholas blinked in the darkness. He realized that his eyes were still soaked with tears. "What?"

"I was just asking how much you knew about your childhood," she said. "Have you seen any pictures from back then?"

He felt his anger creeping back. "Of course I've seen pictures. What do you think? There's a million pictures of me growing up all over our house!"

"Oh?"

"I've got a million baby pictures of me!" he snapped. He was anxious enough to argue with her now that he didn't realize how much of it was not, strictly speaking, the truth. In reality his mom had informed him, so long ago that it now registered as a simple fact, plausible or implausible, that neither she nor his dad owned a camera for the first two years after he was born. Still, he realized that he could visualize a few snapshots, taken by various loaner cameras: Nicky in his high chair, his toothless, grinning face caked with Gerber's mixed vegetables, Nicky crawling across a rug with his diaper falling off his butt, Nicky curled up so tiny in his crib, asleep, with Mother Goose mobiles dangling overhead. Baby pictures, of the quintessential variety that everyone had.

"But your parents aren't in any of them," the voice said.

"Yes, they *are!*"

"Those baby pictures were taken before you went to live with them."

"Yeah?" he said. "By who?"

"Titus," she said. "Didn't he always bring them over?"

"How do you know about Uncle Titus?" he asked. But it was true. Uncle Titus had always brought photo albums to the house, but Nicholas only remembered old pictures of his mother as a girl, of the old house in Wisconsin or somewhere equally dull, of her parents. Nicholas tried to recall if any of his own early baby pictures had contained his mom or dad within the shot. But it wasn't as clear to him as he had hoped. His mind was swimming now, and he felt a little dizzy in the darkness of the van. How could she know about these things? How long had she been spying on him and his family, gathering these little details to incorporate into her story?

"No," he said. "You're lying. I know it. You're lying."

He was disoriented, that was all. After being snatched right off the street, thrown into the van and socked in the jaw, who wouldn't be? The woman in the front seat had just taken advantage of it.

He took a breath and tried to regain his bearings. Judging by his internal clock, he guessed that they had probably been driving for an hour or two now. What time was it? It had to be about ten, maybe a little later. Third hour back at school. Kids were already getting antsy for lunch. He wondered if anyone besides his friend Louis Skye had noticed that his desk was empty yet. He wondered if the police had started their search yet. Didn't you need to be missing twenty-four hours first?

In twenty-four hours he could be almost anywhere.

Nicholas was suddenly able to imagine, very vividly, his own face stamped in fuzzy black and white across the side of a dripping, waxy milk carton. *Have you seen this boy?* it would say, and underneath, all the columns of vital statistics, as if the fact that his eyes were hazel and his hair was brown would somehow speed the rescue. As if someone who *happened* to see him and *happened* to buy that particular carton of milk might *happen* to put the two together—

It was too much to think about right now. He crept toward the back of the van, reaching his fingers into the darkness. His fingers found substance, and he released a soft groan of disgust. A wet mattress lay there in a pool of water that might have leaked in from the roof. The springs sounded rusty, and the padding was in shreds. The whole thing stunk of mildew, a place where vermin might feel right at home.

He found a bundle of rope, a few crushed cans and what felt like a stack of soft and pulpy papers. As he turned around to feel his way back up to the front of the van, his knees dropped into a puddle of cold water that had collected back there. He squirmed and pushed himself forward.

"Hey," he said loudly. He realized that he felt more self-assured when he spoke loudly, and decided to continue doing so as long as his voice held out. "Where are you taking me?"

"We're heading west," the voice said, and he could hear that reassuring tone again. "We're going to California."

"California." The word felt foreign in his mouth. "Why?"

"Your father wants to see you again."

"My—" he started, then forced himself to lower his voice. "Look, I'm telling you for the last time, my father and mother live in Michigan. My name is Nicholas Danzig, I'm fourteen years old—"

"He's been waiting a long time," the voice chimed along implacably. "You could say we're in somewhat of a hurry."

"So you're driving me all the way to California in a *van*?"

"Why not? I drove all the way here in it."

"When?"

"Just a few days ago, actually," the voice said. Then she paused, as if in reflection. "I didn't even stop to pay a visit to our dear Uncle Titus."

"How do you know about him, anyway? How do you know about my family?"

"Because," she repeated with that same calm patience, "I'm your sister."

"Stop saying that," he hissed back at her. "That's a lie."

"It's true. You're afraid to think about it too much, because you know you'll start to remember it too, and you're probably not ready for that yet. That's all right. Sometimes that's for the best. But the truth of it is that Titus—"

He leaned forward with all his strength and slammed both fists against the plywood which divided them. But it was reinforced, and bounded back without cracking. "You don't know Uncle Titus!" he said. "You don't know anything!"

"He's my Uncle Titus, too, you know."

The voice was deadly calm.

"I grew up in a little town in Iowa, with a woman I called Mom, and a man I called Dad. They told me cute stories about when I was a baby, and Uncle Titus would stop by every few months. He always knew I was a special kid. And he said he was in the kid business."

Nicholas felt his heart flutter in his chest. "What?"

"Uncle Titus supplied plenty of pictures for these people's photo albums, a ready-made history and a new birth certificate with my new name on it. Just like you've got a birth certificate with 'Nicholas Harrison Danzig' written on it . . . even though that's not your name."

"That's—" His throat was too dry, and his voice choked off. "That's a lie, too. I know my own name. I know where I'm from."

"And Uncle Titus came by on all the holidays, Thanksgiving, Christmas, the Fourth of July, my birthday. Just paying a visit, he said, and he'd always ask my mom and dad casually about how I was doing in school, if I had a lot of friends, if there were any problems on the home front."

He forced himself not to say anything. He remembered that his schoolwork and homelife were always of interest to Uncle Titus. Titus had used the same phrases, too. Special kid. Home front. Kid business.

"Then one day, when I was getting to be a little older and I'd grown into this family unit of mine, Titus' health started to fall apart. He was on oxygen, and he had to stay in a wheelchair because of his arthritis. He couldn't come see us as often anymore. He sent birthday cards on my birthday with plenty of money in them. He promised to pay surprise visits. Just to check up on me. I had started to go through some changes at that time . . . something I'll explain to you later. It has to do with our family and why we're so special. Don't worry, we'll have plenty of time to talk during the drive west."

He sat silently for a moment, a little bit lost, and then caught hold of reality again by one of its many ragged ends. "You said Nicholas isn't my real name."

"Right," she piped up, sounding absurdly happy to be answering a question. "We were all given new names. My real name is Anthem. And even though you've got a birth certificate with the name Nicholas Danzig on it, that isn't the name that our real parents gave you."

"Oh, really? What's my *real* name?"

"It's Virgil."

"Virgil?" he repeated in sheer disbelief. In just a few short seconds his mind reeled off a long and ruthless list of all the variations the kids at school could find for that name. It wasn't pretty. It wasn't even funny. "Now I know you are crazy. Virgil."

She laughed. "Mom had a thing for unusual names . . . now, maybe *she* was the crazy one, huh? Naming one of us Anthem and one of us Virgil and another one Ovid. But I'm getting way ahead of myself here."

"You mean there are more brothers and sisters waiting for us at the other end of the line?"

"Yes." It was silent for a moment. "One other."

"And Ovid, you said his name is?"

Anthem made a soft grunting sound that might have been assent. Nicholas sensed that he was somehow treading on shaky ground here, perhaps on the cusp of asking some question he didn't want answered, but curiosity insisted. If he could catch her in a lie, make her story sound as crazy to herself as it did to him . . . well, at least it would give him a foothold. Someplace to start.

"So this mysterious other brother of mine, why didn't he come with you to get me?"

Anthem was quiet for a very long time. Because Nicholas couldn't see her during this time, the silence was doubly frustrating. It was as though she were actually conferring with another inaudible partner, someone he hadn't yet seen.

"Anthem?" he prompted. "Hello?"

"It would have been impossible for Ovid to come," she finished vaguely, but there was an edge in her voice, a very definite anxiety. "There's something between the two of you, a kind of invisible barrier. And it isn't easily penetrated. When you do come in close contact with each other, there are consequences to be considered . . . some very serious consequences. You'll learn about them soon enough. But it has to do with distance, and brotherhood. And weather." Something manic entered her voice during that last word, making her sound unintentionally humorous, but a little scary at the same time. "Have you noticed yet that it's getting colder? It's getting colder outside, I really think it is."

"Can we pull over for a minute?" Nicholas asked, after a few more seconds of silence.

"Yes, of course we can." She sounded relieved to be off the subject. "Do you feel all right?"

He said nothing. He *didn't* feel all right. Not at all.

5

"I'll pull off to the side," Anthem told him through the plywood.
She felt a thin pang of frustration in the pit of her stomach.
Judging from Nicholas' abrupt withdrawal from the conversation, she
had already told him too much and probably too quickly. From the
beginning of her journey eastward she had warned herself over and over
to break the news to him slowly, not to get overzealous and tell him
everything all at once. But it was difficult, trying to guess when his mind
might reach its saturation point, when she herself felt electrified with
the sheer power of the truth. She wanted to reveal everything.

But blurting out everything at once would only alienate him further.
People would not always believe such talk. People required *plausibility*,
even when the truth itself seemed utterly implausible.

She pulled the van over to the side of the road and rolled to a stop.
She had to admit that her expression, reflected back in the windshield,
was calm and confident. Her lips, a smoothly curving bow of coral pink,
turned upward into a hopeful little half-smile, and she smiled back at
her reflection, her green eyes glinting behind the lenses of her glasses.
The glasses themselves were black-framed and owlish, almost a disguise
of the beauty that lay beneath. When she put them on, they imposed a
harsh geometry across the more natural smoothness of her cheekbones
and brow, and when she slipped them off, it was as though a strange,
wild creature leapt into view. What had before been normal, shoulder-
length blond hair seemed more manelike, leonine.

She stopped the engine, took the keys and climbed out.

Sunlight broke through the oaks and spruce that grew along the road,
dividing it from the fields and farms on either side. For a moment she
just stood still, inhaling and exhaling, taking a moment to attempt to
banish any tiny trace of doubt from her mind. Then from under her seat
she removed a pair of chrome-plated handcuffs and carried them around
to the back of the van.

"I'm going to let you out now," she said, turning the key in the
rear door handle. Outside all around them, the robins and crows fell
momentarily still, and she thought her own voice sounded small in that

vast, windy silence of the countryside. "I am going to restrain you. I know you don't trust me yet. Please don't try to run. If you want to scream for help, go ahead, but it won't do any good. We've been traveling back roads, and I guarantee the only living things around to hear you are cows and sheep."

She opened the door, ready for him if he should decide to come out kicking. But inside nothing moved. After a few seconds she looked carefully in. He had curled himself into the shadow where he glared out at her, his chin resting on his knees, looking like a starved and cornered animal. His eyes had taken on a feral shine.

"What's the matter?" she said.

He laughed. "Oh, no complaints back here."

She would have to be patient with him. She remembered something that Saint Jack had said to her before she had left: *You don't remember what it was like, do you, when I came for you? Oh, sugar, you will. Virgil . . . Nicholas, they call him now . . . he'll make you remember who you were then, just as you'll make him realize who he is now. You'll remember all of it.*

Anthem, at the time, had just laughed pleasantly at this warning, but for some reason now it frightened her a little. Had Jack meant for it to sound so foreboding when he'd said it?

She watched Nicholas slide himself toward the tailgate, then without a word she closed the cuffs on his wrists and led him out. He continued to stare at her; memorizing her features, she presumed, so he could describe her for the police after he escaped. She thumbed her glasses back up the bridge of her nose. When he glanced over his shoulder at her, she noticed for the first time the slight purple bruise that had formed between his lower lip and chin. The pang of guilt in her stomach came back at the sight of it.

"How's your chin feel?"

"How do you think it feels?"

"I'm sorry about that. I thought you were going to get away."

"I was," he said. He was working his wrists around in the handcuffs. "Maybe I still am."

"It wouldn't be wise," she said quickly, and stopped herself before the threats started pouring out of her. She didn't want to get angry with him. But all of Saint Jack's serenity remained a mystery to her. In retrospect she wished she had allowed him to come with her.

They made their way into the trees, the barnyard smells of honeysuckle and manure growing progressively stronger ahead of them. The earth was still soft from a recent rain. She found herself instinctively following in his larger, deeper footsteps so that it looked as if only one of them had come through here. If an accident happened to him later, she could tell the police he escaped here, alone and on foot.

Oh, and what sort of accident are you expecting? she asked herself.

She was just being realistic. Fate didn't always side with the just. If something happened, and any number of small complications could arise—

But that wasn't what she was afraid of. Realistically she was planning for the biggest, baddest inevitability of all, the possibility that he might die on her. Despite all of her determined enthusiasm, she had long and secretly suspected that she would never find him, and if she did find him, she would never bring him back where he belonged, and if she did start to bring him back, he would die somewhere in transit. Before she could tell the truth about who he was.

Unfortunately but realistically, Anthem had finally come to terms with the fact that sometimes things simply fell apart. It was simply the nature of things to fall apart, just as she was convinced that her family had fallen apart. Entropy was a fact of the universe. Perhaps the first fact, easily the most inarguable. Every family, every individual person, seemed to contain the seed for its own betrayal, and sometimes the center could only hold for so long. There had been a time when she herself would have called such an attitude cowardly, relinquished to failure. But if she was going to undertake this mission to bring him home, she was going to have to be realistic.

They walked out of the shadows of the oaks, and he turned to look at her.

"If you're my sister," he said suddenly, "why didn't you just come by and introduce yourself this morning? I'm sure my folks would be interested to meet their son's long-lost sister."

"I did try that once," she told him. "It wasn't such a rip-snorting success."

Nicholas worked down his zipper with his free hand and began, after a few seconds, to water the grass in the other direction. Anthem stood behind him, their wrists linked by the handcuffs. After a few seconds she saw that her brother was looking over his shoulder at her.

"I don't remember ever seeing you coming around to my house before, saying you were my sister," he said, sounding slightly peevish.

She nodded. "It was a long time ago." Here in the breezy silence of an autumn field, with the two of them so close together, the scene seemed oddly bucolic. The air around her felt warm and swarming with tiny beads of golden light.

"What happened when you did it?"

Anthem averted her head slightly so that her hair swung in front of her face. She knew a few stories about what had happened, but certain questions about the past, particularly the distant past, gave her a vague twinge of discomfort, like a wound that hadn't quite healed properly. She didn't like the sense of potential weakness there. Instead she concentrated almost exclusively on looking forward into the future. A future when they could all be together again.

"I mean, come on, when was the first time you realized I was your brother, anyway?" Nicholas pressed. "Maybe you got the wrong kid in the first place. Is that possible?"

Stop it, Anthem thought, her head starting to throb slowly. The beads of light had begun to precipitate, darkening the air. *Please, Nicholas, you don't want me to hurt you.*

"How old was I? Was I just a baby? Because sometimes babies don't look much like—"

We're going to California, she told herself carefully. Her free hand had already closed into a fist at her side, where it trembled, still tightening. All at once she felt the earth slipping out from under her feet, crumbling away into thin air, and the only way to hang on was to grab him, to grab the source of unsteadiness, as hard as she could. She had to steady herself. *We're going to California together because you're my brother and Nicholas please I don't want to hurt you, it is the last thing in the world I ever want to do.*

"—plus, how did you know I was the same one now? How come—"

He turned to face her and his voice broke off. Anthem's stomach gave a nauseous wrench, her vertigo heightening until she knew that her next move would be purely instinctive, no matter how hard she tried to restrain herself. ". . . wait . . ." she croaked, a last, weak plea. "I can tell you about what happened later . . ."

Every bit of her strength went into her fist, as it clenched tighter and tighter. She held her breath. Letting the fist fly upward would be her next inevitable act. She could visualize it so clearly. There would be nothing she could do to stop its flight upward. Where had all her strength gone, all at once? It was *maddening*. How had he been able to disarm her so easily, with just a few questions?

Her free hand leapt upward, across that small space between them, and then fell away. Blackness swirled for what seemed like forever around her head, muffling sound and vision and finally thought itself. She could almost hear the whisper of its passage, just for an instant, before she lurched backward, gasping for air but unable to breathe.

The handcuff chain went tight and almost pulled Nicholas off his feet. He lost his balance and piled into her with a surprised grunt.

Anthem stared at his face so close to hers before he pushed himself away. Memories flooded inexplicably through her mind, flashes of the night eight years ago when she had first become aware of how her body was going through its fabulous changes, as though the images themselves had been waiting for her to emerge from her fugue. She felt startled, but not surprised. Almost every "awakening" such as this one seemed to have been accompanied by a rush of memories, although she was usually too disoriented to wonder why.

Nicholas was staring at her. "What's wrong with you?"

"Nothing," she murmured. "I'm just . . . tired from driving, that's all."

"Your voice sounds different."

"Come on," she urged, "get back in the van."

She tugged him back, not yet willing to trust her voice again, and at the last second saw the slender muscle ripple through the back of his right arm. He made a soft grunt, pivoting on his heel. She ducked easily, his fist not even grazing her . . . if, she thought, he had even made a fist at all. She was convinced that this baby brother of hers was a peaceful boy. He'd probably never hit anyone in his life. Anthem couldn't suppress a giggle.

"You're laughing!" he screamed, sounding dangerously close to tears himself. His face was pale, except for two bright red spots high on his cheeks. "You're crazy, that's why! You're nuts!"

"Are you ready to come back to the van?"

"Am I . . . ready . . . ?" He was shaking his head, his throat warbling. She felt him yank hard on his end of the handcuffs, but she held her arm steady. He yanked backward again. And again. His eyes burned, red and frantic with rage, boring holes into her chest. But she did not move until he finally threw himself, sobbing, against her, and she caught him tight in her arms. Moving together, awkwardly, they started the long walk back across the field and through the trees.

He hardly resisted. Enfolded in her arms, he shook and sobbed, seeming so terribly thin and vulnerable that for a second Anthem just held him against her and wondered if it would have been much better if she'd never seen him at Titus' farm, chasing around the white chickens, eight years ago.

He didn't resist as she led him back to the van. She stole a glance over her shoulder. She could almost hear the chickens clucking behind her now, the memory surrounding and engulfing the present moment with all the smells and sounds of Titus' farm from eight years back.

Even that hadn't been the real beginning of things. There were memories older than that. As they walked back to the van, Anthem remembered how her life had first begun to change around her.

But *change* wasn't really a strong enough word for what had happened, was it? Upon reflection, *change* wasn't a strong enough word at all.

Back when she was twelve, her life had started to *collapse* around her.

"Listen," she said to Nicholas as she opened the back of the van and guided him inside. "I'll tell you how it all started for me, eight years ago. I'll explain it slowly, until you understand."

"Wait." He looked back over his shoulder at her. "I'm really scared, Anthem. I'm not so sure I even—"

"Shh." She touched his cheek, which was still burning hot. "I was scared, too, when it all started . . . even more scared than you, because there was nobody around to explain it to me the way that I'm going to explain it to you." She curled her hand around the chrome door handle. "I'm going to shut this now so we can get moving. It will be dark back here. But when I get up front, I'll keep talking to you until you understand. I love you, you know. I won't lie to you, ever. And that's a promise."

"And you'll tell me everything?" he whispered uncertainly.

"Everything," she repeated, starting to close the door a little. "All right?"

He nodded. "Okay, go ahead and close it. And start back at the beginning."

Anthem nodded. That was the only place that she felt like she could start.

Back at the beginning.

6

The pain had started when she was ten years old.

With it came the moral certainty that she was being lied to by the people who called her Gertrude and called themselves her parents.

Physically it was an aching throb in her back, nestled into the muscles on either side of her shoulder blades, particularly while she was waiting to fall asleep. Sometimes it hurt her all night long. She'd be unable to arrange herself comfortably in bed for more than a few seconds at a time. Other nights it was just a subdued ache, and that was all right. But increasingly, as she drew nearer her eleventh birthday, the throbbing would become unbearable. She would awaken in the morning exhausted and sore, her temper like a swiftly fraying rope.

At the school she attended in Iowa City she had begun picking fights with other girls, screaming or bursting out crying in the middle of class, suffering head-splitting migraines for whole nights at a time. Her grades had dropped, her appetite vanished, her normally clear complexion began to cloud over with blemishes. At the time, her parents had seemed hostile and ignorant, offering not the slightest idea as to how the situation could be remedied.

But she herself had known.

She needed to escape. Something inside her body was developing but wouldn't be fully developed as long as she was trapped here in a house with parents who didn't understand her pain or her potential for becoming something beautiful.

Every time they called her "Gertrude"—her parents or her teachers or the other kids at school, the minister at church or the rat-faced boy who delivered the afternoon paper—the name sounded increasingly foreign and artificial. For a short time she had entertained the notion that she was going crazy, but then she realized with dawning certainty that crazy was what she had been *before*. Now it was like waking from a long and terrible dream of madness.

She had known of only one person who might help her.

When Uncle Titus had come to visit, she had pleaded with him desperately to take her with him, wherever he was going. She had seen pictures of his different houses, his mountain retreat in Colorado, his summer cottage up in northern Michigan. To her they seemed like dream palaces, and she certainly felt like a tragic princess who deserved to escape to one of those palaces.

"Please," she whispered to him. They were all standing in the mud-room of the house in Iowa, saying their good-byes to Titus. "They won't know, they'll just think I ran away."

Titus had smiled amiably around the Marlboro tucked in the corner of his mouth. "Oh, is that all they'll think? Well, in that case you can just hop right in." He'd seen the crestfallen look on her face and added, "Darlin', you're all your mom and dad have, and they'd go to the ends of the earth to find you."

"But they *wouldn't* if you didn't *tell* them," she'd told him desperately. Actually, it seemed to her that her parents would be relieved to have her simply disappear. Mostly they communicated to her through notes and frozen meals, and when they were together they both seemed as sullen and self-absorbed as she herself felt. "You could just say you hadn't seen me either."

"Gertrude?" Her father had stooped down to deposit Titus' garment bag into her arms. "Why don't you carry this out for your uncle, would you, please? Gertrude? Please?"

"That isn't my name!" she had screamed. The words had just come out of her, from some deep pit of her unconscious mind, without any real certainty of what her name truly *was*. But now that they were spoken, they seemed much more real, if not exactly convincing. They were out there. They could not be taken back.

She had thrown Titus' garment bag to the floor. With a weary sigh, her father simply gathered the bag back up into his arms and continued his conversation. Titus had laughed in his rough, easygoing manner. She had kicked open the front door and gone bounding down the driveway, but then stopped halfway past Titus' long black Lincoln. The trunk was already open, ready to receive the last of Titus' bags, but it remained mostly empty. She glanced back toward the house, then into the roomy darkness of the trunk.

Uncle Titus had said he was driving straight up into Michigan from here.

For an instant Anthem closed her eyes, seeing vivid images of cabins and pine trees and cold, clear streams running through miles and miles of unexplored territory. Strange, fat-leaved ferns dripping with morning dew. Rimes of autumn frost on pumpkins. Her brow wrinkled just slightly in confusion. However had she obtained such images, if she had never been there? Clearly her escape was meant to be.

What if it took longer than she thought to get there? Looking down into the deep trunk of the Lincoln, she had felt a new sense of maturity awakening in her mind. It had been frightening and strange, but it was also undeniably exciting. It had *power*, this new feeling, and, although she wasn't consciously aware of it, she had felt the same thrill as she had just months before, during the summer, when she'd first discovered a faint spotting of blood on the inside of her underpants. Something deep inside her stomach had rolled lazily over, and she'd thought, *Oh. This is the woman I'm becoming, this is me, the grown-up me. This is what being a woman is like. It is like escaping from where I used to be.*

But this was not *like* escaping. This was actually it.

So, are you going to do it or not? she had asked herself daringly.

She had stared deep into the trunk.

Yes . . . or no?

Her heart pounding, she had reached into the trunk, pushed aside one of Titus' soft leather suitcases and slipped down inside. From where she lay snuggled next to the plush lining of the wheel well, it was possible to arrange his luggage around her, covering her up entirely.

She lay still, trembling with anticipation. By the time Titus actually discovered her here, they would be in Michigan and he would have to let her stay, at least until her parents had time to come and retrieve her. What little she knew about her Uncle Titus indicated that he was a busy man, and could not be forever driving people cross-country. Or perhaps he would see by then that she was an adult. Perhaps he would let her stay.

But what if . . .

Locked inside the trunk, she was Titus' prisoner, whether he knew it or not, for however long it took to drive to Michigan. Could such a drive take more than a day or two? What if she needed water?

She squirmed free of the suitcases, climbed out of the trunk and ducked alongside the car, running back up the driveway and into the garage. Her eyes scanned her father's immaculately organized storage shelves, displaying garden hose nozzles and oil cans, until she found what she was looking for. Inside the house she could still hear Uncle Titus reciting for her parents a complicated story about a subway train conductor who kept closing the doors on his passengers, and was tried for murder and condemned to die in the electric chair. Thank God he tells long jokes, she thought frantically. Her parents were laughing nervously along with it.

She ran back out of the garage, clutching the water bottle under her arm. She unscrewed the plastic cap, which had a long plastic straw built into it, and filled it to the top from the water faucet on the side of the house. Across the street a pair of neighborhood boys had stopped on their bikes to observe her, curiously, as she crept back down the driveway along the far side of the Lincoln, then climbed back into the trunk and lay down.

Lie down still, she told herself. *Lie down dead.*

Just as she had pulled Titus' biggest suitcase in front of her, she heard him opening the front door of the house and announcing his final farewells in a loud, laughing voice. She rearranged her body and prayed that every part of it was somehow concealed by the luggage. For an instant she was convinced that her pounding heart alone would betray her presence here; it felt as though it were shaking the Lincoln back and forth on its frame. She heard Titus shuffling down the driveway, heard the loose change jangling in his pockets. And all at once she was aware that he was standing somewhere over her.

With a grunt, he dropped the last garment bag, the one that she had refused to carry, over the row of soft-side suitcases. She froze beneath its unexpected weight. The last of the sunlight disappeared. She heard him standing still, his breathing slightly belabored, and pictured him surveying the bags. Her insides went suddenly cold. She wondered if he had somehow noticed that the suitcases were arranged differently.

She held her breath. The seconds crept by. What was taking him so long?

"Hey!" he bellowed out finally. "Hey, goddammit, *hey!*"

She felt her blood turn to ice water. It sounded as though he were just a few inches away from her face, close enough to reach out and touch.

"Hey, Stephen! Check and see if I left my camera case on the table! I don't see it back here!"

Far off she heard her father's voice make a sound of muffled compliance. She felt sure she would squirm somehow and betray her position. She could almost feel herself losing motor control as her nerves came unsprung.

"Can't leave town without m'camera, no sir," Titus was mumbling under his breath. "Screw *that* noise." Then something in the trunk shifted, just above her. She fought to keep herself motionless. Before she understood quite what was happening, he had started to unpack the trunk again in search of the camera. It seemed to be happening very quickly. All around her the protective layer of darkness began to brighten toward daylight, and any second Titus would see some part of her here, her shoe or one of her hands sticking out from underneath the luggage.

Her throat seized down to a pinhole. This was it, she would never escape—

No. It's going to be just fine. Just be still.

"Titus!" Her father's voice, approaching, as breathless as a little boy's. "Here, it was back on the counter."

She heard her uncle thank him, replace the few bags that he had pushed aside, and then the trunk came down with a *whomp!* that pushed her eardrums in. It was suddenly very quiet. She drew a shaky breath, and then another. Slowly her muscles began to loosen, her body uncoiling to fill the space around her.

The Lincoln's engine turned over and began to idle confidently as Titus rolled backward down the driveway. He stopped, put it in gear, but then halted sharply before moving forward. Anthem could just make out the mingling of excited boys' voices outside the car, and Titus' lower voice.

"No, mister, really, there's a lady in the trunk of your car!"

Titus' window whined down. "Oh, is there? A real live lady in my car?"

"Yeah! Really! Under the suitcases!"

"Well, I guess I'm one lucky fella, then, aren't I?" He chuckled, waving them off, and then slowly the Lincoln began its inexorable advance up the road, toward the interstate, gathering speed until Anthem was certain that she was safe here, at least for the time being. She had taken a sip of water from the bottle and tried to relax.

And in that quiet, dark space, she began to feel something underneath her skin, on either side of her shoulder blades. Growing.

7

Portion of the testimony of Ian Danzig, October 23.

I don't exactly know when I started talking to Titus in private. It happened sometime after That Night, eight years ago.

That's all we called it: That Night. It needed no other name. It had frightened Shelley and me so badly that we hardly talked about it for several years afterward.

That's how people are, I think. We hoard what truly scares us, what truly shocks us. We have nightmares about it. We almost seem to gloat over that obsession. I know that I did, and still do.

It was late in October 1985. Late October, the same time of the year that Nicholas would disappear, eight years later. That was the year the teachers' strike felt like it would last forever, and my homelife was taking a decidedly surreal turn. We were staying at Titus' cottage up north for a week, trying to make the best of a bad situation before the weather became unbearably cold, as it does, well, shockingly early in the fall up north.

It was late at night, past eleven, and Shelley and I were getting ready to retire for the evening. Nicholas had been put to bed hours earlier. He was safely tucked away, fast asleep, when we heard a knock on the door.

God, such a loud knock! I thought. And so close to midnight!

But I'm certain that Nicholas did not stir in his sleep, as I went to see who was at the door. He did not wake up, my wonderful son. He did not, I'm sure, hear a word of what transpired after I opened that door.

Thank God. Thank God.

8

"You're telling me you really rode in the back of a trunk all the way to Michigan?" Nicholas asked in stark amazement. She had just begun to tell him the story of how she had first seen him, eight years ago. "I mean, you just climbed right in?"

"Sometimes it's the secret passenger who sees the most," Anthem's voice answered cryptically. "You'll see what I mean later."

In his darkness behind the plywood barrier, Nicholas sat and turned this over in his mind. He was her secret passenger, too, he thought, and finally he felt himself beginning to come to grips with the situation. It had taken him what seemed like hours to calm himself down after his hysterical outburst of tears. What had unsettled him most was how easily he had collapsed into the woman's warm embrace, how utterly comforted he felt by her kindness. It had been impossible to resist.

And, let's face it, he thought, she was beautiful. It was nothing like what he thought of as traditional beauty, something fragile and fixated on self-preservation that seemed every day to wrap itself more heavily in gauzy effects. Nor was it the knobby prettiness of the girls he saw at school and sometimes thought about late at night. When this woman had shaken back her blond hair, lifted her chin into the cold autumn air, Nicholas had heard himself think, *She's like some kind of goddess*. And then he stopped, awed to have discovered such a thought, because he'd never used that word before, not even in his own mind.

But she was. And the dreamlike fascination with being here in the darkness, in her possession, had not only lingered through his tearful outrage but intensified, as if tempered. *She's wild, like something that people would go to see in a cage. Or*, he amended almost without realizing it, *in a glossy magazine*.

"Well, do you want to hear what happened then?" she asked him.

He sat up. He had not made up his mind about what she was saying, about whether it was true or not, but he felt compelled to hear it all. "Yeah, okay."

"Let's just say that what happened then was as close to eternity as I ever want to come," she told him, her voice sliding effortlessly back into its patient, narrative tone. "Imagine lying in your own coffin, unable to push it open, while you wait for someone to discover that you're still alive. You wait and wait, because the discovery is inevitable, and at the last moment when you absolutely can't take the stillness and silence any longer, you start to scream *I'm alive, I'm alive*, and you push on the top of the coffin with all your strength, and a few crumbs of dirt fall in. You've been buried. You were buried the whole time. Your wait has just begun."

"Jeez," he whispered, helplessly impressed. The image would not have been nearly so effective, he realized later, if he hadn't been sitting in the dark of a moving vehicle himself just then, traveling along endless stretches of road. "Did you—"

"I didn't scream," she said. "Don't ask me how I kept from doing it, but I didn't make a sound. I lay still, falling asleep and waking up a thousand times, my muscles cramping . . . given time and the means to prepare, I would have had some kind of tranquilizer with me so that I could have just slept through the whole ride. But I didn't. I was awake. I drank my water. To occupy my mind I made lists, lists of people I knew, lists of places I wanted to go, lists of cars and colors and animals. Lists of books I had read and all the movie stars I wanted to meet. The geographical fact of it is that Iowa City is only one long day's drive from northern Michigan . . . a very long day. To me it seemed like forever back there. And as time passed, I became aware that something inside of me was changing. Actually a couple of somethings."

"What?"

"I remembered my name, Virgil. That was one of the changes."

His chest jolted as if under the weight of a double heartbeat. Hearing himself referred to by that name was like a sharp poke in the stomach.

"My real name is Anthem," she told him proudly. "But like I said, I had another name that I thought was my own, back then."

He lifted his head. "Which was . . . ?"

"Gertrude." She said the name quietly, like a dead woman's name, and repeated it more audibly. "It was Gertrude."

"Gertrude—" And then in spite of the tension that had been mounting between them, or perhaps because of it, he felt himself starting to giggle. Before he could hold it in, the giggle went toppling forward into a belly laugh, and he rolled backward, kind of slipping off the side of the mattress and into the pool of cold water, but he still couldn't stop laughing, was in fact laughing even harder, actually howling now, until there were tears pouring down his face and his belly ached. "Oh *Ger-*

trude!'' He was yelping in a parody of a motherly falsetto, clutching his stomach all the while. ''Jeez oh Pete, you were really stuck between a rock and a hard place, huh? Anthem or *Gerrrr*-trude!'' And he flew off into another gale of laughter which more or less left him lying flat on his back, a few seconds later, light-headed and gasping hastily for breath. ''Oh, man. I'm sorry, but that is *good*.''

''Really, I'm charmed you find it so funny,'' she said, and she actually did sound charmed by his display. ''But then again, your name is pretty unusual too. Vir-gil.''

''When—'' He stopped and cleared his throat. Only after a moment of quiet was he able to speak again in a normal voice. ''I mean, when exactly did you discover what your name really was?''

''It happened at some point between the moment that Titus opened the trunk, and when I first saw you,'' she said. ''It's actually a difficult period of time for me to recall, probably because so much seemed to be happening all at once. That brings me to the second major change that I noticed during that time. After Titus opened the trunk and found me there.''

Nicholas reflected that she didn't *seem* to have any difficulty recalling it. In fact, she seemed to plunge into what she was saying with such energy that he felt himself—at occasional intervals, mind, and never for very long—transported back into the world that she described. Part of it was knowing the players. And whoever she was, whether she was lying or not, the fact was that Anthem had learned to do a passable imitation of Titus' flat midwestern snarl. Nicholas realized that he could very easily imagine the shock on Uncle Titus' face, blossoming open like a comical white flower, as the trunk popped up.

And he could visualize how that shock could turn nasty, in a split second's time.

''So the good news is that, yes, we finally arrived at his cottage in the Upper Peninsula of Michigan,'' Anthem said. ''By that time I was actually in a sort of stupor, black-and-blue from being knocked around against the spare tire and sick on carbon monoxide from the exhaust. And, also, there was this other thing, the second major change.'' She paused. ''During the last stretch of the trip, my back started to hurt very badly. It was the one thing that, no matter how hard I tried, I simply couldn't ignore. My shoulder blades and muscles felt like they had been tied into knots and then set on fire. There was nothing to relieve the pain. And then, right before we stopped, I reached around my shoulder and my hand found the shape of some kind of . . . deformity, I suppose the word is."

"What do you mean?"

"I didn't know what it was at the time," Anthem said. "I could only think of some spinal disorder that I had finally incurred as a result of being closed up tight after years of slouching." She sighed. "That loathsome woman who called herself my mother, back in Iowa City, God rest her university-educated soul, had told me that I would turn into a hunchback if I didn't straighten up my shoulders. I might have heard the words 'spinal meningitis' from her, too, spoken in all seriousness."

"Yeah, I've heard my mom talk about that, too," he said. Actually his mother had only threatened him with the relatively mild perils of scoliosis (she told him that she had a touch of it, although he couldn't ever tell) and told him that he looked like a delinquent when he slouched.

"Oh, she was a real charmer, all right, a real warm woman," Anthem said. "Anyway, the point is that I thought I was going to double over and spend the rest of my life in a wheelchair, that's how awful the muscles in my back felt. And then when I reached back and touched these lumps . . . well, I was just about petrified by the time Titus stopped the car and cut off the engine, petrified and dazed at the same time. And then he opened the trunk. It was totally quiet."

There was silence spinning out smoothly from the world of her story into the immediate reality of the van. Nicholas could visualize the moment clearly. For a moment he almost felt as though the two worlds were interconnected so that he could look from one into the other.

"Titus took out a few of the bags, and then just as he was lifting the camera bag out of the trunk he must have seen just a flash of me, laid out behind the spare tire, and he dropped the camera on the cement— I heard it crack."

" 'Well, I guess you're buying me a new camera,' he muttered.

" 'Help,' I said to him. 'There's something wrong with my back. I've got spinal meningitis, I'm going to be a hunchback, I'm going to die—'

"He reached down into that trunk and he used both arms. Looking back on the event, I believe that as he reached for me he was still digesting the fact that I had been his secret passenger all the way from Iowa, because every passing second seemed to give him more strength. He grabbed me in both arms and hauled me out of the trunk. Suitcases and soft-side bags were tumbling out of the trunk, too, as he held me up, up over his head, and then threw me down onto the ground just as hard as he could. I screamed, both from the pain and the shock. After that, I lost consciousness.

"He must have carried me inside and up the stairs while I was passed-out, because when I woke up I was locked in a back corner bedroom of the house. It was morning. From my window I could see the side of the house, past the breezeway down the shore of the lake. Although I was all aches and pains from the ride in the trunk, and from being thrown down on the ground, I realized that my back had stopped throbbing, that the pain had receded away to almost nothing. Instead of pain I just felt . . . a *heaviness*. I reached back behind me, up underneath my old University of Iowa sweatshirt, and my fingers brushed against something folded back against my shoulders, a folded, angular shape that was downy soft and warm to the touch. At first I thought Titus had wrapped me in some sort of bandage. I reached further back, stroking my fingers along it, and I realized all at once that I could *feel* my fingers stroking it." Her breathing was audible, not paced at all, but fast and excited. "And whatever it was, it was attached to me."

Nicholas rocked backward, as if from a physical blow. Thoughts clashed in his mind, not new thoughts but the same old ones, one of them saying, *She's crazy, she's making it up*, and the other, irrationally, saying, *Listen, listen. Just be still, and listen.*

"There were no mirrors in the room where he'd placed me. I could not look at myself. I could just barely manage, if I stretched my arms behind me as far as they would go, to brush my fingertips against the shapes." Her voice broke off again, considering what lay before it. "I began, I guess, to question my own sanity again, like I had when the pain had first started, and who wouldn't? After being locked in the trunk for twenty hours, the bedroom seemed like the entire universe to me, but it was still a locked room with no one in it but me, and now I was starting to transform somehow . . . and the worst, worst, worst part of it was that I liked it. And he knew I liked it. I really think he knew."

"Who knew?" Nicholas asked.

"Why, Titus, of course," she said. "Late that afternoon he came upstairs, and I guess he was still pretty furious with me. I had been stomping the floor, pounding on the walls, demanding he come let me out and explain to me what was happening. He'd been ignoring me until then, but finally he . . . he . . ." She swallowed, her throat clicking, and regained some semblance of composure. "He came upstairs, and he kicked the door open wide without even stopping to unlock it. 'What's happening to me?' I screamed at him.

" 'Hey,' he said, 'you know what happens to little girls who go spying? You went spying, didn't you? You don't think everybody's been completely up-front about everything, do you? Do you, now?'

"I told him the truth. I told him that something was happening inside of me, something that seemed to make it physically impossible for me to ever go home to Iowa City and speak to those people who called themselves my parents, ever again. And I threw myself at his mercy. I was certain that I was going crazy, what else could I do?"

Nicholas squirmed. She seemed to actually be aiming the question at him. He could not think of a single instance where he would throw himself at his uncle's mercy. Never in a million years.

"And Titus crossed the floor of the bedroom to where I was, sunk back in the far corner. He was huge, looming bigger than life—this was long before the arthritis and the emphysema actually began to lay him low. He reached down and his hands clamped onto my shoulders, drawing me up to my feet, and then he took my head in his hands and brought us so close that our noses were nearly touching.

" 'You ain't going crazy, Anthem,' he said.

"It was the first time I'd ever heard that name spoken aloud. I think we spent a long, long time in silence, poised that way in the corner of the room. Titus finally said, 'What you think you got, that's what you got, all right. It's real.'

" 'It is?' I asked. I was too stunned to feel relieved.

" 'Yeah, as a matter of fact, it is,' he said. 'And 'parently there's just some things in the world that aren't meant to stay secret. I won't say any more to you right now, but I ain't going to punish you for what you've done. You just picked a bad time to do it, that's all. It happens I've got company coming to stay tonight.' His eyes had a faraway light to them: they were sort of glittering, as though he were withholding some deep inner irony from me, savoring it. 'Now you stay up here, and don't make a sound for tonight. I don't want these people knowing you're here. I don't want them seeing you or hearing you for the rest of the night.'

" 'Who are they?' I interrupted.

" 'Isn't any of your concern who they are,' Titus said, 'but I'll tell you about it, anyway, once they're gone. For now, you stay silent, you hear me? I mean it. There'll be trouble for you if you don't.'

"I agreed to stay silent. He hadn't explained to me about the shapes that I felt straining against the flesh of my back, but he had assured me that I wasn't going crazy. He wasn't going to send me back to Iowa, and for that night, it seemed like it was enough. I put my nose against the window and looked down at the white chickens that Titus kept around, down by the breezeway.

"Time passed, I don't know how much. After an hour or so, just as afternoon was turning into evening and the room was starting to go cold, I started to shiver. I curled myself up and shivered harder and harder, until it felt as though every muscle was stretched as tightly as piano wire, my skin pulled tight . . . and that's when I heard the fabric in the back of the sweatshirt tear open. It made a low, purring sound. And I heard another noise, felt a rush of air past my face, and . . ." she breathed, almost panting, ". . . they *opened*." She sounded ecstatic just saying the words. "Do you understand? There isn't any way I can explain this away or put off telling you about it any longer. It sounds crazy, I know. It sounds like something out of an Anne McCaffrey fantasy novel. It sounds like everything but the truth. But I actually had wings sprouting out of my back."

Her voice dropped, and only then did Nicholas realize that it had gone up more than an octave in pitch. "Wings," he repeated slowly.

She didn't seem to hear him but continued on, her voice becoming more feverish as she spoke. "Down in the breezeway, I heard the sound of a VW beetle rolling up the driveway toward the cottage, and as I looked down through the window, I rolled the muscles in my shoulders, lifting my shoulder blades upward underneath that old sweatshirt, and I brought the wings together over my spine, then pulled them apart, then brought them together again. I couldn't get over how heavy they were, how developed and adult they felt. I could smell the air they stirred up, and it was a fresh, living smell, totally out of place with the smell of autumn. I moved my shoulder blades up and down, very slowly. I realized that it wasn't exactly my shoulder blades that I was moving, but these slim, developing muscles alongside of them. The wings moved right along with those little muscles, and a breeze began to blow right through the room. I was stirring up a breeze! Me! I remember seeing the sheet lift off the bed and gradually begin to billow like a ship's sail. I was hardly aware of how fast they were beating. I looked out the window, then took a step back.

"The VW beetle parked behind Titus' Lincoln had stopped, and I watched three figures step out of it. Titus' chickens were running all around, clucking their heads off. The man was already lugging a suitcase out of the backseat. He set it down in the dusty driveway. He and his wife weren't speaking to one another. She saw where he'd dropped the suitcase in the dirt and said, 'That's great, Ian, that's just great.' She didn't look happy. Neither of them did. If Titus hadn't told me he was expecting company, I would have thought that their car had just broken down here and forced them to ask Titus for help.

"Then I heard laughter. A child's laughter."

Nicholas felt his heart beating very hard, all the way up in his throat.

"This small boy, he couldn't have been more than six, came tumbling out of the backseat, all tousled hair and bright colors and noise, and then he looked around and fell into this awestruck silence. I remember when he spoke again, his voice was a squeal of excitement. 'Mommy! Chickens! Lookit the chickens!' And then he discovered the cows wandering through the field by the garage. 'Take me to see the cows! Dad, I wanna go ride on a cow!' "

Nicholas held his breath. At home, in one of his parents' photo albums, there was a picture from about eight or nine years ago taken at Uncle Titus' farm. His uncle and he were out in the middle of a pasture, and Titus was holding him dutifully astride the bowed back of a spotted holstein cow. This much, he knew even in the most logical quadrant of his brain, was true.

"So I stood there, up in the bedroom, with parts of my body moving that I didn't know I'd had," she said, "and I realized that I knew the name of the little boy running around the breezeway. It was just a flicker, but I had it. *Virgil*, I thought. That's a funny name. But that was it. I felt pieces beginning to connect in my mind, all these fragmented thoughts about people that I'd never met and places that I'd never seen, all of it came back while I stood there watching you run in circles around the yard. I knew that your name was Virgil, and that you were my little brother. A few seconds later another name came to me—*Ovid*. After Ovid, I didn't have another flash for what seemed like a very long time. But when I finally did, it was like all the darkness between me and the truth had not only lifted, it was like it had never been there in the first place. I heard myself say it: *Anthem*. Uncle Titus was right. Anthem was my name. And like you and Ovid, I was part of a miracle."

"Wait a second," he said. "What's the miracle part about me and Ovid?"

But again she didn't seem to hear him. "I couldn't wait for you to come and go again. You were the reason I had come here in the first place, although I hadn't known that at the time I'd crawled into the trunk of the Lincoln. I waited just as long as I could, up in the bedroom, listening to all of your voices through the floorboards, and later, as the night came down, I saw you and your parents making your way back up the road toward, I guessed, a guesthouse where Titus would be putting you up for the night."

"What did you do?" he asked.

"When I couldn't wait any longer . . . ?" She laughed that soft chime of a laugh again, making Nicholas feel dizzy. "I opened the window as much as I could, and—"

"But you said you were on the top floor of the house."

She laughed again, and he sensed this segment of her story, true or false, drawing itself to a close.

"Well," she said, "what better chance to try my wings?"

9

Portion of the testimony of Shelley Danzig, October 23.

I'm surprised Ian talked to you about That Night at all, actually. My husband can go on forever about the problems of the world, but his heart's a secret he keeps to himself, and what happened That Night stayed with him a long time. Just how long, I wouldn't find out for years.

I was sketching out a design for a card—it was a birthday card, but not for the Hallmark people. This was for Nicholas' birthday, which was coming up the day before Halloween.

I remember looking up from my design as Ian leapt up to answer the door. My husband is by nature a jumpy man.

"Eleven-thirty?" I heard him mumbling to himself, glancing at the tall oak grandfather clock by the door. "Who the hell—"

I heard him turning the knob and flinched. At home we've got a peephole in the door, of course: I told Ian I couldn't—wouldn't—open the door to just anybody. But out here at his cottage, I don't think Titus had locks put on half the doors, let alone peepholes. Ian told me we wouldn't need them, out here in the woods. Bears can't turn doorknobs, honey. Ha ha.

So he opened the door.

The girl on the porch had blood all over her. It was streaked across her pale face and through her hair. She was scraped and slashed very badly, as though she'd fallen through an entire garden of rosebushes. Ian seemed to stand in the doorway, just a silhouette against the cold clear night, for a long time before he turned and looked at me. "Oh my God, Shel—" he said. "Come here, quick."

The girl began to scream. At first it just sounded like random, hysterical babbling. If Ian had seemed to stand, mute, for a long time before responding, it took even longer for either of us to understand what she was screaming now.

"Where is he?" she screamed. "Where is he?"

She reached for Ian's shirttails, as if to implore him, and I pulled him back away from her. I remember very clearly the image of her hand, her hooked fingers groping at the air where Ian had been.

"Who are you looking for?" Ian said. He spoke in an absurdly calm voice, I thought. A teacher's voice. "Are you looking for Titus?"

That name seemed to bring her out of her hysteria like a slap. She stopped screaming and lifted her head, and now her eyes looked clear. For an instant she almost seemed ashamed of herself. She pushed her hair away from her eyes. "My brother, where is he? I've got to find him."

"Well," I said, "whoever he is, he doesn't live here."

"His name is Virgil. You call him Nicholas." Suddenly she stood up, cupping her hands around her mouth and bellowing. "Virgil! Nicholas! It's me! I'm here to take you back home!"

At that moment it didn't cross my mind that she knew Nicholas' name. My only thought was that this girl was crazy. She had come from out of the woods, and she wanted to get inside our house. I pushed past Ian to close the door in her face. That's when I saw a figure running up the gravel driveway behind her, a stout, heavyset man only half-dressed, the straps of his coveralls sliding down off his shoulders from underneath the dark cloak he was wearing. It was Titus.

Under the circumstances, I was glad to see him. Ian was calm, cool and collected . . . but Titus had been in the Army. He was strong back then.

In just a few strides he was on the steps, then he leapt up onto the porch and, just as the crazy girl was turning to see him, he grabbed her by the elbows, pinning them back behind her. They looked at each other. There was a sense of instant recognition. She fought him, struggling to get free, but he held her and started to pull her back down the steps.

"Titus," Ian said, "what's going on here?"

"Aw, hell, Ian—" Titus' face peered over the girl's shoulder. "Just some personal crap. Hell of a thing, I'm sorry about all of it."

"Let me go!" the girl screamed. "I'll kill you! I'll kill Uncle Titus! Where's my brother? Virgil? Virgil?"

Titus clapped his hand over her mouth, holding her elbows with his free arm. The girl's feet kicked as he pulled her down toward the gravel driveway. Ian and I stood there, watching Titus take her away, with a strangulated look of apology on his face.

"We'll ask him about it in the morning," I said to Ian, and I shut the door tightly, and wished I could lock it.

I could tell Ian wanted to go out there and ask questions, but I was not about to let him open that door again, not for anything. Not That Night.

10

"Hey," his voice said clearly, from behind the plywood.

Anthem blinked. The world leapt back into focus.

They had been riding again for nearly an hour since she had finished telling him how she had plunged through the window out into the night. At first she had been a little anxious talking to Nicholas after cradling him in her arms—they seemed to have shared a momentary closeness that could only be smothered by talking—but the memory had syphoned her into its world . . . syphoned both of them in, if Nicholas' spellbound silence was any indication. And she thought it was.

In the meantime, since she had finished telling about her maiden voyage from the window, they had been making miles. She had kept the pedal down at a steady seventy-five except when the road became excruciatingly bad, waiting to hear him speak.

"What?" she said. Her voice was rough and shaky. She expected him to comment on its unsteadiness, but he did not.

"What time is it?"

"It's"—she glanced at the cheap wristwatch that she had strapped to the steering wheel—"two forty-five in the afternoon."

"Come on," he said. "You said it was three o'clock a long time ago."

"We're in the central time zone now."

"Oh," he sighed, and she heard a sound of settling weight as he leaned against the plywood. "Illinois?"

She looked at the odometer, making the calculation. "Coming into Iowa, actually."

"Your home state," he said. "You want to drop by and pay a visit to dear old Mom and Dad in Iowa City?" Apparently she hadn't completely charmed him into submission just yet.

"I haven't been back there in eight years," she said, saying it straight out. His reaction was a risk she would have to take. "And I cut my last tie to them when Uncle Titus brought me back to Michigan."

There was a silence from behind the plywood, as though this last remark needed to be translated.

"He didn't try to send you back after he found you . . . flying around?" Nicholas asked. "Why did he keep you around?"

"He was very, very loyal to his employer."

"Who was her employer?"

"A woman named Maria," she said. "Our real father's ex-wife."

"Our—"

"It was Maria who separated you and me and Ovid," she said, "and hid us all from our father."

"You lost me somewhere back there."

"I expected that I probably would at some point." She tried to gather up some of the salient details. "Okay, as you've probably guessed by now, Titus was more than just our great-uncle. He was the guy—" She stopped, her lips still moving in the attempt to form words. "Look, could we just talk about this later? I mean, I can tell you everything else when we stop for the night."

"How did you find out about me?" he asked, as though he hadn't heard her. "How did you find out where I lived and what my name was? Did you just go to Titus' house and start asking him questions?"

She sighed. "I knew that Uncle Titus was the one who connected us in the first place, so he was naturally the one I used to help find you. I was at Titus' farmhouse for a few days, and I learned a lot. I knew if I ever wanted to find you, I would have to go through him first."

"Why? What did Titus really have to do with you and me in the first place?"

"I'll explain that later," she said. But some part of her already knew that she would have to explain it *now*. Already she was clutching the steering wheel harder than necessary and perspiring enough so that her heavy glasses seemed to be slipping perpetually off her nose. "If I were ever going to try to contact him now, I would have to break into his house to find him. He's kind of paranoid."

"What's he got to be paranoid of?"

She smiled. "You and Ovid, for starters." She felt something taking slow, almost sensual possession of her, the feeling not entirely unpleasant. What had Saint Jack called it? Cataclysmic certainty. Bringing Virgil and Ovid together again would start a chain reaction that would almost certainly destroy Titus before it was over. Judging from the weather outside, the cataclysm had already begun. In another few hours, perhaps by tomorrow, all they would need to do was look out the window, at the blizzard. Virgil wouldn't be able to look out the window now, of course, from the back of the van, but she would let him sit up in front by that point.

He would see the power that was building, as inevitably as an electrical charge, between his older brother and himself.

Nicholas cleared his throat, talking in that loud voice he seemed to favor. "Are you saying that this guy Ovid and me together . . . we could kill Uncle Titus with this thing, this force field?"

"That's exactly what I'm saying."

"What makes you think that I want to kill him in the first place?"

"It doesn't matter what you want," she told him flatly. "Once the two of you come together, the choice is going to be out of your hands."

11

It was dusk when they headed out around Iowa City and into the network of secondary roads beyond the outskirts of town. Green, gently sloping hills carried the van along so that half the time Anthem only needed to finger-tap the customized accelerator mounted on the steering wheel. Gravity did more than its share. She drove deliberately below the speed limit, waiting for the sun to set, and when it had she turned around and headed back up the one-lane dirt road at the same speed she'd gone down it until the gravel driveway appeared on the left. She had seen no other traffic for the last twenty minutes.

The driveway back through the woods to the house was nearly a quarter mile long. Up at the end of it she parked behind the small, two-story structure crouched among a few dead willows. It was utterly secluded, its paint colorless and peeling, and had a certain devious slant that indicated it might collapse before it saw another spring.

She stepped out, cocked her head, listened. Yes, the creek was still there. She could hear the white water clattering over the rocks and fallen trees that cluttered its bed. Wind gusted through the field on the other side of the road, rattling through the cornstalks and then dropping back down again. She could smell the rich, rotting banquet of autumn in the Midwest all around her. It was nearly dark.

He rapped on the plywood behind her. "Where are we now?"

"Middle of Iowa." She reached under her seat for the handcuffs, and now a small flat automatic pistol that hardly seemed to weigh more than a few ounces in her hand. It belonged to Saint Jack, and he had taught Anthem how to shoot tin cans and seagulls with it down on the beach last summer. She inserted the clip, fully loaded, and heard it drop into place. "I can show you a map if you want to know where exactly."

She opened the back for him again with the gun in her right hand, but not aimed at him. He just stared.

"What, are you going to kill me here?"

She shook her head. "Just insurance, Virgil. We're spending the night here. I won't be able to hold on to you every single second."

He turned and looked at the unfortunate house that hid the van from the road, not resisting when she took his right hand and clapped the bracelet over it. As a reward she hardly tightened it, just enough so that he couldn't sweat himself loose. "Would you even be able to kill me if I'm really your brother?" he asked. He sounded genuinely curious.

"I don't know," she said. "I've never killed anybody before."

He offered up his bitter laugh again, then hugged himself, a surprisingly childlike gesture coming on the heels of adult cynicism.

"It's cold. I don't even have a good jacket, just this stupid windbreaker."

"Let's go inside," she said, nodding. "There's no heat, but I stocked the place with blankets and food on my way through here a few days ago."

"Whose house is this, anyway?"

"Well, as it turned out, Titus owned this place too, but most of the time he lived in the city. After he took me to Michigan and I saw you for the first time eight years ago, he took me back here. It became our secret place kind of by default, after he sat me down and told me everything I was already starting to suspect about who I really was, about our real mother and father and what happened to make things turn out the way they did."

"I guess he wasn't such a faithful employee after all."

She couldn't tell whether he was actually catching on or trying to make fun. She supposed it didn't matter. Nothing she could say at this point could change how he received the news.

They made their way through the willows and across the neglected backyard. The grass had shot up almost knee-high in places along the gravel driveway, and tall, tough-looking weeds sprouted up even higher. On the back stoop she reached above the broken latticework into a hanging rain gutter and produced a key. She turned it in the lock and swung open the door on a hundred sour memories. They stepped inside.

"I know it looks pretty bad," she said. Actually it looked worse than she remembered. A three-legged couch sank into one corner. The carpet was worn through to expose dull patches of the floor. Tattered curtains floated in a draft from the picture window. She thought she saw a mouse scramble across the floor and disappear into the wall. From his expression, Nicholas had seen it, too.

"Like I said, the furnace doesn't work, and there's no electricity." She led him into the kitchen. "But I did bring a white-gas stove if you wanted to heat up anything, and I've got coffee . . ." She paused. "Why are you looking at me like that?"

He blinked at her in the dim light. "What?"

"You're staring at my shoulders."

"I'm looking for your wings," he said. "I don't even see any kind of lump underneath the back of your sweater. What happened?"

"Ah," she said, nodding. "Another story."

"When do I get to hear this one?"

"Right here," she promised. "Tonight."

12

Portion of the testimony of Ian Danzig, October 26:
Uncle Titus. God, but that man was an enigma.

You know, of course, that he was a very rich man. He had his quirks. But for giving us Nicholas, I thought I could forgive him anything.

Shelley wouldn't have asked about That Night, I don't think, if I hadn't continued to bring it up. That's the way she is. She knew Titus had visitors out here on his farm, and that he also had his girlfriends. Gradually I discovered that she had drawn her own conclusions. She thought the girl might have been the daughter of one of Titus' girlfriends, or some visitor that he hadn't told us about. An unstable visitor, to be sure. Insanity runs rampant in these little northern towns, Shel says. It's like a plague.

Maybe. But I wasn't satisfied, and I wouldn't be, until I found out more about the girl who wanted to take Nicholas away. The young girl who had claimed to be his sister. I didn't think she was the daughter of one of Titus' girlfriends, and I didn't think she was just another visitor at the farm, either.

So, yes, like a man undertaking a lifetime's obses.ion, I started asking Titus questions. And I got answers I didn't like, not one damned bit.

13

She led him deeper into the house. Inside, the kitchen and dining room looked to Nicholas' eyes as though they might have been almost elegant at one time, with their high ceilings and a crystal chandelier dangling high above a long oak table. But now roaches flitted from open cupboards and a bluish moss had begun to crawl over the dirty dishes piled in the sink. Rain had seeped through the ceiling, causing the wallpaper to peel and the linoleum floor to buckle and heave so severely that they had to step over its little valleys and ridges.

He was still preoccupied with thoughts about her wings. He had the distinct feeling that she had plenty left to tell him. Where the wings had come from. What happened to them.

He realized that he was staring at the telephone affixed to the kitchen wall.

"Go ahead and see who you can raise on that," Anthem said, trying to lighten the mood with her voice. "Nobody's paid a bill on this place in years." She opened the pantry door in front of her, beside the icebox. "Are you hungry?"

He was looking out at the coral-colored moon through the window.

"Virg? Do you want something to eat?"

"What I want is for you to tell me what this is about," he said. "I mean everything, all the way to the end, as well as you know how to tell it. That's what you promised to tell me. The whole story. And that's what I want."

She walked with him into the dining room and sat with him at the table. "Don't worry, I will."

"Then do it. Don't stand around asking me if I want food. Just tell me."

"I will," she repeated, a little taken aback, "but first I want you to know that even if you can't accept it, it doesn't change anything. I'm still taking you with me."

"As your prisoner?"

She locked the other bracelet around the arm of her own chair. "All I can do is hope that you *will* accept it, eventually."

He said something that she didn't quite catch.

"Coffee," he repeated. He'd had it only a few times before, but right now its bitterness appealed to him. "Can you make some on that little stove? I guess I'd like something warm inside me."

She had some instant, which she added to some boiling water, and when it was made, she sat down again and began to talk to him, steadily for almost two hours. Occasionally he glanced out at the moon, but mostly he looked right into her eyes through her thick glasses and the shining green eyes behind them, and listened to what she said.

14

"Back in 1978," Anthem said, "a long time before people like John Gotti and the Lucchese family were going up in front of grand juries and organized crime was still going strong in New York, the woman who would be our stepmother was married into one of these families. The union racketeer that Maria married—you wouldn't recognize the name—disappeared during the first year that they were married. But he didn't disappear for long. Somebody found him in Queens, in the trunk of a car, with his hands tied behind his back and three bullets in the head. Maria left New York not long after that. Titus told me that she had already taken an interest in another man. I have no reason to doubt what he said. Titus was her bodyguard. He worked for a crime syndicate in New York, but the mob kept track of her all the way up to Boston."

She saw Nicholas blink. He was listening intently, his head cocked in a way that might have been comical had he not looked so frightened. Ever since his questions about her jumping down from the window, he had looked like someone making his way across thin ice, waiting to hear it crack under his feet. She averted her gaze and pushed on with the story.

"The man she met in Boston was named Jack. Saint Jack, that's what they called him at the jazz clubs he played around town. He played at Wally's, he even played at the Blue Note and the Vanguard in New York one time, opening for Dexter Gordon. Have you ever heard of Dexter Gordon?"

Nicholas shook his head.

"Well, anyway, that was the first time she saw Saint Jack, actually, at that show. Titus was with her then, and he told me that she spent the whole show bugging the bartender for Saint Jack's phone number. I guess she had a thing for musicians in general, piano players in particular. Well, finally the bartender got so tired of it he picked up the telephone receiver and held it up in the air until Jack finished his song early, before he was finished playing the set. Jack didn't even get mad at her when he found out it wasn't a phone call. He just sat and talked to

Maria while the rest of his band finished playing. The two of them kept talking and she kept buying him drinks all the way through Dexter's set too. Afterward, Dexter's quartet finished and Dexter sat down next to him and said, 'Man, that was *hot*, why'd you quit playing in the middle?' " Anthem laughed. "In the meantime, Jack was afraid to say anything too nice to her, because he was afraid Titus was the guy she came with and that he would mop the floor with him." She shook her head. "Poor Jack."

Nicholas sipped his coffee. It was getting cold.

"For a few months Maria pretended it was nothing and didn't say anything to the family about him. After all, she was still supposed to be in mourning. But on the weekends she told them she was going to visit her mother up in Boston. Well, after a month or two she was going to Boston during the week, too. Titus was wise to her by then, and finally she decided to tell the family outright. All right, she said, his name's Jack, he's a widower. His wife died recently giving birth to his youngest son. He's a composer, but makes most of his money giving lessons at his flat in the Back Bay. He's got a little girl and two boys, the youngest is just a few months old. The oldest is Ovid; the middle one, Anthem, is the girl. The infant's name is Virgil. You.''

"Virgil. I still can't get over that. Can't I just keep my old name?"

Anthem noticed that he was trembling. All at once, she felt a wonderful rush of light-headed exuberance. *Thank God*, she thought, *I think I'm getting through*.

"We can decide that part later. Right now I have to tell you about what's between you and Ovid."

He shook his head, brow creasing in confusion.

"I told you about my wings, didn't I?" she said. "We were born into a family of miracles, Virgil. You and Ovid had more between you than brotherhood. You could call it magic or magnetism or the spirit of the womb, but when you and Ovid were together, something extraordinary always happened. It was a sense of things being slightly off, a little jig in the natural order, if that makes any more sense to you. The temperature in the room went way up. Another time, I looked into the playroom, and I saw you and Ovid sitting on the floor together . . . you couldn't have been more than six months old, so Ovid was probably ten. You'd torn a bunch of pages from one of your coloring books, and they were all flattened up against the ceiling like they'd been glued up there, but I could feel something like a really strong draft, blowing them up." She saw him raise his eyebrows. "No, I'm not making this up." Now she was trembling too, as though a magnetic current were thrumming between them. "Another time there was an electrical storm, a real frog-strangler, as Titus might say. It brought on one of the worst blackouts in the history of Boston."

"Look, I'm sorry, but . . ." He was shaking his head. He seemed, at least, to be grappling with what she said and not simply dismissing it. "This whole thing is crazy. I mean, that's just really crazy."

"Nobody ever claimed to be able to explain it," she conceded. "But when you two were together in the room, everybody noticed a kind of barometric change in the air. It was like you and he weren't supposed to be brothers, but halves of some whole organism that never fused together right when you were in the womb. Ovid was born, and then ten years later you came out . . . like the second half of him. I was stuck in the middle. It's not so crazy, really. When a woman is pregnant, and the child she's carrying is male, her body first responds to it as if it were a malignancy, like some kind of a tumor. The same cells that would fight a cancer will attack the fetus of the boy and try to kill it before it can develop. No one really knows why the mother's body does this. It sort of falls into that trench between real and make-believe that people refer to as 'unexplained phenomena.' Now, the biology of two brothers isn't so different. If, in the very early stages after fertilization, our mother's body realized that the cell growth inside of it was altogether out of hand, not just a boy but some sort of a biological runaway—"

"Hold it," Nicholas said. "You're saying that she tried to . . . cut us apart, or something like that? That I'm only half a person that should've been born whole, ten years earlier?"

She shook her head vehemently. "You're definitely a whole person, Virgil. What I'm saying is that maybe together, you and Ovid were much *more* than human, just like I am more than human, and that sometime very early in your development our mother's body realized that. So instead it went to war with the thing inside of it, and in the end, it lost."

"So what? So when me and this other guy, Ovid—"

"Your *brother*, Ovid."

"This brother and me, what's going to happen when we get together again? The end of the world?"

"You know, that's probably not so funny," Anthem said. "Because the fact is, we're heading in a southwest direction, but every mile we travel it seems to be getting colder and more like winter."

He didn't reply. He had noticed that it was much colder outside tonight, but hadn't given it much thought after that.

"Look outside the window tomorrow morning, and I'll bet you'll see frost on the grass. You know, mid-October isn't outlandishly early for frost, but it is something of a surprise. By tomorrow night, as we get closer to California, I bet we'll be seeing snow. Maybe even a few roads closed. You and Ovid haven't been together for a long time now, so you'll probably whip up a pretty big blizzard when you finally do see each other again."

"Anthem." Nicholas sank his face into his hands. "I don't think . . . that I believe any of this."

"Let me finish telling you what happened before," she said. "Saint Jack, our father, he knew about this . . . connection, I guess you could call it, between you and Ovid. Or at least he was aware of it on some level. But he didn't mention anything about it to Maria when he married her later that year. I think you can understand why he was hesitant to try to explain it."

"You mean because it's crazy."

"It sounds crazy," she corrected, "but the fact is that after she married him, she started to notice something between you and Ovid almost right away. She used to get headaches, migraines, whenever you two were together in the same room. From what she told Jack, she also heard a sort of high-frequency whining in her ears, the way your head feels on a jet as they're pressurizing the cabin, except that her ears never popped. The pressure in her head just continued to build, to the point that she didn't want to be around you two at all during the day. After a year and a half the marriage was really suffering, and she wanted to go back to New York, where the family was offering to protect her. They had never liked Saint Jack, or his children, from the start. He certainly wasn't perfect. He drank too much and spent most of the best years of his life, right up until he met Maria, trying to stay sober and failing miserably. And to top it all off, she started to suspect that Jack was taking one of his piano students to bed with him. Later her suspicions were confirmed, and there were serious consequences."

"Consequences," Nicholas said. "Consequences like what?"

"It's my opinion that his screwing around wasn't the last straw for her. It just gave her the excuse she needed to go to New York, back to the syndicate. She was furious. They understood. She wanted to kill him, which they wouldn't do, but they agreed that such a man should be hurt. Revenge was clearly in order. So one night they sent Titus up to Boston, to break into Jack's flat and take his three children away. It was an ideal situation from their vantage point. We were all very young.

All Titus had to do was find foster homes for all three of us in a place where no one would ask any questions. He had to watch over the kids from a distance as they grew up, preferably in three different parts of the country. So Titus took me to an old business associate of his, in Iowa City. I was almost seven years old, and I was told that these were my natural parents. I was told that my name was Gertrude. He took Ovid to a Methodist minister and his wife in Boulder. And he found a couple in Michigan, where he deposited you, under the new name of Nicholas Harrison Danzig.''

"So he really is my uncle, but . . .''

"Well, he's really your *adoptive* uncle,'' she said. "But mainly he is an employee who stayed around to watch you and make sure you never found out who you were, or that Jack never got you back. Or most important of all, that we never had a chance to recognize each other. I never would have gotten very far with my conclusions if I hadn't seen you running around the breezeway with those white chickens all around you.'' She smiled at the familiar image. "But eight years ago, I did.''

"How did you find out about all of this?'' he asked.

"It happened after I had jumped from the third-floor window and gone drifting down to look at you in the guesthouse.'' Anthem nodded. "And yes, before you ask, the wings served me perfectly well.'' She grinned. "It was like . . . I can't explain the sensation of leaping out into the night for the first time, feeling your feet leave the windowsill and then balancing, just for half an instant, on the precipice of the darkness. For that half instant you're sure you're going to crash. And then, *voom!* The wind caught me and lifted me upward again. My stomach just plunged, and at first I thought I was still going down. It was like an express elevator shooting me up ten floors in a second and a half. I was probably a hundred and fifty feet up before I knew what was happening. When I looked down I could see Titus' entire estate spread out below me in the night. The field, the farmhouse, the guesthouse, the beach . . . I just started laughing hysterically at what I was doing. There was almost no period of trial and error, of crashing into trees or flying into the wind. The wings themselves seemed to recognize the *shape* of the wind, the way your hand would immediately recognize the shape and texture of an orange or a lightbulb. They knew it even before I knew it. And they shaped themselves so that the wind filled them.

"I started experimenting with elevation, dipping and swooping down the shoreline where the waves were breaking. The wind on the water was less reliable, but I found that I could move about six inches above the surface, skimming just above the waves. Then I banked right and went back up—I was gasping for air, I still couldn't believe I was doing all of this—and went back into the woods, just above the tree line, until I found the guesthouse where Titus was putting you up for the night. I went up to your bedroom window and hovered. I could see you curled under your sheets, just your little face exposed, and I tapped on the glass very softly. I almost hated to wake you up.

"As it turned out, I never got the chance. Titus had seen me go, and followed me back through the woods. From down below me in the trees I heard him laughing, saying, 'Anthem, come back down from there. We've got business to take care of.' I didn't want to come down, I never wanted to put my feet on the ground again, but out of curiosity for what he had to tell me, I finally did." She shook her head. "Sometimes, now and then, I wish that I'd never come down, that I'd just flown away."

"It would have been all right with me," Nicholas said.

Anthem ignored him. "He made me walk back to the house. Walk! After being up in the air, walking felt like crawling. When we got there, he sat down with me at the kitchen table and confessed everything. He told me about Maria, and the New York syndicate, and you and Ovid. As he spoke, he kept looking at his watch as it got closer and closer to midnight. When he finished, he told me that he'd made arrangements to meet a man who had been looking for me for a long time. The man was Saint Jack, our father."

"How did they find each other?"

"That part wasn't hard. As part of his job, Titus had been keeping track of Saint Jack for the last five years or so out in California, making sure that he never got too close to finding out where we were. But the fact was that Titus was getting old. Over the years, his hard-and-fast vigilance had started to soften. I think he actually started feeling little pangs of guilt. On more than one occasion, I get the impression that he had actually met with Jack in bars and had dinner with him, and toyed with the idea of betraying the syndicate. I think he actually grew to like our father, an old nemesis from years back, and both of them sensed that a reunion was inevitable, at some point.

"And Jack had been ready for this particular meeting. Apparently my hiding in the trunk of Titus' car wasn't such a surprise as I had thought. In fact, I think if I hadn't gone up to Michigan on my own, Titus would have eventually taken me up there, because Jack was also up there waiting for me. Titus had warned him that the syndicate was still interested, and had advised him to keep a low profile. Jack had taken a job playing piano in a local bar on the night Titus told me all of this. Just before midnight Titus stood up and said we were going to drive out to the bar, where I saw our father for the first time in five years."

"What was he like?" Nicholas asked.

"He was dead drunk!" Anthem said, in a rush of nervous laughter that lasted too long. "In fact, what I think I recognized first about him was the whiskey on his breath. When we pulled up, we were late, and Jack was just giving up on waiting for us. He was standing out in the parking lot trying to fit his house key into his car door. He—"

She swallowed, then exhaled more of the same nervous laughter.

"But it was him. It was Saint Jack. It was our father. I sat in Titus' Lincoln, watching the two of them talk casually in the dark parking lot, almost like friends. Suddenly Jack burst into all these wild, angry gestures. I couldn't imagine what he had to be angry about. He was about to get his daughter back! Finally he nodded, like he was giving in. Titus came back to the car and tapped on my window. When I rolled it down, he told me that he and Jack had made a deal, and that I could go with Jack back to California on one condition. Titus hadn't gone completely soft, you see. He'd gone dangerously soft, because there was still a diamond-hard streak running through him, from head to toe. And God help you if you had something that he wanted." She stopped a moment to catch her breath. "Anyway, that was the night I went back to California with our true father and, incidentally, that was the last time that Jack ever took a drink in his life. We began to make plans for getting you and Ovid back, too." When she looked up at Nicholas again, she noticed that he wasn't looking at her face at all, but back at her shoulders. She nodded, indicating that she was finished talking for a while. A single teardrop slipped from the corner of her eye and rolled down her cheek. "And now I guess you probably understand."

"I—" Nicholas cleared his throat and tried again. "I'd like to see your wings, if I could."

"My wings." She looked at him, almost sympathetically. Then without another word, she turned her back to him and reached around behind her, lifting the sweater up over her head and then pulling her white T-shirt up too. Fabric whispered across bare flesh and then fell silent.

Nicholas stared at the long, beautiful curve of her back, the gentle cleft of her shoulder blades as they appeared from underneath the fabric of the T-shirt. Then his eyes stopped, fixed on the white scar tissue that gathered, crudely, in a rough parenthesis shape between her shoulder blades.

"So now you know Titus' final condition," Anthem's voice said, from over her shoulder. The voice was sad, but stable, the voice of a woman who has lived with, and lived through, some singular tragedy. "Before we left the bar that night, Saint Jack held me down in the backseat of the Lincoln and covered my mouth. And while he held me down, Titus used his pocketknife to cut off the wings."

15

Portion of the testimony of Jennifer Clara Wiest, October 16.
   Sure, I remember the girl but not by the name Anthem. We were probably the closest thing to neighbors that the old man Titus ever had, at his farm. That was before he moved north to the Upper Peninsula. I was twelve or thirteen years old then—no, more like almost eight, because I'm twenty now, and that was 1980.

The first time I saw Gertie was that summer. She was out in the middle of the cornfield that stretches across Titus' property, toward ours, running like crazy. I didn't see her very often—maybe once every four months, as the seasons changed. I recall walking with Poppa through the little elm grove behind our house in May, or October, and seeing him sniff the air. "Well," he'd say, "I expect we'll see Gertie running soon." It was sort of a family joke, but also kind of spooky. None of us knew how the girl and Titus fit together, or how often she came to visit, or even who she was, but I knew that the moment I smelled a change of seasons in the air, especially summer into fall . . . well, you couldn't drag me into that cornfield. I was afraid I'd cut across a row of corn and see her standing there, with her eyes gone wild and tatters of cornstalk sticking in her hair.

"Somebody said she's his crazy niece," my mother told me once. "Somebody heard Titus saying he tried to have her committed, but they can't keep her away from him. They say she's tried to kill him once." Well, I don't know about that—

What?

Oh, yes, I did meet up with her once. But not in the cornfields, like in my

nightmares. It was the second-to-last time I ever saw her. I was in Cleary's
Toy and Hobby downtown. I felt very bold, on my own turf. And that's why,
when she'd walked up and down all five aisles at Cleary's and brushed past
me again on her way to the door, I whispered, "I saw you take that."

Not loud enough so that Mr. Cleary could hear me behind the counter. Just
loud enough for Gertie to hear, as she walked out the door. I wasn't even sure
what she had slipped into her pocket, but I'd seen her hand slide out, plain
as anything, and slip the tiny box from the shelf into her dirty back pocket
while Mr. Cleary was talking to his wife on the phone.

When I went out, there was Gertie, waiting and staring at me. I felt a little
unnerved, but not afraid: it was daylight, and familiar faces filled the store
windows and shops up and down the street: Cole's Barbershop, the Village
Grocery, the Happy Town lounge. I said, "Who are you, anyway? Does your
daddy know you steal?" Those two questions seemed linked, the second giving
me a right to ask the first.

She just glared at me.

"He's not my father," she said sullenly. "I don't even come from around
here."

"I seen you running through the fields," I said.

That's when she turned and walked away from me. I never found out what
it was she stole that day. The box was too little to be much of anything, anyway,
I never said anything.

16

Anthem screwed a thick white candle into the mouth of the Coke
bottle and lit its wick, then rose from the table in silence. The
house seemed to regain some of its old elegance by candlelight. Stains
on the wallpaper weren't so obvious, the carpet's manginess was obscured by indigo pools of shadow.

Nicholas didn't know whether or not to believe what she had told
him, but still he had questions. "All these years," he asked, "why did
my mom and dad . . . why did they keep lying to me?"

"Lying to you was just part of the deal. Uncle Titus was instructed to
find a young, childless couple, far away from New York. People who
wanted children but couldn't have any, for whatever reason. And there

are a thousand reasons, you know. Adoption isn't an easy process, especially for newlyweds on a tight budget.''

"If I was still a baby, and Ovid was twelve, and you were only six—'' He stared at her. "How old are you now?''

"I'm nineteen years old.'' She blushed lightly, and her fingertips traced the wrinkles and worry lines that had formed at the edges of her mouth. It was the first sign of self-consciousness that he had seen in her. He had thought she was much older.

"It's all the stress of what happened when we were separated from each other,'' she said. "When I lived with my old family, before the wings, I couldn't sleep at night, I was moody and depressed and unhappy almost every second of the day. When I think back on all the days that I spent being angry . . . terribly, violently angry, as if something of mine had been shattered and brushed away . . .'' She shook her head. "I was always getting in Dutch, I had trouble in school, I started fights and shoplifted. Little Miss Look-out-here comes-trouble.''

She swallowed, and he heard her throat click. Only her eyes shone now, in the darkness.

"Upstairs in the playroom, you'll find all these models I put together when I was a kid. You know, those plastic Aurora kits, cars, planes, battleships, the kind of thing that you'd think only boys liked. But when I was about nine, I loved to assemble those pieces into something whole again. I think Uncle Titus knew what I needed. I spent my whole childhood trying to put something back together again, never knowing quite what it was. And when the pieces wouldn't hold together''—a frown pulled back over her mouth, as though the thought itself were pushing outward on her skull, stretching her skin back tightly, and her eyes seemed to flare up with rage—"I just *couldn't stand it.*''

He took a step back, not even meaning to, really. It was the sort of reflexive retreat he might make from a snarly dog. He watched the anguish drain slowly out of her face again, and at last her expression seemed suffused with light, but it seemed to him like a false, untrustworthy light. His own, limited knowledge of human behavior had no means of qualifying it.

"My favorite things, though, were these two little magnetic dogs. Titus gave those to me, too. He bought them at a little toy shop here in Iowa. They were the cutest little things. They looked like little terriers, and . . . and they'd . . .'' Her voice faded into silence, and her eyes looked empty and thoughtless. "Well, now I can't remember whether they'd stick face-to-face, or turn around and push each other apart, but . . .''

Again, the silence, the blankness filled her eyes. "Anyway, there was one way that you'd put them, either nose-to-nose or tail-to-tail, and they'd stick. If you put them the other way, they'd push each other apart so hard that you could hardly force them within an inch or two of each other. And do you know what?"

He looked at her, waiting. Was she smiling?

"I even gave them names, those two little dogs. I called them Virgil and Ovid! Virgil Dog and Ovid Dog!" She *was* smiling, almost beaming, at the memory of it, and then the smile faded. "I didn't even know, at least consciously, who Virgil and Ovid were—I mean, I didn't—"

"Maybe Uncle Titus mentioned it to you once," Nicholas suggested carefully.

"It's possible." She sighed. "It's possible, but I doubt it. I think that some part of me, the same part that wanted to put things together, remembered two little twin brothers, Virgil and Ovid. You know?"

"Yeah," he nodded distractedly. "Sure."

"Oh, *Virg!*" she said. The squeak in her voice surprised him, because now Anthem was back again. Her eyes shone. "You'll do fine! I know when I first . . . I mean, when Titus first told me who I was, I thought I'd never be able to accept it. A different family? Two brothers? But it was so wonderful to go out west to California and start out a new life with Jack. It was such a feeling of being . . . *restored.*"

He felt himself starting to go numb. Information overload. To put it mildly.

"You look exhausted," she said. "You'll be able to cope with all of this a lot better after we head upstairs for a night's sleep, I'm sure."

The dingy walls were beginning to swirl into uncertain hues of gray. With little choice but to comply, he shrugged and allowed himself to be led toward the stairs.

17

Portion of the testimony of Jennifer Clara Wiest, October 16:
The last time I saw her was not long after I talked to her out in front of Cleary's. It was in the fall. That last time I did not speak to her, or even come close to her.

She was running through the cornfields, like she always used to do. Running along the rows with the wind blowing through her hair. She had roses in her cheeks. Also, I remember one other thing.

She was wearing glasses. Very thick lenses. It's a weird thing to recall, but when I saw the glint of those lenses in the afternoon sun, and realized she was wearing glasses, I remembered how she'd conducted herself when we'd met face-to-face. She'd had an uncertain, squinting way about her that I'd always chalked up to her being plain old country-style crazy. But I'd rather believe it was just nearsightedness. The Christian woman in me would like to believe that, anyway.

18

Ovid, my older brother, he thought, repeating the words over and over as they mounted the stairs to go up. He wondered if he fit Anthem's profile of a displaced child. He tried to recall any hostility, any insomnia or nightmares of his own throughout the last few years, and was a little disappointed to realize that he had almost none; nor was he obsessed with assembling models. Nothing like that.

You never sprouted wings, either, some mental voice cackled crazily at him. *Not even a few loose feathers under the bedsheets. Bummer.*

He could doubt her about the wings all he wanted, of course, but what about the scars on her back? Those were real. He had seen them with his own eyes.

They reached the top of the stairs, and she led him into a small, dark room not much bigger than the back of the van. In the half-darkness he saw the outline of an old canopy bed, a highboy and nightstand, a cracked window. He thought he heard something rustle under the bed.

"Don't lock me up," he said. "What if rats come out and start nibbling on my toes?"

"There aren't any rats up here."

"I saw mice in the living room. There are crickets in the carpet. Why not rats under the covers?"

She crossed her arms. "There's no food to be had under the covers."

"There will be if you handcuff me there." He imagined himself awakening with small, furry gray bodies clinging to the foot of the bed, creeping closer as he tugged vainly at the cuffs clamped to the bedpost. The image was all too clear in his mind. He felt a shudder run over him. "All the Nicholas you can eat. Yum."

She rolled her eyes, seeing he wasn't going to give up on it. "All right, look, no handcuffs, okay? But you're going to have to sleep with me, because I don't want you running off."

"With you?" He blinked. "In the same bed?"

"Titus' room has a double bed with clean sheets," she said. "Why not? We're family, aren't we?"

He didn't say anything.

"Let me put it this way," she said. "It's me or the rats."

"Such a tempting offer."

They crept down the long hallway, the candlelight swooning over cracked plaster walls and the corners so thick with cobwebs that they seemed rounded, not angular at all. At the end of the hall Anthem nudged a door open with her elbow, keeping the candle upright.

"I think . . ." she started, setting the candle down and groping for something on the nightstand. "All right, here we go." A white flashlight beam cut across the darkness of the room, moving over the ruined ceiling, then down to the bed. He had to admit, after the mattress in the van, and the bed down the hall, the sheets and blankets did look clean, and even the pillows looked soft and cool and full. Only then did he realize how a day in the van had exhausted him. Just the darkness of the house was making him feel sleepy.

"We'll be getting up early," Anthem said. "Don't worry, I'll wake you."

"I'm sure," he said. He held up his still-cuffed wrist. "Could you—"

She nodded, inserted the key and turned it. The bracelet popped open and fell away. He massaged the raw patch of skin where the metal had been clamped for the last hour and a half, then sank down onto the bed. The mattress gave in around him, and any remaining reluctance to sleep in the bed with Anthem vanished. He sighed deeply and slipped his sneakers off his feet, stretching out until the muscles in his back and neck and arms began to tingle with relief. He sighed again and stretched luxuriously out across the clean sheet and yawned.

Anthem watched all of this attentively, as if she wouldn't be comfortable until he was fast asleep. He heard her slide the pistol from her belt and lay it on the bureau on her side of the bed. She was humming softly to herself. It was the only sound in the room, besides the crickets chirring downstairs. He heard her unzip her jeans, and the rustle of her sweater as she pulled it off, then, at last, the glasses with their thick and heavy lenses, as she folded the bows together with a soft click. She set them on the nightstand next to the gun.

Finally he heard the grunt of tired bedsprings as she sat down on the edge of the bed. He felt a gentle tug on the blankets as she drew them over to her side to cover herself, then she coughed once and fell silent. A few minutes passed and she started to breathe regularly through her mouth. Drowsily Nicholas realized that he was allowing himself to be hypnotized by the slow, mild susurrus of her breathing. He took a slow breath himself and waited for the queer, half-dreamt thoughts to come as his mind exchanged currency on the borderlands of deep sleep.

Then all at once she took a quick breath, almost like a gasp. The bedsheets shifted. She made another, breathless sound, like a swimmer gasping for breath. His heart skipped. What was she doing? Crying in her sleep? The bedsheets moved again, sliding urgently to her side now, as if she were trying to cover something up.

"Anthem?" he whispered.

Another cry in the darkness. More movement on the bed.

"Anthem?" Sitting up, looking over, he saw her face in the pale moonlight through the window. She was muttering something. Her shape heaved almost convulsively on the bed, and her arms tore at the blankets until they slipped down, exposing the smooth, flattening shapes of her breasts. Her body was tensed, as if she were struggling with some invisible enemy. "Titus?" he heard her mumble. The muscles in her exposed stomach tensed suddenly, then slackened. "Titus, no—no, stay away . . ."

Her hand swung up to the nightstand and grabbed at the pistol. It clattered and disappeared under the covers. He winced, waiting for the shot.

He held his breath for what seemed like minutes, but she had slumped back into bed and remained still. He counted passing seconds. Whatever bad dream she'd been having seemed exorcised from her mind.

"Anthem?" he repeated.

No response. Slowly he sat up on his side and swung himself around to the edge of the bed. The room was full of moonlight now . . . either that or his eyes had readjusted to darkness. He said her name again and waited for some indication that she was awake. Nothing. Then he stood up as slowly as he could and crept across the floor. The wooden boards squeaked now, which he didn't remember before. But Anthem still did not move.

His eyes flicked to the nightstand. The pistol was gone. It was still clutched in her hand. But the flashlight stood upright on the far end of the nightstand. Silently he picked it up and stepped through the doorway.

Behind him he heard Anthem snuffle up a deep, troubled breath. He froze.

"Virgil?" she murmured.

He held his breath, trembling. His throat was dry. He wanted to cough.

"Virgil?" she repeated. He heard her sit up. Then came the unmistakable snick of the pistol's hammer being cocked back. "Who's out there?"

In the blackness he heard her stand up, take a step and pause. His pulse was racing, his nervous system perched on the brink of total rebellion. In another step she'd be in the doorway, looking right at him. Dimly he remembered a closet here behind him, though he had no idea how deep it was, or whether it was empty enough for him to climb into and hide. He grasped for the doorknob, turned it and opened the door behind his back without an inkling of where it led.

"Is there someone out here? Titus? Titus, is that you?" He realized that she had to be dreaming still, at least in part. It was hardly comforting.

In a single step he was inside the closet. Distracted, feeling their way, his stocking feet crunched over shards of something—

Pain spiked through him instantly. It was broken glass, he realized, sucking air through his teeth. A scream welled up in his throat until he couldn't stand it an instant longer, until he was sure he'd wail out loud, shifting helplessly from one foot to the other like a little kid who desperately needed to pee. Tears sprung to his eyes. The flashlight slipped from his fingers and clattered to the floor, but he didn't hear it. He felt like he'd jumped out of his body for a moment to give the pain enough room, like for just an instant he'd actually gone deaf, dumb and blind with the pain. Great thick layers of agony seemed to be peeling away from his face and forehead.

Then the pistol shot exploded, and a single shot whined past him. He felt a warm wetness as his bladder let go, streaming down his thigh.

"Titus," her voice murmured, edging softly into the echo of the blast. "I've been looking for you."

His body tensed, straining against the passing seconds, while Anthem pulled the hammer back again. For a moment he lost consciousness. It was something like mild shock. He waited for what seemed like an hour, feeling the blood beginning to ooze from the pads of his feet, trying to balance out the pain and dread so that neither got the better of him. He leaned back into the closet, felt the slick feel of old winter coats brush against him. He waited until he heard her turn around and step back into the bedroom again.

". . . kill you . . ." she murmured, but he wouldn't have recognized the words if he hadn't heard them before. They were muffled, buried in sleep.

The pistol clattered across the nightstand, then the house was suddenly silent again. He could smell the burning powder from the single shot she'd fired in the darkness, but he had no interest in finding out how close she'd come to hitting him. He had to save his feet. That came first, even before he made his escape. Gingerly taking a step out of the closet, he lifted his foot and felt for slivers of glass from the blood-soaked sock. He groped for the flashlight. There wasn't any glass lodged in his feet, and the cuts looked shallow but felt very bad. Where would he scream? When would he finally get the chance to release that scream he'd been containing from the beginning of the day?

He wouldn't turn the flashlight on until he was sure it wouldn't disturb her. He had to find a hiding place. He started down the hallway on his hands and knees, keeping his weight off his feet. Eventually he found an open doorway. He slipped inside and shut the door behind him, then turned on the flashlight and glanced briefly around for a place to sit.

Shelves lined every wall of this room, caked with a half inch of gray dust. In fact, the room itself seemed at least partially constructed with dust. It had collected across the wooden floor like a loose rug and now, stirred up by his intrusion, thick colorless motes revolved in the moonlit air like toys on a ghostly mobile, drifting in listless circles around the light fixture overhead. He could taste the dust in his mouth, too, already lining his throat and lungs. He slumped to the floor. The cuts in his feet were long but not deep. They were throbbing now, which he hoped meant they would soon go numb. He started to cry, to really sob, and forced himself to stop it.

In the corner of the room he found a few slips of paper: first, an old black-and-white picture of Uncle Titus, smiling a rare smile. Underneath was a map of Michigan. A single red circle marked, very roughly, the location of his hometown on that mitten-shaped slab of land.

He stood up, wincing at the pain that sparkled in his feet, and was about to switch off the flashlight when the beam glanced for just a second over something shiny in the corner of the closet. He stepped closer, brushing aside a long, gossamer cobweb from his face, and turned the flashlight on the closet, flooding it with light.

Here were all the models Anthem had told him about. Dozens of them, maybe a hundred, maybe even more. For a moment all he could do was stare. They were gathered into a pile that rose up to his knees. Whole years of painstaking effort and artistry had been spent here, gluing tiny wheels and doors and windshields into place, painting and detailing exhaust manifolds and running boards, and—

He reached down to study one of them, and that's when he saw it.

They had been destroyed. There were dozens of them, smashed into some unspeakable traffic jam of outscaled Chevy convertibles, ocean liners and Stealth bombers. Carefully assembled 4x4s had been pulverized under some relentless stomping boot, their plastic white sidewalls blown clean off, their plastic windshields shattered. A vintage World War II bomber had been rammed impossibly through the windshield of a black Lamborghini. A tiny Batmobile had been bashed almost perfectly flat. It all looked like the world of a monstrously frustrated child. Cobwebs stretched over the entire, jumbled pile, showing the age of this disaster.

At the bottom of the pile was another photograph, or part of one.

It had been torn down the middle. He found the other half not far away. He put the flashlight under his arm and pieced the two halves of the picture together in the dust. When the halves were together he gasped out loud.

Two children sat in the grass of some anonymous front yard, a little boy and a little girl, frowning very seriously at the camera. He recognized the familiar, pinched expression of Anthem immediately but it took a moment before he registered the boy's face.

Of course, it was his face.

He looked at the photo for a very long time. He wondered where Ovid had been at the time the photo had been taken, if Ovid even existed at all except in Anthem's imagination. Nicholas had not decided whether he believed in Ovid or not. It seemed quite possible to him that Ovid was dead. More than anything else, it bothered him that he had not yet made up his mind about Anthem, whether or not to trust her version of his life's history. She had shown him scars, but scars weren't enough. Particularly not when you claimed that they once had been wings.

But if you go home now . . .

Well, the simple fact was that he couldn't escape now, not with his feet in the condition they were. Anthem had been driving the back roads. He couldn't walk a mile, let alone ten, or however long it took him to reach the nearest freeway. The pain would become excruciating a long time before anyone found him.

He wasn't sure if people were supposed to be aware of such things, but he wondered if some small part of him had seen the broken glass in the closet earlier, and had led him in there deliberately.

That's crazy!

Well, it sounded crazy, okay, it sounded *insane* . . . otherwise he would have been able to escape right now. Did some part of him not want to escape yet?

If he ran now, he would never hear the rest of it. Whatever Anthem had told him, whatever she had left to say, would fade back into a gray zone of allegation and ambiguity, and a year from now he would be left with bad dreams, police reports, psychological evaluations. Educated guesswork, at best. *Unsolved Mysteries*, at worst.

He looked down at the torn photograph again. *Was* he keeping himself here on purpose?

It was a long time before he switched the flashlight off, hobbled back to the bedroom and slipped back under the covers. If Anthem stirred in the darkness, Nicholas did not hear her. He lay still. His feet hurt very badly under the blankets, and he didn't fall asleep for a very long time.

19

Portion of the testimony of Ian Danzig, October 26:
The last time I spoke to Titus about the girl Gertrude was about a year ago. He was in a wheelchair by then and couldn't travel very easily, except in a van he'd had custom-designed, and he hated that van. I had heard him refer to it as the Gimpmobile.

So I made up a story for Shelley and Nicholas about a teachers' conference, and flew up into Burns Mills in the U.P., and met Titus in a lousy little wharf bar overlooking Lake Superior. I had questions. Over the years the identity of the girl had become a pet project of mine, though I think my wife would have called it an obsession, if she'd known. Men are alleged to spend their lifetimes grappling with such things. On and off for seven years I had been spending evenings alone in my den, sometimes pestering Titus over the phone, sometimes working over my account of That Night. I told Shelley and Nicholas that I was writing a novel. Well, the name of the novel was That Night, *and the girl that Titus had called Gertrude was the only character.*

It was a year ago, in that dirty wharf pub, that Uncle Titus said, "I ain't talking about her any more after tonight, Ian. That's it."

"Then for God's sake, tell me," I said. "For seven years you've been evading the question. Shelley thinks I'm crazy for not forgetting the whole incident."

"Yeah?" With his good hand he reached up from his wheelchair for a dirty shot glass of rye whiskey. The oxygen tank lodged in the chair behind him was whistling softly as it blew fresh air through the tubes up into his nose. "Why don't you?"

I looked at him steadily. "I'm afraid."

He simply nodded.

"Titus, I know Shelley and I agreed eleven years ago not to ask any questions about Nicholas. Adoption was a difficult business then, especially for an underemployed schoolteacher and his wife, and it's even more difficult now, and—" I felt myself choking back the words, all the words I'd been rehearsing, by myself in the den, since That Night at the cottage up north. None of them were coming out right. "—if you hadn't been able to cut through the red tape with the state, and put us in contact with Nicholas . . . I don't know what we

would've done. We were struggling financially, but not just financially. We needed . . . something . . . so badly then, something to make it worthwhile. We're more grateful than I could ever tell you that you recognized Shel and me would be good parents. God knows we have tried. We've done right with Nicholas . . .'' Now I felt my eyes focusing right on Titus', almost beseechingly. Shel would have detested the weakness of my gaze, I thought, and my voice. ''. . . haven't we?''

''Yeah,'' he said softly . . . at least, softly for Titus, who hardly ever spoke below a bold, bluff tone. ''You and Shel have done real good.''

I nodded, anxious to be encouraged. I'd had a few drinks, too, by then, and it had loosened my tongue. ''Titus,'' I said, ''you're in your sixties, your arthritis, well, for God's sake, it's got you riding around in a wheelchair—''

''Go ahead and say it,'' he said, smiling. ''You want the truth before I up and croak, right? That's it, ain't it?''

''We'd never say a word to Nicholas, if that's what you wanted. We consider him our son, and he knows us as his parents. But for me, Titus, for my sake, just for my own peace of mind. If she was his sister . . .''

And I looked at him, waiting, hopeful.

''There have been women,'' he muttered. ''Three different women in my life over the years . . .''

''I know,'' I said. ''Were they—''

''Be quiet. You don't know. You don't know a damn thing.''

''I could tell she was crazy,'' I said boldly. I could feel waves of heat radiating from the pores of my skin. ''What I don't know—''

''Gertrude's my daughter,'' Titus said. ''Nicholas . . . had a different mother.''

He slipped a pack of Marlboros from his pocket, tapped one free and tucked it in the corner of his mouth. The fact that he was hooked to oxygen never seemed to faze his smoking habit, but I think sometimes he used it as a shock tactic. You don't expect someone sitting so close to a leaky tank of compressed air to strike a match, but he would do it with some frequency. He liked to put people on the defensive.

He was watching me very closely, which Titus does quite often. The arthritis had turned his fingers to clubs, mostly, and hooked his hands into spade claws, but those eyes of his are always clear, always looking out for a possible lie. But this time I got the feeling—and a strange feeling it was, too—that I wasn't getting the whole truth about Gertrude and Nicholas.

Titus was watching me, to see if I would believe what he was saying.

''All right,'' I said at last. ''I suspected that much, I suppose, or I wouldn't have come up here to hound you about it.''

Titus lit his cigarette, and his gaze slipped away.

"Are there any others I should know about, since we're on the subject?" I asked him, almost offhandedly.

The question took him totally by surprise. Surprise isn't one of his more pleasantly conveyed emotions, as you might have gathered. He stared at me down the bar.

"Now, why in the hell would you ask me that, Ian?"

"Well, I mean, since we were already discussing this one sister, it just seemed like maybe we could get all our cards on the table."

"Cards on the table?" he snarled. Strangely, almost miraculously, it was when he was most emotionally engaged that his grammar seemed to improve. "Listen to me, Ian. First of all, we are *not* discussing *anything*. You asked me a question, and I answered it. Second, I'm telling you straight up, you don't have to worry about any other brothers or sisters anymore."

"Why anymore? Did one of them—"

He closed his eyes. "Enough, Ian."

Finally I nodded. He would say no more. "But Titus, I don't want another incident like that night. I still have nightmares, you know. I still wonder what would have happened if this girl you called Gertrude, what if she had come in through the window in Nicholas' room instead of knocking on the door. She was a mess, you know, blood all over her . . . All I'm saying is, I don't want to have to worry about her coming back and taking him."

"She ain't coming back," he said. "She's put away, Ian. Trust me, so long as I'm alive, she ain't ever gonna find her way back to getting a second chance at Nicky. Why do you think I arranged for him to grow up with you and Shelley in the first place, anyway? Hey, look, Ian, I know you're concerned, but I promise you, nothing like that is going to happen again." His face was obscured in a gust of smoke. "I swear to God."

"Put away?" I repeated. "Why, Titus? How did she get—"

"Never you mind," he said.

"Titus?"

He seemed to explode. His cigarette tumbled from his lips, and I saw his knuckles go dead white, squeezing the dirty shot glass until I was sure it would burst between his stubby fingers, spilling whiskey and blood across the bar.

"Never you mind," he repeated, and that was all.

20

Anthem rolled over just as the morning light was starting to brighten the corners of the room. She stretched and was instantly awake. She felt better than she had in months. After spending yesterday on the road, a full night's sleep had not only refreshed her, it seemed to rebuild her nerves and her mind back to the point where she could think clearly and confidently about what needed to be done. She sat up and rubbed her eyes, wondering what time it was.

That was when she noticed the blood smeared across the bedsheets.

For an instant there was the breathtaking sensation of free fall. She heard her mind whispering, *I'm back, I'm back at Titus' again on the rust-spattered sheets, I'm twelve years old and he's coming up to get me any second now. He says he only wants to talk to me but—but—*

But no. She was here at Titus'. With Virgil. And all this blood.

"Virg?" She pulled the sheets away from his body on the other side of the bed and shook him. No response. "Virgil? Nicholas?"

He lifted his face from the pillow with a groan and peered over at her. His hair was a crazy nest from sleep. He blinked at her as if he both hoped that she was a remnant from some unfinished nightmare and knew that she was not. His head dropped back to the pillow again with a disgusted grunt.

"What happened to you last night?" she asked.

"What?" One red-rimmed eye studied her from the pillow. "You're telling me you don't remember?"

"Don't remember? Don't remember what? Virgil, what did you do to your feet?"

He hitched a breath and held it, slowly gathering up consciousness as he spoke. "Broken glass in the closet . . . I stepped on it . . ."

She drew away from him, and inside her stomach she felt something drop, as it had the moment she had first taken flight. She had the awful feeling of doing something during the night that she could not recall.

"What else happened?"

"You shot at me," he said. "You shot at me in the dark."

She lifted the pillow, but she didn't have to eject the automatic's clip and count the shells inside. The chamber still reeked faintly of powder. It began to tremble in her fingers. She felt a tightness in her temples.

"Anthem—"

She held up her hand, cutting him off. This was going to require a little more thought. The old feeling arose again. The very old, terribly familiar sense of self-loathing.

"Anthem," he said, "I'm getting scared of you."

Her hand jerked up again as if to ward off a blow. First, she thought, she had to take care of his feet. If she could take care of the physical consequences, it would at least give her time to consider the psychological ones, which would be more complicated.

"I've got a first-aid kit downstairs," she said, not meeting his eyes. "Stay up here and I'll bring you some antibiotic cream and bandages we can get on your feet before they get infected and then . . . then you can put your shoes back on."

"It's not that I think you'd really try to hurt me on purpose"—he was talking too frantically, she realized, trying to placate her—"but, you know, when you're walking around in your sleep you don't have any control over what you're going to do next . . . you know? I mean, maybe you shouldn't take the gun to bed with you, or—"

"Excuse me, did you hear what I said?" she cut in. "Your feet need attention."

"No, you're the one that needs some attention." His voice was breaking as he pulled himself to the other side of the bed. "Because you know why? You're some kind of psycho! You don't even know it! You should listen to yourself sometimes when you talk! All that you were telling me about, what, your little magnetic dogs, Virgil and Ovid? Does somebody have to spell it out for you?"

Crouched on the other side of the bed, panting, he waited for her counterattack, but she just blinked back at him. Now the pressure under her ears was pounding almost rhythmically. Her vision was compounded into a weird, fly-eye view of the room so that she could hardly see. "What . . . magnetic . . . dogs? I didn't tell you about . . . any . . ."

"Oh, come on!" he pleaded. "You remember! You must remember that!"

"Virgil, please . . . don't antagonize me like this." She knuckled her eyes hard, then looked up at him again. "I . . . had . . . wings, can't you understand that?"

"You're losing your marb—"

Suddenly she grabbed him and pulled him down to the floor with her, knocking them both breathless. He looked at her, irritated, and saw that she had the pistol in her hand again, aimed at his chest. "Now what?"

"Look," she said. "Out the back window. But don't you say a word."

He lifted his head and peered through the dirty glass and across the backyard to the gravel driveway that curled around the old house to the place they had parked the van last night. The heavy willow branches hung suspended in the morning fog. Beyond them he could make out the vague dark shape of the van.

There, behind the van, barely visible, was a car with an unmistakable rack of blue and red lights affixed to its roof. Two cops stood in silhouette between the cruiser and the van. They were inspecting the van. Nicholas started to stand up and she grabbed him.

"Stay down," she said.

He glanced up again and took a breath of surprise. The cops had left the van behind and were emerging out of the fog. Dawn spread out just behind them, filling the willow branches with an ethereal light.

"They're coming down the driveway," he said.

Why was he so afraid of being caught? He looked down at his wrists. He wasn't handcuffed here. Cut feet notwithstanding, he saw that he would never be able to explain why he hadn't gone through with his escape last night. He had made a terrible mistake. They would be suspicious of something going on between them. They would interrogate him like a fugitive, make insinuations and implications. He felt a weird sense of shame creeping over him.

"Now what are you going to do?" he murmured.

"It's we, not me," she said. She lifted the pistol to face level and thumbed back the hammer. "And we are just going to wait."

21

Portion of the testimony of Ian Danzig, October 26:
For eleven months after that night at the wharf, I wrote letters to Uncle Titus. Inquiring, demanding, cajoling, pleading, threatening. I needed to know more, the details that I was sure he was withholding from me.
Titus made excuses, told jokes, changed the subject.
And still I waited.

22

"I don't want to hurt these men," she said. "I won't have to if you keep quiet."

With the pistol back in her belt, she took him back toward the bed and snapped the cuff around one leg of the oak bed frame and, without a single word, turned and walked out. He found her own silence very unsettling. It was as if her behavior occasionally skipped, bypassing the motivation or small talk that connected the things that normal people did.

He tugged experimentally at the handcuff, then sat back against the bed, listening for details. At some point during his walk last night he had gotten a sense of what was essential. If he survived this trip, he thought, it would probably be attention to detail that kept him alive.

He heard Anthem shuffle down the stairs just as the cops rang the doorbell. He heard the door open. He held his breath to listen for the exchange of words. In all the suspense movies he had ever seen, the guilty person always chatted away gaily with the police when they first arrived, then somebody—it was usually the silent partner of the detective asking the questions—noticed some minute detail out of place. A drop of blood on the shirt cuff, a handprint smeared on the wall. After that everything would come unraveled.

But Anthem sounded unraveled as soon as she opened the door. In fact, it didn't sound like Anthem at all. It sounded like a completely different voice.

"What do you people want?" he heard her ask suspiciously.

"Morning, ma'am." The first cop had a high, fluty voice. It sounded like he might have had a head cold. "Do you know about the van parked down the road, down by the creek behind your house?"

"It's been there all night," Anthem said. "I should know. I've been watching it since it pulled up, and I could hardly sleep worrying about it. Why? What's going on?"

"You don't know anything about it?" the second cop's voice interjected, in a lower tone.

"It's turning me into a nervous wreck, I know *that*. There's hardly any traffic along some of the roads, you know, so when my husband noticed it last night, just parked there . . ." She paused, and it was during this unfolding silence that Nicholas realized just what a splendid actress she could be, intentionally or otherwise. "Officers, just what is this all about? It was a murder, wasn't it?"

"A kidnapping," the fluty-voiced cop said squarely. He sneezed.

"Ma'am, would you mind terribly if we came in and asked you a few questions?" the other asked. "Maybe even took a quick look around?"

"I suppose not," she said. "With my husband gone, I should be glad you're here, shouldn't I?"

Nicholas heard them step inside and scrape mud off their shoes, then a muffled clanging sound he couldn't identify right away. His eyes roved around the bedroom, and then abruptly he lost all interest in the conversation downstairs. In the far right corner of the room, something rustled, and he heard the muffled crumbling of old plaster. The wallpaper seemed to bulge, then pucker and finally split open with a wet ripping sound as a hunched gray shape began to pry itself free.

"Oh—" He stared at it. "Oh boy."

The body of the rat was long but very thin, as though it had not eaten in a long time. It pulled itself from a narrow crevice where the walls should have come together, its tiny nails clawing at the plaster as its belly squirmed free, then its hindquarters, and finally its naked pink tail, whipping carelessly behind it. It sat up and regarded Nicholas with its dull black eyes.

He felt his buttocks clench, his stomach and throat constricting with drawstring suddenness. He could not get up on the bed. There was nothing for him to stand on, no freedom short of cutting off his hand at the wrist. He felt his testicles come crawling up between his legs. He shrunk away, toward the door, but the handcuffs caught him and held him there, almost seeming to draw him back. He sprawled out on his stomach so that his entire body was behind him. The chain was tight. He tugged it violently, and it held.

The rat took a brief, limping step toward him. Its tail wickered and swished along behind, arching into a weird pink question mark.

Well, the question is simple, his mind announced with a sort of mock calm. It sounded almost academic, a teacher's voice. *Is Anthem crazy enough to shoot the cops if you screamed? Because this is not between me and the rat, or me and Anthem, or me and the cops. It all happens in Anthem's mind. And the simple question is, would she shoot them?*

And the simple answer was, he just didn't know.

23

"I'm sorry to be so rude," Anthem told the two men. She set the pan back on the kitchen counter. The conversation was going surprisingly well. Nicholas hadn't made a sound upstairs yet, and she was becoming more glib. She hoped he was listening to this. "Like I said, I've been on edge since we noticed that van. Of course the first thing that goes through your mind is murder. A kidnapping, though . . . that's another thing altogether. I haven't heard anything on the radio about any kidnapping. Still I guess I had good reason to be worried, didn't I?"

Neither of the cops said anything. Were they still behind her?

"You know, I could make you some coffee if you'd like that. Or . . ." She let her voice trail away. "Well, if you need anything, I guess you'll just let me know?"

For a moment she stood in the hallway, and it was quiet. In a house this old, though, the silence itself was filled with small, comforting sounds of the foundation settling, even the soft clicking of the willow leaves blowing in the wind.

She crossed her arms and smiled at the two badges. "Take your time."

24

The rat lurched forward again, its long whiskers quivering as if it were receiving signals. His eyes were riveted to it, to the greasy, bristling hair and its long nose.

Ten feet between them now.

At this distance, the rat seemed both fascinated and perplexed by his presence here in its parlor. As it took a few more steps he saw its flat belly waggling beneath it. Pickings had probably been slim for a long, long time, he thought.

Another step. And another. At eight feet, the rat no longer looked fascinated or perplexed. It just looked hungry. In fact, was that a bit of drool glistening from its lip? He was going to scream. Oh yes.

"No," he muttered to himself. Apparently he'd answered the one big question, without even knowing it. Yes, Anthem, or whoever was in charge down there, would shoot the cops if he screamed and gave away his location up here. So, in conclusion, he could not scream. He had the right to remain silent. Silence was golden. Children were to be not seen and not heard.

The rat took three more loping steps and stopped directly in front of him. Nicholas could feel the sweat trickling down the sides of his ribs. His hand groped blindly behind him, trying to find the familiar reassurance of the flashlight. If it got closer, he could bash its head in, but in this house, every sound was an amplification of some guilty deed. And he could not locate the flashlight.

Suddenly the rat began to squeal horribly, as if it were working up its courage to attack. He watched its gray hindquarters tense. His entire body went rigid as it leapt at the knuckles of his cuffed hand. He brushed it aside and felt its sleek coat, its weight resisting the push he gave it. He could see its eyes were black and shiny now with its own excitement. Screams were coming up in his throat until they gagged him. He realized that his legs were flailing behind him, his feet thumping on the bare floor, and forced himself to hold still.

In the terrible quiet that followed he thought he heard Anthem's voice, ". . . take a look upstairs if you want . . ." Maybe he was imagining it. It was quite possible that he was imagining it. Every one of his senses was sharpened to a pencil point. The bedroom was melting into hues of gray around him, his body wriggling through shock after shock, as the rat lunged again at his hand. He saw it freeze, poised over his thumb, glaring.

He saw his opportunity there and took it, swinging his free hand down in a tight fist, happy to kill it with his bare hand in this way. Its eyes opened, agog, and its head turned as if to accuse him, and he hit it again, afraid that it was not dead yet. The second time he felt its sleek coat in a way that he knew he would never forget, stiff and very thick and very greasy and awful to the touch. For a long second he lay still, three-quarters unconscious, and then was sick, and then sick again, over the remains of the rat. Its hind leg stirred, and he was sick yet again and began to retch drily until he thought his throat would burn and blister and peel. He clutched his free hand to his stomach and wept like a baby.

He heard Anthem coming up the steps.

She was still talking.

25

"—What you call your basic handyman's special." Her voice rang out from halfway down the stairs, and she laughed. "Of course in this family my husband's the only one handy enough to do more than locate a stud in a wall. Are you coming up?"

No reply from the officers.

"Well, I'll be up here. Look around all you like, and if you want to ask me anything just give a call and I'll tell you anything I can. I hope you find those men, or whoever's doing the kidnapping. You might look out by the creek in the back."

Nicholas could hear her voice coming from the top of the stairs now. He wondered why she was leading them up here. He wondered if she intended to kill the cops right here in front of his face.

He heard the door open and waited.

Anthem was looking down at him. She could not see the mess that lay in front of him. A furious smile stretched her jaw forward, her eyes glinting with some weird, canny sense of humor. There were, he saw, no cops behind her. She had come up here alone. She couldn't seem to contain a snicker at the joke. Maybe, he thought, it was no joke to her.

Her eyes cleared. "Virgil? What happened up here?"

Then he shifted to one side so that she could see the body of the rat, lying on its side. He rattled his cuffed hand to draw her attention. She saw the rat. He heard her gasp for breath.

"Oh my God, Virgil, I didn't have any idea. I'm sorry. I would never have taken so much time getting up here if I knew what was happening."

"Stop it," he said. He tasted the sourness of bile in his mouth and felt queasy again. "Where are the police?"

"Don't worry about them." She took a step back into the doorway and drew the pistol from her belt, aiming it at his chest. From her pocket she took the handcuff key and tossed it at his feet. "Unlock yourself from the bed and cuff yourself. We're leaving right now."

He waited, not obeying immediately. Something had happened to the police. He was not sure what just yet. He looked at the rat that he had killed with his hand, and he knew that, whatever happened next, he would respond like a different person to it. Only a certain number of screams could be swallowed, he realized, before they started to tear a hole into the wall of the soul, damaging it permanently. By not scream-ing he had kept Anthem from shooting the cops, and he had saved his own life. But it didn't feel like his own anymore.

"No," he said. "I'm not doing it."

"So you saw a rat," she said with a sort of forced brusqueness. "We have to get going. I'll bandage up your feet, and we'll stop by a clinic somewhere this morning and get something to disinfect them."

"My feet are all cut up," he said. "In case you haven't noticed, they've been doing some serious bleeding. I almost had a freaking heart attack with that rat. I'm starving, I feel sick, I just want to go home—"

"Where do you think we're going?" she asked. "Don't you want to meet your real father?"

"Shut up," he said again. His voice was so croaky that it frightened him. "Nothing's worth this."

"Not even that power I told you about?"

He looked at her face wearily. "What the hell are you talking about?"

"I explained it to you last night." She came back into the bedroom with the pistol still trained carefully on him, and sat down on the edge of the bed. She was running her left hand through her hair over and over like a girl trying to comb out an especially stubborn knot. "Something elemental is happening here," she said. "I'm beginning to think . . .

well, I was listening to the transistor radio downstairs, and the weather's gone out of control all across the West Coast, and—"

"Oh, come on." He shook his head. "You really should try listening to yourself sometime."

"I'm telling you," she said. Her voice was warbling. "It has to do with you and Ovid, and some kind of power between you. Like those little magnetized dogs. I do remember telling you about them now. I don't know what I was thinking before. Dad told me about it. He said that there was a sort of electricity generated between you two, like I said, some kind of elemental *push*. It was very slight when we were all separated, but over the years that we were apart—"

He covered his ears with his hands. He was crying again. At least that was no surprise.

Anthem looked down at him and stopped. Her face looked torn between fury and despair. She was crying, too. The tears seemed huge, cartoonish, spilling over her mouth. She licked them off her lips and swallowed them.

He let his hands slip a little, so he could listen to her. If she was crying, it would make him feel better just to hear it.

"This is just the purpose of my life, you know?" She sobbed a wet, desperate sob and mopped her eyes with her sleeve. "Just to get everybody back together again. There's a power between you two that could . . . I don't know what it could do. Heal people. Or maybe just make rain. I don't even know what it is. But that's the real reason why I went to find you, not for myself, or for Daddy. For you and Ovid. To take care of Titus once and for all. I always thought after I did that I could just lay myself down and die happy."

"You could die now," he said. "I wouldn't care."

She nodded so frantically that the tears flew. "I know! I know you wouldn't, and who'd blame you?" Her eyes scanned him, and her lips rippled into a horrible kind of sneer. "Look at what I've done to you."

He watched as she grabbed two handfuls of her own blond hair. "I deserve this," she said, and jerked it out by the roots without so much as a gasp, then scattered the hair in front of him, watching his expression.

"Gertrude . . ." he said in spite of himself.

"My name is Anthem!" she roared. *"Can't you at least remember my name?"*

And before he could interject, she slapped herself sharply across her face, once, twice, again and again until her lip began to darken and bleed. Her glasses slipped from the bridge of her nose and hung, swinging, from one ear before she reached up carefully and took them off, folding them and sliding them into the front pocket of her jeans. Then she made a tight, hammerlike fist and slammed it immediately into her right eye. He flinched back helplessly.

"Stop," he said hoarsely, "stop doing that."

She lifted her red fingernails to her face and raked them sideways across her cheek, carving its smoothness into long, ugly furrows which turned white, then red, and began to fill up with blood. Her eyes remained on him, riveted, as though there were a code word they both knew which would stop her from destroying herself. With both hands she clawed at her forehead until blood flecked her hair and eyelashes. Her nostrils flared with every breath, her lips sputtering but saying no more.

He shook his head. *"Anthem—"*

She fired the pistol. He saw it jerk in her hand behind a burst of light, and heard the bullet sing past his ear. He went limp, as though he had been shot, and saw her leveling the barrel at his forehead.

"It would be so much easier this way," she said, removing her glasses from her pocket and hooking them back around her ears. "We'd never know about what was between the two of you. No one would ever have to *worry*."

He imagined that he could see up into the barrel of the gun to the bullet that would kill him. If it were possible for his body to surrender itself any further, it would have. He felt melted, spent, drained. Anthem's madness seemed contagious. He was losing his mind, too. She'd poisoned it for him.

Slowly she lowered the pistol, and he let her cuff him again. He believed now that she would shoot him if he didn't. It seemed to him that a very old, very deep wound in her sanity had reopened and been reinfected here, in this terrible old house. With a careless tug she brought him back up to his feet, down the hall to the stairs. Down in the kitchen, he saw a heavy cast-iron pan freckled with bright, undried blood sitting on the kitchen counter. He craned his neck and looked again. He saw the policemen.

It must have happened while he was locked in mortal combat with the rat, he thought, because he hadn't heard anything like what had happened down here. The bodies of the two policemen were sprawled facedown across the tile of the entranceway. One of them had gone down with his fingers beginning to curl around the butt of his pistol. The other had turned his head to the side, his mouth half-open, as if to make a sly remark to his partner. Anthem stepped over their bodies without glancing at them, and pulled him along at the same speed.

"Are they dead?" he asked her.

"Just unconscious." She looked hurt. "We never killed anybody, Virgil."

"Well, maybe you should shoot them a couple times," he said, "just to keep them down for the count."

"I think that rat left you with a bad attitude," she said. The remark seemed absurd coming from her bloody, battered face. "It's going to be a long drive west if you hate me all the way to California." She pulled him along to the front door, until he stopped walking behind her. "What's wrong? Your feet?"

He nodded. He wasn't going to talk any more than he had to.

"Poor baby." She stuffed the gun in her belt, reached one arm behind him and one around his neck and swooped him up all at once, carrying him through the front door and out into the cold morning air. Her arms were strong. The gun in her belt poked against his stomach. She carried him down the walk and across the yard, toward the black van and the empty police car behind it. The radio inside crackled with the voices of policemen far away from here, and burst into static with an occasional flicker of lightning overhead. The sky was a stormy gray, the clouds rolling across the horizon. A cold autumn wind ran its fingers through his hair.

Anthem dropped him to his feet long enough to unlock the back of the van and open it up. She reached for the pistol again.

"Don't bother," he said. Awkwardly, using both his cuffed hands as one, he pushed himself up inside the back of the van, hardly aware of what he was doing. He sank back on the wet mattress, no longer caring that it was wet. In fact, the dampness, the softness, seemed somehow perversely comforting to him.

She slammed the door behind him. In the darkness, he could hear her attacking the police car. He heard the windshield smash, then the cackling voices on the radio stopped a moment later. He could hear her breathing heavily from the sheer physical exertion of it. Finally there were four distinct gunshots, with an interval of silence between them, as she blew out each of its tires.

It hardly bothered him. All he knew was that he was once again safe inside his little black box. There were no rats back here. No broken glass. No dead people, with the future exception of himself.

It was soft and dark. It was rather comforting. He realized that he had begun to cry again. How long, he wondered, until he went crazy? How much more could anyone take, not knowing and not knowing and not knowing some more?

After a while he heard the van's engine start, and they were on the road, enveloped in darkness once more.

26

Portion of the testimony of Shelley Danzig, October 27:

Believe it or not, I had no idea what Ian was doing, writing those letters to Uncle Titus this last year. First of all, I had no idea he'd written so many, and second, I was sure he'd given up asking questions about That Night. Titus wasn't the most open person in the world. Nicholas had received the requisite Christmas and birthday cards, and occasionally we got a short note, but Ian always acted so . . . disinterested.

I know I was supposed to stay out of his desk. I won't lie and say I was dusting, or anything so obvious. I was snooping. That's the long and short of it. I was curious about this novel of his, more than anything. I wanted to know if he was writing about me, and if so, I wanted to know what he had to say.

Anyway, I found the letters that Titus had returned to him.

All of them.

Ian, why didn't you throw them away? If they hadn't already been sitting there, I wouldn't have sat down in your expensive swivel chair and spent most of the morning and afternoon reading them to myself, each one, every word.

". . . Titus, I can't help but press for more details regarding Gertrude . . ."

". . . what could possibly have possessed her to . . ."

". . . any history of schizophrenia in your family that might manifest itself later in Nicholas . . ."

". . . I think we have a right to know . . ."

". . . would be completely respectful of your wishes for confidentiality . . ."

And finally, of course, the question I should have known that you would arrive at, schoolteacher that you are.

". . . what, Titus? What do you have to hide?"

That took gall for Ian to ask that question. After all, he was the one with the secret drawer of his secret desk in his secret room, and all his secret correspondence. His secret obsession.

Why didn't he tell me about what he was doing?
I would have tried to help him. I mean it. I would have tried to help.

27

I t was hunger that thrust him awake.

He had been dreaming, he realized, about Ovid in California. In the dream, he saw Ovid far off in the distance on an endless beach, the sun pounding down on his head and shoulders. To his right the ocean rolled and boomed, the foam seething up toward his ankles and refilling tiny tide pools. The sky was a lighter blue that came down to press against the gorgeous cobalt of the sea on the horizon.

The two of them began running toward one another across the perfect white sand with the sea stretched forever out beside them. Nicholas fetched up deep breaths and ran faster and faster, the sand hot underneath his feet. As Ovid grew near, Nicholas could make out the other boy's face, and his features were like his own, but leaner, older, more deeply tanned. Ovid was smiling back at him. Nicholas started to sprint.

But the ocean beside them was retreating, evaporating in the sun as they neared each other. It was as if God were drawing back some vast blue cloth from the face of the world. The sand under Nicholas' feet was suddenly scalding. He watched Ovid's face, a mirror of his own, shriveling as the sun blazed down brighter and brighter, as though it had been intensified through magnifying glasses and mirrors. The ocean crept back even further, receding to reveal beds of seaweed, then great flopping piles of fish, then sharks and whales and the skeletons of wrecked ships, and the heat from the sun was unbearable, turning his brother's face and then his own into husks as the white sand burned the soles of his feet, his bare feet, cooking them pink.

He jerked his head upright. The air was cold, but his face and chest were damp with sweat. His stomach growled loudly. His feet were on fire.

He rapped on the plywood. "Hey," he said weakly. "I need to eat."

Silence from the other side of the plywood.

"I guess I probably should have had something last night," he said. "I'm thirsty, too."

Still no reply.

He made his way back to the rear of the van. Had it been only yesterday that he'd been so revolted by this cold water? He scooped up a handful and splashed it over his face, careful of his wounded jaw from the day before. Images from the dream began to fade, though his throat remained parched. The water didn't smell too bad, he thought, with only the faintest metallic tang to it. He scooped up another handful and brought it to his lips, sipping at first and then pouring it down his throat. It was cold and good. He trembled, his eyes watering, and rubbed his cold hands vigorously over his cheeks until some energy began to tingle back through his face and scalp.

Still on his hands and knees, he crawled back away from the puddle and the mattress and leaned against the plywood to peel off his socks. Somewhere he'd lost his shoes. Back in the bedroom? The memory wasn't completely clear yet, but he sensed it would return eventually. When he had his socks off, he found a few tiny pieces of glass that were still in his feet—none of the shards were nearly as large as they felt—and returned to the puddle to splash water into the cuts as gently as he could.

He knocked on the plywood again. "You promised to bandage my feet," he said. "I need some more disinfectant, too."

Still she said nothing. He imagined an empty driver's seat, a van cruising by itself down some desolate back road with a kid trapped in the back, talking out loud to nobody. It was a crazy thought, so he tried to forget it. He had worried about going crazy before, in moments when his entire perspective had failed him.

He remembered last year when his father—if Ian Danzig truly was his father, and at the moment it was more comforting to assume that he was—had convinced him finally to join the school's little intramural basketball team, which Mr. Danzig coached. Nicholas suspected that his father had always been disappointed that other kids played when he could never convince his own son to do more than pick up a ball and take a halfhearted shot, sometimes missing the rim completely. Last year, finally, he resorted to bribery: there was a comic book convention in Detroit in January, and he'd drive Nicholas there along with his friend Louis Skye. He'd even give him a hundred dollars to spend if Nicholas would "at least try basketball for a season."

But he'd lied. Ian Danzig had lied.

He hadn't wanted Nicholas to "at least try." He'd gone into the season with the heartfelt intent of carving out the basketball player that he thought was trapped inside his boy. He seemed to think it was a matter of making Nicholas enraged enough, or frustrated enough, to stop losing and start sinking baskets.

So Nicholas practiced with the team in the afternoon. Then at night, after dinner, he and his father would come back and shoot baskets in the empty gymnasium. On those nights he saw a new side of Ian Danzig . . . or maybe, he thought later, it was just a very, very old side of him. His father ran him through drills, coached him on layups, rode him through a hundred games of one-on-one, watched him shoot a hundred air balls from the free-throw line. And then there had been the push-ups. His father had started him doing ten or twenty right before practice, and the twenty had become thirty, then forty. Nicholas had never understood how push-ups affected his basketball game, but he did understand that he was getting better at them. *Push-ups are an angry kid's exercise,* he had thought in a moment of acute awareness, and Nicholas *was* angry—at his opponent, at his father, most violently at himself, for refusing to give up as his father's exercise routines had become more and more demanding.

Ian Danzig—a soft-spoken English teacher until you got him on the basketball court—had worn his silver coach's whistle around his neck and he blew it until Nicholas wished he'd choke on it. He heard that whistle at night, in his sleep, after they'd left the gymnasium and he was up in his room, trying to work through algebra problems. Usually he'd fall asleep without finishing, and have to copy somebody's homework the next morning before class. But he hadn't given up. He was starting to notice his own improvement. Even the push-ups had become easier.

The discovery came gradually, like the suspicion of being followed or watched by a stranger. Unlikely muscles were starting to develop on his calves and thighs. His biceps, once wiry, had become small cables that jumped when he curled his arm. Shots were occasionally sinking through the hoop. He could run up and down court without gasping for breath.

He was turning into something that pleased his father.

One night he had come home from practice, his stomach already starting to ache from the thought of practice with his dad the next day. He had fallen asleep after dinner, and his mother had let him sleep right through the evening. He woke up frantic. He thought it was dawn, and was certain that he'd missed practice with his dad, and now he was going to miss team practice this morning. He'd raced out the door and was almost halfway to school when he noticed that the darkness overhead was dusk, not dawn. It was night. The day had turned itself inside out. And he had stood there on the sidewalk, his Adidas bag slung over his shoulder, wondering if he was going to lose his mind.

The next day he'd refused to practice with his dad. Ian Danzig threatened to cancel the comic book deal. Go ahead, Nicholas said. His father did.

"Honey," his mother had said later, "don't worry. You're a long way from going crazy."

But at that moment, and now in the back of the van, he didn't think anyone ever was.

28

The next time he heard Anthem's voice it came out of nowhere, without any warning.

"I'm so sorry about the way I've been acting," she said calmly. "It's just that I've been doing some serious thinking. We've both been under a lot of stress for the past day or so, I know. I don't want you to remember this trip as a complete nightmare."

Nicholas laughed. It sounded like a choke.

"I told you that Ovid had a family, just like we both did," she said. "Titus found him a home in Boulder, Colorado, and then built himself a place an hour or so away from there to keep an eye on him. We'll be at his house late tonight and we can stay there. It's nicer than his place in Iowa. And I've got a key."

"The cops will catch up to us before that," he said.

But he wasn't so sure anymore. Why hadn't they caught them yet? Even back roads couldn't make the van completely invisible to the eyes of the police, yet they had made it almost halfway across the country without once being stopped. It had to happen soon, if for no other reason than the fact that Anthem had already left the two cops behind her in Iowa. He kept wondering, waiting for the moment when the sirens would come screaming up behind them.

To his surprise he found he could imagine every scene. He imagined being bucked around from one side of the van to the other, a hostage in some high-speed chase that would end in a violent shoot-out with the state troopers. Again he saw images from the movies. Anthem would die in his arms, pleading for forgiveness with her last breath. The police would cart him back to Portage, where the mystery of who he was would haunt him for years. Some monumental conclusion like that.

But none of it happened that way.

His hunger faded eventually, the way hunger does after it reaches a certain point. He sipped more water from the pool at the back of the van. His body moved through periods of intense warmth and cold, and his throat started to feel raw when he swallowed. He was getting nauseated, but when the nausea peaked he could only open his mouth and retch. Nothing left in his stomach but water.

He lay down his head and dozed.

Dreamed of the ocean, and the scalding white sand.

And a boy named Ovid.

29

Portion of the testimony of Shelley Danzig, October 27:

Reading over those letters that Ian had written to Uncle Titus, I felt pangs of guilt—the first pangs I'd felt in years—for never telling Nicholas he'd been adopted. We had agreed to keep silent, you know, when Titus had offered us that laughing little boy twelve years ago. Uncle Titus had made us promise. We were prepared to do anything. We couldn't have children of our own, a sad fact we had begun to suspect by that time. Titus told us that we could raise him as our own . . . but only if we were willing to do exactly that. Our custody would even include the creation of a few harmless stories regarding my pregnancy and his birth. Uncle Titus said he could even provide some baby pictures for us to show Nicholas, when he got older.

Even then, of course, Ian had asked who the real parents were. I was never as interested as he was. Soon enough Nicholas seemed like our very own. It took Ian longer to let Nicky into his life—I think he could've waited another five years to become a father, even though I felt utterly prepared for motherhood—but by Nicholas' fifth birthday, I knew that the risky "adoption" had paid off. I would, I decided, have no trouble telling an occasional harmless fib about Nicky's birth. He truly seemed like ours, and I think even Ian believed that in his heart.

That's why That Night upset him so badly that he never recovered, really.
We had hidden the fact from ourselves—Ian not so well as I—that Nicky
wasn't our own child. There was this girl Gertrude now. Ian suspected from
his continued interrogation of Titus that there had been a third child too—an
older brother of Nicholas'—who had died at birth. Ian wasn't sure. But there
was no denying the presence of Gertrude.

And when Nicholas vanished, we realized that Titus was not strong enough
to protect us from her.

Maybe he never had been.

30

Around noon, while Nicholas was still asleep in the back, Anthem
pulled off to the side of the road and got out to stretch her legs.
They were reaching her favorite part of the country, the part that made
her ache most of all for her lost wings.

She walked to the edge of the bluff overlooking a valley thick with
orange, yellow and gold foliage. The air was getting unmistakably colder.
The smell of pine and cedar surrounded her with its pleasant association
of camping and cooking on an open fire. But beyond that was the smell
of wind and dust and storm clouds crowding in on the foothills on the
horizon. The sky ahead looked gray, ready for snow.

The beauty of her face was distorted by long, ugly scrapes and abra-
sions. There was blood encrusted under her fingernails.

In a few hours they would be leaving Nebraska and entering Colorado, but she couldn't see any mountains yet. She considered the slim
possibility that they were lost. It had been a long time since she had
seen a road sign whose markings she'd been able to translate. In part,
she believed, this was because her mind was fatigued from driving.

She shrugged mentally. Her mind was still fixated on what had happened to her eight years ago, when Titus had taken her to see Jack.

On that night, when she had seen the pained look on Jack's face, she
had known that Titus had given him no choice. Then she had seen Titus'
face, grinning, saying *Get back in the car, girl*, the corners of his mouth
looking like deep, bloodless punctures. *Jack, you get back there and do*
what I told you.

Her eyes had flashed to Saint Jack doubtfully. *Daddy?*

Just do what he asks you, Anthem. It will be all right.

Daddy, did you come to take me home again? Maybe I shouldn't have come here—

That was ridiculous, because she hadn't gone alone, had she? Hadn't Titus brought her there? Or had she been sitting in the driver's seat the whole time? It wasn't clear.

She remembered hands, throwing her backward into the backseat of the Lincoln. Her father's rough palms coming up from behind her, trying to cover up her mouth, *ow, Daddy, you're pushing down on me too hard, be careful with me!* Just as her vision faded, she felt Titus pushing her onto her stomach, heard the metallic click as he opened up his pocketknife.

Daddy, why are you holding me down? I can see you, I know it's you—

Titus, grunting. *Jack, cover her fucking mouth.*

DADDY, I KNOW IT'S YOU!

Now her wings were gone. Chopped off. She tried to remember how it had felt, skimming out along the surface of Lake Superior and up across the beach. It seemed an impossible fantasy, a dream, like being able to walk into a library reading room and hear what the people around her were thinking.

Jack had held her arms forward and covered her mouth. Since that night, he must have apologized a thousand times, or tried to, for the damage that he and Titus had done that night. Usually he never progressed past the overwhelming surges of guilt that seemed to surround his entire memory of the incident. He would despise forever the part of himself that had given in to Titus that night. But what else could he have done? Titus had demanded that he hold her arms while he cut off her wings. If Saint Jack hadn't done it, then Anthem would have gone back with Titus, back to nothing, and Jack would have lost his window of opportunity. And so he had done it. He had muffled her screams.

Tonight, she had decided earlier, she and Virgil would stay at Titus' house in Colorado, where Ovid had occasionally visited. She closed her eyes and tried to envision Titus' face, but saw only a pale, doughy blur with a shock of gray hair and a few yellow teeth plugged into his mouth. His other features blurred, indistinguishable.

It didn't matter. He would be dead soon. When she brought Ovid and Virgil together, the cataclysm that followed would destroy him. She believed this as deeply and dogmatically as she believed anything in her life.

Occasionally she felt a pinch of genuine regret about having to kill him as a result of bringing the two brothers together again. It had never been her intention to exact revenge, but only to find the whereabouts of her remaining brother. Saint Jack, whose sole act of violence had been committed under duress in the back of Titus' Lincoln, had warned her years later about the nature of revenge before she left:

"You're talking about a willful suspension of sanity, honey," he had said. His was a face that she could envision easily, his gray eyes and his graying, carefully trimmed beard. "Listen to me, because on this subject I know whereof I speak. I waited for a long time while the police wandered around and did nothing. When you give in to the urge for revenge, you're permitting yourself to go a little insane. You're giving up part of your mind to a universal spirit of madness that circles the world, starting little wars and turning them into big wars. But you can't do that."

But she was going to do exactly that. She was going to kill Titus.

"I'm sorry, Daddy," she whispered into the wind, above the valley. "I know I'm never going to be as good a person as you."

From behind her she heard a pounding sound from inside the van. Apparently Virgil was awake. For a moment it startled her, and then she remembered that, yes, he was trapped inside with the handcuffs still on his wrists. Handcuffs that she had put on him.

She made a soft, miserable whining sound in her throat. Everything that she did was turning into a crime long after she had done it. How, back in Michigan, could she have thought so clearly and calmly about how things fell apart without lapsing into despair? Her original fears were proving correct. Nothing held together. Ovid and Virgil had not held together before. If the weather was any indication, they would not hold together now.

She extended her hand out in front of her. A snowflake drifted down and landed on her palm, then melted into a tear.

Now it sounded like he was hurling himself against the inside of the van. The entire vehicle was rocking back and forth slightly on its rusty shocks. Anthem felt the corners of her mouth turning down into a grimace, and she was abruptly on the brink of frustrated tears herself. Her cause seemed hopeless, and she was surprised by a tinge of jealousy: he would always think of himself as Nicholas Danzig, and not Virgil, because his false life had been so very good to him. In a fundamental sense, he didn't even want to know the truth about himself.

And why would he? When your main providers both have solid jobs that anchor you securely in the upper-middle-class tax bracket, why start trouble? Why would you ever believe that somewhere, halfway across the country, your real father occasionally went to bed crying because he knew that he would never see both his sons in the same room again? Why would you care?

She looked at the van rocking back and forth, as if it contained some hostile animal that would kill her if it escaped. Absently she ran her fingers over the crusted cuts across her cheeks, letting her fingernails trace the bruise under her right eye.

She remembered approaching Saint Jack in his practice room in their old seaside villa two weeks ago and telling him what she wanted to do. The villa itself was very old. Only the practice room maintained its pastel beauty, its bay windows overlooking the rocky California shoreline below. Her father's baby grand sat by those windows. Most days the sea was calm enough for him to keep the windows open while he composed at the keyboard so that he could hear the waves bursting against the rocks below. His percussion section, he called it. Shelves lined the walls all the way up to the cathedral ceiling, the topmost books up so high that Anthem couldn't read the titles stamped on their spines.

Jack also kept candles on every shelf and table. He wouldn't allow this room to be "electrified." He said that he wanted to know he could work if there was ever a blackout, and left her to decipher the implications of that.

She hadn't knocked that afternoon, not wanting to break his concentration, but had just slipped through the doorway between the long string of notes that was his next song being born. The practice room smelled more strongly of the ocean brine than any other room in the villa; also of coffee and sour perspiration and sometimes frustration. It did not smell of alcohol anymore. Jack had dried out from years of alcoholism in this room, and here he made enough money for them to live. It was journeyman's work, done for money, not love. He had a good agent in L.A.

Over the music stand she saw his long, careful hand appear to lift a cup of espresso steaming up the shafts of morning sunlight. She heard him snap a match to light a cigarette and decided to interrupt, anyway.

"I thought you quit for good," she said, walking toward the piano with her heart already beating hard in her throat.

He didn't look up. "Nobody ever quits killing themselves for good." He was always offering up his most cryptic comments while he was in the middle of composing; it was, she realized, the diplomatic, Saint Jack version of a brushoff. He switched the cigarette to his left hand and began to pencil something onto the pad of blank staff paper in front of him, the long straight lines waiting to become music. The paper fluttered gently in a random ocean breeze.

"Daddy," she said, and he stopped writing and looked at her. His gray eyes looked very sharp, the wrinkles that drew away from them only making them look more intense and aware.

"What's on your mind, little bear?"

"Daddy, it's—" She caught her breath, entirely unprepared for the prospect that she might cry in front of this man who had himself experienced so much loss and sorrow. Jack wasn't stoical himself, but something about his presence seemed to inspire a vicarious sort of stoicism in the people around him. "I've been thinking a lot lately about Virgil. I think it's time I went to go find him."

"Oh . . ." Jack took a slow breath and then blew it out. "Oh, Anthem, honey—"

"Before you say anything else, let me at least get it out, all right?" She watched the gray eyes carefully; this was a genuine question that she needed answered before she went any further. "After I tell you, then you can do your best to convince me not to go, okay?"

He nodded and slid down the bench a space. "You want to sit?"

"Thanks, I'll stand," she said, then waited a moment to see how she would begin, and thumbed her heavy lenses up the bridge of her nose. "Daddy, I want to find Titus. I think I can convince him to help me out. He's getting on in his years, and I think I can convince him, somehow . . . if not to tell me where Virgil is, at least to contact him and tell him that I want to see him. We wouldn't even have to say we're his family, you know. We could just say we were old friends of his family or something. At least we could see him again." She caught her breath; her lungs seemed to be able to hold only a little puff of air at a time. "Or we could just tell him the truth about everything and let him make up his own mind for himself."

"Well, yes, you could," Jack said seriously, "but doesn't it occur to you that he might already be living with parents who love him, in a good home?"

"But you're his father—" She stared at him. "How can you be so . . . so . . ."

"So fair about it?" Jack said drily.

"That's not like you," she told him, "to be so cold."

"I'm just asking you to consider the facts. The only reason that I was able to find you was that Titus allowed me to, back in Michigan. He had been watching me for years, almost since the moment he took you away from me, and we had even met a few times to negotiate a deal. But there's no reason to think he would do it again."

"But you don't even want to try!" she said. "Why don't you even want to *try*?"

He took another drag on his cigarette and set it down in the marble ashtray on the piano. "Don't forget that I knew Titus Heller for a short time back in Boston, during the time that he was working as Maria's bodyguard. Of the different syndicate guys that I was forced to deal with during that time of my life, Titus was one of the most stubborn . . . or the most loyal, I guess, depending on how you look at it. So frankly it doesn't surprise me at all that he hasn't caved in and told Virgil the truth . . ." His eyes flicked away, the nearest he seemed to come to grief since she'd known him. "I always expected that Titus will take that secret to his grave."

Anthem took a few steps back from him. She felt herself beginning to get upset. Normally she led a quiet, introspective life in Vallejo Beach, cooking for Jack and renting movies with him in the evening. She had expected that her father's response to this proposal would be hesitant, even startled . . . but she had not anticipated such utter and total resignation.

For the first time she noticed the weary, tired tone in his voice, and his eyelids seemed to droop just a little; he looked so terribly *old*.

"Look at me," she said, her voice as strong as she could make it. "Look at me and tell me that you don't cry for him at night."

He waved his hand at her. "That's beside the p—"

"That is not beside the point! You don't know what it was like when I first met Titus, or what he did to me, or what I had to think while it was happening just to keep from giving up. I've seen Virgil before—"

"Honey, I know—"

"—right before you cut off my wings!" She hurled that at him with a vicious satisfaction, and almost immediately regretted it. Jack flinched hard.

"But I've made my peace with that," she added. "The whole time I just thought about how I'd actually found my brother. But it wasn't just that I'd found him. He was the key for everything that came later. When I saw him running through the white chickens, laughing and talking, I recognized his voice, and I remembered him and Ovid and you and—" Her voice broke off, permitting the tears to come, then she forced herself to continue. "Daddy, I know you feel bad about what you had to do to me, on the night you got me back. But it was worth it to me. It didn't kill me."

"You say you've made your peace," he said. "But does that mean you could forgive me for doing it?"

"Yes," she said. And perhaps it was the truth. She had only flown once, on that single wonderful night, and sometimes she could almost convince herself that the flight itself was only a dream.

But there were other times when she stood before a mirror with another mirror in her hand, and studied the dead-white scar tissue rippling down her back. During those times, after she stared at the scars long enough and ran her fingertips across the perfectly smooth and dead white tissue, her heart would begin to pound in her throat and finally subside into a hollow, aching sensation. She would think, *You are never forgiven. You are never forgiven.*

But right now, at this moment she had wanted nothing more than to let herself sink into Jack's embrace, to have him soothe her and dry her tears. But she knew that the issue was too serious now. It was rooted too deeply in both of their hearts for any kind of sentimental quick fix.

"Listen, kiddo," he said at last, "I know we're swimming into murky territory here, but have you thought of what might happen if you bring Ovid and Virgil back together again?"

She nodded. Of course she had thought about it. She knew that Jack himself had, too; had thought about it once for every candle he had on the shelves and tables around the practice room. Apparently he had even considered the possibility that Virgil might appear on their doorstep without warning while Ovid was around. She realized that that was the blackout he was expecting.

"I remember the blackout in Boston and the electrical storms," she said. "I remember Maria's headaches."

"It's just so goddamn unbelievable." Jack looked uncomfortable, balanced on the edge of the piano bench. "If I were going to write all of this as a story for some magazine, that would be the one part that I would cut out."

"I can see why," she shot back ruthlessly, without any warning. "You already helped cut out the other implausible part eight years ago in the backseat of a Lincoln, didn't you?"

He withdrew again, unable to face her in the silence that followed, until finally the moment threatened to collapse underneath its own weight. "Anthem . . . look, I can't quite comprehend why the three of you kids turned out as you did, and for some reason it still scares me silly to think about it. Once I said something to a physician I know about Ovid and Virgil being connected at some point and he said I had to be lying."

"I don't mind if I get a headache," she said tonelessly. "There's such a thing as aspirin. And we could always read by candlelight."

"What if it's not just barometric changes anymore? What if—"

She looked at him. She had been waiting to earn this tone of voice from him.

"We're talking about high drama here." He wiped his eyes. "What if we get them together again and they crack open the San Andreas Fault? What if they touch off another series of race riots? How do we know what will happen?"

"Don't say things like that."

He aimed a finger at her like a gun. "*You're* afraid they could happen."

"Don't say things like that," she repeated more forcefully, pushing her hair out of her eyes and tilting her chin slightly upward. "If I decide to go, I won't trouble you to convince me otherwise at the last minute."

Shaking his head, he said, "I don't think anyone could."

"You could, Daddy, but you won't . . ." *You can be a weak man,* she wanted to add, *and I love you for that just as much as for being the other way.* There was a feeling of pride, for having overcome that other, hateful voice, at least for now. *I do love you, you know, so much.*

But she knew that he wouldn't understand, and that it would only wound him more when, on the morning of the next day, she walked out to the van and began to head east, toward Virgil. By now Jack would have read about the disappearance of Nicholas H. Danzig in the newspaper, she thought as she walked back to the van. He would see a photo. And no matter how he felt about it, he would need to prepare himself for Virgil's arrival.

Snow was swirling past her on either side by the time she stepped back up into the front seat of the van. In the back, Virgil had stopped throwing himself against the sides, but now he was talking to her through the plywood in a low, growling voice that made her wonder if she would ever be able to open the back gate again without his tearing her throat out.

"I need to eat," he muttered, placing a savage emphasis on each word. "C'mon, please, I'll eat anything you give me, just give it to me soon . . . I'm starving back here, for God's sake . . . and I need water . . ."

"Sometimes I wish you wouldn't be so melodramatic," she said. "This trip is hard enough without your theatrics."

He cackled back at her, then began hammering against the plywood with his fists. He was raving about the rat and the cuts on his feet and God only knew what else. Once she even thought she heard the word *Ovid*. He was delirious.

31

"Colorado," she announced that night. "Gateway to the West."

They had continued to make miles throughout the rest of the day, having stopped only once for burgers and fries at McDonald's, where he had inhaled a fabulous amount of food she'd handed him through the slit in the plywood. A few miles later she had stopped again and opened the back door just enough to pass a large Coke into his hands. His cheeks and forehead were burning bright with fever, his lips cracked and parched. For the rest of the afternoon he had murmured and made incomprehensible sounds, and finally around dusk had fallen completely silent. Even now, after bucketing down three miles of bad road to Titus' mountain retreat, she doubted if he was awake to hear her.

"Colorado," she said again. "Virg, wake up."

She looked up the road that eventually turned into the private drive-way and disappeared into the trees. Titus had kept secluded counterparts to every one of his town apartments, but she suspected that this had to be the most inaccessible of the three. Even during the summer, motorists had to contend with fallen trees, loose gravel, massive potholes and a relentless thirty-five-degree grade; after the first snow of winter, travel would be impossible. During the last mile, the engine had taken on an ominous wheezing sound, but she had coaxed it along, slower and slower, until finally the gravel driveway appeared ahead of them on the right. She angled the van carefully into the breezeway and looked at the house in her headlights.

Hard weather had worn away most of the paint, but it was still in much better condition than the Iowa house had been. She wondered why Titus had chosen to make his home where life was so hard. She walked around to the back of the van and opened it, and Nicholas stumbled out.

"I can't move very far," he said. "My feet."

"I'll walk with you up to the house. I've already got the key."

He pushed his face against the side of her breast, allowing her to drag him up toward the porch. Shifting his weight into the crook of her elbow, she opened the storm door and rattled the key in the lock. The keyhole would not receive it. Immediately her hands began to tremble.

"Maybe somebody else bought the place and changed the locks," he muttered into her breast. "People . . . come and go, y'know."

She let him slide down to rest on the porch, then withdrew the pistol from her belt and pointed it a few inches away from the brass doorknob. She could feel the pistol straining heavily in her hand, how it wanted to be fired, the bullet contracting all at once to embed itself deep into the mechanism of the lock. She squeezed the trigger. The barrel blasted and jerked in her hand and everything jolted as the lock cylinder burst open through the door. She kicked it in, then took him by the arm again.

"I promise I won't run away again," he said. "Please, my wrists are killing me."

She popped the cuff from his wrist, then glanced inside the house at strangely colored walls and noticed odd smells. She stopped with one foot through the door. There was the smell of a recently prepared meal still lingering in the air. She looked to either side at the floral-print wallpaper running through the vestibule.

She moistened her lips. "I hope this is the right house."

"You hope—" He looked up at her, the drawn expression of his face making it difficult to tell whether he was smiling. "What, do you mean you aren't sure? You just shot the doorknob off."

She tried to think. She had only been here a few days ago, on her way out, and she had been positive that this was the house. Nothing could coax the actual address from her mind; she recalled it only as a certain familiar distance upward through the winding paths leading away from town. The gravity just seemed *stronger* there somehow.

She glanced to her right. A small pushbutton console was attached to the wall, the word *Honeywell* lettered across it. A single red warning light stuttered from somewhere deep inside its plastic casing. She heard him say, "I think—"

The alarm system began to wail. The sound seemed to connect with her like a punch. She dropped down into a crouch with her heart cowering in her chest and looked up in time to see Nicholas go springing out the doorway and toward the open road, the bottoms of his feet flickering out into the darkness.

"Stop!" she tried to scream. "Stop or I'll shoot!"

But he didn't hear her over the alarm. He didn't stop. Anthem rose up into the open doorway with the pistol extended in front of her, clutched in both hands. He was already halfway across the yard when she fired on him. He went tumbling as if he had tripped over something hidden in the tall grass.

Somewhere far away, sirens started to rise up in the night.

32

Huge jerks of pain spasmed through his knee and thigh, up through his groin to the base of his backbone. He could see the pain as vividly as a Roman candle hissing and spuming showers of red and bronze-colored sparks, brightest in his ankle, then fading in waves through his entire body. He felt the pavement as he fell.

Anthem's face filled his vision, though his eyes were swimming with tears, and he heard her voice saying *my fault my fault it was all my fault*, almost accidentally, because he wasn't paying attention to the words, or even the sounds, just to the pain, the rocketing, endless pain that made everything that had happened until now seem like a dream. He rolled on the pavement, still screaming, feeling the world sink into a pool of blood.

He saw the sky above, galaxies of stars overhead, fading in and out of view amidst the coming storm clouds, and the branches of trees bowing over in the wind. He felt Anthem's arms, cradling him. And he was still screaming.

He went inside the van, rolling awkwardly across the mattress, feeling the heat of his wound gouting blood up his pant leg over his belly and chest. He got another glimpse of Anthem's face. Where was all this blood coming from? *This can't be very good for me*, he thought, eyes rolling wildly.

Then the back of the van slammed shut.

And he was still screaming.

Sirens, fading back. Out of the darkness, floating like dusty images projected onto a screen, he saw his parents' faces, their day-old ghosts, his mother hanging up the phone and looking at his father and him at the breakfast table. He could taste the Frosted Mini-Wheats soggy in his mouth, the milk and juice he was having with breakfast, and he could smell his father's coffee about to burn his mouth, as his mother said, "It's Uncle Titus . . . you want to say hello?" He heard the sharp squeal of the rat, and he saw Ovid himself embracing him like a slightly aged reflection leaping free from a mirror. He drew back, still screaming. It was his scream, he thought; the only thing that he could really call his own.

The van jolted to a halt, and he heard the wind wailing on either side of it. The wind picked them up and began to carry them along. So that's why the cops never found us, his mind gibbered. We rode the wind. We've been riding on the wind the whole time. Just like Anthem with her wings that night on the beach.

"Stop it," she was saying calmly. Her voice was sweet, gentle. "Virgil, please, stop screaming. It just grazed you . . ."

She was tearing strips of bedding from the mattress and wrapping them around his leg, just above his knee, then cinching them tight. He saw the first shadow of blood soaking through already, after just a second or two. The back door of the van was open behind her, and he could see the snow spilling down in torrents of night wind. A few of the flakes were melting in her hair. She looked flushed and darkly beautiful as she pushed it back out of her eyes and finished knotting the cloth strips over his wound.

"Stop *screaming*, Virgil," she repeated.

She wrapped a wide swatch of the bedding around all the smaller strips, then knotted it off too. He watched the stain spread over the dirty fabric, then he fell backward against the cold metal, waiting for her to lift him up again. But she just crawled out, slammed the back doors behind her and started the engine.

The wind seized the van, and they flew up into the air, far away from the eyes of the world. Later they stopped, started, stopped again, started up again. Vaguely he felt Anthem's arms underneath him, lifting his weight and setting it down again.

When he awoke the third time, he was riding in the passenger seat, looking through the front window at the storm.

33

"My God," he mouthed. No words came out, just his rasping breath. He hadn't simply screamed himself hoarse, he realized with tired astonishment. He had screamed himself *mute*.

The windshield in front of him seemed huge, as though it encompassed the entire world. Snow skidded and danced across the glass in thick flakes the size of quarters. Above them, the sky rolled with thick black clouds, occasionally parting to uncover a vast gray sky stretched out across the hills and the unpaved two-lane road ahead. It was impossible to tell what time it was. Here in front of him all times of the day collided and intertwined, morning, afternoon, twilight.

He realized that Anthem was next to him, alternating glances between him and the road. When she saw that he was awake, she nodded toward the landscape outside.

"Arizona," she said.

He shook his head in disbelief. It was the first movement he'd made since swimming back up into consciousness, and the pain rushed up into the muscles of his neck and shoulders like antibodies attacking some foreign invader. He gasped silently and crumpled against the seat.

"We're just passing through the northern tip of the state," Anthem said. "They've shut off all the main freeways from here to the coast. They don't have the equipment to keep them open. Nobody can believe what's happening."

He nodded cautiously to indicate his agreement: *I can't believe it either.*

"It's only getting more serious as you and Ovid get closer together."

He opened his eyes wide, wrinkled his brow like a skeptic: *How much worse can it get?*

"Oh, this is just the start," she said. "Now I remember the way my little magnetized terriers were. You could never get them face-to-face. They'd shoot each other backward across the room before you could get them face-to-face. That's you and Ovid."

His eyes studied her, then narrowed, then finally closed in resignation.

"It's all true," she said. "Everything I told you. You'll see."

He thought of how she had continued to speak to the cops after she'd hit them with the frying pan. She hadn't seemed to be playing a practical joke. How often, he wondered, did Anthem hear voices responding to her in the silence? Did she hear his voice responding to her right now? If so, what was he saying to her? He felt a thrill of fear reverberate through to the pit of his stomach.

"You'll believe it when you see the Pacific Ocean stretched out forever, and the beach, and your brother," she said. "That's when the real storm will break, and afterward we'll all be together again. You'll believe me then."

He rolled his eyes. Anthem was holding the steering wheel steady with her knee and reached over to thrust a half-folded map in his face. "Look for yourself. I highlighted the back roads we're taking. It's a good thing, too. They say on the radio that there's head-on collisions and cars off the road all over the West Coast. They can't even land planes at the airports, and pretty soon those jets are going to be falling out of the sky."

An absurd, destruction-hungry grin lit her bruised face at the thought of the wreckage. Even her sleepless green eyes managed to twinkle, like a pair of dusty jewels laid across a mottled velvet background. He remembered the jumble of smashed model planes and cars in the closet of her old playroom, and her unending frustration with things that just wouldn't hold together. And now everything was falling apart.

"I came prepared, though," she continued proudly. "I wasn't sure what would happen when I tried to bring you and Ovid back together again, so after we left Colorado last night I stopped and put chains on the tires. I figure, what's hard to separate is even harder to put back together, right? So even if a blizzard hits L.A., we can stay on the back roads clear to Vallejo Beach."

He pushed the map aside without looking at it and mouthed three words: *How much longer?*

"Oh, Virg." She giggled with the sisterly delight he hadn't seen since yesterday, but now it looked like a ghastly pantomime played across her beaten face. "You're still just like a little boy—"

The pain was back, striking red and yellow sparks against the base of his skull. He mouthed the words again, with exaggerated care: *How much longer?*

"Tonight," she said hopefully. "We'll be there tonight."

He sank back against his seat and continued his vigil out the front window.

The storm intensified. Anthem finally slowed down to forty-five, but reluctantly. He could feel the van veering toward the shoulder, and then toward the yellow line, as crosscurrents rose and fell along the hills and valleys. Sometimes the entire windshield seemed white with snow, then the wind would whip it all away, flashing a clear view of the road ahead. Strange as it sounded, they actually seemed to be riding just inside the boundaries of the blizzard itself.

At some point during the long night, Nicholas noticed, Anthem had stopped for fast food. He poked at what remained of the cold McDonald's french fries and cheeseburgers, feeling too queasy to eat much but knowing that he wouldn't stay awake unless he tried. And he felt as if he'd won a victory by sitting up here with her, enough of a victory that he didn't want to pass out if he could possibly help it.

But he did lose consciousness, at least three times. His head nodded, and he dozed, no longer dreaming of the beach and the pure white sand, but the snow in the windshield and the California blizzard. When he woke up, his leg had bled through its bandages.

The storm bullied the van back and forth across the blacktop, and he tried not to think what would happen if they went into a skid and rolled off into a ditch. He would die in the cold with Anthem's body piled on top of him; he would die without ever finding out who he was for sure. Perhaps it was only light-headedness, but he found himself thinking more and more about a certain visit to Titus' house up north, years ago. He thought of a scream that he'd thought to be part of a nightmare, something that he had almost erased from his mind but that lingered in his unconscious, fading. Had he awoken, eight years ago, and heard a voice crying his name downstairs? It was uncertain. He no longer had the means for separating the truth from the craziness.

To distract himself he considered that name she'd spoken so casually. He wished he could speak, so that he could hear it himself in his own voice: Vallejo Beach, California.

He wished he could believe what they'd started would end there, magically, but somehow he could not.

In his dream the rats had his legs and feet. They were tearing flesh like fabric from his bones. He couldn't speak or scream or cry for help. His body lurched awake, wheezing and trying desperately to produce some sound beyond a papery rasp. His mouth was full of phlegm. There was blood from his throat on his lips.

Anthem's hand gripped his knee, squeezing it in reassurance. She was smiling over at him. "Virg," she said, "you are going to ruin your vocal cords in your sleep with these nightmares."

He pulled his leg away, unwilling to accept her sympathy.

"We made it into California an hour ago," she said.

This could not be California, he thought quite rationally. They had been on the road three days, hadn't they? It was simply impossible to drive to California in three days.

Besides, it was not the landscape of his dreams. They were still driving through that strange twilit storminess of dry snow and gray skies. The ground looked desolate, matted with pine needles and plugged with a thousand ugly tree stumps like soldiers across a flattened battleground. The sun was gone. It had been completely blotted out by clouds. Thick, colorless sleet lashed across the windshield, faster than the wipers could brush it away. Although the road ahead wasn't drifted shut with snow, it looked glassy with patches of ice, and when they hit those patches the van's tires, despite their chains, spun wildly out of control. Nicholas watched as the tachometer needle jumped spastically upward, then dropped back down, fluttering. Anthem struggled with the wheel, barely keeping them on the road.

He waited for her to look at him, fighting off unconsciousness until he could mouth his question to her again: *How much longer?*

"Two hours to the beach. And we're home."

He thought of the storm outside—the storm they were bringing with them—as it grew steadily more furious.

And what happens then?

34

Portion of the testimony of Jennifer Clara Wiest, October 16:
What else do you need to know?

Gossip? I never heard of a police investigation where they wanted to hear town gossip. But I'll tell you what I know.

We thought she was the daughter of an old girlfriend, somebody who wouldn't leave him alone. Titus had sired his share of bastard kids, I'm sure, by country girls around northern Michigan. Most times their fertility got them as far as the bus station with a round-trip ticket into Windsor, where a girl could get such a condition taken care of. That was the only option Titus offered his girlfriends . . . the ones that wanted to stay in town, that is.

It's hard to imagine him being so reckless about his offspring, though: for all his womanizing, he had a kind of country-style reputation to live up to. They say he started up that chain of retail sportswear stores in the Midwest, and I know he liked to cruise around in that Ford truck of his, looking in on the different stores in Michigan, Indiana and Ohio. But they all knew he'd made most of his fortune on Wall Street.

He owned cottages, farms and land around the state and up into Canada, and he was, what's that word, eccentric, but nobody seemed quite able to believe he would let some crazy girl go running around his farm, even if she was the daughter of one of his best girlfriends. A lot of folks were talking it up. Eccentric doesn't mean crazy, does it?

Of course, Gertrude's presence wasn't public for too long: she disappeared off the face of the earth. Eventually the town forgot, I guess.

I don't think it crossed anybody's mind that Titus might have had the girl put away because she was more than just the daughter of an old girlfriend. But I must say it's crossed my mind, from time to time. They say Gertrude was crazy . . . but having Titus for a daddy would drive just about anybody crazy.

Wouldn't you think?

35

Outside their windows Nicholas could hear the wind shrieking. Never in his life had he heard it sound so human, so enraged. White shapes swooped past, shapes he first thought were newspapers or garbage, but then recognized as seagulls.

The sky was black as they crested a hill overlooking a long, empty street below. The street itself was lined with abandoned-looking storefronts, dark alleyways and half-flattened slat fences. Through the sleet and rain it looked like a resort town gone to seed during the off-season. At the bottom of the hill, beyond a single stoplight, the road veered right. Two blocks beyond that, he could see the beach. The boardwalk was gray and desolate. Further out he heard a buoy clanging across the water. A lonely, mournful sound.

Anthem drove down the hill, staring straight ahead. She seemed both mesmerized and jumpy, troubled by the gulls that swung down in front of the windshield. He watched the storefronts pass. Ice-cream shops, souvenir shops, fishing charter offices: all of it boarded up and lightless, deserted. Not a single person on the boardwalk. He hadn't seen another car for what seemed like hours. But just being here at last gave him a chill that was almost exhilarating enough to make him feel like he might be getting better.

"Would you hand me the map, please?" Anthem said.

He reached down and gathered it up from between his feet. The movement didn't hurt much; mostly there was just numbness now, as though his right leg simply ended just below his thigh. He glanced at it and pushed it away in disbelief.

"What?" She glanced at him. "Something wrong?"

They rolled toward the traffic light. It had turned red. She drove straight through the intersection without stopping, already starting to turn right toward the saltbox buildings of the wharf below, and reached for the map herself.

"It's . . ." He was forcing the words through his wounded throat, though every syllable burned worse than the last. "It's . . . not the right . . . map. This is just a map of Michigan . . ."

He saw that strange emptiness floating behind her eyes, like it had the night before. She was not watching the road as, behind them, a blue strobe began to swirl. He looked in his side-view mirror and saw a police cruiser pulling around the corner at the intersection, where they had just run the red.

He waited for the adrenaline rush, sensing at the same time that all his adrenaline was spent. Anthem had the map spread open across the steering wheel, but she wasn't looking at it or the road ahead. Her eyes roamed as if she were following the path of an invisible fly overhead, and her grip on the wheel slackened until it started to turn by itself, slightly at first and then suddenly. The van veered left and caromed off the curb of the oncoming lane. Nicholas went toppling across the driveshaft, steadied himself and grabbed the wheel to straighten it.

"*Anthem!*" he shouted. He couldn't think of anything else to say. The cruiser was right behind them now, tailgating so closely into the turn that, in his side-view mirror, Nicholas could see the confused expression stretched across the face of the man in the driver's seat. The driver had gray eyes and a carefully trimmed gray beard.

Nicholas reached across his lap to buckle his seat belt, his mind reeling with absurd details. He realized that he had never seen a cop with a

beard before, had always assumed that it went against some police dress
code. The man flashed his headlights and pulled into the oncoming lane
alongside them. The van surged ahead, as though Anthem had suddenly
floored the gas pedal.

''Anthem!''

Two things happened at once: the cop hit the sirens and the van
exploded into a newspaper machine on the corner as it plowed across
the sidewalk and down toward the wharf. Newspapers fluttered across
the windshield and blew across the street. The last of the storefronts
blurred past, and he felt the van gain speed as it headed down the
incline. The map flew off the steering wheel and into Anthem's face. As
he reached to grab it off, still trying to hold the steering wheel, he had
time to think: *This is the map she wanted, after all. This is the map she's
been using—*

''Virgil.'' Somehow she was looking at him, her face flooded with
remorse. The steering wheel was revolving on its own again, under the
loose grip of her hands. Her voice was almost a whisper. ''Virgil, I loved
you. You have to believe that.''

The van listed drunkenly back into the road and he saw the ware-
houses of the wharf fly past them, and the dry dock full of fishing boats
in storage. He looked ahead and realized that they were going to run off
the road, that there was no way of stopping the van or even swerving
away from the beach in time to keep them away from the water.

When she looked at him again, he saw something ecstatic flicker in
her eyes, and he thought, *That's what she looked like when she was flying.*
And, as a final afterthought, *I think I almost believe her about the wings.*

She reached over and took his hand, almost tenderly. ''This is for the
best.''

As the front wheels leapt up off the blacktop he glimpsed the police
cruiser slowing down, the strobe lights fading and then gone, and they
shot through a patch of tall grass and across the low dunes of the beach
so fast that he couldn't take a breath before the van dove over the last
dune with a heart-stopping jolt. Then it felt like they hit a wall. He saw
Anthem's body, unrestrained by the seat belt, slam face-first into the
steering wheel. Glass burst out of the windshield. Metal screamed, and
the hard, cold water knocked him backward against the seat cushion.
He gagged, already drowning, and felt his heart freeze up. The water
around him was beyond cold, to the point where it might have just as
easily been scalding hot. He could not move in it. He certainly could not
breathe.

Water rolled past him like a river within the sea itself, bursting the plywood barrier he had once struggled so hard to burst himself, and the current yanked him out of his seat to the rear of the van. Here the back doors trapped the last pocket of air, perhaps just a few inches of open space between the water and the door, which had now become the ceiling. He tore a breath and sank, his limbs stiff and useless, back toward the driver's seat. Anthem was fighting to dislodge herself, and he saw just a flash of her face. She was gaping back up at him, bubbles streaming from her lips, her arms clawing frantically with the wreckage that had been the front seat of the van.

The doors buckled. When they did, the current that had already knocked him out of his seat drove his body out of the van. He saw the entire vehicle—just a half second's view—receding beneath him into the depths like a whale. He neither saw nor felt much of anything else from the instant that the water hit until afterward, when arms plucked him out of the water, blue and strangling, more dead than alive. He did not remember being laid across the cold sand, a few feet from the water. His first thought afterward was as difficult to specify as the first thought he might have had in his life. He could not separate what he felt from what he thought.

But he remembered one of the last bits of awareness to trickle through his mind, sometime while he was lying sprawled out across the cold sand, just a few feet from where the waves rolled and broke.

The water where the van had crashed wasn't salty like the ocean.

The water was *fresh*.

36

Portion of the testimony of Ian Danzig, October 27:

It was Friday the 15th, about three in the morning, when the call came. Nicky had been missing for three days, and for those three days neither Shelley nor I had slept more than a few minutes at a time. Even then I'm not sure you can call what we experienced "sleep." For me it was more like a moment of dizziness when my mind simply grayed out, like the screen of a television tuned to a faraway station, when the details become too addled to make out anything besides shadows and ghosts. These moments were always over too quickly, leaving me feeling punk and confused, never rested. Finally, after three nights of this, I had consented to taking one of Shelley's Xanax about ten o'clock at night. The tranquilizer had gone to work fast on me, faster than I might have wanted it to, actually. It almost seemed to attack my mind, like it felt compelled to avenge the aching exhaustion that had gathered there in the last three days. My head dropped to the pillow in just a few minutes, and I slept without dreams until Shelley shook me awake. The phone was ringing. It was the police.

I had a premonition, reaching for the phone. It was the first one I've ever had in my life, but I suddenly knew why those who experienced them seemed to trust them so completely. I knew unquestionably about the news that awaited on the other end of the telephone line.

"Hello?" I said softly.

"Mr. Danzig? Sir, this is Sergeant Dryden from the State Highway Patrol . . ." There was a pause, a horrible pause. ". . . Mr. Danzig, I'm afraid I've got terrible news about your son, sir. We just received a call from up north—"

I could feel Shelley's sleep-tangled hair brush against my cheek, as she leaned close to the receiver to listen along with me. I felt this only distantly, like a tickle in sleep. "Ah . . ." I heard myself saying. "Ah, God . . . oh no . . ."

". . . there was a wreck up there . . ." Dryden was saying, and saying quickly, as if he had a certain amount of lines he was required to speak before slipping offstage and out of this particular drama. ". . . your son . . . a girl . . ." I wasn't listening, not listening at all. ". . . van went into the lake . . . both presumed dead . . ."

Next to me, Shelley's shoulders began to tremble. She sucked in a breath, moaned and began to hitch up great, flat sobs from deep within her chest. She fell backward onto the bed, and I think that's when I began to cry along with her in my own whimpering voice.

37

He didn't know how long he slept after that, but it was long enough that he was afraid he might have died. He was aware that his body had gone about the job of healing itself the way his mother occasionally went about cleaning house: it seemed to tackle the problem with a vengeance, neglecting everything else. He didn't dream during this period, except once, and it was really more like a single image that played over and over in his mind:

He was back in the van, traveling, traveling, forever traveling down a bleak and nameless road. In the dream he knew there was no driver, nor were there any other cars on the road, or any other roads in the world: just the pale-faced kid, crouched alone in the rear corner of the van, riding down the dark edge of the world. The only sound was a soft but incessant flapping noise from somewhere in the front seat. He peered through the slit in the plywood. Knotted to either side of the steering wheel were the sleeves of Anthem's sweater. Wind filled it like a sail, so that it expanded to occupy the driver's seat entirely. Nicholas watched the wheel jerking back and forth on its own, making slight corrections in their course. It had a frightening, cartoony sense to it, like an illustration in one of Dr. Seuss' more eerie stories. He jerked awake, completely disoriented, blinking away the image.

His eyes tried to focus on the room where he lay.

Details crept up shyly around him. He saw that he was alone in a bedroom with a single bay window. It was plain, sparsely decorated with only a bureau, a nightstand, a lamp, but filled with bars of golden sunlight through which layers of dust eddied lazily. The door had a well-polished brass knob. It was shut. The air was warm but not unpleasant, a welcome change from the clammy dankness of the van. After a while he could hear the furnace below when it kicked on. It was a reassuring sound, proof somehow that he had not been deserted here. When he turned his head to the nightstand, he found more proof: an empty bowl and spoon on a plastic tray. Someone had been feeding him, or trying.

Most of the day he slept. The pain in his leg ebbed and flowed, and it gave him his only sense of passing time. Sometimes the pain was so terrible he wanted to scream, though he knew from his throat that screaming, even speaking, was out of the question. He could scarcely breathe. His lungs felt full of fluid, and his sinuses tickled with a million tiny bugs swarming just beneath the skin of his face.

He did not think about Anthem, or the map of Michigan that she had been following. When he had those thoughts, his head would start to pound, and it was difficult, sometimes impossible, to stop the pounding. Consequently he didn't think about them. He looked over the bumps of his feet under the blanket, at the bedroom door and its well-polished knob. He waited for the knob to turn, as he knew it would.

And sometime after the leg pain had come and gone a dozen times, maybe a hundred times, the knob turned. His eyelids drew open. He lifted his head.

"Well," a man's voice said. There was the slow whistling of canned oxygen. "Welcome back, kiddo."

The man was Uncle Titus.

He looked older and more withered than when Nicholas had last seen him, but his eyes spun and shimmered with an excited inner brightness. He was in his wheelchair, of course, wearing a red flannel hunting shirt and heavy wool pants that drooped down a little in front to allow for the paunch of his stomach. A pair of plastic tubes ran from either nostril and over his shoulder, where they plugged into a green canister of oxygen. His gnarled fingers clutched the armrests of the wheelchair. He stopped at the foot of his bed to light up a Marlboro, bringing the lighter audaciously close to the oxygen flow, then guided the motorized wheelchair up close to the bed and paused to look at Nicholas.

"I guess you've had quite a couple of days, haven't you, Nicky?"

Nicholas just nodded, certain now that he was dreaming.

"Yeah, well, it's over now. Somehow you survived it . . ." The eyes flicked over the shape of his body under the blankets, as if he could see through them. "But God only knows how. Bullet just nicked your leg, and it's already started to heal up. But you used up most all your luck for the rest of the year, I expect. Count yourself lucky."

Nicholas watched Uncle Titus release a gust of smoke from the corner of his mouth. "While you're at it, you can thank God that worse didn't happen to you, screwing around in that house. I told myself a hundred times to board that damn shack up, I knew she'd be back there screwing around . . ." He took another drag, disgustedly. "Course I never dreamed of nothing like this happening, Nicky, I swear to God."

Nicholas didn't understand what he was talking about. The words jumbled in his mind, raising the kind of questions that brought headaches, so he tried to ignore them. Just leave, Uncle Titus, he thought. Please, just leave so I can forget this so I can drift back to sleep.

But Titus didn't turn his wheelchair around and go. He sat, staring at Nicholas, long after the cigarette was gone, the crazy blue light pinwheeling in his eyes. He seemed to be looking for some trace of knowledge in his face, an answer to some question he couldn't bring himself to ask.

Finally the gaze was too much, and Nicholas opened his mouth, moving his lips around her name. It came out all at once. He waited for Titus to respond.

"Her name ain't Anthem," Titus said at last. "Everything she told you is a lie."

"You know her?" Nicholas asked hoarsely. "You know why she brought me back here?"

"Yeah." The old man offered him a thin seam of a smile that Nicholas didn't like one bit. "Yeah, I guess I do know why."

Before Nicholas could ask him anything else, Titus spun the wheelchair around and rolled out of the bedroom. Nicholas heard the wheelchair rolling down the hallway outside, and then a high-pitched whining sound, like a machine straining at peak capacity. He paid little attention to it, at that moment. His final thought before slipping into unconsciousness was that Uncle Titus had not asked him any questions of his own.

38

Portion of the testimony of Shelley Danzig, October 28:
After the news came about Nicky's death, we wanted to fly up there to Burns Mills, where Gertrude had taken him and where they'd crashed, but the state police talked us out of the trip. They were working as hard as they could up there, they said, looking for bodies, and our presence wasn't going to help. It might just complicate the process.

Survivors, I said. Why can't you say, "Looking for survivors"?

But they say surviving a crash into Lake Superior is next to impossible. And if Nicky had survived, they said, he would have been found by now. It's just too cold and desolate up there for a boy to be wandering around, alone and confused, before starvation and exhaustion set in.

More than once I caught myself starting to think, "We could just stay with Uncle Titus for a few days until the police had finished the search." Somehow we expected magic from Uncle Titus, after all these years. But, of course, Titus wasn't magic. Titus was an old man whose crazy daughter had finally done what we had deeply feared she would. We spoke to him briefly on the phone. He apologized, of course, profusely and energetically, and offered to drive down to Portage. At the time it just didn't occur to me why he was offering.

Finally, two nights after the phone call, it was Ian who suggested, in a soft, tentative voice, that he supposed we should wait another day or two, and then begin to make arrangements.

And I thought of why Titus had offered to drive down to Portage.

For Nicholas' funeral.

39

An uncertain time later, Titus returned to the room. Moving along behind him was a gaunt, narrow-shouldered shape in a dark blue uniform. Vaguely Nicholas recognized the bearded face from the side-view mirror of the van. The cop had been the one chasing them.

As the man drew closer, Nicholas noticed his sad gray eyes. The stranger had a newspaper folded under one long arm.

Nicholas lifted his head from the pillow. The paper was the *Burns Mills Register*. He noticed that the cop had folded it under his arm so that Nicholas could read both the date, October 16, and the headline, without moving more than a few inches.

TWO DIE AS VAN CRASHES, SINKS
Police continue search for bodies

"How's death treating you, Nicky?" Uncle Titus asked.

"It feels like I'm still alive," he murmured. The words came a little easier now, but breathing was still a chore. "I guess I am."

"Sure you are. And you can thank your lucky stars we were all waiting for you two to come tear-assing up through here. Ever since you and Gertie busted into that house down in the Lower Peninsula we been expecting you up here."

"Gertie?" he croaked. "Michigan?"

"You've been on a beeline straight up north since Tuesday. Where'd you think you were headed, with this weather kicking up like this?" He tipped Nicholas a sly wink. "They don't get these early snows like this nowhere but along the lake."

"What . . ." He shook his head. "What . . . lake?"

"The big one. The big lake. Lake Superior. The one you nearly drowned in two days ago, if Jack hadn't been here to fish your sorry ass out."

Nicholas looked at the bearded man, standing silently beside Titus with the newspaper folded under his arm. "You pulled me out," he said. "What happened to Anthem? Is she really . . ."

Both men looked at him silently for a long time, but the cop had nothing to say. Then Nicholas remembered Anthem's face, gaping back at him from the flooded front seat of the van. Nicholas closed his eyes and heard Uncle Titus light another cigarette. The fact that he needed compressed air just to continue breathing did not seem to have affected his three-pack-a-day habit, Nicholas noticed.

"Jack," Titus said. "Gotta talk to you outside."

Before Nicholas faded back into the warm darkness, he heard the cop following his uncle in his wheelchair to the doorway, and shutting the door behind them. At some point the cop had left the newspaper at the foot of the bed. Titus had not seemed to notice, but he, Nicholas, had. Something in him already realized that Anthem's business with him— even if it was all a lie like Uncle Titus had told him, and even if that raving, goddesslike woman who called herself Anthem was truly dead— even if it was all of that, it was not over.

He thought of her face, how helpless and lost she had looked in her final moments.

I had wings, Virgil.

And it was strange, but at that moment he again realized that he could have believed it.

40

Later, when Titus came back into the room, Nicholas felt consciousness spread back across his mind like a hesitant ray of sunlight. He didn't know how much later it was. The furnace had clicked on and then off again. The wheelchair had whirred into the room. The sound of the motorized chair had probably awakened him, but he had rolled over feigning sleep. Only as the old man turned the chair around to leave did Nicholas open his eyes.

Titus halted the chair, pausing as if to reconsider something, some bit of unfinished business.

Nicholas stared at the long green oxygen tank mounted at the back of Titus' wheelchair. He was almost certain that Titus shouldn't be smoking cigarettes so close to pure oxygen, particularly not *compressed* oxygen, but the old man had persisted in doing it as long as he'd had a tank cradled against the back of his wheelchair. In fact, Titus had always seemed to relish the potential threat it presented to onlookers. It looked dangerous. Nicholas recalled his father commenting more than once that Titus smoked more for this effect than for the pure pleasure of it.

"Hey, aren't you afraid you're going to blow yourself up one of these days?" he asked. "Smoking all those cigarettes?"

Titus jerked the chair around and peered back at him, streaming smoke from between cracked lips. "Well, look who's up." He smiled. "Naw, not me. Ain't the worrying kind."

"Well, I am," Nicholas said, and felt the truth come bubbling almost unexpectedly out of him. "I'm worried about why I'm still here."

"Here?" Titus asked innocently. "Here in Burns Mills?"

"Yeah." He tried to sit further up and felt a sharp wire of pain uncoil up through his leg. If Titus saw him wince, he showed no sign of it. "Anthem told me . . ."

"Gertrude," Titus corrected. He seemed so preoccupied with what Nicholas was saying that the correction sounded mechanical. "Gertrude is her real name."

"She said she was my sister, and that my parents at home aren't my real parents."

"Oh really?" Titus said, one eyebrow arched upward. Now he seemed interested. "What else did Gertrude tell you?"

"She told me about her wings," Nicholas said. "She told me about Ovid. And some kind of power we had when we were together."

"Ovid?" It was impossible to tell whether the surprise in Titus' voice was real or manufactured. "Who the hell is Ovid?"

"She said he was my older brother," he said. "She said we were separated when I was too young to remember it because bad things happened when we were together. But I think she was probably . . ." He paused. "I think she was probably a little crazy."

Titus closed his eyes. Although it was difficult to read expressions from his face, Nicholas thought the old man seemed to be half-amused by what he had said, and perhaps a little threatened also.

"So you and this O-vid," he asked, pronouncing the name more slowly, as if he had only now come to realize what Nicholas was talking about. "What did she say it was like when the two of you were together?"

He felt his heart skip and flutter. "I don't remember."

"You're lying." He leaned slightly forward in a gesture of barely repressed force. The plastic oxygen tubes were stretched tight alongside him. "What did she say it was like when you and this Ovid came together?" He leaned even further out of the chair, his face very close to Nicholas'. *"Tell me!"*

"She said something about storms," Nicholas managed. But that wasn't right, was it? His thoughts were getting hazier instead of more clear. The weather had gotten worse just because they were heading north, not because they had been getting any nearer to some mysterious, unseen older brother. "I don't . . . I don't remember . . ."

"You'll tell me," Uncle Titus said. The flesh on his face had become very tight and shiny, as though it might burst at any moment, but his voice remained level. "You'll tell me what happened, Nicky boy. Or, believe you me"—he grinned—"I'll take it out of your hide."

"Things got lost . . ." Nicholas babbled, hardly recognizing the slurry of his own words as they tumbled from his lips. "Things got . . . broken . . . stolen . . . shattered . . . I don't know." He realized that the "power" that Anthem talked about was just a way of explaining the cold weather and snow. He was astonished that he had ever believed this story at all.

Any sense of rebelliousness had vaporized from inside of him. His voice wavered, dissolved into tears. He prayed Titus would just let him cry, that he would stop questioning him. Honestly, he told himself, he knew nothing else to confess.

"I don't even know for sure if he was even real," he said at last. "If you know who he is, I wish you would tell me."

Titus' fingers uncurled from the arms of his wheelchair, the crooked joints of his fingers almost creaking, and he sank back into his chair. "All right," he muttered, and turned his chair the rest of the way around to wheel himself toward the open doorway of the bedroom. "If I ever find out for sure who you're talking about, rest assured I'll let you know about it."

He slammed the door on the way out. Nicholas waited until he didn't hear the wheelchair's tires rolling down the long wooden hall anymore.

He reached underneath the covers of his bed, feeling around for a moment before his fingers found the *Burns Mills Register* left behind by the bearded cop, the one that Titus had called Jack. He read the article that reported his own death, along with Anthem's. It was an amazing piece of fiction. According to the article, the cop had never been near the wharf when the van shot through the metal guardrails, bounded up over the dunes and bellyflopped into the bay. And according to the article, both their bodies were still missing. It finished:

> *Services for Nicholas Danzig, who was reported missing four days ago, will be held next week in the boy's hometown of Portage.*

Services? They were already having a funeral for him?

He relaxed his arms and the newspaper crumpled.

Uncle Titus and the bearded cop had rescued him, hadn't they? So why didn't Uncle Titus call home and tell them he was alive?

Because at the moment it's more convenient for you to be dead, something inside told him cautiously. *It's more convenient in case Titus decides to keep you around here.*

The tail end of that thought startled him badly. Why would Titus want to keep him up here in Burns Mills?

He closed his eyes. All he really knew with any confidence at the moment was that he was still alive. He didn't know if Ovid really existed, or what Anthem had meant by her stories of thunderstorms and blackouts.

And Uncle Titus didn't seem to know any more than he did.

Didn't *seem* to know.

But in the time that he had, he needed to use that leverage to escape. Gestating in his mind was the notion that he had some kind of higher purpose here in Titus' house, a discovery he needed to make first. It sounded a little crazy, phrased that way. But he didn't know what it was yet, and if he couldn't figure it out soon—

"Yeah, I know," he said, cutting off that inside voice by speaking out loud again. "It'll be my funeral."

41

Something woke him up later that day. He pushed the covers aside completely and sat upright at the edge of the bed, slowly shifting his weight onto his good leg and balancing off his bad one. He was wearing only a pair of long underwear and his bandages. He felt badly exposed, especially after how Titus had gone nose-to-nose with him earlier. Holding the nightstand with both hands, he was able to take three steps before the pain hit. It drove long silver spears through his joints, and he saw a blot of fresh blood spread through the dressing of his bullet wound. Instantly the pain overwhelmed any sense of heroism he might have otherwise felt. He was discovering how well pain and heroism counterbalanced each other, as reliably as sugar and insulin.

Even more obvious than the blood, though, was the wooden floor beneath him. Every inch of it seemed to sing a different note when he stepped across it. *Scree-scraw-screep-yaww.* It would be impossible to sneak across the old boards without everyone downstairs knowing he was creeping around.

He took another step, and another. Now the door was in front of him. He clutched the knob with both hands, mainly for support, and felt it turn as the door swung open into the long hallway outside. He looked out. Electric flambeaux were attached to either side of the hallway at five-foot intervals, the light fixtures bolted down against the wallpaper's fading floral print. A red rug, crosshatched with a thousand wheelchair tracks, ran to the end of the hall, where a huge picture window revealed the shoreline outside.

The morning looked gray and miserable, a perfect reflection of his own hazy internal weather. He started toward the window, passing doorways as he went toward it. He imagined throwing himself through it. He began to walk faster, with his head starting to throb.

Then from down the hall he could hear the saxophone music that must have awoken him in the first place.

At first there was just the saxophone itself blowing out slow, smoky notes from somewhere down at the end of the hall, and he halted and cocked his head, listening. He took another creeping step forward. Underneath the saxophone a bass line bumbled along, seemingly disconnected. The sound was muffled but close, as though it were being played only a room away. Nicholas stopped to listen again. Now he could hear the cymbals, too, chattering along consistently behind the saxophone and bass.

One of the doors he was leaning against swung open and he lost his balance and tumbled, sprawling, inside. His head knocked against the corner of a dresser, and the pain came late: it had rerouted itself through his bad leg, which he had landed on. Then it was very bad. Tears burned in his eyes.

When the mist cleared from his vision again, he looked at the room around him. He was in the same room as the music, and he saw the record on the turntable. He was in some sort of storage room. Bookshelves rose up on either side of him, swaying under their freight of books and records, with twin speakers perched at the very top. In the back of the room, shoved up close to the shelves, was a battered-looking piano with a few sheets of music propped up on it, fluttering slightly in the breeze. Stacked around the piano were towers of cardboard boxes. The boxes were dusty, but he could still read the marker scrawl across several of the smaller ones stacked on top:

GERTRUDE

He walked toward the "Gertrude" boxes and noticed a coffee cup steaming on top of the piano. He stopped in his tracks.

Behind the piano the bearded cop pushed back the bench and stood up. He studied Nicholas with his sad, gray eyes but said nothing for a moment. Behind them in the stereo's speakers the saxophone started jerking back and forth like a fast, brassy fish.

"That's Dexter Gordon," Jack said quietly with a nod. "Have you ever heard of Dexter Gordon?"

"Yeah," Nicholas said, "I've heard of him."

The bearded cop took a sip from his espresso and produced a sigh.

His gray hair stood up on the side of his head where his hand had been pushing it up.

Nicholas allowed himself to recline at a moderate angle against the door frame to rest his leg while he looked at the man. His wound hurt, but it wasn't bleeding. He met the cop's gaze across the room. "You're the one she called Saint Jack, aren't you?" he asked. "Anthem told me a lot of stuff about you in the last few days."

"I'm going to ask that you don't bring up her name." Jack looked at the cup tilting in his hand and snuffled up a laugh through his nose. "Whoops, look at that, almost got espresso on the piano." He snuffled again. "There's a sonnet in that, I do believe. Or I'm not the celibate and celebrated poet laureate of Burns Mills, Michigan, population 1,280."

"She said you were our father," Nicholas said. Why were they having this crazy conversation? Now his head was hurting him again, and he felt the tension developing in the cords of his neck. "She said you named me Virgil. Is that the truth?"

The bearded man looked quickly away from him as though he'd heard his name called among the saxophone notes. Then he disappeared behind the piano again. Over the music on the record player Nicholas could hear the thumping of keys being pounded and pumped, but no music being produced from inside the piano. He limped in a wide half-circle around the room until he saw the man's long fingers pouncing up the keyboard, then back down again, then stopping as he glanced back at Nicholas.

"Titus had all the wires removed from inside the piano after she tried to hang herself," Jack said. "But you know, she claimed she could still hear the music all through the house, so I kept coming over and playing from the sheet music just like those strings were still there, and sometimes she could even identify the piece." His fingers began to move again. "Me, all I can do is just listen to records. I try to listen to myself play but I can't hear anything."

"She said you had me and another son," Nicholas said. "My older brother, Ovid."

The long fingers began to strike at the keys more violently, almost bludgeoning them. Underneath, his feet stomped on the pedals as though he were working an old harmonium, but the only sound was the same sullen thumping. All at once Jack's head snapped up to look at him. When he stood up again, Nicholas could imagine the entire piano tipping forward with a crash. High color had rushed into the man's cheeks so that his salt-and-pepper beard looked almost white beside it.

"She said you were our father," Nicholas repeated. "Is it true?"

"Go back to your room."

"You have to tell me the truth here!"

"No, I don't," Jack said. The words came more smoothly, but no more easily. "And unfortunately for you, Nicholas or Virgil or whatever your name is, even if I did have to tell you anything, I think you'd find that most of what she told you is only partly true around here, and it's never the part that you suspected in the first place."

The manner in which he spoke reminded Nicholas absurdly of the White Rabbit in Lewis Carroll's story. And in fact, he thought a little dizzily, at the moment that they crashed through the surface of the lake, he seemed to have fallen through some looking glass all his own, where actors were hired to impersonate all the people that Anthem had described to him. Again there was suddenly the question of what was real. His Uncle Titus was real, of course; the pain in his leg, ah, that was very real indeed. He winced, because the memory of it was enough to bring back the pain in full force. Jack seemed to notice this immediately.

"Titus did leave some medication for me to give you," he said. "You know you shouldn't have been walking around on that leg in the first place."

"I just had to go to the bathroom," Nicholas said. "I heard the music and it woke me up."

"It's good music," Jack said testily, as though Nicholas had attacked it. "Well, listen, if you were heading for the bathroom, you went too far. It's just up the hall across from your room." He glanced up and watched Nicholas take a few limping steps toward the door, then sighed and stretched out his hand. "Here, you can lean on me, I'll help you."

Nicholas looked at the open hand and wondered suddenly why he alone had been rescued from the crash, and not Anthem.

"Like you helped her?" he asked. "Out of the lake?"

The bearded man raised his eyebrows. "Are you really trying to provoke me, Nicholas?"

"I just want to know what's going on here," he said. "I'm really just trying to get some answers."

He stopped in the doorway, pretending to be catching his breath. Really, though, he was thinking about the strange, cowering tone in Jack's voice. He couldn't quite define it. It was a sort of apologetic inflection, but he couldn't come up with the correct word at the moment. He knew that his mother had accused his dad of acting in this manner sometimes, when Ian Danzig's students' parents occasionally called to complain about his teaching methods. What it meant was that Jack was trying too hard for something he didn't really care about. And the question was why.

As he stood in the doorway, Nicholas looked at the details, meager though they were. He realized that the left side of his brain had made the decision that Jack was not his father. Whatever else he was, Jack was an outsider to this business between him and Anthem and Titus. There was too much the sense of this—whatever the word was—mingled in with a strange wishfulness. A melancholy. A weakness. He considered whether Jack had helped Anthem escape from here before. He looked at Jack, and for the first time, Jack appeared useful to him.

"Actually," he said, "you could give me a hand."

Called to duty, Jack regarded him cautiously. All the authority had drained from his facial expression, and his gray eyes now seemed soft with fear and fret. "What?" he said anxiously. "Do you want a pill? Something for the pain?"

"Maybe just one," Nicholas said.

"After the bathroom," the cop told him. He wrapped his long arm around Nicholas' shoulder and stepped with him back toward his bedroom at the end of the hall. He opened the door across from the bedroom, revealing a plain, closet-sized room with a sink, toilet and shower inside. "You go ahead and do your business. I'll get you that pill from downstairs."

Nicholas went inside and shut the door behind him, took a seat on the throne, but didn't bother lifting the lid first. What he needed was just to think for a minute. He heard Jack's footsteps padding quickly, doglike, down the steps to the downstairs he had never seen, and his mind grasped the full meaning of the word that he hadn't been able to come up with a moment ago.

Servile. Servility.

Jack was smart, but Jack was also servile. It probably meant that he owed Uncle Titus something. Nicholas guessed that a lot of people had owed Uncle Titus *something* in their lives—in the backhanded way that he himself probably owed Titus his life itself—and Jack seemed to owe him on that same large scale. Large enough, anyway, that Jack would have been willing to call Portage and tell Ian and Shelley Danzig that

their kidnapped son was probably three hundred feet under Lake Superior, when in reality he was cozied up in Uncle Titus' house with Dexter
Gordon on the stereo.

Maybe for the rest of his life.

Nicholas realized that the trip north with Anthem had changed the
way he saw things. Adult gestures no longer divided themselves neatly
into the formal and the irrational, but blended into one stereoscopic
view. There was only the useful. He could sense opportunities, and right
now he saw an opportunity in Saint Jack. One of the reasons that his
mom hated it when his dad was *servile* was that it often made him act
another way later, and the term for that was *resentful*. His thoughts were
rushing very swiftly and clearly now. He knew what resentful meant.
Resentful meant slow-motion hate. And if Jack was *resentful*, he might
be able to help him, whether he knew it or not.

Nicholas heard him trotting back up the carpeted steps, then a dull
thud and a soft clattering of pills. Jack was reciting a litany of curses
under his breath. Nicholas stood up from the toilet, flushed it, and
opened the door and stepped back out into the hallway. He looked
toward the end of the hall and saw Jack hunched over the banister, his
expression a little hangdog, plucking individual pills from out of the rug
like tiny yellow wildflowers.

"It seems Titus has allowed the steps to fall into disrepair," he said,
trying unsuccessfully to cover his anger with words as he gathered the
rest of the pills in his hand and started toward Nicholas. "I think I got
most of the pills. He really should fix that loose step."

Nicholas took one of the pills from his hand and made a gesture of
throwing it back into his throat. It was small enough so that he could
hide it under the ball of his thumb, for the moment, while Jack walked
him back into the bedroom. The gray eyes observed him carefully, and
he shifted his weight from one foot to the other while Nicholas sat down
at the edge of the bed.

"All set?" Jack asked. He looked anxious to make a run for the door,
the moment that Nicholas lay back down between the sheets.

He nodded. "Hey, Jack?"

"What?"

"Did you call my parents?"

The gray eyes narrowed, and the vague, servile expression on his face
sharpened into a look of distaste. "That honestly isn't any of my affair."

"But it's your job," he said. "Isn't it? And you saved me, didn't you?
Fished my sorry ass out of the lake, like Titus said?"

"Isn't any of my affair," he muttered again, like a refrain. "You swallow that pill?" Nicholas nodded. "Good, then go to sleep. And try to avoid asking questions that don't concern you."

Nicholas shook his head. "I've got to get home again somehow. I'll tell Uncle Titus whatever he wants to hear, I'll give him whatever information it is that he thinks he needs, but—"

"Nicholas," Jack said, "if you're really as intelligent as you're supposed to be, you won't tell Titus a damn thing." His voice lowered even further. "Not that it'll matter, one way or the other."

"But I don't even know what he wants to hear," he said. "I don't know anything about—"

"That's exactly what he wants to hear."

"Look," he said, trying to use the same frank tone he had used with Anthem, when he wasn't quite pleading or commanding, either. It was not a kid's voice, not at all. He had screamed that voice away for good. That voice was gone. "You could help me."

Jack closed his eyes and shook his head, tugging at the seams in his navy-blue trousers until they fell straight again. "No," he said.

Nicholas raised his eyebrows. "At least tell me what he's got on you . . . maybe I can help."

"Don't talk craziness." But for just an instant, as he tugged at his pant legs, Nicholas thought he saw Jack pause while his eyes flicked up with just a glimmer of hope. Then he dropped his head again, and the feeling was gone. "You don't know what you're talking about," he said softly. "Just rest your bones for a while. Titus'll be back later tonight."

"Are *you* going to be back?" Nicholas asked him as he walked out.

"Do yourself a favor," he muttered before shutting the door, "and forget about me."

Lying back in his bed and depositing the Percodan underneath the corner of the mattress, Nicholas listened to the man's footsteps, clumsy and off-kilter, as he skulked back down the steps and let himself out the front door. The Dexter Gordon record had ended a long time ago. The house fell silent.

No, Jack, he thought. I'm not going to forget about you.

He must have dozed, because the next thing he heard was the door downstairs opening and shutting again. Gradually he was getting more attuned to the sounds of the house. Now the *snick!hmmm* of the furnace clicking on and off was just one of a hundred distinct noises crowding the hallway. Water burbled through pipes deep in the walls, and somewhere downstairs he imagined a heavy pendulum swinging with a loud, hollow *tocktocktock* sound. Judging from Jack's remark when he tripped over the loose step, Titus had some sort of staircase elevator for his wheelchair, a kind of platform that slid along on its own track, like the kind he had seen advertised in Sunday newspaper supplements. That probably accounted for the weird, mechanical whine sounds he had heard earlier.

On several occasions, between moments of unconsciousness, he had heard Titus' voice itself, muffled through the floorboards, giving orders over the phone. He realized that he could sometimes make out a few telltale words—"sell," "brokerage," "market"—because Titus was shouting them excitedly to the party on the other end.

Nicholas was intrigued in spite of himself. His parents had told him that Titus had made several million dollars in the bull market of the eighties. Now, whatever his involvement with New York crime syndicates, it appeared that in his way he was still an active businessman. If the phone calls were any indication, Titus was still in possession of a small fortune in blue-chip stocks. IBM and Ford were two of the more prevalent names he heard mentioned through the floorboards, along with several others that Nicholas, with passing knowledge of the stock market, didn't recognize.

Tonight, however, he heard none of the market phrases, nor the commanding tone that Titus seemed to use along with them. In fact, his voice sounded calm, almost friendly. A stranger might have called it charming. Nicholas slipped out of bed and put his ear to the creaking floorboards, listening.

". . . Ian?" Uncle Titus was saying, then hurriedly adding, "It's . . . now, Ian, cool yourself down, yes, I . . ."

Nicholas couldn't believe it. Was Uncle Titus actually talking to his own parents while he was up here, not fifty feet away? Did he dare?

". . . you . . . now, Ian, I know it ain't . . ." He heard Titus sigh an exasperated sigh. "Look, put Shel on the phone, will you, if you can't get a grip on yourself. Oh, for Christ's sake—"

Nicholas stood up, his heart hammering, and when he had his balance, he took a deep breath and screamed, "MOM! DAD! I'M HERE! I'M UP HERE! I'M ALIVE! HELP ME!"

42

Portion of the testimony of Shelley Danzig, October 28:
  "What was that?" I asked Uncle Titus. I was sure I'd heard something, a voice, in the background, just a second after my husband handed me the phone.

He chuckled. Nobody chuckles indulgently like Uncle Titus. It sounded like a magician who'd just reached up his sleeve and whipped out a bursting bouquet of red flowers in front of a gasping audience. "I think you and Ian are just a little shook up by my calling, maybe you're hearing things," he said. "I got the TV set on, but that's about it."

"It sounded like Nicky," I said. Those were my exact words. But you've got to understand something else, too: Ian and I had been hearing Nicky's voice almost everywhere for the last week. It was the same perverse sort of hopeful hallucinations that caused us to reach for every slightly familiar boy in the mall or grocery store, and spin him around on his heels, stare into his face . . . and then turn away, muttering apologies. And when you're talking long-distance you sometimes do hear other voices in the background, straying in from other conversations somewhere else in the world. It didn't surprise me that this one sounded like Nicholas.

When I explained it to Titus, he tried to sympathize.

"Shelley," he said in his best circle-the-wagons voice, "I'm grieving for him, too. And I do want to come down for the funeral service next week. The girl Gertrude—well, I don't know what Ian's told you about her—"

"Enough," I said, and paused, wishing for a second that both of us could stop talking, and I could just listen to that voice I heard muffled in the background. Because, I swear to God, it sounded just like our boy Nicky. Long-distance. Very long-distance.

"The service for Nicholas is Tuesday, at four o'clock, at Truesdale Funeral Home," I said mechanically. "You're invited, of course."

"Thanks, Shel," he said. "I'm so sorry, babe—"

I nodded, and listened, and tried to convince myself that I wasn't losing my mind.

43

His door flew open as if someone had kicked it open, and that, as it turned out, was exactly what had happened. Uncle Titus' wheelchair plowed across the rug to the foot of the bed. The wheelchair hit the bed frame and halted, but Uncle Titus himself did not stop at all. In fact, to Nicholas, he seemed to launch himself headfirst out of the chair, heaving his entire body forward and landing on top of him. The oxygen tubes snapped right out of his nostrils. The heavy slackness of Titus' stomach crushed against his chest, driving his breath out. He gasped and tried to squirm free. He could feel the man's body, rigid with hideous angles, his one arm squeezing him in a vicious, grinding hug. The weight alone was enough to pin him to the mattress.

Titus shoved his face into his, so near that the tips of their noses brushed, and he smelled the old, sour tobacco smell of Titus' breath. "Kiddo," he fumed, his chest expanding, "that was the dumbest thing you could have decided to do, and you did it. What the hell were you thinkin', anyway? That Mommy and Daddy could reach through the phone lines and pull you back home again? Is that it?"

"They'll come and get me," he said. "They heard me. They'll come—"

"You are dead," Uncle Titus wheezed. He spoke the words with an odd, deliberate emphasis, then pushed himself up and jabbed his chest with his index finger extended like a gun. He grabbed the tubes and reinserted them into his nostrils. "Dead, Nicky boy, do you get me? All I gotta say is, that's my television turned up too loud in the background, and they believe it. You know why? Because you're *dead*."

He shook his head. "Why?"

Titus swung himself over to the edge of the bed, relying totally on his good arm and leg. Despite his frustration, Nicholas felt a little prickling of fascination at how easily he manipulated the joints that the arthritis had immobilized. In just a few seconds Titus had pivoted himself on the foot of the bed and deposited his large, square-shaped butt back in the wheelchair again. There he sat, chin in hand, and contemplated him with a look of dull amusement. Behind him the oxygen tank hissed contentedly.

"I think you know something," he said, keeping his chin cupped in his hand. "Gertrude told you something. Didn't she?"

"I don't know what you're talking about."

"Oh, can we please cut the crap," he said, waving the words away. "You're a kid, and kids remember everything."

"Maybe when I was blacked-out she might have said something . . ."

"But you don't remember," Titus said impatiently.

"If you let me go . . . maybe I'll remember when I'm not so . . ."

"Stressed-out? Is that the word you kids have for it nowadays?" Fires were lit behind his cheeks and brow, Nicholas noticed, the first flames of the rage he had seen earlier. His eyes bulged frantically, widening almost until Nicholas could imagine the lids puckering and spitting them out like grapes. "Nicky, if this amnesia routine of yours keeps up, then you'll see some stress. I promise you." He nodded once, sharply. "Oh, yeah, kiddo, you've got my word as a *gentleman*."

What was wrong with his voice? Suddenly it sounded false, as if he had to force the anger this time. What was the anger supposed to be hiding? Relief?

He remembered his conversation with Saint Jack:

I don't know anything.

That's exactly what he wants to hear.

"I guess I went about it all wrong with you, Nicky," Titus said finally. "I should have either given you up completely or kept you secret. Now you're the bad penny that came back. And believe me, I'm glad you did."

Nicholas shook his head. "I don't know what you're talking about."

"Don't matter." Titus reached over and tousled Nicholas' hair. "You're mine again. You're what I sent Gertrude out after, and she did exactly right to bring you back to me."

"Are you going to tell my parents that I'm alive?"

"What?" Titus asked. "And ruin this cozy little situation we got right now?"

"I know about you," Nicholas said on impulse. If pleading ignorance couldn't get him free, it was time to try a different strategy. "I know all about how you worked for that woman Maria in New York, and how you took Anthem—Gertrude—how you held her down and you cut— you cut off—"

"Aww." Titus smiled with mocking sweetness. Behind the smile, fire blazed in the feverishly lit eyes. "What, did she tell you how I cut off her wings? You believe in people with wings, Nicky?" His countenance darkened. "Listen to me, kiddo, because I'll only say this one time: Gertie was crazy, and whatever she might have told you is straight out of the Brothers Grimm and down the yellow brick road." He shook his head. "What's real is what you see in this room, and right now, it's just you and me. And some very . . . thick . . . walls." A smile cut across his face. "I'll be seeing you."

"It wasn't all a lie, though, was it?" Nicholas asked abruptly.

Titus made a startled sound.

"She told me stories because she couldn't tell me the way it really happened," Nicholas said. "So I guess that's my job."

"I'll see you later, Nicky boy." He snapped his head around. "She was crazy as a bedbug, and you know it."

But his smile was gone without a trace.

44

Later that night, the man that Anthem and Nicholas had called Saint Jack was driving south, out of town.

He shifted the squad car into fifth at the outskirts of town, carefully obeying the speed limit. Tonight he had a drive of some length ahead of him. He would begin to investigate the disappearance of Nicholas Danzig. He was not serving in his official capacity, as Constable Jack Tornquist. If he needed an official title for what he was doing tonight, then he supposed that "Saint Jack" was as good as any.

After all, it would be as Saint Jack that he wanted to betray Titus . . . if he didn't lose his nerve first.

He was driving toward a small farm community on the other side of the Mackinac Bridge, where a house had been recently broken into and the alarm system triggered. It was a long drive. On the way to that town, he would pass through another town where, a day earlier, two cops had been found with concussions because some crazy girl had bashed them across the head with a skillet. State police believed that the alleged assailant had also kidnapped Nicholas Danzig from his home in Portage earlier that week, but by now the state police and anyone else who read the paper knew that Nicholas and his abductor had crashed into Lake Superior, where they were presumed dead.

Constable Jack Tornquist had not given them any other information. He certainly hadn't told them that Nicholas was alive and well in a back bedroom of Titus' house. He hadn't breathed a word about what happened to Gertrude after the crash. His motives for silence were sufficiently convoluted so as to be criminal.

Slowly the outskirts of Burns Mills gave way to the open two-lane highway. Jack pushed the pedal down and shot out straight ahead into the night. The weather was sleety and cold, and he seemed to have the highway to himself tonight. He reached into the passenger seat, and his fingers found the Sony microcassette recorder and switched it on.

"Saturday, October sixteen, eight-thirty P.M.," he said. His own voice by itself sounded unfamiliar and unpleasant. "Beginning to solicit testimonies for the implication of Titus Heller."

He thumbed the pause button, concentrated for a moment, then started the tape again. He wanted a drink very badly.

"Great God, I don't know why I'm doing this."

At first it had been just a germ of an idea. He had wondered if it was possible to betray Titus without his knowing it. Once there had been the possibility of Titus becoming the closest thing Jack Tornquist had to a friend. Now the old man employed Jack's services, in a very unofficial capacity. They had first met when Titus had moved to Burns Mills with his daughter, a little girl named Gertrude. At that point Jack Tornquist had not known the whole story. Even now it was doubtful that he would know the whole story. Part of the reason why he was doing this was his obsession with seeing the full dimensions of what he had gotten himself involved with, eight years ago, when the girl Gertrude was thirteen.

Now that Titus had the other kid, the boy, Jack wondered if he could somehow blackmail him the way that Titus had been blackmailing him for years. The old man certainly had more to lose. A year or so ago, Titus had confided to Jack that, by a conservative estimate, he was worth almost eight million dollars, most of it tied up in high-yield municipals with some common stock thrown in to keep things interesting. With money like that it hadn't been difficult to buy just about anything he wanted, including a small-town cop like Jack. But Titus hadn't bought Jack Tornquist with money. He hadn't needed to.

Jack Tornquist had grown up in a poor rural town in northern Michigan, one of the thousands of people whose communities had straggled along behind the advancing years of the century after the lumber industry had collapsed. His father had also been a cop in a town not far from here. He had conducted himself as a cop in his home, too, as brusque and indifferent to his wife and children as he was to the outside world.

The exception to all of that was the piano in their old dirt-floored basement. One winter, a long time before Jack's birth, his father and his grandfather had gotten drunk and stolen the piano from a roadhouse in Mackinac and, later that same night, brought it across the ice in a horse-drawn cart. Even at that time, his father had said, the instrument seemed very old, and it was notched and sanded and repolished as though it had been in someone's family for years.

When Jack was fourteen years old, he had found some very dusty sheet music inside the piano bench, and although his father claimed to have taught him how to play those first, very basic five-finger exercises, Jack himself could only recall the old man standing over him, a great, boozy-breathed shape with heavy hands reaching underneath Jack's undeveloped arms, guiding his fingers over the black keys. Slowly, almost reluctantly, Jack had arrived at the conclusion that his piano playing made him different from his brothers. Not better or worse, but just distinct, as though fate were singling him out.

Now all of the Tornquist brothers were dead except him: two of them had died for their country, one of the cancer, and one of them, his little brother Quentin, had shot himself last Easter. Eight years ago, Jack had resigned himself to the bachelor's pleasures of jazz and alcohol—the good folk of Burns Mills understood alcohol, but they did not by any stretch of the imagination understand jazz—and his position of town constable. In town he could drink and do his job, but if he wanted to play the blues he needed to drive about forty miles south of Burns Mills, to a crappy little tin-roof roadhouse where, depending on the time of year, the clientele consisted of summer people, deer hunters or cheating spouses on the prowl. The place had no name, nor did it seem to require one. Jack himself went there for two reasons.

The first was to play.

The roadhouse piano keys were loose and feather-light under his fingers, and the stage lights overhead seemed to burn very hot. Four or five nights a month he hunched over the piano where all the smoke and heat and noise and faces rose up and his fingers would start to jerk and hammer on the keys. He would play until his sweat-soaked hair tumbled across his forehead and his back ached and his neck ached and he lost all sense of time and place underneath the hot lights, until he felt good and empty and achy. Toward the end he didn't think of his father or his dead brothers or his audience. He didn't seem to think of anything but the piano and how he could use it to scare them all until they couldn't even get up and walk to the bar but they had to stare at him and listen to him play.

And afterward when it was quiet he would drink.

One night in October eight years ago, after he had finished playing, a graying giant named Titus Heller had shambled up and introduced himself at the bar. Jack and Titus had closed the place that same night, still deeply embroiled in an argument about jazz pianists and saxophonists and by now both drunk as lords. After endless drinks and the ultimate last call, Titus had wandered out into the empty parking lot, where he began to urinate against a rain gutter while still holding his beer and his cigarette carefully in his other hand.

"I know I can't get back in the car and drive myself home," he said over his shoulder to Jack. "Guess you'd probably pull me over and take away my license before I got out on the main road."

"You know who I am?" Jack asked, stunned. Some of the nights that he drove out to the roadhouse, especially the ones where he had as much to drink as he'd had this evening, he *himself* seemed to forget that he was a cop. "You from Burns Mills?"

Titus nodded. "You ain't sober either," he observed. "How you planning to get yourself home, anyway?"

Jack realized he hadn't thought about it until now. It wasn't like him to be so nearsighted about such things; but on the nights when he came out to the roadhouse to play, unfamiliar personality tics sometimes asserted themselves long before he drank his first drink. It was as though the part of him that had fallen in love with the bottle had a full-blown personality of its own. It hadn't really occurred to him before that night. In some dim way he sensed that Titus, this man he had only met hours ago, saw something about him that no one else had seen, or at least taken the time to tell him: he, Jack Tornquist, was probably on his happy-go-lucky way down the road to alcoholism.

"I'm fine to drive," he snapped back at Titus, but he felt for the first time like he was on shaky ground. He fumbled out his keys and lurched against the side of his old Chevy, trying to locate the keyhole in the darkness. The paint on the driver's side was already scraped all around the door handle from many nights of this, although he could not recall more than one or two occasions when he had actually driven drunk.

Drinking, yes, maybe even drinking too much. But not falling-down, word-slurring, three-sheets-to-the-wind *blotto* the way he felt right now.

Titus shook his head slowly. "Just wait out here," he said, "and I'll go back inside and call us a ride."

Jack kept trying to find the keyhole with his house key. Suddenly it seemed vital that he get out of here before Titus returned. He leaned against the side of the car and closed his eyes for just an instant, and he wondered if it was still evening or morning or what it was now, because he realized that he had fallen over into the gravel and had been lying there next to his car for a few minutes, actually, looking up at the shadows of trees at the edge of the parking lot. He had cut his hand, and for a long moment he looked at his blood, a strange, black pool on the gravel.

The pain helped him focus his thoughts. He stood up. He felt certain that if he could only get inside the car, he could navigate his way back into Burns Mills without incident. With his eyes narrowed, he went back to work on the lock again. By the time that Titus came back out again, Jack had wedged his house key into the car door and finally snapped it off in the lock itself. He stood holding it a few inches in front of his face, examining his half of the broken key stupidly while a thin stream of blood trickled down his wrist to his elbow and dripped on his shoes.

At some point later, another car rolled into the parking lot. It was a long black Lincoln, and the girl's face, still blurry to Jack's eyes, studied him calmly from behind the windshield. Titus half led, half carried him over to the backseat. But he did not let Jack get in just yet.

"Gertie, get out of the car," Titus said.

Jack had stared, mesmerized, at the girl who had stepped out into the parking lot. During the eight years since then, he must have told himself a thousand times how he had not known that she was only thirteen, that she was Titus' daughter, that she was already very emotionally unbalanced. At the time, his intoxicated understanding was limited to the small and hazy sphere of what he saw before him: a nubile young woman, her lips slightly parted, her long blond hair tumbling behind her in a great copper frenzy. The details were far from focused, but he thought that he grasped the essence of it.

When the overcoat she was wearing fell open, Jack stared in astonishment at her pale nakedness beneath it. Already he could imagine how his hand would feel sliding along the bare smoothness of her leg into her thigh.

"Well," Titus had said, unfolding his pocketknife with a horribly casual gesture, "looks like our ride is here, huh, Jack?"

If ever a man could have turned back time and changed what he had done by sheer force of regret, Jack Tornquist thought he was the man to do it. He had been drunk. He had been misinformed. But he hadn't been either to the extent where he had forgotten, or misunderstood, the precise moment when Titus had told him to hold the girl down in the backseat. Or when he had said, *Jack, cover her fucking mouth.*

Because the fact was that he had done those things.

Titus didn't have to cut the overcoat to get it off her, but he did it, anyway. He cut the girl herself through the coat, along either shoulder blade, and seemed to enjoy it. Other things happened afterward, with the torn coat discarded. And somewhere behind him, just beyond his field of vision, had been Titus with his camera, its shutter whirring busily away. That was all it had taken.

He could almost hear the auctioneer's gavel fall. He, Jack Tornquist, was *sold*, to the man in the flannel shirt. For a handful of photographs.

Jack wasn't formally introduced to Gertrude until the following morning when he awoke to find himself on a couch in Titus' living room. She was a shy, silent girl with tangled blond hair and constantly shifting eyes, and from the first Jack understood without asking, without needing to ask, that something was missing from behind those eyes, some crucial connection with the rest of the world. One of Jack's brothers had been the same way: Quentin, the one who had finally shot himself a year ago. Jack realized that he had not thought about Quentin for years. As he spent increasing amounts of time with Titus and Gertrude, the memories of his brother returned like dark, unwanted guests.

A half-wit, that's how they had all referred to Quentin. When the boy was five, two of Jack's older brothers decided it would be funny if they closed Quentin in an abandoned barn with a mean-tempered old junkyard dog. They informed Quentin that the dog was rabid. In reality, of course, the dog hadn't been rabid. It was just an old mutt, nearly dead and hopping with fleas, that had been safely leashed to one of the roof beams on the other side of the barn. And Jack's brothers had not intended to leave Quentin locked in the barn. Initially they had intended to climb up into the crotch of a nearby oak tree for a spell to enjoy the sound of Quentin screaming and pleading from inside the barn. When Quentin started pleading, "Good doggie, good doggie," in a high-pitched voice, they had nearly fallen out of the oak tree laughing.

But after a few minutes that had lost its novelty, and maybe a couple of kids from down the road had wandered by asking if Jack's brothers wanted to play a little ball. Even then, Jack's brothers had told themselves they would come back in a half hour . . . but as the day had gotten hotter and hotter, they had kept playing ball, and it wasn't until midafternoon that one of them remembered Quentin in the barn.

Curious by that time, Jack had followed his brothers back to the barn. Inside the hot darkness, through the shaft of light thick with floating hay and dust, the scene seemed unremarkable, even innocent. Jack saw the dog first, where it had finally curled up and gone to sleep in its corner of the barn, and then behind him, Quentin, also curled up but with his eyes wide-open and clotted with hay dust. He did not seem to have blinked for hours. After yelling at him, shaking him and slapping him across the face, Jack's brothers had begun to grasp the severity of what had happened inside Quentin's head, and they had gotten scared. Jack had never seen either of them so frightened in their lives. If he had not been there, he thought they might have thrown Quentin down an empty well and pretended innocence.

But Jack had been there in the barn that afternoon, and that night, their father had administered to Jack's brothers the worst beatings they had ever taken in their lives. One of them walked with a limp for several months afterward. The town, in its countrified way, had looked at what had happened to the two brothers, and then looked at Quentin, drooling, clucking, jerking his head right and left at phantom sounds as he shuffled up and down the streets of town, and no one had ever accused Jack's father of child abuse. It simply had never been an issue. Justice had been exacted, and their small corner of the universe had adjusted itself accordingly.

Inevitably Jack brought memories of Quentin with him on the occasions when he went over to Titus' to play the piano. The occasions themselves became increasingly frequent. A perverse companionship had developed between the two men. It was Titus' considered opinion that Jack could have made a living playing the piano, and a damned good one, if he lived in a larger city, say Chicago or New York. Eventually he gave Jack a key to the house and invited him to come over whenever he wanted to play the piano in the upstairs library; and that was how Jack had eventually discovered that Gertrude liked his music, too, in a way that she seemed to have some difficulty expressing.

When Titus was not in the house, Jack would occasionally look up from the keyboard and over the cup of coffee that was invariably resting on the piano and the cigarette smoldering at the edge of the saucer. Up in the doorway Gertrude would have her chin pushed slightly outward, her face struggling for some tint of sophistication. After Jack had started to come by routinely, she appeared routinely, too, like some shadow that fell across the doorway when the sun reached a certain point in the sky.

"Do you like jazz?" he had asked her. "You can come in and listen if you want."

It had been months of seeing her from the corner of his eye while his fingers jumped across the keys, months before she had entered the room to sit with her back pressed to the far wall and her chin resting on her knees. Had she forgiven him? Did she even remember what had happened that night, in the back of the Lincoln?

Her head nodded, her feet tapping, totally out of time with the music, hearing different notes and a different rhythm in her head. Sometimes Jack would stop the song abruptly, listening to the last notes fade from the room while Gertrude continued rocking back and forth, eyes half-closed, as though she had learned to listen to music from paintings of people posed in the act of listening.

Titus would never let her listen when he was around. "She can't really hear it, anyway," he grunted to Jack, sounding disgusted. "She ain't deaf, but to her, it's all just dah-dah-dah, you know."

Looking back, Jack saw that he had already been rather intimidated by Titus' presence. Intimidated, but somewhat ingratiated. A year after he had first met Titus, both men had stopped drinking completely. As Jack had dried out, he became more acutely aware that, photographs or no photographs, Titus' company was filling the lonely void that, until then, he hadn't been able to fill with anything but a steady river of booze. Anyone who knew all the details of Jack Tornquist's life over that year would say that he was a changed man afterward and they would be right, but the alcohol had only been part of it.

What had happened between him and Gertrude was the other part.

By that winter Jack had been sober for several months. There was no holiday spirit for him that year, no sense of Christmas at all, just the bleak feeling that the days would continue on with miserably regularity and no spring in sight. Twenty minutes did not pass that he didn't wish for drink.

Just about the time that Jack had stopped drinking, he had noticed that Gertrude had started to look at him with new interest. As the months and then years passed she had begun to talk to him, just a few words at a time, and then whole sentences and laughter. Flattered, he had started to look forward to her appearance in the doorway of the practice room. When she talked, he watched how her pale face was illuminated as she whispered her strange stories to him about who she really was and where she had come from. Jack had listened, and had no idea what to think.

She told him about two brothers, separated when the younger was born, who possessed nearly mythical powers when they were together. She told him how her real mother had been a Mafia princess in New York. She said that she had forgiven him, for cutting off her wings.

"Your wings?" Jack asked.

One night when Titus was downstairs talking to his broker on the phone, she slunk inside and told Jack that Titus was not her father, but that he, Jack, had raised her many years ago along with the two brothers.

"My name isn't really Gertrude, you know," she'd said. "And you should know that, of all people."

"Oh?" He had pushed the piano bench back to devote his full attention to her. There were twenty years between them, he estimated, but like those first winter nights that they had talked, the years hadn't seemed important. "I should?"

"We can stop hiding," she had told him from the other side of the piano. "We can be ourselves now."

"What selves?" he'd asked.

"Starting with our names," she had said. "Why don't you call me Anthem anymore?" Then, seeing the look of confusion on his face, "Before you say anything else, let me at least get it out, all right?"

Later on, Jack had decided that he hadn't interrupted her at that moment for a crazy medley of reasons that he could never explain. He had been thinking of Quentin, poor crazy Quentin, and had found his heart had been filled with old, untasted bitterness; he had been thinking of Titus, and how he treated his daughter so cruelly; mostly he had been thinking of Gertrude herself and how soft her chest looked rising and falling a few inches away, as he wondered how it would feel to bury his face again between the warm globes of her breasts. He had watched her growing up, sick with an old memory, and hated himself for what he was feeling in spite of it all, but there it was.

He had nodded and slid down the piano bench, offering a seat. She had never come near enough for him to offer before.

And sitting there next to him on the piano bench, with Titus' voice muttering through the floorboards beneath them, she had told him the entire fantastic tale, embroidered with such elaborate detail that all of it seemed as though it might have been some journalistic account in a parallel world, something from a science fiction novel. At first, in the immediate world, all that she required was that he call her by her "true" name, Anthem, and that she be allowed to call him Saint Jack. Only later did he realize that they were still laboring under the pretense—oh how very humorous—that he, Jack Tornquist, was her true father. This, too, he had secretly agreed to with an amazingly flexible sense of the absurd. It had become even more flexible after the first time he had laid his hand on the soft swell of her breast.

But eventually it had all gone too far.

They had gone too far.

To give all of it words was simply beyond him right now, but he had not thought Titus was in the house, and they had done something, and they had done something else, and then afterward . . .

Jack Tornquist sat in the front seat of the car, feeling sick to his stomach but not turning the car around. It would start tonight, he had convinced himself. Tonight he would begin to make recompense for the crimes he had helped commit, in Titus' name.

Gertrude had left him no choice.

Just a few nights ago, she had come into the piano room while he was playing and announced, in no uncertain terms, that she was going to find and bring back her brother Virgil. Jack did not know how she recalled this. In retrospect he didn't know how she remembered much of anything that had involved her. He could only look back in dismal regret for the first time he ever indulged the fantasy, and could only try to prevent its consequences from becoming too catastrophic. The effort felt futile.

Later that same night Jack became the first of several police officers to visit and take testimony from, among other people, Jennifer Clara Wiest, regarding the strange childhood and adolescence of Gertrude Heller.

What he recorded on the microcassette recorder eventually became part of the public record. He gave the cassettes to a mutual acquaintance of his and Titus', a former doctor in town, for safekeeping.

What he didn't record, no one ever discovered.

45

S unday morning.
   From his bedroom window Nicholas could hear church bells gonging distantly, and the overtones of a pipe organ playing hymns in some nearby church. It brought to mind thoughts of sanctuaries, hymns, cemeteries. His funeral was two days away.

He heard the whine of the staircase elevator and then the front door opening and shutting, and being locked. He wondered if Uncle Titus attended church. The old man never had, as far as Nicholas knew, but maybe recent events had convinced him he should repent now that he was in his last days. Confess all his sins: *Forgive me, Father, I got my great-grandnephew locked in the upstairs bedroom of my house. I know it's terrible but I think the little fella knows something about me, something awful—*

"Yeah?" Nicholas asked the dream Titus. The ringing solitude had made him remarkably unself-conscious about engaging himself in conversation. "What? Just tell me, I'll admit or deny it or whatever you want, just so I don't have to spend the rest of my life listening to that damn furnace click on and off all day, what do you say?"

Forgive me, Father, I just might have to mess him up a little, you see, I think he's hiding something—

"No, you don't," he said, sitting up in the bed. "You think I'm really in the dark, don't you? You're starting to think I'm really telling the truth. Right?"

He stepped out of bed. His bad leg wasn't throbbing quite so insistently this morning. Maybe the pain slept late on Sundays. That was fine by him. It might be a long walk to the phone. He didn't want to wear himself out. He crept across the floor on tiptoe, ignoring the squeak of the floorboards, and slipped out the doorway and down the hall, stirring himself up for the journey downstairs.

Then he passed the room where Jack had been yesterday. The door was ajar, and he could see in, at the cardboard boxes marked "GER-TRUDE."

A chill prickled across his shoulders and neck, spreading irrationally across the rest of his upper body.

Not "Gertrude's Clothes" or "Gertrude's Models" or "Gertrude's Little Magnetized Terriers, Virgil and Ovid."

Just "GERTRUDE." As if it contained the body itself.

"Stop being such a dork," he muttered to himself. "Just keep walking."

But he didn't keep walking. Not just yet. Not even when he instructed himself that he could open those boxes *after* he made the phone call to his house in Portage, which was the primary order of business for the morning.

Looking at those boxes, stacked like twin towers halfway to the ceiling, he got an immobilizing sensation of knowledge dawning in his brain. It happened fast. One second he was just standing in the doorway with his leg beginning to ache just a little as he looked at what seemed like normal cardboard boxes, and the next second he could almost feel the rays of light brimming over his mind's horizon. The realization was sudden, like the sudden sense he'd once had, last year, as a basketball left his fingertips, arced in the air . . . and then came swishing through the hoop, so sleekly that the net itself seemed to recoil afterward soundlessly with the absolute perfection of it.

Whatever it was that Uncle Titus did not want him to discover was waiting for him in those boxes.

Breathless, he hobbled across the floor to the spot where he had stood yesterday, where he had first caught sight of Saint Jack behind the piano. But this time, as he touched the first box, there were no intrusions into the solitude, only his mental voice with a single crazy thought:

Maybe this is what crazy old Anthem wanted you to see, after all, it said. *Whether she knew it or not.*

"Maybe," he murmured, already pulling open the flaps of the first box. He looked inside. The box was full of neatly folded children's clothes, sweatshirts and footies and blue jeans with elastic waistbands. He sifted through it and found a few pairs of tiny shoes at the bottom, but nothing else. He set the first box aside and opened the next one, only to find more clothes. They were a few sizes larger, but other than that, no different from the items in the first box. He tossed it aside and opened the third: more clothes. Nothing in the bottom. Nothing special, even for clothes: no names inscribed on the tags of the underwear, even. He dropped that box in dismay. Was this it? Box after box of old clothes?

He ripped open the fourth box and stole a quick breath.

"*My Family Photographs*" was printed in gold-embossed letters. He reached in, curled his fingers around the edges of the album and lifted it out in a great cloud of dust. It was even heavier than it looked. He sat cross-legged and opened it across his lap. More dust rose, then settled over the pages. He wiped it aside and looked down at the faces pressed beneath the dry, nearly crackling cellophane.

The first photo was familiar. It was he and Anthem. It was the picture that he had found torn in half back at the first house, featuring the two of them frowning with their little Victorian-looking faces at the camera. Behind them stretched some mysterious street of some unnamed suburb, somewhere. Brother and sister.

He turned the page, wanting instinctively to cut the thought short before it could swallow him up entirely. Pasted across the next two pages were four more photos of the boy and girl together, playing with a Tonka tractor in that anonymous yard behind them. Anthem looked six or seven years old. She was just grown enough that the first distinct facial features were starting to develop.

He turned another page, stared at the picture, then at the caption below it. Then his eyes went back to the picture of the more formally arranged figures, as if to study it for alteration, though he knew it was true. Anthem and a younger Uncle Titus sat on a fireplace hearth, smiling politely at the camera, just as if they had been asked to do so a second before by some dim-witted photographer. Titus had her balanced on his knee. Still she sat there, straddled, the picture of obedience.

Daddy and me, words next to it read. She'd written in pencil right on the sticky cardboard underneath the cellophane, so they were more engraved than written, actually. But he could read them well enough.

Daddy? his mind asked, reeling. *Uncle Titus?*

He made himself turn the page again. And again.

Most of the pictures focused on Anthem, riding bulky plastic Big Wheels down a sidewalk, somewhere; lingering a little shyly behind a folding TV table with a printed sign advertising *Lemonade only 5 cents a cup*; swinging on swings at some county park in front of a massive bandstand draped in colorful bunting. Occasionally he found a picture of him by himself, and some of the snapshots were familiar. Here he was curled up in his crib or falling asleep at the table with his face squashed against his little crustless peanut butter and jelly sandwich. Yes, a few of these photos he had seen before, in the albums that the Danzigs had at home in Portage. His mom and dad had shown them to him. They had told him funny little anecdotes along with each one.

He drew a deep, shaky breath.

The photos came in chronological order, he realized from the dates printed in their corners. March '79, June '79, September '79, May '80—

The book slipped from his fingers and lay listlessly across his lap. After May '80, the boy appeared in no more pictures.

He was *gone*.

Sometime after May of 1980, he had become Nicholas Harrison Danzig.

He closed the photograph album and gazed at the walls of books that towered around him on all sides on the very threshold of imbalance. Was this what Uncle Titus did not want him to discover? Not just that he had been adopted, but that he was in fact *his son*?

As if in answer, a thin stack of loose-leaf sheets slipped out of the back of the album, where they had been folded beneath the back cover. They spilled out across the dusty wooden floor in a slatternly pile. He set the album aside and gathered the loose pages together, glancing at the one on top and then the others in turn.

They were pictures, but not the photographic kind.

They were crayon drawings.

Child's drawings.

Looking at them, he reflected that Titus had probably saved them, and given them dates, as parents sometimes do when they save their children's drawings. For some reason this gave him a chill. The three subjects of the first drawing weren't exactly stick figures, really. The artist—Anthem (or, as she had signed her drawings at the time, Gerti)—was apparently a little old for stick figures at the time she'd drawn these. But the figures in the drawings were rough and disproportionate, with large round heads drawn in peach crayon, narrow trunks, long spindly arms and legs. Anthem had labeled herself *ME*, and on either side stood two shorter bodies, labeled *VIRGIL* and *OVID*.

She had been painstaking in rendering the faces of *VIRGIL* and his older brother, *OVID*, exactly alike, with Ovid's body drawn twice as large. Her commitment to detail was impressive and exacting, to the point where she had even repeated the same brown and yellow crayon strokes from the first circular head onto the second.

I AM HAPPY, she had written underneath.

WE ARE TEGETHOR, she had scrawled beneath that.

Unlike the photos, Anthem's drawings were not just illustrations of Titus and his children. She had taken it upon herself to re-create the entire world in painstaking crayon, including whole pages of dogs, houses, cars and trees, signs (*MCDONALDS*) and then-current movie ads copied from the newspaper (*YOU WILL BELEEVE A MAN CAN FLY SUPERMAN THE MOVIE*). Titus had dated some of them accordingly. Nicholas flipped past these until he found more of Anthem's drawings of him and his brother, Ovid, where Titus had apparently gathered them together.

Except these later drawings—Anthem had to be ten or eleven—were usually labeled *OVID* and *VIRGIL*, and the *ME* became *ANTHEM*. The three of them, he noticed, were also spending more time hanging around with unicorns, witches and castles, with an occasional periwinkle dragon traipsing through the imaginary crayon landscape, exhaling great banners of magenta-colored fire. There weren't any more pictures of dogs or cars or trips to McDonald's. Nothing from the real world seemed to have ever found its way into these middle drawings.

Occasionally, Nicholas noted, Anthem had taken the time to draw an increasingly large set of wings on her back.

Feeling the first tears welling in his eyes, he laid that set of pictures aside and glanced down at the next one in the stack. His eyes were fixed on the two figures she'd drawn there.

"Oh, wait," he whispered under his breath, feeling the sadness wane a bit. "Wait just a second."

ME, read the label over the scrawny, sketchy girl figure. *VIRGIL*, read the label over the not-quite-stick figure standing next to it.

But there were only two of them now. There was *ME* and *VIRGIL*.

SOMETHING VERRY BAD HAS HAPPENED, Anthem had written beneath that, in reckless red crayon.

WHERES OVID?? she demanded below that.

GONE, she had slashed underneath.

The two of them that remained in the picture had different expressions on their faces. His face—Virgil's face—had that same curly grin she had drawn in the other crayon drawings: happy, cheerful, oblivious Virgil probably still slaying dragons and chasing elves through some imaginary fantasyland they had created back then. Virgil didn't seem to have a care in the world.

But the *ME* figure was frowning. No . . . Nicholas looked at the expression that Anthem had drawn on the self-portrait . . . the *ME* figure's mouth was open, and its eyes were huge, bulging circles that dripped blue tears. The *ME* figure was *screaming*.

Hurriedly he flipped past another drawing of the two of them— Anthem wore that same, terrorized expression on her face—and found the one beneath it, the one that he had been waiting for. He stared at this picture for a long, long time.

It showed the *ME* figure by herself. Anthem had drawn her head with a huge, hydrocephalic circle now, so that it dwarfed her body by comparison. The bulging eyes still dripped aqua-colored tears: the corners of the horrified mouth were pulled down even lower into a grotesque grimace.

ALONE, it read simply.

And the wings were gone.

Below that, in Uncle Titus' more adult scribble, was the date: June 1980. It was probably around the time that he, Nicholas, had gone to live with Ian and Shelley Danzig, and Anthem had been left with Uncle Titus.

Daddy, his mind corrected instantly. *Daddy Titus. You've been coasting long enough, Nicky. Don't you think it's time to begin looking at the facts before you go any further?*

"All right," he said softly. His hands folded Anthem's drawings together and slipped them back inside the cover of *My Family Photographs*. He stood up, hardly aware that he was doing it, and dropped the album back into its box, wanting nothing more than silence for a moment. Silence to sort through what he had seen.

But there was just one box left. He opened it and looked inside.

Birth certificates.

Three of them.

The name on the first was *Gertrude Heller*, the second was *Nicholas Heller*. And the third was made out to *Ovid Heller*, all three the children of Titus A. Heller.

What did she say happened when you and Ovid were separated, kiddo? Tell me! TELL ME!

Ovid had not died at birth as far as Nicholas knew, but there were no pictures, just the drawings Anthem had made until that day—was it dated?—when SOMETHING VERRY BAD happened. When his older brother Ovid was GONE.

Something being stolen. Taken away. Shattered. Ruined.

A final photograph dropped out of the back of the album. It was stiffer, somehow more formal than the others that were underneath the cellophane. It was a glossy black-and-white, developed in a private darkroom.

Nicholas lifted it up and looked at it.

It showed a plain gray wall, a *basement* wall, he thought with a sharp sense of recognition. Cinder blocks formed an orderly gridwork of lines that opened three-quarters of the way up the plain cement floor. The opening was a rectangular space where the final cinder blocks had not yet been laid. There was not quite enough shadow to cover what hung inside the wall.

He brought the photo closer to his face, angling it slightly as though he could adjust the light within the scene itself. Just inside the half-constructed wall, behind the freshly laid brick, Nicholas saw the profile of a boy's face, the lean cheekbone and brow, rising out of the darkness within. The boy's head hung slightly to the left, as though he bowed in prayer. Nicholas saw a single arm, a manacle clamped tightly around its limp wrist. He saw the vague whiteness of the boy's face, an unnatural pallor that had never seen enough sunlight in its terribly short life.

Nicholas held perfectly still, utterly oblivious as the photograph slid from between his fingers and seesawed lazily to the floor.

Somewhere, chained inside one of the basement walls, there was a body.

And, God help him, he thought he knew whose body it was.

I need to stop this right now, he thought. *I need to put these away right now.* The thought echoed back and forth through his numbed mind with idiot persistence, like a closing announcement through a long-vacant shopping mall. *At this moment I am in more trouble than most people would be capable of believing.*

But he only watched in amazement as his hands went back into the box, his fingers searching, probing for substance. He had thought that the birth certificates had been the last of its contents, but now something at the very bottom of the box caught his eye, a glint of gold-embossed lettering that until a moment ago had been covered up by shadow. He stared at it, uncertain.

It was a second photo album.

Finally he knelt down and reached into the box to retrieve it.

46

Like the first album, the second book read, *"My Family Photographs,"* and from the outside it looked exactly like the first: same fake-leather binding with a plastic seam running along the outer edge, same gold-embossed letters on the cover, same dust arising from the first page as he lifted the cover and looked down at the first snapshot on the first page.

He was still badly shaken from the photograph he had seen of the body behind the wall, but he couldn't help but notice certain things about this new album he held in front of him. Like, for instance, the pages were not pressed as closely together, making the second album twice again as fat as the first. The pictures inside were thicker, because they had been taken by an instant camera. They had not been sent away for developing.

He looked at the first photograph.

It was a picture of Anthem, lying across the same scruffy-looking couch she had been sitting on in a September '79 photo. In fact, although this picture wasn't dated, he had the odd feeling that the two photos were probably taken on the same day. Anthem was wearing her new glasses, and they still sat a little crookedly over the bridge of her nose, as if she weren't quite yet used to them there. He turned the page and stopped.

At some point between shots they had stripped her clothes off.

"Oh no," he whispered. Something was suddenly terribly wrong with this photo album he grasped in his hands. It was not "family photographs" at all, it was—

He tossed that page over and glanced at the next picture helplessly. His hands were trembling. It was Anthem again. Now she was on her back. Her photographer, her captors, were just shadows behind her. He felt a little whimper escape his lips. He could see a glimpse of her face.

SOMETHING VERRY BAD HAS HAPPENED.

Yes, he thought. Something—

Something broken. Something stolen. Some very, very precious thing—

In the corner of that photo, just barely included in the picture, was a man's hand, grasping Anthem's ankle. It was a red, chapped hand, thatched with strands of black hair the way men's hands sometimes are. Nicholas had no reason to believe that the hand was not restraining her, holding her down for these pictures—

And he had no reason to believe that Anthem's—Gertrude's—other ankle, which was not included in the picture, did not have a similar hand clenching it, holding it down.

These were the diametric opposite of baby pictures. These were the pictures of what happened on that unspeakable day when Anthem or Gertrude had stopped being a child and had to grow up. Maybe that's how it happened. First came Ovid, until Ovid was worn out or used up, and then it would have been Gertrude's turn to satisfy Titus' monstrous demands—

And Nicholas had no reason to believe that the grasping hand did not belong to his Uncle Titus. His father Titus, he corrected. His father, whom he finally knew. His father, who had given her a pair of glasses but taken from her everything else.

He wondered if Ovid had tried to stop him.

Maybe, his mind answered. *But probably he had served his purpose at that point, and Titus had already killed him. That's probably how it happened. First came Ovid, until he was too old to satisfy him, and then there was Gertrude, and eventually she shattered, too. Shattered just like crystal.*

And now there's me.

Chilled, he felt himself beginning to tremble.

He looked at a few of the other pages, but not many. He could not turn many more of the pages, because his fingers were trembling so badly. He had been shot in the leg, he told himself, and he had killed a rat with his bare hands, and he had survived a terrible car crash . . . but nothing was like this, seeing these pictures of Anthem in front of him.

In the next picture that he looked at, Titus and his daughter were together. Titus had forced her across the couch. The pocketknife glinted. The scars told a story that Anthem herself had not been able to tell, no matter how badly she had wanted to.

So she had become Anthem. She had given herself wings, and tried to fly away.

Nicholas looked at the blurred images and felt a rush of sickness starting in his stomach and squirming up into his throat. In the next photo Titus was sitting in his wheelchair. Nicholas couldn't see much of his sister's face, but he could see enough, the curve of her cheek and brow, the glasses and how they hung half off her face. He saw that Titus had seized a hunk of her hair in one of his great ham-shaped hands. He might have been grinning.

He felt himself choke. It was a clicking sort of sound, like the clicking of the furnace when it came back on. He remembered traveling with Anthem those few long days, all the moments that he'd wanted to scream and dared not, the flickering instants when the screams had welled up and welled up and spilled over and he still hadn't screamed. How he had felt the results like some chemical imbalance in the very logical left side of his brain.

He tried to imagine what it was like with no one around to hear Anthem's screams for those days, those countless days, those months with Titus here, and all he could do was imagine it, because those screams were gone, just like Ovid and Anthem herself; they were pressed, flattened and just plain gone now. That was all the childhood she'd had, and now it was over. They were a glossy memory under faintly yellowing cellophane and nothing more.

"Anthem," he murmured, "oh God, ah my God—"

The stack of remaining pages in the photo album was so *thick*. The pictures left to look at—

"Jeez, there are so many," he croaked. A few tears broke in his eyes, and the light of the room refracted and blurred.

He let the pages flip along between his thumb and forefinger, unable to stop himself now. In front of his eyes the pictures flew by, and Anthem rolled in the couch beneath the red, chapped hands as they directed her. Always she was naked. Sometimes with Titus, sometimes with someone he didn't recognize.

But nothing about her nakedness could distract him from the expression on her face, of mounting grief and anguish, of disbelief that *this was happening to her, that someone—her father—was doing this to her, that someone else was just standing there watching, and taking pictures.*

"There are so . . . many . . ."

His voice broke off in his throat.

Moving as deliberately and steadily as he could, Nicholas stood up straight. He looked up into the doorway.

"Here I am, Anthem," he murmured, apparently to himself. The very least that he owed her was the respect to call her by that more exotic name that she'd picked for herself, the infinitely more beautiful fantasy that she had developed as the abuse had started, as she had drifted further and further from the moorings of reality.

And in the end, Nicholas thought, Titus had sent her out to get the youngest child, the last of his three children. Compliant, terrified Gertrude, who had never had wings to fly or known anything beautiful about the world. Titus had assumed, rightly, that Gertrude wouldn't resist his demand. After all, she was terrified of Titus, so deeply traumatized that the very idea of rebelling against him felt like blaspheming God.

Yes, Nicholas thought, nodding with terrible certainty. Titus' plan had probably looked effective from the beginning. Send out your daughter . . . oh, excuse me, your *slave* . . . for what appeared to be a simple abduction. And if she does happen to get caught, her personal history has already established a motive for trying to contact Nicholas. She had done the exact same thing eight years earlier. How could anyone accuse Titus of masterminding anything so sinister?

But the old man had left himself vulnerable to a single possibility.

Somewhere along the line as Gertrude had been driving south, Anthem had taken over.

Michigan had become an entire continent in Anthem's eyes. She had asserted herself, insulated herself, with her story about the wings and the Mafia and a wonderful, unbelievable power to change the weather. And that had changed everything, transforming a command from Titus into a mission of personal redemption.

It might have been a fantasy world she'd assembled for herself, but some little part of her tattered sanity had been able to reach out and bring him back here. Some part of her had wanted him to come here—north, south, east or west, the directions themselves hardly mattered anymore—to obey what Titus had told her to do. To bring Nicholas home. Home was home, and he was back here again.

And now somebody had to pay.

47

"It's not a complicated question, is it?" Titus said. "All I'm asking is where you went last night."

Jack Tornquist sat behind his cluttered desk, looking scared. Sitting in his wheelchair on the opposite side of the desk, Titus paused to savor the moment. Jack's office was not much more than a single room partitioned off from the Burns Mills Community Center, a telephone and a typewriter surrounded by a chaos of paperwork and empty coffee cups. A bronze plaque glinted from the wall, proclaiming him Kinderhook County's Civil Servant of the Month, October 1989, and next to it hung an Audubon calendar almost as outdated. There were no windows and only one door. But the office, squalid though it was, had always seemed to provide him with a home-court advantage when Titus met him there, and at the moment Titus enjoyed seeing all the confidence drain from Jack's face. What was left, he saw, was just unadorned childlike fear. And that suited him fine.

Finally Jack rocked backward, his swivel chair making an absurd squawk beneath him, and spread his hands. Titus noticed that his long fingers were trembling. "Police business," Jack said. "I told you that."

"But you were gone all night."

Jack summoned up his voice. "Look, sometimes what an investigation entails—"

"You can *fuck* what your investigation entails." Suddenly Titus' fingers drew into a gnarled fist and he slammed it down violently against the desk so hard that the Styrofoam cup in front of Jack jumped into the air. "In this town, you don't *fart* without consulting me first, do you understand?"

"Titus, now—"

"Continuous telephone contact, Jack," Titus growled. "That is what we agreed on, isn't it?"

The bearded face slackened, weakening. "Yes, but you have to understand—"

"*Continuous* telephone contact." He nodded along with the words. "Which means that you call me before you leave your apartment to come here, and you call me before you leave here to go anywhere else." He grimaced, his head pounding now in time with his heartbeat. Tiny beads of sweat had gathered at his hairline, where the white of his scalp met the brightly flushed cleft of his furrowed brow, and he reached behind his back to give the oxygen gauge another quarter-turn. It began to hiss louder. "Otherwise, any number of photographs could begin to appear in very inconvenient offices down in Lansing. Now, do you understand *that*, you shit-eater?"

Jack nodded. His face sank into his hands and he made a small, grunting sound that Titus assumed was yes. After another long moment of silence, the old man leaned easily across the desk. The pain in his joints was hardly there at all now. The oxygen flow left him feeling exhilarated. Usually it was excruciating when he had to spend any length of time in the filthy little office, but at the moment he was experiencing almost unrestrained freedom of movement and thought. It was a rare delight.

"Jack," he said softly, grasping the constable's hand. Jack stared down in barely suppressed revulsion at the twisted, swollen fingers clutching his own. "Jack, for Christ's sake, you're shaking all over." His voice sank to a conspiratorial whisper. "How about a little something just to calm your nerves, huh?"

"You—"

"Shh." Titus grinned. From the wheelchair's side pouch he produced a pint bottle of Jack Daniel's and held it slightly above the desk. The bottle seemed to shine, talismanic, even in the dim glow from the fluorescent lights overhead. "Picked it up on the way over here. Seal isn't even broken yet. Is there anything better than that?" His eyes held the constable's closely as he withdrew his hand from Jack's and snapped the top off, then waved the bottle under his own nose. "Whew, remember the smell of this? Been on the wagon awhile, haven't you?"

Now Jack was starting to perspire, too. He had pushed himself back from the desk, tugging his tie loose, but his eyes were riveted to the bottle.

"Firewater, the Indians called it." Titus decanted a few ounces into the empty Styrofoam cup on Jack's desk and smiled again, benevolently. "Tell you what, you go ahead and drink up, and then we'll head up across the border to transact some business. I've got some Canadian clients coming down this week for a little party, and . . . hey, Jack? Hello?"

But the constable appeared hopelessly distracted, his eyes flashing back and forth between Titus and the bottle and the cup that sat in front of him. Titus couldn't see Jack's hands under the desk, but he wondered if the constable's knuckles had turned white yet from clenching his chair.

"Y'see, now, that's exactly what disappointed me the most about your sudden disappearance last night," Titus said with a world-weary sigh. "The way I figure it, I give a numb-nuts Deputy Dawg like yourself an important job, it's all you can do just to get it done right, but instead you go shooting off to Christ knows where on short notice and I—" Suddenly something caught his eye, something shiny on the table behind them half-buried in the rubble of Jack's weekly paperwork. "What's this?" Titus asked coyly, wheeling around the desk to reach for it himself.

"New tape recorder, Jack? Is this one of them new Japanese gadgets, with the digital audio whatzit?"

"It's just a tape recorder, Titus," Jack answered carefully. "I've had it for years."

"Really? How's it work?"

Jack's voice had begun to waver. "It's broken, I'm afraid."

"No, it isn't either!" Titus announced happily. "Look at that! Little spools are going around, see? Must have been the battery or—"

All at once Jack whipped around in his seat, faster than Titus would have ever given him credit for, and the tape recorder disappeared from his hand. Spinning backward in the chair, Jack hurled it across the office where its casing burst open against the wall, just below the Civil Servant plaque, and landed in a scattering of wires and magnetic tape. It left a sad little pockmark in the wall. He looked back at Titus with desperate, red-rimmed eyes but said nothing.

"I hope I'm never up at bat when you're pitching, Jack," Titus said with a sigh. When Jack defied him, it was always with these abrupt and childlike gestures, and it left him feeling more weary than suspicious. It was a game they had played, on and off, for far too long. Still, he made a mental note to check into Jack's tapes, and what he might be doing with them. "Drink your drink, and head up into the great white north and see what's shaking there, what do you say?"

Jack Tornquist said nothing. Having momentarily relieved the pressure of an impending sense of heroism, he reached for the whiskey, his first in more than six years, and threw it back in one swallow. After all that time, he was at least expecting it to leave his eyes watering, but it didn't. It didn't burn much at all.

48

Outside, the day was cold and bleak, the streets that ran through the northern outskirts of Burns Mills were nearly empty.

Jack rode shotgun, reeking from just a few tablespoons of whiskey. Titus had steered the specially designed Lincoln through Burns Mills' single stoplight, over the bridge and up the winding main street toward the edge of town. With his other hand he worked the Lincoln's custom-mounted hand throttle, keeping their speed a good fifteen over the limit. Within half an hour they had crossed the St. Lawrence Seaway and cleared customs into Ontario.

"Just another few minutes now," Titus said as the highway opened up in front of them. "We're meeting this fella halfway. Enjoy the scenery, why don'tcha."

Jack didn't like Canada, never had. He particularly didn't like it with a buzz on. Between the doughnut shops and the somehow ominous absence of police, the reality seemed thinner here, with greater space between sane thoughts. He watched the open woods spread out on either side of them, miles and miles of desolate forests that broke occa-sionally to show a flash of Superior's gray shoreline. In two months these coastal routes would all be closed down, snowed shut until spring. Not that it mattered, he thought. The land was government-owned, unoccupied for miles in every direction. The road itself was rarely trav-eled, and Jack hadn't seen another car for the last fifteen minutes, since they had left the main freeway.

Titus was slowing down, his eyes focused on the gravel shoulder a half mile ahead, a scenic overlook with a picnic table and a rusty oil-drum trash can. "Get ready," he told Jack. "Get that folder from the backseat for me."

Jack reached behind Titus for the manila folder, and it fell open in his slightly unsteady hand. Several slippery-looking black-and-white pictures fell out and spread themselves across the leather upholstery.

Jack turned one of them over and saw that they were photos of Nicholas that Titus had taken while the kid was still unconscious. Titus had carefully photographed the boy's face from the front and either side, using shadow and perspective to conceal the occasional bruise or cut that the crash had left on his face and neck.

"Kid's body was a little too beat-up yet to take pictures of," Titus was saying as the Lincoln slowed to a halt, "but he's a quick healer, and by Wednesday I guess he'll be more or less presentable." He cut the engine and snapped the photographs from Jack's hand, dropping them into the side pouch of the wheelchair. "You ready?"

Jack looked outside at the little gravel area where Titus had stopped the car. Next to the picnic table was a phone booth. Far away through the spruce trees he could hear the surf thundering. He reached down, unsnapped the holster strap from the .38 at his hip and nodded once.

"Good." Titus opened his door and kicked down the metal ramp.

Jack felt cold wind off the lake blowing into his face, the air that smelled like solitude and motor smoke. It was a Titus kind of place, he thought, as the ramp landed with a crash against the loose gravel. "This shouldn't take but a minute."

Jack watched the old man navigate the whining wheelchair down the nonslip surface of the ramp and across the gravel. Tiny chips of gray stone lodged in the chair's treads. *Evidence*, Jack thought, almost absently. He watched Titus steer the chair past the picnic table and the trash can to the telephone, the wind stirring the old man's shaggy hair.

Presently, the phone began to ring. It was a strange, lonely sound, out here in the midst of all this emptiness.

Titus picked up the receiver and spoke into it, smiling broadly from the first word. Jack sat still with his hand resting on the butt of his gun, glad that he couldn't hear what Titus was saying. It was the Pitch, and he had always hated those occasions when he actually had to listen to it. Sometimes, especially with Gertrude, the Pitch went on for an unbearably long time, with the old man heaping on outrageous offers, describing services that Gertrude would perform for certain additional amounts of money. Now that Titus had Nicholas to offer, he thought, negotiations could conceivably last all afternoon.

He saw Titus nodding, smiling and then hanging up the phone.

A few seconds later, a car rose into view in the southbound lane. Jack glanced at Titus, and the old man gave him a single, reassuring nod in response. The car, a long, cordovan-colored sedan with smoked-glass windows, swerved over to the right shoulder and came to rest on the opposite side of the road from Titus' Lincoln.

"Okay," Jack murmured under his breath. He had the .38 in his hand now, his palm perspiring against the wood-grain grip. "Come on out and let's get this over with."

The driver, a slightly familiar-looking boy in worn navy peacoat and a spiky haircut, climbed out and ambled around the side to open the door for his passenger. The Canadian stepped out, his gloved hands buttoning his overcoat, and then turned toward Titus' car and fixed Jack with cold sea-green eyes. A warning. He walked across the deserted highway, nodded at Titus and took the folder of photographs from him, riffling through them. Titus said something and laughed, and the Canadian shook his head, handing back the photographs. Titus threw up his hands. The Canadian began to walk away. Titus spoke again. The Canadian stopped and turned around.

Titus showed him the pictures again.

After another few minutes, he returned to the Lincoln and piloted the wheelchair back up the ramp, working it around, back and forth, until he was behind the steering wheel. He looked anxious and flushed, and Jack saw that he had cranked the oxygen up to four liters, so that the tank was hissing steadily. On the other side of the road, the Canadian had disappeared back into his sedan.

"What's up?" Jack asked.

"Goddamn Canuck," Titus muttered, starting up the engine again. "Guy's going to follow us back down to Burns Mills. He wants a closer look at the merchandise before he and his partners lay down a deposit." He shook his head and turned the Lincoln around as the sedan crept up behind them. They began to head south again. "I sure hope the kid's feeling spunky, Jack. Because it's showtime."

49

Portion of the testimony of Ian Danzig, October 28:
So, with nothing else left to do, we arranged his funeral.

Uncle Titus had asked that we have it later in the week rather than earlier, because he had some urgent business that he had to attend to, although he definitely wanted to come. Coming from anyone else, the request would be an insult. Coming from Titus, we agreed. The funeral would be Thursday afternoon.

We had spoken to him again early Sunday, and he had given us his most sincere apologies, none of it making Shelley or me feel any more together than we had for the last week. None of it seemed right, or possible, in what I'd always assumed was an orderly, rational world. None of it seemed licensed to happen. None of it seemed approved. Instead, everything seemed to be coming unraveled. Shelley refused to stop talking about the voices she'd heard in the background of Uncle Titus' previous phone call. Nicky's voice, she said. I argued with her spectacularly, mainly because I had heard them, too—in my mind, if not over the phone lines. And I was worried that if somebody didn't jump to the defense of rational thought, and fast, we were going to lose hold of it completely.

That night I made dinner for the first time in six years. It was spaghetti, and it was horrible. We tried to talk about the funeral arrangements, but all

I could do was cry—the one thing that my wife seemed incapable of. She had wept once, when the police had first called about Nicky's death. Since then she had seemed to exist in a gray world all her own, clinging like a child to the last thing she had left—that voice, crying for help, on the phone.

I tossed both our plates of spaghetti away and stared out the window over the kitchen sink for a long time, still crying. I couldn't think of anything else to say. I didn't have the strength to argue about the voice on the phone anymore. Instead I just shook my head, running the hot water from the tap until the steam rose up into my face, watching the street as parents called their kids back inside for the night. Tomorrow was a school day, as I'm sure I'd told Nicky on a thousand Sunday evenings in the past. Another weekend over, another working week begun, but don't fret too much, there's next weekend to think of . . . another weekend, always another weekend before the winter snow flies, and when it does we can take your red plastic sled out to Northern's hill, panting clouds of our breath every step of the way to the top, and we can go shooting down with you on my lap screaming happily, we can build a snowman, we can—we—

I guess I probably would have stood there running the hot water all night if Shel hadn't come up behind me and put her arm around my side, and squeezed me tight against her. But that was all it took. I slammed my hands against the rim of the sink, empty, useless hands, idle hands—

"Oh God!" I burst out, turning to her, and my little tears were now swamped in whooping sobs as I felt myself collapsing into her arms. I would probably never stop crying for him, I thought. "Shelley, I miss him so much!"

She had no words of reassurance, not yet. But she could embrace me, and I suppose I could embrace her. It was not enough—I wondered if it would ever be enough again for the rest of our lives—but at the moment it was a little better than being alone.

50

Looking back on that long Sunday afternoon and evening, Nicholas could only wish that he had spent less time upstairs in the storage room and just a few minutes more hunting for the telephone downstairs. It wasn't an easy search, and finding it sooner would have saved him a lot of bad dreams later on.

Nicholas Danzig, Boy Detective, he thought glumly. *Gets the goods on his uncle and then trips over his own shoelaces.*

True, he was still reeling from the shock of what he had discovered upstairs. He was so edgy, so anxious from what he had just seen, he was bumping into corners with his shoulder and nearly tripping over his own two feet. Limping down the staircase, he had told himself sternly he had to push ahead—for Anthem's sake if not his own.

And then there was Ovid's body, down in the basement. What was he going to do about that?

I don't want to go down there. Even if I did want to, I don't think I could.

Deep inside of him, the anger and the shame were percolating to a full boil.

Of the two, it was the shame he hated the most. It was also the hardest to put out of his mind. In its own perverse way, it was more satisfying than anger. His anger was directed at Titus, but the shame was eating at him. It was a horrible, complex feeling that he couldn't even come close to understanding.

Cut it out. You're not doing yourself any good having these thoughts.

At the bottom of the stairs he found himself in a paneled vestibule, a massive oak coat tree in one corner with a greasy CAT baseball cap on one hook. Framed hunting prints hung underneath carefully positioned track lighting. The front doorway was a giant old-fashioned arch with leaded-glass windows that looked out into the dirt driveway. The Lincoln was nowhere to be seen.

Nicholas walked down the hallway. "Uncle Titus?" he shouted. His voice volleyed back and forth through the empty corridors. "Hello? Is anybody home?"

Down the hall was a great, immaculate kitchen with a butcher block in the middle of the gleaming tile floor. The surface of the long Formica counters had been teased to a high polish. Constellations of brass pots and pans and assorted cookware hung from hooks just overhead, among green plants, and Nicholas realized that he was touring not just a house but the estate of a country gentleman. Just how much money did Titus have, anyway? Did he make it all in the market, or did he have other irons in the fire, so to speak?

On one side of the kitchen, through a pair of glass French doors, he could see the dining room, its terra-cotta walls spangled and flecked with reflected light from the candelabra overhead. On the other side, through another set of doors, the ceiling soared upward, the paneled walls opening into a library that seemed to consume the entire west side of the house. Nicholas padded across the tile floor, turned the handle, and the library door opened silently. He went in.

Whole shelves, whole *walls*, of books loomed from every side. Rich velvet curtains drew back from bay windows overlooking the rocky shoreline below and the overcast sky above it. Nicholas looked outside, through the beveled glass. A flock of Canadian geese were flying over the water in a loosely formed, barely recognizable V. He was used to hearing them honk as they passed over, but the glass was so thick that he couldn't hear them even faintly. He couldn't hear anything outside, actually, even the wind gusting through the eaves. Stillness and silence ruled the library unchallenged, and held court. Down here, he noticed, even the floorboards were silent.

Everything bore the faint, unmistakable scent of tobacco. At one end of the room, behind a long mahogany table, a small fire flickered in the hearth. Nicholas saw Titus' breakfast dishes sitting next to a neatly folded copy of the Sunday *New York Times*. The business section was on top, stamped with a light brown crescent where Titus had obviously set his morning coffee. Next to it was an ashtray, half-full, and a cardboard pack of matches which he picked up and slipped into his sock thinking vaguely that he might put them to use later. Maybe, he thought, he could burn the place down.

There was no telephone here, either.

Nicholas wasn't sure how he first came to think about the possibility of an alarm system rigged somewhere into the house. At first he scoffed at the idea—which authorities would such an alarm system alert, besides Jack?—but then he realized that he might have already tripped something that would indicate to Titus that he'd been snooping around, and Titus could be on his way back now. He scanned the walls for anything resembling a motion detector, but he couldn't see anything obvious. And anyway, he thought, the odds were if Titus had anything more sophisticated, say photoelectrics rigged into the walls, then Nicholas had already made his presence here hopelessly well known. He was already bagged.

In searching the walls for an alarm, however, he did notice something he hadn't seen before. At the far end of the library, more or less obscured by the great stone hearth, was another doorway leading even further back. At first it seemed too narrow even for a wheelchair to fit through. Nicholas tried the handle and found it was locked.

The lock itself was probably ancient and easily broken, but he couldn't give himself away yet. Instead he stood there and stared at it. The door handle looked very old too, and somehow familiar . . . from upstairs in the bedroom? No, that door had a real doorknob, eccentrically egg-shaped though it was, and this was an actual handle that jutted, hook-like, from the brass plate affixed to the heavy oak door. There was probably nothing behind it, just a woodbin full of chopped cordwood or maybe a back door that led down to the shoreline. A blind alley. A dead end.

Or maybe Titus' office, he thought. And a telephone.

He knew that he was standing almost directly below his bedroom, from where he had heard very distinctly Titus calling his broker. Odds were good that this door led to that office. Thoughtlessly, he started to reach for the door handle again, just to make the physical connection, and suddenly he recalled where he had seen such a handle before.

Back at the first house where he and Anthem had stopped, in the house that had been Titus' a long time ago, the bedroom door had had a handle like this one. It had locked on both sides.

And once Nicholas remembered that, he saw very clearly the handle on the other side of the door, and the key that remained in the lock on that side.

He walked back to the kitchen, forcing himself to move slowly enough that he didn't knock anything over in his excitement. He started opening different drawers around the kitchen, not quite sure of what he was looking for until he laid his hands on it. A plain old paper clip would do half the job for him, so he took the biggest one he found from Titus' household junk drawer—rubber bands, twist-ties, dead batteries—and unbent it to its full length, then unfolded a section of the *Times* and slipped it underneath the locked door in the library.

Shouldn't I be saying a prayer for this to work, or something?

He wriggled the paper clip into the keyhole. For a second his heartbeat stalled in his chest—the clip wouldn't go in more than half an inch, at most. Then he jiggled it just a little to the right, felt it scrape against the tumblers and pushed it the rest of the way in. There was a soft *click!* and he heard the key on the other side drop to the floor. He pulled the newspaper back out from under the door and saw it lying there like a prize. He felt a burst of renewed enthusiasm at his success.

Almost enough to make you forget that your father was raping your sister, and taking pictures of it, right here in this house, isn't it? his mind exclaimed with a sick sort of glee. *And that you were looking at pictures of it yourself? Pictures, man, can you believe it?*

"Shut up," he told himself. A black fog had begun to crawl over his enthusiasm again. "Can't you just shut up awhile?"

Working carefully, he tugged the paper clip free without breaking it off in the lock and then inserted the key itself and turned it. The door seemed to leap open in front of him.

Standing in the doorway, he found himself peering in at the marble slab of Titus' desk. At once he felt drawn into the shape of the office. It seemed to be all glass, with windows offering an uninterrupted view of the entire shoreline below and horizon beyond it, designed so that the person behind the desk would feel as though he were floating somewhere beyond the world, in the middle of some vast, impenetrable cathedral of silence. Above him, the ceiling rose up and up, spiraling into a whirling dervish of open space.

Nicholas wandered across the room, his feet sinking into the deep gray pile, his eyes everywhere at once. As he walked, he kept his hands outstretched before him, as though he were feeling around in the darkness for a familiar shape to support him. His fingertips brushed against the frictionless surface of Titus' marble desktop, which was arranged with neat, almost compulsive precision: a pen set, a box of stiff, creamy monogrammed stationery, a small remote control for the television console built into the wall behind him. A cordless microphone topped with a black foam baffle. Nicholas picked it up, glanced at it and frowned. Mr. Microphone?

Behind him the television screen was lit, with Friday's stock quotes scrolling in silence across the bottom of the screen. To his left, curving alongside the sleek surface of the wall, stood a plain oak bar. Just beyond that, a chrome ticker-tape machine sat, gleaming with anachronistic elegance. Nicholas had never seen one in real life before, but he knew that it had to be an antique. Titus got all his stock prices from the television.

He looked back at the desk and saw the telephone sitting next to a stack of papers. He reached down for the receiver and put it to his ear. It was dead.

He followed the cord down with his fingers and pulled it up from where it hung loose against the floor. Dropping to his knees, he searched the wall until he found the phone outlet.

The small, square opening in the middle of the plastic plate was covered with a second plastic shield, bolted directly into the wall. Nicholas was about to stand up and search through the study for a letter opener, or anything flat enough to go to work on the bolts, when he heard the unmistakable sound of the front door of the house opening. He froze, his heart vaulting in his chest, his lungs locked.

You were wasting time looking around! Now it's too late!

From the other side of the house he heard Titus' voice, soft and melodious, persuasive. Although the sounds were muffled, Nicholas thought he recognized another voice that wasn't Jack's. This unknown voice was asking questions. Titus would chuckle and answer them.

Nicholas' eyes flicked around the office, abruptly confronted with its smooth surfaces and slowly uncoiling curves. There was no place to run, nowhere to hide, not in the office, anyway. He ducked his head out the doorway, surveyed the cavernous library beyond it and sprung out across the carpeted floor toward the first of the huge bay windows, his feet hardly touching the ground.

He ran halfway across the library, light from the beveled glass flashing over his face. Jumping up onto the windowsill, he curled himself up against the glass and pulled the curtain shut in front of him, hugged his knees and sucked in his breath. The cold windowpane against his body heat began to fog up, obscuring the view so that he felt walled in on both sides. He held perfectly still. Only seconds later, the conversation of Titus and his mysterious visitor began to echo back and forth through the hallway. Gradually they were working their way toward the library, and Nicholas realized that he could make out some of the conversation.

". . . you'll understand our hesitancy," the voice he didn't recognize was saying. It had a detached, businesslike tone. "This is totally different from what we discussed. Utterly unexpected."

Now Nicholas could hear Titus' oxygen tank whistling from the other side of the French doors. He was reminded oddly of the sound of a bomb plummeting downward through the air in a World War II movie. He heard the wheelchair's motor droning forward into the library, but Titus had not yet spoken.

"Certainly we appreciate the specialization of your . . . services," the voice continued, drawing closer still. Nicholas could hear the man's shoes clicking slowly across the library's hardwood floors. "But there comes a point at which the buyer must see what it is he's paying for, wouldn't you say? It is, as you would surely agree, the *American* way?"

Nicholas gripped his knees more tightly than ever, as though he might be able to collapse himself into nothingness if he tried hard enough. Now he was sure that he did not like the voice's easy impassivity, nor did he like the way he continued to refer to himself as the buyer. He was shaking, clenching himself tighter and tighter, but unable to stop shaking.

I'm the product. I'm the thing for sale. He's talking about me.

He swallowed drily, his throat sliding like a handshake between two nervous strangers. His mouth tasted coppery. Soon, he knew, his trembling would become severe enough to shake the curtain and betray his hiding place. Still he couldn't stop.

I can't stay here.

As quietly as he could, he rubbed an oval in the foggy windowpane and gazed down at the shoreline, wondering if he could somehow smash the glass and make a jump for it now. How far up was he? Distances had never come quickly to him, and they weren't coming any quicker now with his mind chasing itself in panicky little circles. He looked down at the grass and wilting flower beds that gave way to the pale gray sand and the rocky coast. How many feet down? What could he use to estimate it with? His mind flashed on Ian Danzig, who Nicholas knew was six feet tall, and he looked down again. How many Ian Danzigs, stacked up end-to-end from the grass? Five? Six? Say thirty feet, at the least. Could be forty.

Nicholas shook his head. No. At forty feet, he would break his legs, or whatever he landed on first. Maybe it would be his head.

But if I stay here, I'm going to get auctioned off to the highest bidder like some stupid lamp or something.

Was that what Gertrude had been thinking when she jumped out her window?

No. I'd rather die before I ended up like her.

And for just a second he felt that terrible closeness of death drift across his heart. Self-destruction was always possible. He had just never realized it so effortlessly before now, how easy it would be to drive his elbow out through the beveled glass and dive headfirst out into the cold air as the ground rushed up at him faster and faster until at last there came the single, sickening crack—

No. Sorry. Rejected. Absolutely not. Killing yourself is not *an option.*

Nicholas relaxed his arms, and realized that he had been squeezing himself so hard that his biceps were throbbing. He wasn't going to kill himself. He was the last of three, and he wasn't going to let Titus win. Whatever happened next, he thought, the old man was going to leave this world wishing like hell that he had never tried to bring his youngest child back in first place.

All at once something popped into his mind, something that Ian

Danzig had once said to him in a fit of fatherly wisdom: *There are two*
kinds of mistakes you can make, son—little ones and big ones. Make all the
little ones you want. Just avoid those big ones when you can.

Titus had made his one big mistake twelve years earlier. Whether he
had been driven to give Nicholas away because he loved him more than
Ovid and Gertrude, or whether he felt some obscure pang of guilt . . . it
didn't matter. The old man's game was over.

Suddenly he was aware that Titus' customer had stopped talking, that
he was awaiting some reassurance. But Titus had not yet spoken.

"Mr. Heller?" the customer prompted. "Are you quite all right?"

"Yeah," the old man's voice said at last, and Nicholas jumped. The
voice was right next to him on the other side of the curtain. Titus had
switched off both the wheelchair's motor and the oxygen tank, and
maneuvered himself silently up to the window. He was only inches
away, close enough to touch.

Nicholas watched the two nicotine-stained fingers curl inside the edge
of the thick velvet curtain and draw it open, just an inch or two at first.
He saw a corner of the old man's face, his yellow grin and the corroded
green oxygen tank. And those eyes, whirling and dancing with ecstatic
blue sparks.

"Nicky," he said in a husky whisper that was somehow intimate,
"why don't you come on down from there?"

51

Nicholas let out his breath.

Titus drew the curtain open. Nicholas heard its smooth rings
clicking together along the teak curtain rod like beads on an abacus. He
watched as Titus reached back to readjust the oxygen tank's gauge,
giving the knob a full three turns before the hissing began again and then
slumping back into the chair, his eyes watering with glazed satisfaction.

"Been out exploring the house, huh?" the old man asked. "Must be
feelin' pretty sprightly, then."

His wheelchair was flanked by Constable Jack Tornquist on the right,
the unfamiliar visitor on his left. The stranger's face was pink and clean-

shaven, his expensive topcoat draped over narrow shoulders. He blinked curiously up at Nicholas, then looked down at Titus, beaming with barely repressed excitement. "Ah, Mr. Heller. Always the showman."

A slow smile opened across the old man's face. "C'mon, Nicky. Don't make Jack have to pull out his gun. Get down from there."

Nicholas slipped down from the windowsill. His stocking feet hit the hardwood floor with a muffled bump. He could see that Jack already had his hand on the butt of his pistol, but the constable's face was wrenched into an almost comical mask of indecision.

"Jack," he said, forcing his voice to stay calm. "You're the cop here, you're going to stand by and watch them take me like this? You gonna shoot me if I start walking away?" He raised his eyebrows. "Huh? Jack?"

"Constable's been working for me a long time, Nicky," Titus said. The oxygen rush seemed to be making him slur his words a little. "He'll do as he's told, and I guess you will, too."

He turned to the Canadian. "Fine-looking boy, isn't he?" His voice rose with carnival barker's pride. "What I got for you here isn't just your average, ordinary fourteen-year-old boy, you see . . . and I know you *can* see it, too, because you and your partners have always been what I'd call discriminatin' types. They sent you down to check the lay of the land because you've got an eye for talent. You know what I'm sayin'? You know *quality*. This is a very special boy, with very special abilities. A very *capable* boy." His eyes flicked back up to the constable and he took a long, luxurious breath of oxygen. "Jack, give the man a little taste of what we're talking about here."

Jack moved forward in a startling blur of activity. Nicholas said, "Hey, wait—" but before he could withdraw into the open space behind him, Jack tore open his T-shirt, exposing his body to the waist. Nicholas pulled himself free and tried in vain to close the torn shirt around him again. The library was silent for a long moment except for the hiss of oxygen.

"Look at the smoothness of him," Titus whispered.

The stranger nodded and blinked. "Yes. Oh, yes. Quite good."

Titus chuckled and sucked oxygen, his fingers fumbling for the crumpled pack of Marlboros in his breast pocket. "Boy's been playin' basketball for his school last summer . . . now, you wouldn't believe what I had to do just to get him involved in it, so don't even get me started." He lit a cigarette, and the flame at the tip of his chrome lighter puttered and flared, hungry for the nearby flow of pure oxygen. "But, for Christ's sweet sake, look at the line of the stomach, wouldja? See how the abdominal muscles are just now startin' to develop underneath there?" He glanced back up at the visitor. "Not an ounce of fat on him—hell, you can see that for yourself—but not scrawny either. Can you see ribs? I'm asking you, is this quality or is it quality? Just like them pictures I showed you. Told you I wouldn't waste your time with inferior goods, didn't I?"

"What's wrong with his leg?"

"Oh, that." Titus waved with the cigarette. "Nothin' that won't be healed up by Wednesday."

"He is a bit . . . lean."

"Look, I told you, he ain't fat. But there ain't a pimple on him yet, not a blemish, not a scar, and by God, that kind of skin's rare as hen's teeth in a fourteen-year-old." Titus gestured impatiently for Nicholas to turn around. Nicholas held still. Titus sighed. "Jack?"

The constable grabbed Nicholas' shoulders and whipped him around on his heels. They stood looking each other in the eye while Titus continued the Pitch, his voice hushed and conspiratorial.

"Okay, okay, tell you what, for every pimple you show me on this kid, I'll . . . I'll take off a hundred bucks from the fee." He spoke slowly with the air of one presenting his final offer. "Every pimple, every rib you can see, hundred right off the top. You show me more than one or two, I'll give you and your partners an extra hour with him, free of charge, do anything you like. What the hell, bring cameras if you want to, capture the moment. Call it a special introductory offer. Because what we got here is something that you boys will be able to come down and enjoy exclusively whenever you like for a good few years, before—"

"Before what?" Nicholas interrupted. His face was burning with rage. "Before you have to bury me in the basement next to Ovid?"

Titus' voice broke off, midswing.

"You better keep your mouth shut when you don't know what you're talking about, kiddo."

"And what if I do know what I'm talking about—" Nicholas spat. "—Dad!"

He turned back around to see the Canadian businessman take a careful step backward, the heel of one black oxford clicking across the blond hardwood floor. His pink face had gone ashen. "Mr. Heller . . . ah, perhaps now isn't a good time."

"No," Titus said. His hand slipped into the side pouch of the wheel-chair and reemerged wrapped around the stock of a chrome-plated automatic, its slotted detail work flashing in the afternoon sunlight. He leveled the pistol at Nicholas, its bore looking as big as the mouth of a garden hose, and he smiled. "So you've been doin' more exploring than I thought, huh, Nicky? You been lookin' at pictures?"

"Yeah, that's right," Nicholas said. His heart was hammering merci-lessly underneath his breastbone, and the heat from the sun behind him seemed to have doubled its intensity in a matter of a few seconds. "I saw it all. I haven't been down to the basement yet, but believe me, that's next."

"The youth is . . . quite rebellious," Titus' customer said warily, mea-suring another step backward. "Perhaps—"

"Oh, he'll do as he's told," Titus said, his eyes never leaving Nicholas. "Don't worry about *that*. By Wednesday he'll be flying behind enough Percodan to drop an elephant. I'll leave him a little feisty, though . . ." He glanced up at the Canadian. "'Cause I know you like 'em that way. But he'll do as he's told. Won't you, Nicky?" The blue eyes flickered and capered brightly. "Why don't you get down and show me twenty push-ups, pump up them muscles a little?"

Nicholas glared at him in silence. He felt like a human thermometer, the quicksilver of his own rage rising steadily up his spine into the nerve center of his brain, lighting tiny fires as it surged upward. His fists hung at his sides, clenched so tightly that they dug little half-moons into his palms.

Titus worked the action on the automatic with a cold metallic snick and aimed it directly at Nicholas' face. "You hear me talking at you, Nicky?"

"You better do it," Jack advised from behind.

"Wait a second." Nicholas looked at the faces of Titus and the Cana-dian. Beneath the mounting fury, there was still something in him that wanted to at least try reasoning with Titus, something that couldn't believe what these men actually expected him to say and do. It was as though, crazily, he expected that one of them, either Titus or Jack or the customer, would burst out laughing and declare the whole thing an enormous practical joke, or at least a kind of punishment that Nicholas could somehow talk himself out of. "Wait a minute, now, just hold on—"

Titus' pistol blasted once, a blurt of white flame leaping from its barrel.

Everybody jumped, and behind him, Nicholas could actually feel the paneling shudder and burst. His ears were still ringing as he looked over his shoulder at the hole in the wall.

"Twenty push-ups *now*," Titus repeated, his blue eyes dancing. "So the man can see what he's paying for."

Nicholas lowered himself to the bare floor, the torn T-shirt fluttering around his chest. He put his hands against the wood, went down and up again. Down and up. Push-ups were a form of exercise all their own, intense and relentless. He had done his fair share during basketball practice last year. Had Titus been the one behind all of it, the one who had told Ian Danzig to push his son *hard*, to make him develop muscle and endurance and stamina?

Yes, I think it was. Even back then, even before I knew it. He had his eye on me. Call it product development.

In basketball practice he had known guys who could run for miles without stopping for breath, who could do sit-ups all afternoon, but who couldn't make themselves do ten push-ups. Push-ups were an angry kid's exercise, he remembered thinking. Because they demanded so much energy so quickly, you could whip off a set of ten or twenty with a single adrenaline rush and then just keep going until your arms collapsed.

And of course, Ian Danzig had continued to push him.

Now, lying on the hardwood floor of Titus' library, Nicholas pushed back. He pumped himself up and down while Jack counted them out. They weren't difficult at all. He had enough adrenaline for a hundred more. He just imagined that the floor was Titus' face. That made it easier.

"See those shoulder muscles at work?" he heard the old man marveling from above. "I put together an exercise regimen for him last year, made his dad a basketball coach and just put him through the paces. See the leg? By Wednesday, good as new. Word of honor. And look at the quadriceps. See how they slide? Just like pistons. Kid's a little machine just the way he is, but I'm gonna start him on the gym downstairs this afternoon just the same."

"You're going to work him out for three days?" The Canadian sounded amused. "Why bother?"

"When you and your partners come back here, you will see a difference, and that's a guarantee." Titus sounded dead serious. "So what do you say?"

Nicholas stopped and rolled over onto his back again, looking up at the men.

"All right," the Canadian said with a contented little sigh that seemed to indicate that the outcome was never really in doubt. "We'll take him."

52

It was night and Nicholas was back up in the bedroom. He lay in bed exhausted and was skating along the very precipice of sleep when he saw the figure step in the doorway. He pushed himself up on one elbow, the muscles aching with protest, and looked up, although the absence of the wheelchair's whine had already told him whom to expect.

Moonlight squiggled across the profile of Jack's high forehead and down the aquiline bridge of his nose, peppering his beard with tiny prickles of light. For what seemed like a long time the constable stood in the doorway, as though he were waiting for the silvery darkness to recognize his face. Then he dragged a chair over to the bed and sat down, keeping a safe distance. He laid his service revolver across his lap, its barrel glinting faintly. When he spoke, his voice was surprisingly clear, the words delivered on an acrid breeze of vinegar-smelling booze.

"J'get enough to eat?"

Nicholas nodded. "Yeah. It was pretty good."

"Good cooking makes for a haaappy bachelor," the constable mumbled. "That's what my mother used to say, anyway. Roast chicken's about the only thing I can make, to tell the truth." He squirmed in his seat, obviously uncomfortable, then curled his fingers in front of his mouth and burped. "You sore from downstairs?"

"Just a little," Nicholas lied. Actually, his body felt as though it had been stretched twice its normal length, one muscle at a time. He sensed that Jack was drawing him into conversation, but didn't try to resist it. He sank back down into the pillows, closed his eyes and watched the events of the late afternoon and evening as they reran themselves through his mind in sleepy detail.

After the Canadian businessman had walked back out to where his sedan had been waiting for him, and Titus had disappeared back into his study, Jack had drawn his pistol and suggested they go downstairs to the gym. "Back through the kitchen," Jack said. Walking single file, they had followed a flight of peeling linoleum stairs down from a hidden kitchen doorway, the odor of stale sweat rising up from below to meet them as Jack flipped on the light switches mounted at the bottom.

For Nicholas, who had expected ugly cinder blocks and bare cement floors, the basement had been a revelation. Two large, mirror-walled rooms opened on either side of him, the fluorescent tubes overhead sputtering for a second and then spilling a hard white light across the bright chrome plating of the exercise machines themselves. Two industrial-sized ventilation fans, their blades the size of biplane propellers, occupied either corner. A glowing neon clockface hung on the far wall. He stood at the bottom of the stairs, blinking in surprise.

"Christ, it looks like Christmas morning for Jack La Lanne down here," Jack mumbled, gesturing him forward with the barrel of the pistol. "You probably don't remember who Jack La Lanne is, do you?"

"I never knew in the first place." Nicholas had his arms crossed self-consciously over his exposed chest, although the furnace seemed to keep the gym itself warm enough. "Did Titus buy all this stuff for me to use?"

"No. Gertr . . . his daughter, she used to use it too."

At the mention of his sister's name, Nicholas felt a fresh switchblade of hatred spring open in his stomach. The sensation was both painful and satisfying at the same time. "Have to keep her nice and marketable, huh?" he snapped. "Right up to the minute she died."

Jack sighed. "Look, Nicholas, I'm prepared to let you in on a little secret: you're only making it harder on yourself. You're stuck here, and you won't be leaving for a long time. Everybody thinks you're dead. Titus brought you here for a purpose, and as long as you serve the purpose, he's not going to let you walk away. Just keep your mouth shut, and when you feel that anger coming on"—he gestured toward the row of exercise machines—"work it out down here."

Nicholas followed him past the machines, stunned into momentary silence by the level of Jack's subservience, as the constable introduced the machines to him one at a time.

"We'll start with the Nautilus here," the constable said. "Fully functional multipurpose ass-kicking machine. You can work every muscle in your upper body with these weights. Lower body we'll hold off on until that leg starts to show some progress. Just make sure you follow the directions on the thing. Careless misuse could get you hurt."

Nicholas laughed out loud, but Jack ignored it.

"Rowing machine . . . pretty self-explanatory. Tension control knob on the top there. Incline bench, good for high-impact sit-ups, of the variety that will make your stomach into a box of muscles."

"I don't want a box of muscles on my stomach."

"Titus will." He continued down the row, listing slightly to the right and then catching himself on a steel support beam. "Okay, lookit, here's your free weights, your bench press and barbells. Tough stuff, but I guess you already know that. These you're going to need for detail work. Meaning that you can do push-ups and isometrics until you puke, but it still won't make your nipples point down."

"I don't want my nipples to point down."

"Ultimately what Titus has requested," Jack continued implacably, as though he were afraid to listen to what Nicholas was saying, "is for me to get you started with some light weights tonight—some easy curls, just to introduce your body to it. Nothing with your legs, of course. See, if we start this afternoon, by Wednesday you'll have something to show the Canadians when they come. After the free weights we'll move over to the Nautilus . . ."

Nicholas listened to the constable prattle on about Titus' long-range goals. He had decided that Jack was pretty close to blotto. Upstairs, when the constable had first grabbed him to turn him around, Nicholas had noticed that distinctive smell mingled into his stale sweat, his breath, even his pores, the cloying reek of sour mash. He guessed that the constable had been drinking pretty seriously before they arrived with the Canadian, and it occurred to him that if he was going to try to earn Jack's trust, now would be a good time to start. He thought Jack's level of resentment had to be reaching its apex soon.

But he couldn't just demand that Jack help him escape. Not yet. He had to make it as hard as possible for the constable to refuse.

But when am *I going to ask him?*

He would know, when the time was right. Until then, he needed to choreograph the most impressive display that he could come up with, starting with what was right here in front of him. A way of bonding himself with Jack.

While the constable was still talking, Nicholas lay down on the bench and picked up a five-pound barbell in each hand. He lifted them upward with a muffled grunt and brought them together over his chest. They clicked. *Like a pair of magnetic dogs,* he thought wildly. *I will call this barbell Virgil, and this one Ovid.*

"Oh, hey, careful now," Jack said. "You don't want to start out—"

Nicholas hoisted them again. They felt heavier this time, but he kept his elbows locked. The adrenaline left over from his confrontation with Titus stirred in his biceps and pecs. Deliberately he called up the image of Titus' smiling face, the wheeling blue light in his eyes, the steady whistle of leaking oxygen. He found his anger and pushed it through every muscle in his arms and chest. The weights clicked together a third time. A fourth. A fifth. And again. And again. What had started out impossible had become a little easier. He forced himself to do three more, then lowered the barbells back down to the rubber mat underneath him. His upper lip was beaded with sweat, his triceps and biceps were on fire.

When he sat up again, Jack was gaping at him. "Wow, that's—"

"What's . . . next?" Nicholas panted. "Incline press? Lat pull-downs? What?"

"You better slow down," the constable said. "Or *you're* going to pull something."

Nicholas told him that he didn't want to slow down. His heart was racing. The fury in him wasn't going to slow down anytime soon, the heartfelt desire to attack Titus and destroy him for everything he had done to his older brother and sister.

"Okay," Jack said, "but go easy, pace yourself."

Despite Jack's warning, he moved from the bench press to the Nautilus machine, from the Nautilus to the rowing machine, with just a minute or two between each one. Even he was a little amazed by the sheer brute strength of the rage within him. It was a little scary, as though he had discovered a second personality inside himself, one that already had a raging endorphin addiction . . . an addiction to the physical tension of the weights.

Being careful to let the constable guide him, spot him, make suggestions for his technique, he took breaks when Jack told him to, but always tried to push himself just a little bit past what the constable clearly expected. If Jack asked for ten sit-ups with the incline bench at a thirty-degree angle, Nicholas moved the bench up a notch higher and did fifteen. His leg had started to bleed, and he ignored it. He cranked down the tension a full revolution on the exercise bike, and pedaled until Jack snapped the clamp down on the wheel, forcing him to stop. Twice Nicholas caught him taking a drink from a silver flask while he thought Nicholas wasn't looking. Every time he saw Jack take a drink, it gave him the extra little boost of strength that he needed to finish a set of reps, to do another minute or two on the exercise bike or the rowing machine.

Keep drinking, old boy, he thought. *Just keep drinking.*

And there was something else interesting as well. As Nicholas developed a rhythm between exercises, time became plastic, formfitting itself to his body's new cycle of exertion and rest. He was only distantly aware of his own exhaustion, creeping up on him. Titus had called him a machine, and in a way, Nicholas thought, the description fit. He *felt* like a machine, moving the weights up and down, pushing his muscles until they screamed at him.

They spent almost two hours downstairs, by the neon clock on the wall. It was almost seven o'clock. By the end, Jack was staggering noticeably when he walked, and no longer bothering to hide the flask. He stared at Nicholas through thin-slitted eyes. "My *Gawd*, son, aren't you tired yet? How much longer can you go?"

Nicholas tried to smile. "Done." His body felt dishrag-weak, perhaps even too weak to carry himself up the stairs. He had stripped off his T-shirt, and his thin chest shone with sweat, his lean arms gleaming softly like lumps of sculpted wet clay. The room blurred dangerously around him. "Can't do any more."

"Well, I'd frigging well guess you can't," Jack said, shaking his head. "You'll sleep well tonight, though, I bet. Give yourself a few minutes to settle your pulse and then we'll go upstairs and get you some dinner."

Dinner, Nicholas thought. He hadn't eaten breakfast. Yes, dinner would be good. "Can you cook drunk, Jack?"

The constable threw back his head and laughed. "Nicky, drunk or sober I can outcook any man in this house. Why, you just wait, you won't believe the culinary artwork in store for you. You'll eat till you puke!"

"Is that a promise or a threat?"

Jack gestured him toward the stairs with his gun. "Titus wants you five pounds heavier by Wednesday," he said. "But first you better get showered. I'll start the chicken going, then you can eat. Come on."

Up two flights of stairs, he had escorted Nicholas to the bathroom halfway down the hall. Inside, Nicholas turned on the hot water full blast, stripped naked and stood for a long time with the shower cascading down over him while the steam rose up over his body like a gentle, comforting hand. He began to scrub himself with more puritanical fervor than he'd ever felt before in his life, washing carefully around the spot where the bullet had grazed his leg. Whole layers of filth washed away, whole scenes from the last six days swirling down the drain before his very eyes: the back roads, the photographs, the birth certificates and the terrible knowledge that accompanied all of it.

I've got three days, he thought as he worked a handful of shampoo suds into his scalp. *The Canadians come back on Wednesday. Thursday is my funeral.*

Jack's voice, echoing, inflectionless: *News flash, kiddo: you are stuck here.*

. . . Ah, look at the smoothness of him . . .

In Gertrude's crayonscript: *WHERES OVID??*

. . . the smoothness of him . . .

. . . news flash: you are stuck here . . .

. . . it's the secret passenger who sees the most, Virgil; you'll see what I mean later . . .

"Secret passenger," Nicholas said aloud. Shampoo trickled into his mouth and he spat it out. Suddenly his mind was on Anthem's story, the way that she had escaped with Uncle Titus before. "Yeah, I'll see what you mean later." He finished rinsing himself, turned off the water and toweled off, his mind still reeling from the possibility of it. He was almost afraid to think about the idea too much at this point. It seemed fragile, something that could die from being handled before it developed more fully. But maybe tonight, or tomorrow . . .

He stepped out into the hall in a billow of steam, with the towel wrapped around his hips. While he had been in the bathroom, the entire house had filled with the aroma of roasting chicken. Nicholas heard the busy clink and clatter of kitchen sounds from below, where Jack was drunkenly making dinner and singing to himself.

Nicholas went to the bedroom, where he found his clothes laid out on the bed, cleaned and pressed with new white socks. He shut the door and something caught his eye. Hanging by its strap from a brass hook on the back of the door, looking spuriously consistent with the rest of the room, was a cheap transistor radio. It had not been there this morning.

Some kind of gift, he thought, a trinket from Titus to show his appreciation for his performance earlier today. He wanted to smash it to pieces, the way Gertrude had smashed her model cars and trucks.

What if I tried to leave right now? he wondered abruptly. *Jack's too drunk to follow me out. Maybe if I ran I could make it to one of the main throughways, or at least to a working phone.*

But what about Titus himself? Titus wasn't drunk. Titus was some-where in the house, maybe even waiting for Nicholas to attempt his escape. What would the old man do to him if he caught him trying to run?

He couldn't lay a hand on me. Can't bruise the merchandise, you know. Skin like mine is rare as hen's teeth on a fourteen-year-old.

But there were plenty of other things he could do that wouldn't leave a trace afterward. Plenty of them. Nicholas had seen these things being done to Gertrude, in the photo album.

With a shudder, he began to get dressed. After pulling his windbreaker on over his T-shirt, he walked over to the window and looked out where the sky had started to turn a pewter color. In a few minutes it would be full dark. His mind pulled back and forth in a frantic tug-of-war of self-doubt. He was trapped here by a drunken constable and a crippled old man on oxygen. Escaping should have been as easy as walking through the door. Except that if Titus had Jack Tornquist on his side, then he probably had most of the town working for him, too, in some way or another.

But all I need is a phone!

The simplicity of it was all the more maddening. He needed a phone, but he couldn't get out of the house to use one. And even if he could, his parents would not be able to respond right away. Even the state police couldn't drive up into the desolate wastes of Burns Mills immedi-ately. And Titus would have plenty of time to—

To kill me. Yeah, I think if it came down to that, giving up his last child, he would probably kill me first. Then maybe he'd turn the gun on himself.

Was the old man that crazy? Nicholas didn't think he was, but—

Something crackled behind him: *"Hey, Nicky? You're sure takin' your time up there, aren't you?"*

He whirled around, his pulse pounding in his neck. His eyes went to the transistor radio, where it hung from the back of the door. Titus' voice came raspily from its plastic speaker. Nicholas remembered the cordless microphone that he had seen downstairs in the old man's study.

"You better come down here for dinner, toot-sweet. You're makin' me nervous. And old Jack, he's afraid maybe you're questioning his cookin' abilities. So get your ass in gear, huh? And Nicky, one other thing—"

"Oh, screw off," Nicholas muttered, giving the radio the finger.

"—after you and Jack eat, come back and meet me in my study. I guess you know where it is. We gotta talk."

The speaker popped and went dead.

Nicholas put on his shoes and started down the stairs for dinner.

Afterward came the final images of the day, receding into darkness. He was falling asleep, releasing the last handgrips of consciousness and toppling into the void beneath and behind him, toppling further and further back without the slightest resistance . . .

Jack shifted his weight in the chair, the moonlight altering its pattern subtly over his oblong face. "What did Titus want to talk to you about, anyway? After dinner?"

". . . mm?" Nicholas blinked, uncertain whether he'd actually heard Jack's voice or just dreamed it. "Huh?" Then his nostrils caught the familiar sourness of alcohol and he knew that Jack was still here, half-crouched into his chair next to the bed. "Oh . . . he . . . he was just telling me the same stuff he told you. The exercise program . . . the meals, you know . . . all that stuff . . ."

"Oh." The constable looked relieved. "So he didn't say anything about me?"

"No, nothing about you . . ."

"When you were looking around at those pictures today—"

Nicholas lifted his head an inch off the pillow. ". . . burned them . . ."

"What? What did you say?"

"Those pictures of you and Gertrude together," he heard himself murmuring. Exhaustion and the nearness of a long sleep helped him with the improvisation; he was too tired to have planned it or felt nervous. The words simply slipped from his lips. "I found them, Jack . . . and I burned them all . . ."

"You . . . you're lying," Jack said uncertainly, half out of his seat. "Nicholas, there *are* no pictures like that."

"Not anymore, anyway," Nicholas mumbled, and dropped his head back into the pillow's warm depression. ". . . g'night, Jack."

"Hey, no, wait just a minute now—"

But Nicholas had already shut his eyes. His own exhaustion had washed over him as powerfully as any sleeping drug that Titus could offer. Behind his eyelids, he saw the lingering afterimage of the constable starting to rise up so quickly that he nearly knocked the chair over behind him. By the time Jack had caught the chair, set it right and tried to ask another question, Nicholas' heart rate had slowed, his breathing became more regulated and he escaped into a vast and depthless sleep.

53

L ong, dusty daggers of morning light had just started to slide through the blinds when Nicholas awoke to the sound of white static sizzling through the transistor radio across the room. He lifted his head and then dropped it again, unable to believe that dawn had come so soon.

"Gooood morning, Nicky boy," Titus' voice crooned, sounding as far away as he always had coming over the phone. *"Hope you slept well. Slept like a baby myself, always do . . . must be that sweet country air, you know . . ."* With that he treated Nicholas to the sound of his lungs filling up with oxygen from the whistling steel tank. *"Ahhh . . . if there's anything better than that, I don't know what it is . . ."*

"You could try sticking a firecracker up your ass," Nicholas told the radio. Titus couldn't hear him talking back—it was just a normal transistor radio the old man was broadcasting through—and that allowed Nicholas to vent all the aggression he wanted. He had plenty. His muscles were sore and wire-tight from yesterday's exercise, and every day it was growing harder to convince himself this was all just a bad dream.

"—gotta get an early start, you know, get you downstairs working out in the gym," the old man's voice roared along merrily. *"I'm gonna be too preoccupied to keep an eye on you today personally—stock market's open this morning, y'see, and I'm busier'n a one-legged man in an ass-kicking contest— but Jack's around, he'll be checking in on you. Just stick to the routine we talked about last night. Keep the radio with you and just . . . stay tuned, good buddy!"*

He rolled over and put another pillow over his head. "Shove it, good buddy."

"—got a nice big breakfast waiting for you downstairs. C'mon down, get some food into you, and let's get you started. Just like we talked about."

After a few minutes of drowsing in and out of sleep, Nicholas finally dragged himself out from between the blankets. His body groaned, particularly his leg, but he knew if he stayed in bed, Titus would become suspicious just when he was beginning to think Nicholas would cooperate. For the next two days, Nicholas knew, he had to act the part of the obedient son, and arouse as little suspicion as possible, if his plan with Jack was going to work.

He stretched and looked around the room.

Freshly laundered gym clothes—a clean sweatshirt, gray Everlast trunks and sweatpants—had been draped across the chair where Jack had been sitting last night. Nicholas started to dress without thinking about it. It was amazing how eager he was to put on whatever clothes were available, as many as were available. That had been a side effect of seeing all the pictures that Titus had taken.

Pulling the drawstring tight on the trunks, he remembered the story he'd told the constable just as he'd dropped off to sleep, about the photographs. Jack had denied that such pictures existed, but Nicholas thought they did. Although they weren't in *My Family Photographs*, he had seen their existence reflected even more clearly in the constable's face.

Something else had convinced him, too.

Last night, sitting across the marble desktop in his study with the autumn starlight encrusted across the sky behind him, Titus had given Nicholas an extra advantage that he hadn't had any right to expect:

"Don't bother trying to ask the constable for help again, Nicky," the old man had said, his eyes spinning with that wild blue light. "Jack's mine, has been for years. Maybe you think you mighta seen all the pictures . . . but I've got the best of them locked away where nobody's gonna find 'em unless they know where to look."

"Pictures of Jack and Gertrude?"

Titus nodded, chuckling throatily, sucking oxygen through his tubes. "Hell, I got pictures of a lotta fine upstanding citizens in this town. I'm just telling you this before you go around looking for a helpin' hand. A few people know I'm in the kid business around here, and I think most of them have their suspicions. But the smart ones keep it to themselves." He cleared his throat. "Them that doesn't . . . well, I can't take re- spons'bility for what happens to 'em."

Titus had passed along a few other "helpful hints" that he thought might save Nicholas precious time and energy.

"And b'lieve me, kiddo, you're gonna need all the energy you got in that slim little package o' yours for the next few days before them Canadians fly in. Me and Jack are gonna work those muscles into something memor'ble." He'd gestured out at the house vaguely. "We got magnetic bolts on the outside of all the doors. They work on a remote switch, like the automatic locks on a car door." He'd held up a featureless black box with a single button, small enough to fit on a key chain. "You gotta go outside for any reason, you ask me or Jack. Otherwise everything stays locked up. You start fiddlin' with the locks, I'll find out about it. You're gonna be spending most of your day down in the gym, so you shouldn't need them opened in the first place. You come upstairs for your meals. You keep that transistor radio with you wherever you go in the house and keep it switched on. I don't care what you listen to, just make sure it's on in case I feel like jawin' at you."

His eyes flashed. "And stop looking at that goddamn phone. I got every outlet in the house bolted shut, with the exception of the little portable one right here in my wheelchair. So whyn't you just give it a rest. And Nicky, one other thing—"

Nicholas had looked at Titus, the old man's cobalt-blue eyes becoming something manic and irrepressible now.

"Wednesday night, after the Canadian gentlemen leave, I'm drivin' downstate for your funeral, leavin' you here with Jack." And he had grinned. "When I get back, we're gonna have us a private party . . . just you an' me. You'll learn to like me, Nicky. I really think you will."

Now, with those final words still reverberating through his head, Nicholas opened his bedroom door, slipped the little radio from its hook and carried it downstairs. He could already smell the familiar aromas of bacon and coffee rising from the kitchen.

"I can hear you comin' down the stairs," the radio crackled happily in his hand. *"Have a nice breakfast, Nicky boy. Hope to see you around later today."*

"Hope you drive your wheelchair into a swimming pool or something," Nicholas replied grimly, hobbling around the corner into the empty kitchen. Down at the long pine table, he could see breakfast laid out before him. Platters loaded with bacon strips and scrambled eggs, a plate piled with wheat toast sweating butter. Another platter, this one stacked with buttermilk biscuits and gravy, an Upper Peninsula favorite. All very high-calorie stuff.

He sat down at the table, groping for his appetite. He managed a few forkfuls of the eggs and half a glass of peroxide-tasting orange juice. On the table in front of him, the radio was now playing an innocuous mixture of pop music and morning-show chatter. Nicholas stared out the window where a few gunmetal clouds had already begun to crowd out the sunlight. Bad weather blowing in off the lake. The afternoon would bring snow, he thought, if they didn't get it earlier.

Behind him he heard the muffled thud of the magnetic bolts on the front door. "Morning, kid," a sleepy voice mumbled. Boots squealed and stomped across the floor of the foyer, and then there was a second thump as the bolts shot home again and Jack stepped out of the shadows.

"Jack." Nicholas looked down the hall. "You don't look so good." He pushed his chair back for a better view of the wasted-looking figure as it wandered down through the entryway and toward him. The constable's face, which had always been gaunt, was now positively skeletal, the hollows of his eyes dusted with a faintly purple hue. He seemed to have passed out in his uniform, which was wrinkled to fit against the joints of his knees and elbows. The stink of cheap whiskey radiated from his skin and the nylon shell of his jacket in palpable waves.

"I need coffee," Jack said, shambling across the kitchen to slop some into a dirty plastic cup from the sink. He drew back a chair and sank down across the table from Nicholas. "You seen the honcho yet this morning?"

Nicholas nodded down at the radio. He had to move a few inches back just to breathe. "Just heard him."

"Uh-huh, yeah, he said he was gonna do that." Jack sniffed the coffee with the kind of delicacy that spoke of the worst skull-pounding headaches. "Thinks he's Paul Harvey or something." He slipped the familiar steel flask from an inside pocket of his jacket, unscrewed the cap and splashed a heavy dollop of amber-colored liquid into the coffee. His eyes were glassy and huge, nearly transparent. Nicholas nearly expected to see goldfish swimming behind them. He watched as Jack sipped at the doctored coffee, pulled it back as though it had nipped him and then tugged out his handkerchief and coughed spastically into it for a long time. When he was finished, he put the hankie away and wiped his eyes on his jacket sleeve. "Nick, I think we need to have a conversation."

"Okay." Nicholas laid down his fork. "Let's have a conversation."

"Downstairs. You done eating?"

Nicholas picked up the radio and followed him back through the doorway behind the pantry and down the peeling steps, into the fluorescent glare of the gym. He stopped on the bottom step and watched as Jack staggered across the room, gaping to his right and left at the group of equally battered-looking Jacks that surrounded him, staring back from every one of the mirrored walls.

With a wet sniffle, the constable sat down at the end of the bench press with his hands laced over the compact little potbelly that Nicholas had never noticed before. He looked as though he were trying to decide whether or not he should vomit. Finally he cleared his throat and blinked painfully up in the glaring light. "You—you didn't really burn those photographs, did you?"

"Every one of them," Nicholas said. "I even flushed the ashes down the toilet."

"Nicholas, those pictures . . . I didn't even know who Gertrude was at that point, I swear to God." Jack opened his hands in supplication. It seemed as though the existence of the pictures was as important to him as the question of their destruction. "Titus introduced her to me as his niece, for crying out loud. You know what kind of a joke that sounds like, when a guy introduces a girl . . . you know, she's my *niece*, nudge-nudge, wink-wink? You know?"

Nicholas shook his head. "She was my sister, Jack. That's all I know."

"Well, if you're so fucking upset about it," Jack said with a sudden whininess in his voice, "why did you burn the pictures in the first place?"

"Because I think you can help me."

"Oh no. No way, compadre. You've got another think coming."

"O-kay." Nicholas squatted down in front of him and forced himself to look into the constable's bloody, basset-hound eyes. "Jack, listen, assume for a second that I didn't burn the pictures, okay? I did, but just say I didn't, okay? What if I showed you a way you could help me and not get caught doing it? You just bring me Titus' portable phone for just half a minute, thirty seconds is all I need—"

With a groan, Jack reclined across the padded bench and lay perfectly still for so long that Nicholas wondered if he had simply passed out. His arms drooped on either side, his narrow pianist's fingers half clutched the foam padding that covered the floor. Nicholas could see the underside of his jaw, where his beard thinned down into a forest of single, scraggly-looking gray hairs. They seemed even grayer than they had been just a day before.

"Jack—"

The constable jerked upright again. "Dammit, he told me you'd try something like this. He sat me down, he told me, Jack, the kid is smart, smarter than Gertrude or . . ."

"The kid *is* smart," Nicholas nodded. "But he isn't lying."

The constable cradled his face in his hands. A soft groaning sound issued forth from somewhere in his chest, the loneliest sound that Nicholas had ever heard. "I don't deserve it, you know," he said finally. "I mean, if you did burn those pictures, then you've flown directly in the face of fate, or just desserts, or whatever you'd call it. Jesus, Nick, what I mean to say . . . after all the things I've done . . . my soul is as black as midnight in Persia. Sometimes it seems like what we deserve and what we actually get are so misaligned that it's hard to believe there's any justice in the world at all." He whipped out the flask, tipped it back and set it down with drunken deliberate care next to him on the foam padding. "I shouldn't even be walking around anymore, after being the kind of man I've been. I should be walled up, buried somewhere behind one of these mirrors, next to your brother."

Nicholas felt a tremor of shock run through his heart. What he'd seen in the picture upstairs suddenly leapt into vivid focus before his eyes, and for a minute he was afraid he was going to faint. He sat down in front of Jack, his sore legs folded underneath him. "So . . . he's really . . . down here?" He made his mouth say the words. "Ovid's really down here?"

"Aww, Christ." Jack lifted his head, and Nicholas saw there were tears brimming in his eyes. "What do you think?"

"What happened to him? Did Titus just . . . just murder him?"

The constable drew his long, bony knees up in front of him, hugging them tightly while his shoulders shook. Eventually he produced the hankie again and mopped his eyes and nose. He shook his head.

"No," he said, his voice nearly inaudible now with self-loathing. "The sonofabitch, he'd just flown in a group of his regular clients from somewhere around Detroit. Ovid was tired, he . . . he said he couldn't do it. He was sick with something, I don't even remember what. Pneumonia or something, I think." Jack stared out over Nicholas' shoulder for a long time. "But Titus let them go upstairs, anyway. The guys had offered him double, paid it right up front in cash. There must have been at least three of them, and they didn't want to have wasted the trip up for nothing. So Titus . . . just . . . let them go up."

Nicholas looked away at the mirrors that surrounded them on every side. Everywhere he looked he saw the same thing: the pale, frightened-looking boy and, beside him, the hunched, sobbing bundle of clothing that might have been a man.

"The guys came hurrying down the stairs after just twenty minutes or so, all of them looking as though they'd just seen some kind of ghost. They left Titus the money and tore out of here before the old bastard could even get a chance to go upstairs to check things out." Jack lifted the flask again and drank. "Ovid was up there on the bed. His face . . . oh, Jesus, his eyes were still wide-open and it looked like he had been trying to get some air into his lungs or something. But by the time Titus got to him, he wasn't breathing anymore. Not even a little."

Nicholas stared at him, unblinking, and then without speaking he stretched himself out across the floor, across from the bench where Jack was sitting. Something stiffened within him, between his haunches and his back.

The constable stirred, lifted his tear-streaked face from his hands. "Nicholas, what—what the hell are you doing?"

But he could see it clearly enough.

Nicholas was doing push-ups.

Images passed instead of minutes.

The smell of his own sweat, light and undisciplined, rising up through the air around him; the muted creak and clank of weighted cables, working in counterbalanced rhythm with his aching limbs and ligaments; the lighting, becoming a fluorescent glare, as the flesh directly beneath his eyes became increasingly mirrored with sweat. Counting off the repetitions, Nicholas eventually lost track of the passing seconds and the minutes. Time itself became something that happened between glances at the neon-faced clock above one of the mirrored walls.

He snapped his head around to look at it, the sweat-slicked strands of hair slapping against the back of his neck like a whip. It was a little after eleven.

He struggled to redirect his Titus-anger into a long series of different exercises on different machines. Today it was harder. He had recognized it from the moment he had started with the push-ups. The lean muscles in his arms and legs shot long spikes of pain through his limbs, and he would have to stop and rest, sometimes after every rep, until the cramp went away.

Half-crouched in his corner, Jack watched him and emptied the flask's contents down his throat. It seemed to Nicholas that he could drink himself to the very edge of unconsciousness, but never quite beyond it.

At noon the background squabble of Top 40 from the radio went suddenly silent. The speaker popped and hissed. *"Nicky, Jack . . . whyn't you fellas take a break down there, c'mon upstairs. Take a look outside."*

Nicholas wiped a thin sheen of perspiration from his forehead. He had been trying to do sit-ups on the incline bench, and his right leg was giving him a hard time about it. "Do you know what he's talking about?"

Jack shrugged, too drunk to coordinate it right. "Uh-uh." His face had gone pale except for a pair of scarlet spots high on his cheeks. His lips moved, trying to form words that wouldn't quite come.

Looking at him, Nicholas realized that although the constable could come and go from Titus' house, he'd made himself as much a prisoner here as he himself was.

"C'mon," he said, picking up the radio. "Let's go check this out."

Jack followed him up.

54

"*Pretty goddamn impressive, huh?*"

The kitchen air was cold compared to the gym below. Nicholas stepped into the kitchen with the radio gabbling enthusiastically under his arm, and looked outside. On the other side of the tall, mullioned kitchen windows, he could see the expanse of early winter thunderheads flattening themselves across the surface of the lake. It gave him an odd chill to see the sky that color. The clouds themselves were sheathed in a deep, mottled gray color with an odd pinkish tint beneath, where the sun had once been. Wind rattled anxiously against the panes and fell silent.

Then, before his eyes, the clouds burst open like titanic gray mattresses and began spilling out thick gusts of snow.

Behind him, back in the doorway, Nicholas heard Jack whisper out some breathless, nonsensical curse. He understood. Seeing the elements shift so radically did touch on a caveman impulse of sheer awe.

"*Guess we're looking at our first freak blizzard of the winter,*" the radio crackled. "*Lookee there, Nicky, you ever seen weather like this before? You bring this white stuff with you when you came up?*"

Nicholas laid the radio down on the kitchen table, still sweating from his interrupted workout. He stepped through the French doors into the library, unable to tear his eyes away from the coming blizzard as it spread itself out across the coastline. It was as though the library's windows had been ground into magnifying-glass convexity, enlarging the snowflakes themselves until they looked as big as seagulls, swooping and drifting wildly along the beach, then at the last minute whipping back out to disappear into the waves. They danced, lingered, scudded against the glass. Nicholas stared out at a world that was all gray and white, a world where the air was suddenly crowded, twisting with individual currents and eddies, whole constellations of crystallized light.

"Get back in the kitchen," the radio spattered at him. *"I liked you just where you were."* The speaker popped, sizzled, and continued to play static-softened refrains of some classical piece from far away, violins rising up over the low, brooding sound of cellos.

Nicholas started back toward the kitchen, where Jack was picking disinterestedly at the remains of breakfast. "I didn't know he had cameras around," Nicholas said. This could change his plans seriously.

"Oh, hell yes." The constable nodded. "He's got them through the main part of the house, anyway, running through that TV in his study. Thought you knew."

Outside, the sky had all but vanished behind sheets of white. Nicholas picked up the radio from the table, swinging it by its strap. The music faded in and out periodically, as though such grace had to come from far away from here, and could never be sustained for more than a few precious seconds, never longer.

He laid the radio down again and sat down at the table. He joined Jack in staring out at the falling snow.

The speaker crackled. It caught Titus midlaugh, broadcasting it as little snuffles of static. *"Nicky? Hey, I got something I'd like for you to hear. You're a pretty inventive kid, I know that much. And just in case you did end up laying your hands on a phone, I didn't want you to get any ideas about trying to call home. You listening?"*

Faintly through the radio's speaker, they heard a pattern of electronic beeps.

Nicholas frowned. "What was that?"

"He's dialing," Jack said listlessly, still staring out at the snow. "He's dialing on his portable phone."

55

Portion of the testimony of Shelley Danzig, October 28:

The first of the phone calls came Monday, in the early afternoon.

I was sitting on the living room couch in a sort of daze, watching the sky outside turn a cloudier and cloudier gray. North of here, I was thinking abstractly, all this rain will come down as snow. All my thoughts were coming abstractly lately, as though I couldn't bear a single pipeline running down into my core. I was aware mostly of images and sensations, detached, somehow clearer than ever before.

Besides the overwhelming grief, the obvious reason for feeling like I had left the world behind, I think part of it has to do with seeing yourself portrayed inaccurately in the paper. It sounds trivial, I know, but as I said, my mind was preoccupied with trivialities and abstractions. Reporters from Detroit had come to talk to us over the weekend, fortifying their Sunday editions with page-two photographs of Ian and me, sitting at the table with a picture of an elementary school photo of Nicholas clutched between us—the only photograph big enough, they told us, to be clear in their own picture. ''Mourning the Loss,'' the headline read. The reporters had asked if I had an even bigger picture, an eleven-by-fourteen would be optimal. The biggest pictures we have are the baby pictures that Titus brought over, but when I brought the baby pictures down, they looked at me with that polite sympathy people save up for the temporarily insane. ''Oh, we were thinking of something more contemporary than that,'' one of them said gently.

But when I thought about how we all simplify our lives, providing bigger and more inaccurate images for the world to take pictures of, it all made perfect sense to me. Why not a baby picture? Why not a wall-sized poster of another boy entirely? They would never know the Nicholas we knew.

Strange, to look back and see Ian and me trying to forge some emotion from out of our numbness. Strange and a little horrifying, I think.

Upstairs, that Monday afternoon, Ian was trying to sleep with his earplugs in. I was sitting thinking about the newspapers. I don't even think I heard the phone ringing for a long time, but gradually I became aware of some sound piercing the hood of obliviousness that I'd pulled over myself. I stood up and walked into the kitchen to pick it up. ''Hello?''

"—hello?" The voice on the end was already talking, a shrill, gasping voice whose words I didn't understand for several seconds. "Hello, Mom? Hello?"

I felt something hitch up inside of me. For a second I think I sort of grayed out.

"Mom? Mom, it's Nicholas! I'm alive! I'm alive, Mom!"

There was a long silence while my jaw unhinged. I tried to say something, but all that came through my mouth was a little creaking sound.

"Hello? Hello, Mom? Hello?"

Finally when the word came out, it was little more than a sigh. "N-Nicky . . . ?"

"Yeah, Mom! It's me! I'm here, I'm alive!"

"Where . . . where are you?" The room was swimming around me. The voice on the other end did not sound like Nicholas, but all the logistical equipment in my brain was simply fried at the moment, like a ship's navigational system when it crosses one of the poles. "Where are you, Nicholas?"

"I'm . . . I'm at Disneyland, Mom! I love it! I love it and I'm gonna stay here forever!*" The words shattered into high, manic laughter that clattered across the phone line and into my ear, drawing tears.*

I think I might have screamed. I hurled the receiver away from me, sent it bounding across the kitchen floor and stepped back clutching my arms across my chest as though it might jump up and try to bite me. But it only hung at the end of its coil. The laughing had become a mechanical chattering, like the sound of a machine gun . . . and then it ended with a click.

By the time Ian had woken up and come downstairs—it was the sensation of something striking the floor that had stirred him, he said, not the sound— I was crouched down in the far corner of the kitchen, weeping silently. Sobbing, more like it.

"What is it?" he asked. "What happened, Shel?"

*"I-I-Ian . . ." It was all I could do to lift my chin up and look at him. "It was a juh-juh-juh-*hoke *. . . a tuh-terrible . . . tuh-huh-herrible . . ."*

"Shelley?" He wrapped his arms around me and only then seemed to notice the receiver dangling down toward the kitchen floor. "Did somebody call? Was it another reporter?"

"Nuh-nuh-not a reporter . . . suh-somebody who suh-suh-suh . . . Ian, they said that they were . . . they were . . . Nuh-Nuh—"

His face went white, and every curve in his face seemed to harden and tense. It was a little like seeing plaster dry, in time-elapse photography. He stood up and walked over to the receiver. "Oh God," he said softly. "Who . . . who could be doing this? Who could be doing this to us?"

At the moment his terror was as unnerving as the call itself. "Oh, Ian . . . I was so . . . scared, I thought . . . I thought . . ."

"Shel, we're going to get through this," he told me, setting the receiver back into the cradle for a moment to comfort me. "I promise you, we can be strong, and—"

And then the phone started to ring again.

56

"K nock it off!" Nicholas shouted at the radio. "You're gonna drive them crazy!"

At the other side of the table, Jack jumped in his seat, made a soft, hungover sound like *ohhh* and began to rotate his fingertips against his temples. "Hey, Nick? Let's—let's not shout for a while, all right?"

Nicholas thumbed the volume switch up, but all he could hear was the phone still ringing on the other end. His parents hadn't picked it up this time.

"Looks like they're not gonna answer it again!" Nicholas yelled.

Titus' voice crackled sadly through the speaker. *"Oh well, we'll try it later . . . or, what the hell, maybe once or twice did the trick."* More snuffled-up static-laughter. *"Either way, Nicky boy, if you try calling back home anytime soon, you'll probably push them right over the brink. Your folks don't seem to be copin' too well with your recent departure, huh? Too bad, too bad. I'll be sure to express my condolences on Thursday."*

His voice popped out, replaced by abrupt overtones of Canadian radio.

"That *asshole!*" Nicholas resisted the urge to pick up the radio and pitch it across the kitchen. Hearing his mother's startled voice, even through muffled layers of static, had brought an unexpected flood of emotion through him, and he felt dangerously close to tears himself. He glanced over at Jack, who at first appeared to have passed out with his eyes wide-open. "Where is he, anyway? Back in his study?"

"Sit down, Nicholas," the constable said, without looking away from the falling snow. There was a deadness in his voice, as though memories of Ovid had wrung every remaining drop of emotion from his scrawny frame, leaving only whiskey and exhaustion. *Wait*, Nicholas thought,

don't you have any sadness left for me? I'm the last boy. Didn't you save any
sadness for me?

"What are you going to do, Jack, shoot me? Huh? You're just gonna
pull out your gun and—"

"Oh, shut up." The constable's head sank back into the crook of his
arm. "Whyn't you have a cup of coffee or something."

"I hate coffee! Coffee sucks!" This wasn't exactly the truth, but the
situation seemed to call for absolutes. He was furious again, as angry as
he'd been when he started doing push-ups this morning. "Where's
Titus? I'm gonna go back to his study, and—"

"Nicholas, he might not even be in his study."

He stopped. "What? Why not?"

"He could be anywhere in the house. The place itself is a lot larger
than you think. You probably haven't been through half of it yet, even
after you took that little tour of yours yesterday. He's got at least one
wing added onto the third floor that even I haven't seen in years."

"Third floor?" Nicholas asked. It occurred to him that he had never
seen the house from the outside, and as a result he had no idea of its
actual perimeters. "There's another whole floor above where my bedroom is?"

Jack nodded into the crook of his arm. "With skylights. I'd guess
he's probably got an office up there, too, somewhere, with surveillance
cameras where he just keeps track of things and talks to his stockbroker
in New York."

"Things . . . you mean, me-things."

"Yeah, you-things." Jack tottered unsteadily to his feet and brought
down a clean white mug from one of the kitchen cupboards behind him.
"Sure I can't change your mind about that coffee?"

Nicholas let him fill the cup and took a sip. The last time he had
drunk coffee had been back with Anthem when she told him the history
of Saint Jack and his three children. That coffee had been instant, and
Titus' coffee—fresh-ground, he concluded, from the fine black grounds
scattered across the counter next to the coffeemaker—was much better.
He brought the cup to his lips again, his gaze returning to the falling
snow outside the windows. It moved so silently, so smoothly, billowing
down across the rocks and gray sand below and then disappearing into
the waves far below that for a time he was almost mesmerized by it.

"I'll tell you something," Jack said conversationally, in a tone that
Nicholas liked better than his previous emotional numbness. The only

other sound was the soft drone of the transistor radio, and Jack's voice had an odd resonance to it in contrast to the great, silent turbulence spilling out across the sky beyond the windows. "Titus thinks this weather is just a freak storm, but if it keeps up like this for the rest of the day, there's a fairly good chance that they'll have to shut down Kinderhook tomorrow."

"What's Kinderhook?"

"Kinderhook Municipal Airport, over in Harrisport. Where the Canadians are supposed be flying in on Wednesday."

"The Canadians?" Nicholas lifted his head. "So they wouldn't be able to get here before Titus drives down for my funeral?"

Jack shrugged, another everyday gesture that his drunkenness transformed into a fractured-looking dance move. He scratched at his grizzled chin. "Can't land a Learjet in the middle of a blizzard, no matter how good your pilot is. We'll just wait and see. But I bet you dollars to doughnuts that Titus is going to keep calling it a passing storm for just as long as he can get away with it."

"He stands to lose a lot of money on me, huh?"

"Well, yeah, but . . . it's not really just the money. Most of his money comes from investments he's been making over the last twenty or thirty years. He's set for life, no matter how extravagantly he decides to spend it. Money isn't so much the object as . . . you know . . ."

"Love," Nicholas finished for him. His heart was cold, as cold as it had ever been in his life. "Yeah, I guess with something like this, you have to do it for the love of the thing."

The constable looked startled. "Well, Jesus, Nicholas, I wouldn't call it *love.*"

"Well, what would you call it? He did it to Ovid, he did it to Gertrude, you're watching him do it to me . . . if he's doing it by accident, then it sure is a coincidence, huh? Three times in a row? That's dedication."

"But love . . ." Jack raised one hand, looking comically like a poet preparing a formal oration. "I mean, love is something else, isn't it? Love . . ."

Pop! The radio's speaker. Both of them stopped what they were doing and looked down at it expectantly, until Titus' voice came crackling out. *"You gettin' bored yet? Jack, you might consider fixin' the kid some lunch. He looks hungry."*

"I hope you get leprosy," Nicholas told the radio conversationally. "As a matter of fact, I hope—"

"Good thing I can't read lips, Nicky boy, or I guess my ears'd be burning right now, huh?" More snuffled-up laughter from the radio's speaker, and then the voice dropped down into total seriousness. *"Jack, get your drunken ass up and make the kid a san'wich or something. It's been three hours since breakfast. He looks starved."*

Nicholas rubbed his eyes. "Tell him where to shove it, Jack. Go ahead."

But the constable had already stood up automatically and gone into the kitchen to assemble different high-calorie combinations for lunch.

57

The storm continued throughout the afternoon, and by Monday evening the entire shoreline of Whitefish Bay was blanketed in shallow drifts of white. Wind whooped in the house's eaves, rattling the ice-stippled screens and making the entire structure creak faintly on its foundation like a not-entirely-trustworthy oceangoing vessel. Occasionally the lights dimmed, but never for more than a second or two. Still, when it happened, Nicholas and Jack exchanged an anxious glance that never had time to mean anything.

At dusk they had moved into the library, where the constable spread a Trivial Pursuit board in the middle of the eight-by-fifteen-foot Persian rug on the hardwood floor. Next to them the transistor radio sat, gabbling out the next day's Canadian school closings, signals bleeding over from across the border.

At the moment, Nicholas was more interested in the radio than the game. Despite the storm, he'd discovered, the surface of the lake still acted like a natural transmitter, bringing in deejays from as far away as Thunder Bay to the west. It gave him a passing sense of having escaped for just a moment. On the far left end of the dial, very faintly, he even had been able to hear voices murmuring in French.

"—gonna answer the question or not?" Jack was asking him, from the other side of the board. "Nicholas? Yoo-hoo." He glanced at the card. "You listening?"

Nicholas sighed. He had discovered, to his own muted dismay, that

Jack Tornquist was quite nearly unbeatable at Trivial Pursuit. Jack had
insisted that this was due to the fact that alcohol enhanced his brain's
"information receptors."

"Yeah, okay." Nicholas stopped fiddling with the radio dial and
glanced up at Jack half-sprawled across the rug. "What is it again?"

"It's ridiculously easy, that's what it is. Okay, what Hollywood legend
starred in over forty Alfred Hitchcock films?"

Nicholas blinked. His brain offered up a single, four-color image of a
blond woman with an early sixties haircut, her arms crossed over her
face, being attacked by birds, a movie poster he'd seen once at a brass-
railing and potato-skins restaurant with his parents. He shrugged. "I
think this game discriminates against kids."

Jack grunted and tossed the card aside without providing the answer.
His attitude seemed to be if you didn't know it, you didn't deserve to
know it. He rolled the dice and then moved around the circle five spaces,
landing on brown.

Nicholas drew a card. "In the second level of Sonic the Hedgehog,
what sort of—"

Jack was waving his hands. "Wait a second, wait a second, what the
hell's this Sonic the Hedgehog?"

Nicholas sighed again. "I was just trying to make it a little more
evenly matched." He looked down at the real question printed on the
card. "In Emily Brontë's famous—"

"Bron-*tay*," Jack corrected.

"I haven't even finished asking the question yet."

"I'm just telling you how to pronounce it," the constable told him.
"And the answer is Heathcliff, by the way. I've had this one before."

Nicholas groaned as Jack picked up the dice again, rattled them in
his cupped hands and shook out a pair of ones. "Uh-oh." He blinked
down at them suspiciously. "Snake eyes."

And the lights went out.

58

Portion of the testimony of Ian Danzig, October 26:
It was as though the elements were conspiring to wear us down.

After the third phone call on Monday night—by then I was just picking up the phone, not touching the receiver to my ear, just hanging up as soon as the voice impersonating Nicholas started to gibber away at us—we called the police. It was past midnight when they finished.

"It's just like in the movies," the officer told us, late that night, once the tracing equipment had been installed into the phone itself. Mentally I had started to refer to him as Officer O'Course. "You've got to try to keep the caller on the line long enough for the thing to work. Michigan Bell gives the average time of a little over a minute to trace back any domestic call." He gave a humorless little smile. "But o'course my personal opinion is the little bastards doing this have already found something else to amuse themselves with."

"It . . . it didn't sound like a child," Shelley told him.

"Ma'am?"

"She's right," I said, startling myself with the sound of my own voice. I hadn't written myself any lines in this scene, except the occasional nod or grunt. "I picked it up once, too, and in a way, that was the worst part. It sounded like an adult—male or female, you couldn't tell, because it was so high-pitched—but an adult imitating a child."

The cop closed his eyes. For an instant he seemed to have taken all our sorrows onto his own shoulders, just to try them on for size. "Jesus, there's people out there . . . you don't like to think of them living here in Portage, but I guess they're everywhere. And o'course, the kidnapping did appear in most of the big papers. There was an article in the New York Times, wasn't there?"

I nodded. Shelley didn't do anything.

"Well, we'll be in touch, o'course." He zipped up his jacket. "And maybe you two might want to consider sleeping in shifts. You know, somebody stays up and keeps an eye on the line, the other person gets some rest. Your body needs it, you know, even if your mind doesn't feel like it."

"Of course," I replied automatically.

But after the police left, neither of us went further away from the kitchen than the living room couch, where we sat together, silently, not touching each other.

Outside, what had been a crystal-clear October evening had begun to cloud over. The moon had disappeared behind an apparently endless bank of clouds. I glanced at the digitalized weather patterns on the television screen between sweeps of the radar signal. The outline of the state was being obscured, slowly but inexorably, by colliding warm and cold fronts. Further north, I thought, they'd have snow.

Down here, it would come as rain.

59

Nicholas was halfway across the library when the power came back on again.

Behind him, Jack's voice was lifeless again, and cold sober. "Move and I'll shoot you, I mean it."

"Jeez, Jack—" He looked over his shoulder.

"He's dead serious, Nicky," the radio crackled along cheerily behind Jack. *"See the gun?"*

Nicholas turned around completely, his brief burst of adrenaline spent. Twenty feet away, the constable had his revolver out, his arms extended. He didn't look too drunk to hit his target at this range.

"Where were you gonna go, anyway?" Titus' voice rasped through the radio's speaker. *"The only place I can think of is through one of the windows, and I wouldn't recommend that. Gertrude tried it, and it didn't get her very far at all. You get cut up by the glass, then when you hit the ground you break your legs. Nope, not recommended. Zero stars for the window idea. Two thumbs down."*

Nicholas turned and walked back into the center of the library, scanning the walls and bookshelves for the camera. He couldn't see it.

Jack holstered his pistol. He gave Nicholas a hurt, things-were-going-so-well glare as Nicholas sat back down in front of the game board. They stared at each other for a long moment, neither of them sure whether Titus had finished talking.

"Finish your game, Jack," Titus' voice said through the radio's speaker, *"then lock Nicky back up in his room. Afterward I want you to go out to the*

shed and make sure there's plenty of fuel in the backup generator. You got that?''

"Tell him to stick it up his butt, Jack," Nicholas said sourly. "Go ahead. He can't hear you, anyway."

Jack just raised his hand, his thumb and forefinger circled into an OK gesture. The transistor radio popped, then resumed broadcasting the eclectic mingling of U.S. and Canadian signals.

"Roll the dice and pretend to keep playing," Jack said, not looking up from the board. His voice had changed. "Titus can't read lips."

"I'm sick of this stupid g—" He stopped. "Wait a second, why did you tell me he can't read lips?"

"Because maybe I've got something really important to say right now." The constable was looking down at the game board. "But I'm not going to start talking until you sit down and roll the dice."

Nicholas picked up the dice, shook them and moved his piece across the spaces, waiting while Jack pulled a card from the box in front of him. Just like that, Jack had decided to help him. No bargaining, no arguments, no promises.

"So," the constable said, as though he were reading a question, "you think you have a way I can help you without him knowing?"

Nicholas paused, scratched his head, pretended to be thinking of an answer. His heart rate had started to quicken. "Yes, I do."

Jack nodded and tossed the card aside while Nicholas rolled again, moved his piece and waited. Jack drew another card, pausing to take a quick drink from the flask next to him. "Obviously it can't involve telephones," he said at last. "So tell me when and how you want to do it."

"Wednesday. And it's really simple."

The constable made a quick gesture as if in disbelief at Nicholas' sudden burst of good luck. "Okay," he said. "Roll again."

Outside, it was still snowing.

60

Portion of the testimony of Shelley Danzig, October 28:

Tuesday was workday. Not in the sense that it had ever been before, though: Ian and I stayed inside all day while the autumn rain first drizzled and then lashed against the windows. We cleaned house. Several of our friends who had gone away for the weekend—a couple of them on the Canadian Color Tour that we had planned for ourselves this weekend—came home and read the newspaper for the first time in three days, so there was a new flurry of phone calls which Ian and I took turns answering. At first we were hesitant, not wanting to pick up the receiver, but there were no more phone calls claiming to be Nicholas. So we worked a phone shift, though we should've been able to jury-rig an answering machine that could hold up our feeble end of the conversation.

I found Ian crouched in Nicky's room, looking at his books and toys, late in the morning. He found me there, sitting on his bed and looking at his comic book collection, later that afternoon.

Still, the rain kept coming down. Sometime around four o'clock, Ian unplugged the phone, and we lay down together on Nicky's bed, exhausted by tears and grief and overloaded with the sympathetic words of everybody in the world, and the aftereffects of Monday's awful joke. I was waiting on a knife's edge for the inevitable, the first salesman who knocked on the door, the first friend of Nicky's to call and ask, in innocent oblivion, if he could come out and ride bikes . . . even the next time that the sun had the audacity to rise on the eastern horizon, and dare to start a new day, when we were still, it seemed like, in the absolute blackest night of our mutual sadness and loss.

But no salesmen called on Tuesday. No friends of Nicky's rang the doorbell. Late that night, with the sounds of rainwater trickling through the drainage pipes and off the roof, Ian and I stumbled back to bed and slept like we hadn't slept in days.

And when I awoke in the middle of the night, it was still raining.

"They've lost power in a lot of places upstate," Ian told me, "but now they're starting to get it back. We'll be inheriting the storm tonight."

"I hope we can at least keep the lights on through the service Thursday afternoon," I said.

I can't remember which one of us had the idea first about the candles. Ian suggested that we bring flashlights in case the power went off in the funeral home, and at one point we were actually going to call some of the people who we knew were coming, just to let them know. Then it struck me—struck one of us, anyway—that if the power went out we could just use those cheap hooded candles that they use for candlelight services. The odds were against anything like that happening, but if it did I wanted to be prepared for it.

We called the man who did custodial work for the funeral home. He said they had plenty of candles we could use, although he, too, doubted we'd need them. It was his opinion that the weather would clear overnight.

But in the very early hours of Wednesday morning, when I woke up in a cold, irrational sweat, the clock radio was flashing midnight at us.

Outside, even the streetlights were totally dark.

And it was still raining.

61

O n Tuesday, Jack disappeared.

What woke Nicholas in the morning was not Titus' voice from the radio, which sat serenely on the chair next to his bed, but a steady, mechanical roaring from outside the house, as though a car without a muffler had pulled into Titus' driveway and sat there, endlessly revving its engine. He started to sit up, then realized too late it had been a mistake. His muscles shouted at him, all at once.

"Oohhhh." He flopped back down onto the pillow, listening to the roaring from below, and finally reached over to switch on the lamp next to him. The light came on, but it was pulsating faintly, graying out every few seconds.

The generator, that's what it is.

Now Nicholas understood why the old man had installed it outside of the main house. Even sequestered in an equipment shed in the corner of his property, the thing was still obnoxiously loud. He wondered if Jack had fueled it up as Titus had requested last night.

Nicholas cautiously stretched out his legs as far as he could under the covers, wincing at the familiar tension awakening in his hamstrings and thighs. He could feel himself getting a little bigger down there, particularly in his swollen hamstrings. Ian Danzig would be proud, he thought with a smirk.

Carefully he choreographed his movements out of the bed, trying to keep his arms and legs as straight as possible. But there was no way to leave the bed without bending his knees, which meant tension on the hamstrings, so he slid out as quickly as he could and locked his knees as soon as his feet touched the floor. The pain was annoying more than anything. *This is stupid. Nobody should wake up feeling this sore.* He glanced at the radio next to the bed.

"Morning, Titus," he told the radio.

The speaker whistled and fizzed uncertainly.

Nicholas lumbered across the squeaky floor like a man on short stilts. *Creak-yawww . . . screep . . .* The noises of the room around him were all familiar now, mapped out into a comforting geography of antiquarian wood and plumbing.

He walked over to the window.

Outside, seeping through the slanted venetian blinds, he already sensed a certain blueness in the morning light that accompanied fresh snowfall. Still, as he slipped his first two fingers between the slats and peeled them open, what he saw outside surprised him. The world was utterly white. Thick streamers of dry snow gusted across the window directly in front of his face, and stretched out behind them he could see a landscape sculpted by wind and ice, rows of drifts rising up, hunched across the cliffside and down to the beach. The surf was slate-colored, the waves marbled with white, like deep cracks in smoked glass.

No school today, he thought, and turned back to the room.

No fresh clothes laid out for him this morning either. No smell of breakfast, prepared and waiting for him downstairs.

"What's going on, Titus?" he asked the radio. "Jack quit on you?"

Only static from the radio.

He stopped halfway back to the bed. Once verbalized, the idea of Jack's disappearance suddenly frightened him. What if Jack *had* decided to quit on him—on both of them—after last night? Jack had been amenable to the plan, had agreed that it could work. But what if he had gone home afterward, stopped off at the bar on his way to refill his flask, continued drinking . . . Nicholas could almost *see* the constable's resolve evaporating before his very eyes. Or what if he hadn't lost his nerve, but had just passed out on the barroom floor and knocked himself out? Or spilled out everything to a sympathetic bartender?

Or picked last night to put the barrel of his own gun in his mouth?

That possibility chilled Nicholas most of all, because it rang most true. The constable's mood swings were enough to make a person seasick. Imagine he starts crying, he starts tormenting himself with thoughts of Gertrude and Ovid, and this time he's just unable to stop. He pulls out his revolver, shakes out four of the shells, gives the cylinder a spin and flips it back into place, then raises the pistol back up . . .

"Nicky!"

He jumped, then stared down at the blaring speaker of the radio.

"Good mornin', kiddo! Today is the last day of the rest of your life! I'll make sure to bring you a souvenir from your own funeral when I go down tomorrow!"

Something was wrong. Titus' voice was straining, working too hard for its carefree tone. They both knew it.

"It's Jack, isn't it?" Nicholas asked the radio, with readily dawning certainty. "You don't know where he is either, do you?"

"—expect you know the routine by now, don't you? Just like Sunday night and Monday, get down to the gym and get that heart pumping! Let's go, kiddo! Up 'n' at 'em!"

Nicholas was left with yesterday's clothes. Something fell out of the back pocket of the sweatpants. The cardboard matches. He kicked them under the bed and pulled the sweatpants up, tucking in his T-shirt, then pulling up the gym shorts and slipping into his shoes.

He picked up the radio again and walked from one corner of the room to another, as though he could somehow detect where Titus was broadcasting from in the house. But the signal remained equally clear in every corner.

"Jack will be by later this morning to check up on you. It's good to see you two gettin' along, Nicky. Playin' games." The speaker went silent for a moment. *"Now get your ass in gear. Don't make me tell you twice."*

Nicholas said nothing. Talking back had lost its novelty. With the radio hanging by its strap from his hand, he walked out of the bedroom and down the long corridor, the framework of the house groaning faintly in the wind outside. Tall oak doors stood on either side of the hall, doors he had never tried before, and he wondered which one of them led up to the third floor of the house. He knew which one was the bathroom and which was the room with the photographs, but beyond that . . .

"Keep movin', Nicky."

But with Jack gone, and the plan on hold, Nicholas didn't feel like acting the part of the obedient son anymore. He took another step, his eyes searching the arches of the ceiling for the surveillance cameras that

Titus had to be using. The rows of flambeaux along either wall cast only dim fans of light across the faded wallpaper, so that the ceiling arches overhead were mostly obscured by shadow. He turned around and looked back down the way he'd come, and up toward the darkly ribbed ceiling, and forced a foolish-looking grin across his face. When the radio remained silent, he returned to his original position and grinned again in that direction.

"What's so goddamn funny, kiddo?"

So the camera was in front of him. His eyes swept the arches ahead, and finally he saw it, the faint glimmer of a lens set back into the ceiling like a single dusty eye.

He turned to his immediate right and tried the door. It swung open into another bedroom, this one uncluttered with even so much as a mattress, the single window boarded up. He knew the next door down was the bathroom, and across from that, the room with Jack's piano and the Gertrude boxes. Beyond that, there was just the stairwell leading down. But what about the other direction?

As he turned back, the radio snarled, *"You're not gonna find anything but locked doors down this way, kiddo. Best just to turn around and do as you're told."*

From outside in the utility shed, Nicholas heard the generator coughing, faltering, and all at once the flambeaux faded out to nearly total blackness. The hallway, without a single doorway to permit it sunlight, sank into the dark. He heard a sharp squawk of surprise from the radio, but a second later the generator got a foothold and the power surged back on again. Through the radio's speaker, Titus was cursing softly and extravagantly. Nicholas realized that as long as the old man had to depend on the generator, his surveillance equipment, as well as the staircase elevator, would only be of moderate use to him.

Conclusion: he had to be down on the first floor. Where he couldn't be trapped by a blackout.

Nicholas continued to hobble his way up the hall in the direction he'd come, rattling doorknobs as he went. He could afford to take his time. Titus wouldn't risk riding the staircase elevator up to stop him if there was a possibility that he and his wheelchair might be stranded up here when the generator finally ran out of gas.

It was the first advantage that Nicholas had enjoyed in a while. He intended to exploit it.

"I'm warning you, Nicky . . . go downstairs," the radio snapped, sounding more anxious now. *"I know exactly where you are."*

Nicholas ignored him and kept walking away from the staircase. He wanted to find the doorway that led up to the surveillance room on the third level of the house, where the skylights were supposed to be. Whatever else the space above him offered, it meant a greater freedom from Titus, a delicious sense of climbing his way into a corner of the house where the old man himself wouldn't dare follow. From there his plans blurred out of focus. Maybe he would find a telephone up there. Without Titus hot on his heels, there might be time to convince his parents it was really him.

He listened to the floor creaking under his feet, enjoyed the patient, measured sound of his own intrusion deeper into the house's secret places.

The radio crackled in his hand. *"Last warning, Nicky. Turn around and go downstairs. I mean it now."*

But he could see it in front of himself now, the last door on the left, the doorway that had to lead up to the third floor. A tablet of bright daylight shone from underneath the door and spilled across the thread-bare carpet in front of him, light that had to come from the skylights that Jack had mentioned. Working his way forward, it occurred to Nicholas that he could try smashing his way through it if he had to, if it wasn't unlocked. The top two stories of the house belonged to him.

The light fixtures down the hall began to dim again as he reached out for the doorknob. He took another step, bringing his right foot together next to his left—

Whamp! A muffled gunshot exploded through the half-darkness.

He jumped back from the doorway, his fingertips tingling with shock. Halfway down the hall to his right, motes of dust from the carpet spun through a pencil-thin beam of light that shone from the ceiling. The beam passed down through the gray light of the corridor and disappeared into the floorboards in front of him.

Nicholas stared at the light, transfixed. Titus was using the cameras to shoot wide, obviously firing only warning shots in an attempt to scare him down. Can't harm the merchandise and all of that. But in his rage, the old man was taking stupid risks. What if he hit Nicholas by accident?

Whamp! Another beam of light sprang up behind him, intersecting the first at just about head level.

"Go downstairs, Nicky," the radio growled. It sounded enraged now, beyond humor of even the darkest variety. *"Do not make me keep shooting."*

Nicholas looked at the twin beams of light crisscrossing the hallway.

He wondered if Titus really *was* upstairs, shooting down at him, and he realized there was really no way of telling. The bullets had gone through both floor and ceiling, and he had only heard them in passing.

"Goddammit, kiddo, you are really pushing your luck—"

He heard the fury mounting in the voice and leapt back from the forbidden end of the hallway at the last second, dropping the radio in his haste.

Wham! Wham! Wham! The dim end of the corridor behind him was suddenly a cage of skewed white lines. There was a brief caesura, no longer than a second or two, and then the automatic blasted twice again, and two more beams sprung across the gray light. Almost on cue, the generator outside began to pound louder, as though the heart of the house had been alarmed by Titus' gunshots. The flambeaux stuttered and then blazed brightly all down the length of the hallway, so that the beams from the skylight on the third floor faded into obscurity behind him.

Nicholas glanced back at the radio lying on its side, where he'd dropped it. He could hardly hear it over the generator's racket.

"Pick it up," the speaker was snapping at him, *"and get downstairs, Nicky. Or else the next shot I fire is going straight down your throat."*

Nicholas nodded to himself, took the three steps he needed to reach for the radio. He still didn't think Titus would shoot him deliberately, but his aim might slip.

. . . straight down your throat.

Nicholas took some comfort in what he'd discovered; Titus was shooting from above.

Hands half-raised in the air, he crept back toward the stairs and started down.

62

The generator was louder on the first floor.

Most of the light on the ground level was natural. The sunshine filtered through opaque curtains in the front hall, bathing the hardwood floors with a gauzy white glow, so that the kitchen lights stuttered and surged with little consequence around him. But every digital clock—

the microwave, the automatic coffeemaker, the stovetop—was blinking intermittent midnight. They would let him know when the power went out.

He would also be able to sense when the power started to die by the sounds the generator itself made outside. He felt the radio crackling in his hand and held it up closer to his ear.

"Go on down. Go start liftin' those weights. You know the drill."

But Nicholas lingered at the top of the stairs leading down from the kitchen, swinging back and forth slowly with his fingers clasped around the doorjamb. He knew Titus could see him from at least one angle, from the camera in the library, but he thought that the old man might expect him to be reluctant. The muscles in his arms and legs felt pinched and weak. During the last two days, he hadn't been stretching out properly or taking the extra winding-down time that he needed, and Titus knew it. Just the notion of going back down for another two-hour workout made his body howl in resistance. And with Jack missing, who knew if there would ever be an end to it?

"—guess you ain't been listening to me lately," the old man was complaining, only half-audible now. *"I ain't just yappin' to hear myself—"*

Impulsively Nicholas switched the radio off. Cutting the voice off midsentence brought back a faint echo of the liberation he'd felt stalking through the forbidden corner of the second-floor hallway. As an excuse, he thought, he could always tell Titus that he hadn't been able to hear him over the roar of the generator, or that the batteries had simply died. He wished he'd thought of it earlier.

Walking over to the freezer, he got out a wax pouch of black espresso beans from the inside of the door and poured them into the coffee grinder left out from yesterday's breakfast. The grinder was a stainless-steel cylinder, sleek and featureless except for its brand name, a German brand that Nicholas didn't recognize. The beans were cold and black. Lying in the elegant shape of the grinder, they looked like part of some modern sculpture.

He pressed down on the top of the grinder, listening to the uneven droning sound it made in tune with the unsteady flow of electricity through the house. When the beans were ground, he dumped the thin powder into the gold mesh filter and started a pot of coffee with no idea whether or not he would actually drink any of it once it was brewed. It was more a ritual he wanted to act out for the cameras. He could feel Titus watching all of this from upstairs, anticipating his moves one at a time, like the stylized steps of some larger dance. He was aware that he was acting differently because of the cameras, putting on a small show of rebellion to mask the greater rebellion growing in his mind. Maybe Jack's disappearance had changed what Titus would expect from him.

He sat at the kitchen table watching it snow as the coffeemaker gargled. Like the transistor radio, it was something he felt rather than actually heard, because of the roar of the generator. Gradually the kitchen began to fill with the smell of strong black coffee.

He stared out at the silently falling snow. *The generator* . . .

After a few minutes he found himself wondering where exactly the utility shed was located. He stood up again and put his nose to the cold glass, his breath spreading out in front of him. Although the generator sounded nearby, he couldn't see it from this angle. It had to be on the west side of the house.

He walked back up the front hallway, toward the heavy wooden coat tree where the greasy CAT cap hung on one brass hook, and turned left through another pair of French doors, divided into squares of beveled glass, into a large drawing room where he hadn't been before now.

He stepped inside and shut the double doors behind him.

The floor in this room was bare and very cold, tile inlaid with polished slabs of smooth marble. *I'd like to see him shoot through this*, Nicholas thought, looking down at his own shape reflected vaguely at his feet. The room itself was drafty, almost to the point where he could see his breath, but without any discernible source. It was more like a museum's permanent chill. He could understand why Titus would keep the doors shut.

From its furnishings he guessed this might be the room where Titus entertained his wealthier clientele, a sort of greenroom where drinks were served before the main event took place in the bedroom upstairs. A plushly upholstered divan sat in one corner, flanked by a matching ottoman and an antique recliner, and to his left he could see yet another set of glass doors with the terra-cotta dining room on the other side. Bulky chiffon drapes were gathered with tasseled cords over the windows.

The pounding of the generator had become even louder here.

Nicholas pushed the curtain aside and looked down at the view below, to the west. Tall, white-jacketed pines jutted up from the rocky shelf that separated Titus' house from the unpaved road beyond, spreading their skirts across the length of the property. Their green needles were only visible in small patches, where the snow had accumulated and finally dropped away. Between their branches Nicholas saw the distinct slant of a corrugated metal roof, covered in white. Icicles clung from its edges. Semitransparent trickles of diesel vapor rose from the shed's metal seams, wafting out between the trees. The utility shed.

Lodged in a snowdrift just a few feet in front of the structure, partially swallowed up by blue shadow, was a splash of yellow and red.

It was a gasoline can, mostly buried in snow.

The drift where it lay had turned a crystallized amber color, where the fuel had spilled out through the can's plastic nozzle. Had the constable left it out there by accident? It didn't make sense, especially with the gasoline slopped everywhere. The can wasn't full now, certainly, but when Jack dropped it, it probably was. Why would the constable drop a full can of gas and leave it out there?

"He *wouldn't*," Nicholas whispered to himself, the words becoming a patch of fog on the glass before him.

Not unless he had some kind of accident out there or something, his mind continued. *And he must have, because that generator sounds like it's running on fumes by now . . . if that. Does Titus know about this?*

No. If Titus knew, then he wouldn't be upstairs on the third floor, where the final power outage could leave him stranded.

A second thought, close on the heels of that one: what if Jack was already dead of exposure, out in the snow? Nicholas couldn't see a body out there next to the gas can, but maybe the snow had already drifted up deep enough to cover him, or maybe the constable had managed to crawl behind the shed, hoping for shelter, and simply passed out there to die of exposure, tiny blue icicles hardening around the edges of his beard.

That's a lot of maybes. Question is, what are you going to do about all of this?

What else could he do right now? Only one thing was absolutely certain: the power was going to go out, in this house, and very soon.

Nicholas let the curtain drop, turned around and froze.

On the other side of the French doors, Titus was hunched in his wheelchair, staring at Nicholas through the squares of beveled glass. He lifted the chrome-plated automatic from his lap and tapped its barrel softly against the glass, then pushed the door partly open.

"Okay, Nicky," he said tonelessly. "Let's eat."

63

The old man looked older than ever, pale and exhausted, his clothes reeking of old smoke and stale sweat.

Also, as they moved back up the front hallway toward the kitchen, Nicholas realized how loud the oxygen tank was hissing. Titus was rolling along behind him with the gun aimed at his back, so he couldn't actually see the tank's gauge, but he guessed that the needle had to be quivering somewhere near its maximum calibration point. The rubber tubes in the old man's nose sounded like the high-pressure air hose at a gas station. In its way, the tank sounded as though it were screaming.

"I'm not hungry," he said as Titus followed him up the hall. "I lost my appetite when you started shooting at me upstairs."

Titus was silent.

"It was really stupid of you, you know?" Nicholas told him. "I mean, what if you miscalculated and really hit me up there, then what would you tell the Canadians when they showed up? Sorry, guys, I accidentally shot your new toy?"

No response from behind him. It was as though shutting off the radio had actually shut down Titus' chatter in real life as well. It made Nicholas even more nervous.

He walked around to the far side of the kitchen table and stood watching the old man direct his wheelchair over to the coffeemaker. Holding the automatic steady in his left hand, Titus poured himself a cup with his right and took a sip, then shook his head. "You used too many goddamn beans. Too strong."

"I've never made coffee before."

"I wasn't gonna shoot you up there, by the way," Titus muttered, bringing the cup to his lips again. "Not that you couldn't use a lesson in obedience, but when I do, I want to watch you bleed with my own eyes, right here in living color, and not through some goddamn video monitor." He took another sip from the mug and his lips thinned into a grimace. "My God, but that's bitter. What'd you use in the grinder, birch bark? Sweet *Jesus*."

Nicholas stood for a second listening to the tank whistle and squeal. "The Canadians aren't coming, are they?"

"Not with the weather like it is, they ain't."

"So what's going to happen next? I already told you, I'm not hungry for lunch. So now you're going to shoot me?"

"Not unless you try to run," Titus said, turning his wheelchair to face the table. "C'mere where I can see you better. Out from behind the table. Come on."

Nicholas walked to the center of the kitchen, his eyes fixed on the barrel of Titus' gun as it followed him across the floor.

"Stop right there." Titus directed the wheelchair backward, then began to circle him. There was a long silence while Titus looked him up and down from different angles, inspecting him like an item he was considering purchasing. "You're already starting to bulk up," he said at last, with a trace of satisfaction. "You've been working hard downstairs. You're angry. That helps, doesn't it?"

Now it was Nicholas' turn to be silent. He watched as the old man's wheelchair did another slow half-circle around him.

"See, now, Gertrude wasn't ever angry, at least not on the outside. And Ovid, well, he was angry on and off until he died, but he never learned how to direct it. You're different from them. I guess I knew that all along."

"Let me go, then," Nicholas said.

"No." Titus stopped the chair and shook his head. "No, I'll never make that mistake again." He wheeled back to the counter and set down his mug. "See, you're too beautiful." He reached back and found a second mug and filled it. "You want sugar? Course you do, you're a kid, 'n' kids love sugar." He spooned in several loads of white granulated powder from a porcelain dish next to the coffeemaker and handed the mug across. "You see, Nicky, sometimes you give away something too quick, thinkin' you're making the right decision at the time, and that feeling of loss, it doesn't come back for years and years. I gave you up when I shouldn't have. Whether it was guilt or love, I dunno, but it was the wrong thing to do. Havin' you back here again feels like the right thing . . . at least as right as anything's felt for me in a long time. You're the best of the three. And now you're home again."

Nicholas lifted the cup with both hands and drank. It was still very bitter, even after Titus' sweetening, but it did something to alleviate the chill in his bones.

Titus began to circle him again. The oxygen tank hissed. "Which takes us back to the question, I guess, of what's gonna happen next. We both know the facts: the weather's only gonna get worse, the Canadians aren't gonna be flying in until later this week, maybe not till next Monday or Tuesday. Jack's out there somewhere, maybe he's run away, maybe he's tits-up on the barroom floor somewhere, I don't know. If he's not back here by tonight, I'll have to fax a handful of photos of him to the state police headquarters in the Sault, I guess. I'm not looking forward to it. In the meantime, that generator's gonna run out of gas. And I've got a funeral to go to tomorrow." He stopped the wheelchair. "I guess that about covers it, doesn't it?"

Nicholas took another swallow of coffee. There was a chalky aftertaste that he hadn't noticed before.

"Y'know, Nicky, it ain't easy trying to sleep with that godforsaken thing roarin' away out in the utility shed," Titus said. "Me, I'm used to it—I usually have to use it every winter—but in the beginning the thing used to keep me awake all night. I was thinking you wouldn't have any trouble sleeping either, because of those pills we've been giving you . . . but then I found your little stockpile upstairs. I guess you haven't been taking your pills like you should have. That's okay." He smiled, displaying the row of yellow teeth. "We can find other ways to keep you in bed. If we hold off on the food a little bit—just a day or two—maybe then you'll show me some fucking respect."

Nicholas blinked, and watched the phosphorescent spots dance fleetingly in front of his eyes. Titus' voice still seemed to be droning on somewhere, like a voice in the back of a cave. What he wasn't so sure about was the rest of the room, where the constant rumbling of the generator had faded into the background, where *everything* had faded until it was just a ghost of its former self.

He watched with something like fascination as his fingers came partially uncurled and the mug dropped, shattered and burst across the kitchen floor.

64

Later, as the blackness began to shrink back into the corners of Nicholas' vision, he realized that it wasn't the generator, the burning pain in his arms and legs or even the hunger that had first brought him back.

It was the sound of Titus' voice in his study, across the room.

He looked around and saw that he was back in the library, spread-eagled across the Persian rug where he and Jack had been playing Trivial Pursuit the night before. His arms and legs had been tied off loosely with lengths of spongy rubber tubing. He was surprised to find he wasn't in much pain, except for the hunger that had developed in his stomach during the time he was out. He guessed that some of the painlessness was an effect of the "sugar" Titus had dropped into his coffee. It left his thoughts muffled and cloudy.

All around him, the house was utterly silent, except for Titus' voice in the next room. The generator had run mercifully out of fuel. He saw that Titus had set up rows of candles on the bookshelves and in the bay windows, some of them lit, others guttering or blown out completely. Judging from the light outside, Nicholas guessed it was late afternoon. The generator hadn't gone out too long ago.

He lay still, listening to Titus' voice.

He remembered how he had listened on Saturday as the old man niggled with his broker in New York, but this wasn't niggling anymore. For one thing, it was clear that the stock market was still open. *Must be before four o'clock, then*, he thought, staring up at the ceiling.

For another thing, Titus was screaming. Nicholas had no difficulty understanding every word. He realized that he was even beginning to grasp what it was all shaking down to. Even though most of it was a continuing stream of curses and demands for clarification—*"What? When, goddammit? How low?"*—Nicholas understood enough to know that Titus had lost whatever link he'd had with the market's activity when the generator had died for good. And the market didn't seem to be doing very well this afternoon. The violence in his tone was frightening, but in a way it was also encouraging.

For the first time, Titus seemed to be losing ground. He was cut off from New York. He was also cut off from the rest of the house as long as the blackout kept the staircase elevator out of service.

He tugged at the rubber hoses. Except now it felt more like the hoses were tugging on him. His muscles felt very weak and sore, particularly in his shoulders and arms. But the physical exhaustion didn't bother him as much as the emotional side of things. Strange thoughts kept creeping into his mind, the way they did when you were lying peacefully in bed and half-asleep. Aftereffects of ground-up Percodan.

He forced himself to keep his thoughts aligned, to concentrate on the plan of escape, but it only lasted a minute or two before he realized that he was thinking about Anthem again. Not just thinking about her, but actually visualizing her as clearly as he had in the dream.

Twice he caught himself actually speaking to her in a low croak. Then he would snap awake, blinking his eyes blearily in the gray light of the room, and tell himself to quit. He knew he wasn't going crazy, but that wasn't the point. The point was—

The point was that Gertrude started out this way. She gave birth to Anthem while lying here, probably tied up just like this. The next thing she knew, presto-chango, the woman had wings.

He shook his head. For the hundredth time he caught his body trying to sit up straight, and he was not surprised to see Anthem hovering directly over him again. Her skin seemed to radiate a soft, golden light all its own. She was smiling sweetly, a great succulent chicken drumstick steaming in one outstretched hand. *Hello, Virgil.*

"Hey, Anthem." Nicholas giggled a little shrilly, his eyes following the drumstick that floated just out of reach. He could feel his stomach rumbling. "You doing your Henry the Eighth imitation?" The sound of Titus' voice was just a soft rumble behind him now.

She smiled and offered him the drumstick. When it was close enough, he craned his neck and closed his mouth around it, chewing and swallowing almost simultaneously. The flavor was an unexpected symphony across his tongue. He strained his neck for the rest of the meat. Anthem had a fresh piece, a moist wedge of white breast meat, and she dropped it casually into his mouth. He savored it as long as he could before swallowing.

"Perfect." Tears of gratitude stood in his eyes. "Who would've thought Shake 'n Bake chicken could taste so wonderful?"

She just smiled, offering another mouthful. Steam was rising up from the platter she held in her arm. Behind the steam he was aware of her eyes and mouth reformulating, becoming another familiar face.

"Saint Jack?" he croaked.

He looked up where Anthem's face had been. Now he saw the gray-bearded, sad-eyed man looking back down at him with a forkful of cold potatoes waiting in one hand. Jack had dipped the potatoes in some of the slightly coagulated gravy, and now it was about to drip off the fork and onto the rug. Jack hadn't noticed. He seemed as distracted as a man could be while still remembering to breathe. Surrounding him in a faint nimbus was the unmistakable smell of beer. The tip of his nose was bright red, and his hair looked matted and damp. He sneezed.

"Jack, I thought you ran off on me." Nicholas' eyes darted around the library, across its shelves and candles, to reassure himself that he was back in the real world and not still dreaming. "I—I didn't know what happened."

"Well," Jack mumbled, "the truth is, I took a swan dive into a snowbank . . . for a few minutes, anyway. The storm was so bad I couldn't tell which direction I was going, so I just kept pushing till I found the driveway, and holed up in my car for the night. Woke up around noon today with a hangover and a real sore throat. Frostbite, probably, too." He cleared his throat. "But I didn't come back to rescue you."

"But last night . . ." His mind was racing. "Last night I thought you said—"

Jack scowled, then his face went strangely blank. His eyes seemed to be saying something quite urgent, transmitting a code all their own. "I just came to feed you, Nick. Titus will be coming out of his office shortly, and he'll want me to take you back upstairs."

"Is he just going to stay on the first floor until the power lines are up again?"

Jack shook his head. "I'm going back out to the shed in a minute, and this time I should be able to make it the whole way out there." He looked at Nicholas sprawled out across the floor and sighed deeply. "Here, you want some more food?"

Nicholas nodded, took another bite of the potatoes. He was trying to gauge Jack's usefulness, but it wasn't easy because Jack himself seemed undecided about what was happening. He wanted to ask more questions, without making Jack say anything about their plan out loud.

"I guess Titus is pretty upset about this whole blackout thing, isn't he?"

"That's not even the worst of it anymore. He says the market went into a nosedive this morning, at least from what his broker's told him over the phone. Apparently he's already lost a significant amount of money, and there's no end in sight. And I don't think that's the whole story, either."

Wind screamed against the tall windows, making the candles flicker. Nicholas watched sheets of snow whipping across the glass. Afterward he noticed that Jack's hands were shaking badly.

"Here, I think you should finish up the rest of these leftovers," he said hoarsely. "After I get that generator started, when Titus comes back out here, he might not feel so generous."

"He's leaving for my funeral tomorrow, isn't he?"

Jack nodded. "Before the storm gets any worse. The Canadians aren't coming."

They stopped talking and Jack cocked his head toward the office doorway on the other side of the library. From behind the door came Titus' voice, ranting at the broker in New York, then pausing just a few seconds to listen before flying headlong into another tirade. After a few more seconds the call ended and Titus shouted, "Hey, Jack? What about gassing up that generator? Maybe sometime this decade? I want to catch the closing quotes on TV before five."

"I'm on my way out," Jack called back. He looked back at Nicholas, his voice dropping to a whisper. "Don't tell him I gave you anything to eat—he's supposed to be starving you for a day or two, breaking you down."

"Jack, wait a second," Nicholas whispered. He could hear the words rushing out of him, not the way he wanted them to, but not seeing any other choice in the time remaining. "Tell him you took me upstairs first."

"What?"

"Tell him you took me upstairs. Then go outside . . . tell him the generator's frozen up or something, that you can't get it started . . . he won't be able to double-check to see I'm up there . . ."

"Nicholas, I can't." Jack moaned softly, a soft sound of surrender. "I just can't."

"Jack—" Nicholas looked into the constable's sad eyes, and suddenly he understood more than he wanted to about what he saw. Jack's urgency was a compulsion, an irrational itch for self-destruction. "You didn't really pass out in that snowbank at all, did you?" he asked. "You just sat down in the snow, in the middle of the storm . . . and waited.

Didn't you? But in the end, you just couldn't do it. You came back. *You came back because you promised to help me.*"

The constable was blinking back tears. Snot dripped from his nose into his moustache. "Why not just give in, for Christ's sake? You're not going to get out of this place, and we both know it."

Nicholas shook his head. "No, Jack. When I'm gone, you do whatever you want, but right now I want you to listen to me."

"I—I—"

"Jack," Nicholas repeated softly, at that moment more frightened than he'd ever been in his life. But he forced his voice back into level calm. "Listen to me."

65

Jack's mind was working even faster than Nicholas had hoped. It must have been the adrenaline. The full range of emotions—fear, doubt, longing and finally a steady flickering of hope—all flashed through his eyes in rapid succession.

"Come on," Nicholas urged him. "You're not going to get into trouble for this, just taking me upstairs." He had reduced Jack's involvement to its lowest possible terms, but he was suddenly aware of how far from freedom he still was. He felt a feather of panic tickling his stomach. "I mean, it could have happened exactly like this, with me escaping from my bedroom on the second floor."

"If it could've," Jack said slowly, "then why didn't it?"

But he uncoiled the rubber hose from around Nicholas' right hand. He actually heard the hose snap before he realized that his arm was free. The tubing flapped along behind it. With his one free hand Nicholas reached across the rug and picked at the knot on his left wrist. Pinpricks of feeling began to spread through his hands as circulation restored itself, but his fingers felt clumsy and fat. He realized that Jack was untying the hose from around his ankles.

Suddenly, shockingly, his legs were free. When he had finally loosened the knot from his left wrist, he sat up, stretching, rubbing his sore muscles vigorously. His body felt as though it had been backed over by a truck, several times, and he took a minute or two to stretch himself back into shape. He was in for a long, cramped ride, and he wanted to enjoy this one moment of freedom as much as he could before it was gone again. It was wonderful.

"Andelay, kiddo, andelay," Jack urged, shifting his weight anxiously from one foot to the other. He looked like a tap dancer in some slowed-down musical. "If he gets anxious enough he can climb right out of that wheelchair and crawl up the steps himself, you know."

"I'll take care of that," Nicholas said. He stood up and winced at the tension pulling between his hamstrings and his heels. "You do have the keys?"

He nodded impatiently. "Yeah, he wanted me to load up the trunk for him." He jangled them from his fingertip, and Nicholas saw he couldn't suppress a crazed half-grin, a grin that spoke of madness on the near horizon. "And I guess that's exactly what I'm going to do, huh?"

Nicholas opened the closet door. "Let's just go. Now."

"What—what should I say when he comes out of the study?" Jack asked. "What should I do?"

He thought for a second. It might have been the thrill of being able to move around again, or just the lantern of hope that he saw dangling not far away, but his thoughts were coming very clearly now. He felt inspired. "Go see him," he told Jack. "Tell him I passed out from hunger or exhaustion or something, but that you fed me some of this chicken and I'm doing all right. Tell him I'm upstairs, locked in my room. Tell him he's got nothing to worry about."

"*Jack! Jack, you sonofabitch! What the hell are you waiting for?*"

Jack jumped and ducked his head, like a candle flame in the wind. Nicholas felt his heart hammering in his chest. "The front door," he whispered. "I'll meet you there."

The constable's face was a miserable mask of uncertainty. As Nicholas started down the darkened front hall, toward the door, he heard Jack's voice trailing along behind him. "I'm taking Nicholas upstairs to lock him his bedroom," he was saying. "I just want to make sure he's out of the way before I get the generator started again."

And Titus' voice, snapping back at him: "*Just get it done, for Christ's sake! The market's closing in twenty-five minutes, and I don't have any fucking electricity here!*"

And you won't have any for a while yet, either, Nicholas thought, as he reached the front door. It was locked, of course.

He looked back as Jack came rushing up the hall toward him.

"You all ready?" Nicholas asked. "Unlock the door."

Jack was crying again. Now he seemed unable to stop. "I don't think this is really going to work," he babbled, reaching for Nicholas' shoulder. His face had gone dead white, except for the blots of red in his cheeks. "Come on, let's just—I'll just take you upstairs, and—and we can talk about it tomorrow or something. All right? Let's do that."

"Jack, unlock the door."

The constable's hand rose up, now trembling worse than ever, with the remote locking device in his fingers. He pressed his thumb against it.

The last sound that Nicholas heard in that house was the thump of the door's magnetic bolts, opening up in front of him.

66

Out in the breezeway, he ducked down behind the Lincoln and was not surprised to find himself shaking.

"*Jack!*" Titus bellowed out into the snow, from up by the main house. "You out there?"

Peering over the hood of the car, Nicholas saw Jack's silhouette fill the side doorway. Beyond him, on the enclosed cement landing just across the yard, he could make out the shape of Titus in his wheelchair. The details were obscured by a gust of snow, but his voice came through clearly.

"What the hell are you doing?" he demanded. "Where's Nicky?"

Please, Nicholas thought. Panic gripped his insides and squeezed like a rubber fist. *Please don't let it end like this. Oh dear God, not like this. Give Jack some kind of courage now, just enough for five more minutes, that's all I ask.*

"Well, he's still up in the bedroom, isn't he?" Jack said clearly. "That's where I told you I put him."

Titus said nothing. Through the rain Nicholas thought he saw the old man slump over slightly in his chair. Finally he heard the voice again. "What about the generator?"

"I don't know, Titus," Jack said. Nicholas saw him take another step out of the doorway so that he was now standing in the falling snow, face-to-face with Titus. The wind shrieked and howled, but this time Jack didn't flinch away from it. He stood his ground. Nicholas felt a wild surge of pride for him, something he would have never thought he'd feel for the man.

"I was out by the utility shed," Jack said. "I think the generator's frozen up."

There was another long silence, filled in by the scream of the wind off the water.

"Frozen up?" Titus bellowed. "What the hell do you mean, frozen up? What are you doing out in the goddamn breezeway?"

Nicholas closed his eyes. *Please, Jack . . . don't start crying. Don't break down. Just think of something. Anything.*

"I'm getting a butane torch to heat it up with," the constable answered. "I think it's the only way I can heat it up fast enough."

More silence. Then, without another word, Jack walked back to the tailgate of the Lincoln, inserted the key in the trunk lock, turned it. It popped eagerly open. Nicholas smelled the good smell of new car upholstery, then took a step in. He lay out across the bristling plastic carpeting that covered the spare tire, and stretched.

"It's not too bad in here," he said, but that was mostly for Jack's sake. If he looked as if he was worried about him, Titus would notice. What he was really thinking was, *It's just about the size of a coffin in here. How appropriate.*

"Holy shit, he's coming back out here." Jack snatched a quick breath. He was staring through the trellis in disbelief. "You all right in there? Can I close it?"

"Close it," he said. "Remember, Jack—don't forget—"

"I know, I know . . ." He looked over his shoulder again. "You all right?" he repeated, as if asking enough times would make it so. "Are you sure this is going to work out for you?"

"It worked for Anthem," he muttered.

Jack's eyebrows shot up. "Huh?"

"Never mind. Just shut it. We're out of time."

Jack nodded. "Good luck, Nicholas," he whispered, and slammed the trunk shut, leaving him where he had started out. In darkness.

Waiting.

And in his mind, playing "What if."

What if Jack goes back inside right now and Titus catches him? What if he stabs him with that little pocketknife or shoots him dead with the .357, and Jack never makes the phone call, the one they agreed on so hurriedly upstairs, to the Portage Police Department? What if he, Nicholas, goes totally claustrophobic halfway to Portage?

There was one "what if" more grisly than all the rest, one that refused to be suppressed.

What if Titus just doesn't go to the funeral?

What if he decides the weather is just too nasty, Nicholas thought, *and he'd rather stay home and watch the stock market, while I starve to death in this trunk?*

He tried to banish the question, but the doubt wouldn't leave him. Here in the trunk of Titus' Lincoln there was just him, and the doubt, and the last few Percodan from Titus' medicine cabinet. Jack had brought them down from the bathroom and pressed them silently into his hand. Nicholas had found out who he was, and now he just prayed to God that he could go back to Portage, and make a life out of that knowledge.

Just a life, that's all he wanted: a regular life for Nicholas H. Danzig. Was it so much to ask?

He took a pill from his fist and popped it into his mouth. "Good night, Titus," he whispered in the darkness of the Lincoln's trunk, and waited in silence for the first of the Percodan dreams to come.

67

Portion of the testimony of Ian Danzig, October 28:
  There would be no symbolic burial, we had decided, just the service itself. Besides the sporadic blackouts that continued on throughout the morning, the only unusual thing was that we had been expecting Uncle Titus to arrive at our house sometime that morning, and he had not yet appeared. The weather through the Upper and Lower Peninsulas was turning worse, however, the snow changing to sleet on most of the major highways, and that morning Shelley said he'd probably just arrive in the afternoon. When he didn't arrive then, we started to get worried.

  "Oh, well," Shelley sighed. Like me, she looked as if all the stress and

trauma and terror had been wrung out of her already, and something like electrical failure or Titus' lateness could not squeeze more than a drop of concern from either of us at this moment. "Maybe he'll meet us at the funeral home."

"Maybe," I said, and prepared to take a shower and dress for my son's funeral.

68

Portion of the testimony of Shelley Danzig, October 28:

Ian pulled the Tracer into the funeral home parking lot, which was already half-full, about three forty-five. The storm had become more of a typhoon by then, but the lights were still on in the funeral home itself.

I scanned the parking lot, through curtains of rain. "I don't see Titus' car," I said.

"No," he said. "Neither do I."

He parked and we stepped out, walking arm in arm across the parking lot to the front steps, then up into the funeral parlor. Two days ago we had seen the room where the service was being held, but when we walked in now, the atmosphere was different . . . it seemed charged with the tears of the people who'd come to say good-bye to Nicky.

The room was large and plain, with rows of folding chairs set up on either side of a wide aisle that led up to a podium. Most of the seats were full; most of the faces were familiar. Louis Skye and his father were here, in the front row. Louis himself had called us Saturday night, when the obituary ran in the paper, and asked very simply if he could "talk about Nick" for a moment at the service. Ian had questioned the boy gently, afraid that his father, an overgrown oaf of a comic book collector who seemed to cherish Nicky as much as Louis himself, might have put Louis up to it. No, Louis said. It was his idea. We had been touched and had agreed.

A few of Ian's closer teacher friends had left a little early from Clove Junior High to attend the funeral, and they sat together somberly in their second-best suits and trousers, some of them touching Kleenex to the corners of their eyes. John Tabor, Nicky's teacher at Harris Middle School, had also come. To his credit he had not made a field trip of it: Louis was the only school chum here. There were a few others—Marsha Cooley, a neighborhood friend of mine, and Janice Pendennis, probably my closest friend.

And I saw that they were all holding unlit candles.

Ian reached over and took my hand. His fingers were clammy, the gesture automatic and thoughtless. I squeezed him, and he squeezed back. Then Emily Sjolgren, an assistant minister at a Congregational church that we attended on Christmas and Easter, stood up and went to the podium. The murmuring and sobs died down into silence.

Emily is a rail-thin woman with short black hair and a whistling tone that might have been a lisp. She wore a navy-blue suit and white blouse, all very routine. Her eyebrows were plucked and painted, and they seemed to scowl when she smiled. Her appointment here, like that of Louis Skye, was something Ian had arranged, thinking he was being convenient.

"Friends of Nick Danzig," she began, nodding, "we're here this afternoon to remember Nicky, and to see his living spirit off to a better place. For as Jesus Himself tells us all, Suffer the little children to come unto me, for theirs is the kingdom of Heaven."

I gave Ian's hand another sharp squeeze, and he looked at me apologetically. As I said, we hardly attended church, and had agreed that the service was to be as secular as possible. No prayers, no Bible verses or fond and happy traveling up to the Pearly Gates—we both saw it as false sentiment, and there was too much real sentiment floating around for that. I could only hope Emily was throwing this in for all the good God-fearing Christians, and we could just move it along from there.

My hopes were rewarded. Or so I thought.

"To begin remembering Nicky Danzig," Emily said, "I know there's a friend of his, Louis Skye, who wanted to offer just a few words about Nicky. After all, when else do we have such friends; such fast and true friends, as those days of our youth? And when else—"

I gave Ian's hand another squeeze, thinking that if this was going to be a harbinger of the service to come, I would just stand up right now and take matters into my own hands. I would interrupt this service before I'd seen it turned into a mockery of Nicholas' death. It might sound unreasonably bitter, but that's how I felt.

And for a second, Emily did seem distracted, as though she'd read my thoughts. She halted and looked back to the rear of the room.

Uncle Titus came wheeling up the aisle toward us, the tires of his chair making a soft but urgent crushing sound against the carpet. He was wearing a black suit and tie. The look of anguish on his face was the closest approximation to the misery I felt, myself, at that instant. I felt a bittersweet smile work over my face. We could hear his oxygen tank making a soft, sibilant hissing behind him.

Up at the podium, Emily droned on, but I was no longer listening.

"Scoot over," I whispered to Ian. We both shifted one chair to the right, and I pushed the extra chair aside. Uncle Titus wheeled into the open spot. I turned to him. "It's good to see you again," I said, meaning it.

He just nodded. There were tears in his eyes, and he took the hand that Ian wasn't squeezing, and squeezed it. Unlike Ian's hand, Titus' was warm, powerful and reassuring, despite the arthritis-swollen knuckles. Here, I thought, was a man who seemed to hurt inside as badly as I did. I wanted, in a perverse way, to pass some of that hurt along through our hand-linked chain into Ian.

By now we had both noticed the hiss of the tank, as had the people sitting on the other side of the aisle. It was a strange sort of sound, that seemed to become louder the more you listened to it rather than fading into the background noise of coughs and sniffles. Ian leaned over to Titus. "You've got the oxygen turned up rather high, don't you?" he whispered across my lap. "Is your breathing okay?"

"Ain't nothing to worry about," Titus whispered back, his breath smelling of Marlboros and truck-stop coffee, his voice hoarse. "I'll tell you about it after the service."

Up in front, Emily had finished speaking. She stepped away from the podium, allowing Louis Skye to speak.

Louis vanished for a moment behind the podium, then he must have climbed up onto an unseen stool Emily had placed there for him. His head bobbed up, he adjusted the microphone upward with a surprisingly professional gesture, and started out, "Nick Danzig was my best friend."

Through the windows lightning flashed our shadows out across the wall. Somewhere in the congregation somebody gasped.

I heard a pop and a sizzle, and the lights went out.

69

Portion of the testimony of Louis Skye, October 29:
I thought, Oh great.

First of all, I was so nervous, you know, thinking maybe I should have something written down or something. But Dad said, "Talk from your heart, Louis. Say what you liked about Nick. Keep it simple and honest. Don't be nervous. Be brave." And I was all set to go, too, when that creepy uncle of Nick's came rolling in sounding like a big scuba tank on wheels. That threw me off a little, I sort of forgot where I was going, and I started wishing I'd made some notes again.

But in the end I guess it wouldn't have done me any good to write anything down, anyway, because the moment I stepped in front of the microphone, everything just went black. Outside, the sky was so dark that you could hardly see the faces of people sitting right next to the windows.

"Should I go ahead and talk?" I asked. Of course now it was just my regular voice because the microphone was dead. And it sounded small even to me.

I heard my dad's voice from out of the murmuring. "Go ahead, Louis."

Little pinpricks of light began to flicker all across the room. People were lighting their candles if they had lighters or matches, and people who didn't were getting a light from the rest. It's a strange thing to see, if you've never looked down on it before. In just a few seconds the room had refilled itself with light again, and I could see all the faces out there. Except they had this faint, orangish cast to them. It was kind of spooky, when you think about it. But it was also kind of neat. I thought, Nick, man, it's too bad this has to be your funeral, you know? 'Cause he'd probably think it was pretty cool, otherwise.

"Go on ahead and talk, Louis," my dad said again.

I took a second to sort of pull myself together. I looked out at that funky galaxy of lights. Somewhere out in the middle of it I could hear Nicky's Uncle Titus breathing, that kind of hoarse, raspy sound that lifetime smokers get, except amplified. I took a few deep breaths myself. When I was pretty sure that my voice wouldn't get weird on me, I started to talk and hoped they all could hear me without the microphone.

"He was a good friend for anybody to have. I don't have too many friends at school, but Nick made it seem like I didn't need any other ones except him. He always listened to what I said, and I can't remember him ever taking advantage of me. He had crazy ideas, but they were fun ideas, too. And—"

I had thought of one kind of funny story I wanted to tell, about a time when Nicky and I decided to start up our own pet-sitting company last summer. Nick had tried to take three dogs—I mean these three huge *Dobermans—for a walk all at once, and they'd just about dragged him around the block before he finally got control of them. It was supposed to be funny, but as soon as I thought of it, I felt myself on the verge of tears.*

"—he was . . . he was just . . . just a . . ." Now I felt a little frightened, but I couldn't hold back. The first tears were brimming in my eyes. "I'm really just gonna miss him," I said, and then I choked and couldn't say another word.

I probably would have stood up there bawling forever if I hadn't looked up the aisle through the lit candles and seen those two cops come walking in.

70

Portion of the testimony of Ian Danzig, October 28:
"Excuse us, everybody," the voice from behind us said, and we all looked around. It sounded booming and godlike in the middle of Louis' tearful good-bye.

Shelley, who I could tell had reached the end of her rope, looked around and stood up, staring back at the two police officers in the back of the room. One of them was fumbling with his flashlight, trying to slip it out of his belt.

"What?" she demanded. Her voice sounded frighteningly edgy, and in the guttering candlelight she looked positively cronelike. "What do you want? What do you want from us now?"

"Ma'am," the first cop said, coming up the aisle, "we—"

"You already told us he's gone," Shelley spat back, "so what's left? Who's dead? Who else is dead now?"

I saw Titus reaching up next to her, slipping his arm easily around her waist. With an offhand sense of balance, he was gripping the candle that she had given him. He looked calm, almost serene. "Now, Shel, just relax," he said comfortingly. "We'll get this straightened out . . ."

The cop assumed none of the gentleness Titus' voice had. He had the flashlight out now, its beam splashing across the aisle alongside of us. "We're looking for the owner of the black Lincoln Continental in the parking lot, license plate number 404 YE—"

Titus held up his hand slowly, a picture of aged smoothness. "Officer, that's my ride you're talking about," he murmured, as though there were still some way that Nicholas' service could continue alongside this intrusion. "Now, if you can just wait until we're finished payin' our respects in here for this boy—"

"I'm afraid not, sir." The cop stepped away from Titus. I saw him reach down to the pistol at his hip, unsnapping the holster. A gasp rushed through the group of mourners. "I think we're going out to see that vehicle."

Titus chuckled, that ever-indulgent Titus chuckle. I saw my wife look at him and seem to regard his placidity with something like wonder. "Now, Officer—"

The cop pulled his revolver. "I don't think you understand, mister. You're coming out with us to that vehicle. Right now."

71

Portion of the testimony of Shelley Danzig, October 28:
"This is an outrage," I told the cop. I was almost blind with anger. "Before the day's over I will have the badges off the chests of you two . . . clowns. I promise you that."

But the cop was already reaching down to the handles of Titus' chair, getting ready to push him toward the back door.

"He can wheel himself," I hissed at the cops, slapping the hand away. Then I stooped down and whispered into Titus' ear, "I'm going with you."

He smiled, so very gently. "Shel, really, there ain't really no need."

"I'm going with you," I repeated. "Ian, come on."

72

Portion of the testimony of Louis Skye, October 29:
Well, what would you have done? Well, I got down from behind that podium and followed the cops, Nicky's Uncle Titus, his dad and mom, in their weird parade of light right down the aisle and out the door.

"Louis," I heard my dad say, "stay here!"

But I didn't stop, didn't even look around. And I figure that's when he stood up after me and started down the aisle, too.

73

Portion of the testimony of Ian Danzig, October 28:
It was a mass exodus, to be honest. I was right behind Shelley, so I didn't notice until we reached the outside doors that led into the parking lot that we were leading at least half of Nicky's mourners out with us. They brought their candles with them, filling the center aisle of the funeral home with a river of light. It was the tone in the cop's voice that had done it. That, and the fact that he'd drawn his side arm.

We followed Titus in his wheelchair and the cops out of the great room and down a corridor toward the parking lot. When I saw the weather outside I couldn't believe we were all going to step out into it without our coats. Since Titus had arrived, the sky had gone from gray to completely black. The thunderheads up above were juggernauts, vast and mountainous. I couldn't see where they ended. Rain was hammering down, and it had also started to hail. I remember thinking that it might be the end of the world, and that if it was, I wouldn't really mind.

But we all stepped out into the storm, moving as a group. The wind swept through us, blowing out candles. We cupped our hands around them, and somehow kept a few of them burning. The cops had both brought out flashlights now. Even they looked a little taken aback by the savageness of the weather.

We worked our way across the parking lot. Titus, having arrived late, had parked at the far edge of the lot, but we finally reached it.

We stopped en masse. It was 4:20 p.m., October 21, 1993.

"Yep," Uncle Titus said, his voice so sure and easy it was almost like music. But I saw him reaching around behind his back to give the oxygen valve a final half-twist. "This here's my vehicle."

74

Portion of the testimony of Louis Skye, October 29:
The cop leveled his gun at Nicky's Uncle Titus. "Open the trunk up, sir," he said.

"Don't you aim that gun at him," Nicky's mom said. She was mad.
We all watched as Nicky's uncle got out his keys.
And I saw something else, too.
It sounded like his oxygen tank was really starting to leak.

75

Portion of the testimony of Shelley Danzig, October 28:
By this time, I was just about livid. Rage, misery, confusion, shock, you name it, I was feeling it. I think I must have burned off five hundred calories in those few moments out in the parking lot.

But Titus jangled his keys and slipped the right one into the trunk, turned it, and the trunk burst open.

I was not the first person to scream.

I know that because the moment between the time that the trunk flew open and I looked down inside, and when I heard the first scream from the back of our little mob of people in the parking lot . . . that moment seemed to stretch on forever. I heard some man, Mr. Skye, I think, say, "Oh, holy Jesus Christ Almighty," in a very loud and clear voice, and then other loud and clear voices joined with his, and I think that was the moment when mine joined them. Then the rain was pouring down so hard that I could hardly see anything at all.

But I could see Nicky.

Inside the trunk, he lay still, curled in a fetal hug just above the Lincoln's spare tire. His face was turned away from us and for what seemed like a long time I simply stood there thinking that this thing, this pale little body, could not be my son. He was wearing dirty sweatpants and a T-shirt, with gym shorts pulled up over the sweats. One of the legs of the sweatpants was pulled up, and I could see an old bandage on his leg. His hair was greasy, unwashed for days. He was filthy.

But the worst was his face, as they lifted him out. It looked faintly blue, especially around his lips. Beyond that, it was hard to describe, except for a moment all I could think was He's dead, and on the heels of that, He grew up. That was the most frightening, for that one irrational second. The round childishness of his face, the fine hair, the eyes wide with wonder, were all gone. Maybe I'm seeing an idealized picture of my Nicholas from very early on in life, but I remembered a sort of innocence in him from before. It had been replaced by this indescribable gauntness, this adultness. He had seen something, or something had happened to him, that had left its mark forever.

To my right and just beside me, I hardly noticed Uncle Titus pushing himself slightly back from the rest of us as he reached with one hand to the tank that sat cradled in the wheelchair behind him.

His other hand—well, I suppose you know what he was reaching for.

76

Portion of the testimony of Frazier Skye, October 29:
I know why you're taking my testimony. Because when that trunk opened, everybody else just about took a dump in their pants.. Well, I almost did, too, but I got my balance back faster than most of them, and I saw what happened with Titus. I saw the kid's body in there, and I recognized it was Nicky, about

the same time that most of them were starting to think that the boy was dead.

"Holy Jesus Christ Almighty!" I said, and then the cops took over.

One of them was reaching right into the trunk as soon as Titus had it open. The cop recoiled, just for a sec, when he saw what it was, and then his hand went right to Nicky's throat for a pulse. Under his moustache, that cop's face went ghost-white. "Call an ambulance," he said loudly.

And together they hoisted Nicky out of the trunk.

Ian Danzig stood there, swallowing. At that moment, I thought to myself, That poor guy is gonna spend the rest of his life in therapy trying to make this moment into something logical in his mind. *He was sputtering, the rainwater spraying from his lips and running in a solid stream from the tip of his nose. "Is he . . . is he . . . is he . . ." and that was all, though I'm sure the cop knew the question well enough.*

"His vital signs are hardly there," *the cop murmured, turning with Nicky's body in his arms. His voice slipped, and he spoke to himself.* "Carbon monoxide from the engine . . ." *He took something from Nicholas' hand, and I realized only much later what it was. It was one of those plastic screw-on caps for a water bottle, the kind that had the straw built into it.* "He must have brought the bottle to drink out of, but my guess is he was getting fresh air to himself through this thing. Otherwise . . ."

Shelley, Nicky's mom, put her hands on her face like she was going to claw it away like a mask. Instead she screamed, louder than I'd ever heard anybody scream in their lives. Believe me, I'm an E.R. nurse, and I've heard some doozies. Even if he lives, *I thought,* this woman is also going to do her share of couch time in the next year or two.

The cop moved with Nicky's body away from the car, Shelley right at his heels. I followed behind her. I told the cop I was a nurse, and we laid Nicky down and started to administer CPR, the cop pushing with both hands against Nicky's skinny chest while I put my mouth against Nicky's lips and breathed for him. It's funny—as soon as we laid him down I thought that we'd have to be careful he didn't drown in the pouring rain. It's happened, you know.

I could feel Shelley's hands clutching at my shoulders every time. I put another breath into the kid's lungs. She didn't know she was grabbing me, I don't think. I don't think she was aware of much of anything at that point.

The cop counted out loud and I breathed. Shelley's fingers were really starting to sink into my shoulders. We did five more breaths, then five more, and then after what seemed like a very long time I thought I felt the dry, dead mouth twitch, ever so slightly. After ten breaths, Nicky's eyelids flickered briefly and he started to cough, his eyes filling up with tears.

"Late," he was whispering, his voice hardly there. What I could hear, well, it sounded more husky, not a kid's tone of voice at all. "Late for my own funeral."

All around us the crowd made a sound like a giant, astonished gasp that was like a laugh at the same time. I've never heard anything like that sound in my life, in the hospital or out of it. The cop reached up to help Nicky sit up. He was crying and looking around, his jaw working out silent words and his thin chest trying hard to draw in enough air. I stood up and felt my heart swell in my chest, ready to get down on my knees and thank God for letting him live. At that moment I happened to look around at the people behind me.

"Where's Titus?" Nicholas said hoarsely. He was trying to stand up, pushing back the paramedics with these pathetic little swings of his arms so that he could get a clear view of Titus. The crowd drew back and then it was just Titus and Nicholas facing one another. A bolt of lightning shot across the sky overhead, so close to us that the thunder came almost simultaneously, with a deafening blast.

"Here we are, Dad," he said. I'll never forget it, his exact words. There was so much bitterness in his voice. It sounded like he had tasted something that had made him sick. "Here we are at last, all of us together for you."

Titus screamed something incoherent into the heart of the storm. His eyes had rolled back in his head. I saw the other cop pulling Titus' hands down behind his back.

Uncle Titus yanked his hands away.

The cop made another grab for them.

That's when it happened.

77

Portion of the testimony of Ian Danzig, October 28:
I looked over at Titus right after he started screaming. Shelley and I were both hugging Nicholas, trying not to hug him too hard but both of us wanting him all for ourselves. Trying to cover him up. Neither one of us had quite registered the fact that he had just addressed Titus as "Dad." At that point we had no rational thoughts. Rational thoughts, I suppose, would come later. The only one who was completely aware of what they were doing at the time, I suppose, was Nicholas himself.

Behind us, Titus had pulled something out of the side pouch of his wheelchair. He extended his arm toward Nicholas, standing just a few feet in front of him, and then jerked sideways at the cop that had been trying to catch his arms.

I heard somebody say, "Jesus, he's got a gun."

It was one of those times when events themselves seemed to have bunched up all at once, as though the smoothly flowing film of everyday reality had suddenly jammed in its sprockets, so that images and sounds were superimposed over each other and still piling up behind. Everything literally seemed to be happening all at once, before my mind could even—

Is it that obvious that I'm trying to avoid the facts at hand? Do you need to hear me say how it happened after that, when the police tried to grab his gun away? All right. They tried one last time to restrain his arms, but the rain had soaked us all to the skin by then, and every time they grabbed him, he slipped free. Also, I believe he was still a man of unbelievable strength, arthritis and wheelchair notwithstanding. At one point he shoved one of the police officers away, and the cop went flying backward, arms flailing like a rag doll.

Titus had begun to scream at himself, in a fading progression of different voices. His swung the gun around wildly, then directed it back at Nicholas. It wasn't so much like alternate personalities, but more like a man gradually coming to grief about some old and terrible act of violence.

It was horrible to hear.

"Damn it, Jack!" he howled in the tone I'd come to recognize as his own country intonation. Then, with the same breath, his voice shot up an octave and the words came faster. "She's dead! I don't know what happened! I don't

know what happened to her!'' Then it fell again. ''Nicky! Oh my son!'' Then a middle-range voice, with a ragged Canadian accent. ''You all . . . just leave me alone! DO YOU HEAR ME? LEAVE ME ALONE! IN THE NAME OF GOD LET ME BE!''

He was still shrieking when his dead legs started to kick against the footrests. He kicked them out of the way, his feet sort of flailing, the rain and hail pouring down on him, almost seeming to wrap around him and envelop him until he might suffocate.

When it looked like Titus might stand up, it really became a different ball game for the cops. It was like realizing the pit bull you thought was on a leash wasn't restrained at all. One of the cops had his side arm out again, and I'm confident he would have fired on Titus at that point, just hit him in the leg and taken him down for good, if Titus hadn't picked that moment himself to start shooting.

They say that the first shot bounded off the blacktop in front of Nicholas. Somebody saw a spark where it hit, and the crowd drew back.

One of the cops fired what was intended to be a warning shot in return, but Titus had already started to jerk the wheelchair to the left to aim at Nicholas. His bullet only grazed Titus' gun hand.

But it hit the oxygen tank straight on.

78

Portion of the testimony of Louis Skye, October 29:
Nicky's Uncle Titus kind of exploded.

That's how I'll say it, when you ask me what I saw. I don't know if that's really the facts, but I know what I saw. It wasn't a giant fireball like in the movies or anything, with flying cars and chunks of cement, but it sure was loud enough. There was a sound, like WHOOOSH, and then you heard— kind of felt it, too—this big metallic PAA-AANG! Imagine, like, somebody putting a firecracker under a tin can, maybe that times a thousand.

The cops afterward said it was a good thing people were already down on the ground, hiding behind their cars and stuff, when the tank blew. You know what? They found about eight inches of the rubber tubing, still attached to the green plastic cone that my dad says they call a ''Christmas tree''—they found that thing half a block away. A half-block away, man! That thing must have been moving like a missile. Like my mom is always saying, somebody could lose an eye.

And little chunks of shrapnel everywhere. I counted ten busted windshields and half a dozen flat tires before I quit. The tank blew like a grenade.

Anyway, Titus kind of toppled backward into his chair like a big sack of laundry. There was smoke pouring out of the back of his head, what was left of it. It had absorbed a lot of the explosion. At that point I think he had more metal in him than anything else.

His hands were twitching. Once . . . twice . . . then they fell still.

The cops sort of moved his shoulders back, and that was when I saw his face. It was pretty badly burned, all his hair scorched off, you know . . . and he didn't have any eyes. Just these blank, empty, smoldering holes.

Well, that did it for me. Ten-four, over and out. I was running for the rosebushes after that, and you can put that on the public record. S-K-Y-E, Louis Victor.

79

Portion of the report of Officer Howard Tenielle, October 31:
I tried to catch the suspect's hands and failed. They were moving very quickly. But I did try to pull the suspect's hands away from the back of his head. But he was wet, slippery from the rainwater. He was much stronger than I had suspected. It was not until the oxygen tank had exploded that I was able to confine him. At that point his body had gone limp in the wheelchair. I tested for the suspect's pulse. The suspect registered no vital signs.

By the time that the suspect was confined, the ambulance we had called for the Danzig boy had arrived. We put the suspect in it, although now there seemed to be no particular rush.

80

Portion of the testimony of Ian Danzig, October 28:

As you know by now, Nicholas himself has very little conscious memory of anything that happened to him after the van crashed into the water. On more than one occasion, hypnosis has been suggested as a way of forcing him to remember. Shelley has fought the idea every time it has been put forward. I have joined her, not just because I think Nicholas will remember eventually on his own—he has already begun, thanks to recent developments you can hear about on the nightly news—but also because I don't think the secrets that would be divulged would be worth the trauma they might exact on him.

I suppose this means that I am less of an obsessive man than I was before all of this happened. Or maybe it's just the frightened look that Nicky gets in his eye whenever the police begin to question him about events following the crash. I don't think it matters, frankly.

I do not know what else to tell you about the man we called Uncle Titus. They've been up to his house now in Burns Mills, and even as I speak, the newspapers are still full of what they found up there. Enough sensationalism to keep people busy for at least a week. Enough so that we're trying to keep Nick from reading about all of it all at once.

On Friday morning, the 22nd, state police broke into Titus Heller's house on the shore of Whitefish Bay. In the front hallway they found a body identified as Constable Jack Tornquist.

Constable Tornquist had hung himself from the stairs. On the kitchen table, next to a bottle of Old Crow, they found his service revolver with a single round in the cylinder. Constable Jack Tornquist might have been planning to kill himself in a variety of ways.

Next to the pistol was a short, explanatory note directing them to a certain corner of the basement.

By the evening of the 22nd, two state troopers had removed a wall-length mirror from the basement of Titus' house and torn open the wall behind it, pulling out plaster drywall and paneling in big chunks.

A little past midnight, our telephone rang again.

We plan on bringing Ovid's body downstate for a proper burial at some point next week. Perhaps then Nicholas' mind will begin to reveal further details of last week's ordeal. We all want answers, of course. You asked for a collection of testimony and got it, and I hope that you can, at some point, use it in a way that might help us explain what happened to Nicky between October 12th and the 21st without ever having to hypnotize him. We have spent so much of these last two days recounting details for you that, even with the body they found in the basement and Constable Tornquist's note, I haven't begun to understand what has happened. What, for example, are we to make of the empty photo albums that the police found upstairs in one of the bedrooms? Or the ashes that were still stuck to Constable Tornquist's fingertips?

All I know is that I think Nicky probably found out more in one and a half weeks than six years of badgering Titus ever got me. And I don't just mean family history, I mean reasons, and causes. Or as close as anybody can get, anyway, to the reasons and causes of family madness.

As for myself, I cannot imagine what my son saw, after the crash.

I cannot imagine it.

Someday Nicky might tell us. Now, at this very moment, life seems very long and there is no knowing what secrets may eventually be divulged after every voice has been given a chance to speak.

For the record, I saw the doctor's report that Nicky was almost technically dead when he was lifted from the trunk of Titus' Lincoln. His vital signs were negligible, and might have been fading into nothing at the moment the trunk was opened. Of course, I am not thinking about what might have happened if Titus had arrived later, or if Titus had self-destructed before he had unlocked the trunk, and there had been some delay, or even if Nicky had not found that plastic water-bottle straw they say he breathed through. I have no idea why that was there, because Titus himself never owned a bike, let alone such a water bottle. But I am a very long way from wondering about that. It is possible that I never will.

But I will finish with this. It is a little, half-mad thought of a father sick with confusion but still very, very happy. Very grateful to whatever powers may be.

The doctors say that my son's pulse and respiration began to fail, apparently, just as the trunk was opened, about the same time that the storm began to break, and the power came back to some of the towns that had lost it.

But Nicholas did not die, of course. After he was resuscitated, the storm that he seemed to have brought with him from up north only faded for a moment and then continued to get worse. By the time we got to the hospital that afternoon, they were running on auxiliary generators, but most of the rest of the town was totally blacked-out. This was true with most of the state, as a matter of fact. October 21, 1993, may not go down in history as the worst electrical storm ever, but it was almost unbelievably severe in the western part of the state, all along U.S. 131 up to the Upper Peninsula. That was the way Titus had come down, of course.

But it was a strange day in general. I'm sure something will be made of the two-day stock market crash that stripped Titus of much of his fortune on the 19th and 20th, although I can't imagine what logical connection could be made even by the most imaginative of investigative reporters.

As Nicholas's father, I think I'm entitled to speculate illogically, but I won't trouble you with that.

To my knowledge, my wonderfully alive fourteen-year-old son never knew about this bizarre fluctuation in the climate—financial or meteorological— during the few seconds that he left the earth. But when I told him about it later, he told me a story that Anthem—the girl we knew as Gertrude—had told him, about a boy named Ovid. And about the weather. But as I said, this is just a story, and I don't think it belongs on the public record.

I'll keep it personal, and just finish like this:

Nicholas, I'm so glad you're going to be able to grow up into adulthood.

I love you, son. I love you so much. Yes I do.